ORDER FROM CHAOS

Nick Campanella

La Maison Publishing, Inc.

Maison
Vero Beach, Florida
The Hibiscus City
lamaisonpublishing@gmail.com

Thank you!

A special thank you to my friends and family. My girlfriend and my daughter. My mom and dad. Step parents and in laws. My coaches and teachers. My lawyers, accountants, and employers. I am also grateful to my professional support: editors, graphic designers, marketing experts. My website designer. My publisher. My manager. And my launch team. Thank you!

My biggest thank you goes to the readers — past, present, and future. Without you, there would be no reason to write. Your opinions matter so much. Please leave a short review on Amazon.com and Barnesandnoble.com. Oh, one more thank you to God, for guiding me away from the path of affliction I was running toward twenty years ago.

*Author's note: *Order from Chaos* is the stand-alone sequel to *Path of Affliction*. It is not necessary to read Book One first, but I do recommend reading it next.

*Order from Chaos is **nonlinear story.** Because of this, it will be important to pay attention to the dates at the beginning of each chapter. *Dates in italics represent the past.*

Thank you for reading. Enjoy!

Best regards,

Nick Campanella

"…there is no such thing as a left or right. There is only an up or down. Up to man's age-old dream — the maximum of individual freedom consistent with order — or down to the ant heap of totalitarianism. Regardless of their sincerity, their humanitarian motives, those who would sacrifice freedom for security have embarked on this downward path."

— President Ronald Reagan

INTRODUCTION

Astana, Kazakhstan
March 13, 2007

A figure shrouded in a black hooded robe lifted a vial of red liquid just above her head. "Long live Molech, son of Ra," she repeated the chant, her eyes shifting from her uncle to her father, who were both cloaked in black. "Long live Molech, son of Ra."

As the grandfather clock against the ancient cobblestone wall struck midnight, she tilted the glass tube to her lips, pouring the drink down her throat. Upon setting the empty vial on the marble table in front of her, she briefly bit down on her plump lower lip. "I don't think I can wait ten years for the Great Reset," the woman said sharply. "I wish we could speed up the process." Her voice was sharp like her pointy nose. The creases on her pale face revealed her age, but her squinting dark eyes were still seductive.

The wrinkled old man on the other side of the table brought a burning cigarette to his lips. "Patience is a virtue," he said, croaking out a stream of smoke in the darkness of the candle-lit room. "Our ancestor's plan is proceeding on schedule."

The elderly man sitting to her right rubbed his pale cleft chin. "Significant progress is needed to procure the capping of the pyramid."

The smoking uncle clicked his tongue a few times. "I once thought like you, young lady," he said with a hoarse voice. "You will soon grow to think like me. When you see how this unfolds, when you harness the power of the universe, when you fulfill the prophecy, you will remember this great day…we made your destiny formal."

The woman's arms spread apart. "Pardon my thinking out loud, Master," she said with a touch of mockery. "I fully understand. I've been spoon-fed the ancient text as long as I can remember. Forgive me for craving the power I'm entitled to."

The man sitting next to the woman rested his pale and wrinkled hand on her bony shoulder. "For the next ten years, we need you to grow yourself into a revered public figure." His tender countenance rendered a smile on his only child's face. Her dark eyes were locked with his. Blinking. "We need you on TV more than any politician." Her father leaned back, crossing his arms. "We need you to smile and laugh. We need you to be the champion of America's victims—past and present. Our useful proxies in the media will be sure to destroy anyone who questions you."

The smoking man lit a new cigarette with the cherry of his last. "Your father speaks the truth on this matter." He coughed out a cloud of smoke, snubbing the butt in an ashtray that looked like a human skull. "Anything the media can't fix, my men will do what is necessary."

"Your time will come," the elder man said. "The multitudes will beg to be herded like pigs to the slaughterhouse."

The woman in black laughed a loud cackle.

"Never forget. "The smoking man cut her off. "At most… you will only be a lieutenant. But *you* will bathe in the glory of an empress…while *we* work from the shadows. If you divert from the plan, the demigods at the top will crush you. And I can't stop them."

"Yes, Master." Her voice lowered to almost a whisper. "I'll never forget my role."

1

Fish Lake, Minnesota
March 12, 2017

Frankie Buccetti knocked on his old friend, Ivan Mortenson's door. Giovanni Mariani was standing behind him. Leaning into the door, his tan knuckles pounded louder. Stopping suddenly, he turned to his friend with a scrunched-up face. "Ughhh…what's that smell?" He took a few steps backward.

Mariani sniffled. "It's gotta be Ivan," he said, shaking his bald head. "I haven't smelled that smell since my last tour in Afghanistan."

"No." Frankie jiggled the locked door knob. "Maybe it's just a dead rat."

"Bro, trust me." Mariani pinched his nose with his pale fingers. "That's a decomposing body for sure. Couldn't be anything else. Either way, I'm going in." Lifting his knee, Mariani kicked the door with his boot. With a loud crack, it swung inward violently.

Frankie's thick black eyebrows lifted underneath his dark-gray watch cap. *Damn*, he thought, his eyes following Mariani's long black leather coat into the house. Squinting his eyes, he crossed the threshold into darkness. "Oh, my God. That just stinks." He found the wall, flicking on the light switch with the cuff of his tan parka.

"Holy shit," Mariani said, stopping to look back at Frankie's blank face. "Told ya." His hand popped up to cover his mouth and nose. Turning forward, he peered down at Ivan who was face down on the floor. A dark crusted stain was surrounding his head. "He must have been here at least a month or so." He coughed hard with disgust.

Scanning the room, Frankie tried to put the pieces together. *The TV's on but no volume,* he thought. *A brick of dope on the table. A chrome revolver on the floor. Ivan shriveled up in front of his favorite chair.*

"You all right, bro?" Mariani nudged Frankie, whose brown face was turning pale.

Frankie's mouth opened but no words came out. "Yeah." Frankie's voice cracked, his chin sinking in his chest as he turned away. "I'm good." His head bobbed.

Mariani squinted one eye after hearing Frankie sniffle.

"I-I'm just…trying to figure it out."

Mariani dropped a hand on Frankie's back. "What's to figure out, brother? He sold you out to the cartel for a brick of dope. Then he geeked out on coke before he blew his brains out. Fuck him. He's a piece of shit."

Frankie let out a deep sigh, his lips quivering. "I-I've known Ivan a long time."

"You need to stop sympathizing for this asshole."

"I know." Frankie swallowed hard, slapping his face three times to pull his emotions in rein. "What should we do?"

"Well, first thing I'm gonna do…is find the hush money you gave him last year." Mariani chuckled with contempt. *Money can't buy loyalty,* he thought, shaking his head. "You stay here and try to figure out what happened."

"Make it quick, man. We got to get out of here."

Mariani bolted up the stairs.

Frankie looked over the room once more, his eyes falling on the TV and the subtitles at the bottom of the screen. *China, Russia, Iran, and North Korea just signed a historic military alliance pact. Speaker of the House Heather Roth: This should be a wake-up call to the new president. President Clacher's response: This four-headed dog is all bark no bite.*

Frankie leaned forward, pressing the power button. "Nuke 'em," he said softly, his eyes taking in the neglected coffee table full of dust and ash and cocaine.

Next to the heaping ashtray and the small mound of white powder, there was a brick of drugs with the packaging split down the middle. Underneath the brick lay a packet of documents. The cover was stamped with a symbol in black ink. "What the…"

Mariani stomped down the stairs. "Found it," he said with an olive-green backpack hanging from his wrist. "It's full of cash."

Frankie spun around with the papers in his hand. "Give my share to Brice." A bad memory flashed before his eyes — A brave friend unconscious in a hospital bed. His closed eyes twitching. The tubes in his mouth. All because of his quarrel with the cartel. *Money couldn't repay him, but this will be a start.*

Mariani nodded. "He probably deserves it. Took two bullets for you."

"I can't believe he woke up from the coma."

Mariani nodded. "He's the luckiest dude I ever met."

"It was a blessing. The Lord has plans for him."

"We'll have to go visit him again soon. I heard he moved in with his cousin, Dennis."

"That dude is fearless. In that jailhouse riot last year, he was like a gladiator, battling fools twice his size."

Marinai grabbed the papers in Frankie's hands. "Last will and testament." He laughed. "Your mom is the sole beneficiary of the Ivan Mortenson estate."

"Ivan must have thought the cartel killed me. He actually felt bad."

*****

In Frankie's furnished basement, Mariani unzipped the backpack and dumped stacks of money on the pool table. "I still can't believe you gave Ivan a backpack full of money."

"It was hush money," Frankie said, removing his jacket and winter cap. His bald head looked like Mariani's, but a few shades darker.

"How'd that work out?" Mariani tilted both hands before answering his own question. "He sold you out, and almost got me killed."

"You have every right to feel that way," Frankie said, spreading apart his hands. "I get it. But —"

Mariani raised his voice. "You have no fucking idea what it feels like to have a hot bullet rip through your lung." The muscles on his face were twitching, his brown eyebrows low. "For the last three months, I've been dreaming about how to kill that asshole. Stop sympathizing with this dead fuck."

"But if we can't forgive him, how can we expect to be forgiven for *our* sins?"

"Brother." Mariani shook his head. "I will never…forgive that back-stabber. Never. And if he didn't commit suicide, I would have put a bullet in his brain." He paused, tugging on the two-inch brown scruff on his chin. "And then I would've stuffed him in the wood-burning heater like we just did with Iv —"

The basement door creaked open. Both men turned to see a tall woman with long dark brown hair and royal blue scrubs, cradling a bottle of wine.

Frankie's girlfriend, Conny Bream cleared her throat. "What were you guys just talking about?" she asked accusingly with an elevated tone and low eyebrows. Redness darkened the skin on her face.

Marini covered the mound of cash with Frankie's jacket.

"Nothing," Frankie said. "Just talking about hockey back in the day."

"Bull-shit." With a clunk, she set her bottle on the table, and then closed the distance between her and Frankie with a bouncing finger. "You *ever* stuff someone in a wood-burning heater—we're done. Do you understand me?"

"Don't worry, babe." Frankie laughed shortly, shooting Mariani a warning glance. "We were just joking around. Just venting."

Mariani lifted one hand. "I'm sorry, Conny," he said. "We ain't gonna kill no one. I was just talking shit, ya know? Had a few too many cocktails."

Conny pointed at Marinai. "*You* almost died three months ago." Her finger then snapped in Frankie's direction. "And *you*. You almost went to prison." She swore under her breath. "I thought you both learned your lesson." She scoffed. "What a waste." Turning for the door, she slammed it behind her.

Frankie met eyes with Mariani. "Sorry, bro." He let out an exasperated sigh. "I gotta go calm her down."

*****

In the kitchen, Conny poured a glass of red wine. She set the bottle on the black granite counter, sliding it away from the edge. The tip of her tongue wet her lips. Snatching up the glass, she took a big gulp and stared out the icy window as the tart beverage flowed down her throat. Darkness was all she saw. The wind was all she heard. With her right hand on her hip, she shook her head. "I knew it," she said to herself. "He lied. He wasn't innocent of murder. He just got lucky." She lit up a cigarette, and blew out a stream of smoke. *Why am I so weak for him?* Footsteps interrupted her thoughts.

Frankie strode into the kitchen. "You can't smoke in here."

"Why not?" She shot him a look. "You let that fat carpenter smoke in here, right?"

"Who, Larry Sobek?" Frankie tilted his hand. "That's different. He built this house. He can do whatever he wants. I piss him off, I'd have to pay top dollar from a different company."

"Fuck you, Frankie," she said, taking a sip of wine. "You know what?... You lied to me. It was all one big lie, wasn't it?" She took a drag from her cigarette.

"What are you *talking* about?"

She exhaled smoke in the air above her head. "The murder trial. It wasn't just self-defense, was it?"

"Of course, it was."

"Yeah, right. It was probably a drug deal gone wrong."

"I never sold drugs." The words came out in a low growl.

She opened one hand in a sweeping motion. "How 'bout your house?" She scowled. "How did you pay for this big ass house in the middle of the woods, anyways?"

"I told you." Frankie's eyes shifted to the left. "My great aunt died. My mom inherited some money."

Conny laughed shortly. "You just lied to my face." She lifted the faucet, stuck her cigarette under the stream of water, and then tossed it in the trash can. "How 'bout I call your mom and ask *her*?" She pulled out her phone. "We'll see what *she* says."

"Stop," Frankie said, showing her the palm of his hand. "You got me." He sighed heavily, sinking his head before lifting it again. "I found a bag full of money last year. That's why the cartel tried to kill me." He let out a breath. "I'm sorry, I didn't think you'd understand."

Conny poured another glass of wine. "One lie is a thousand lies." She took a sip. "How can I ever trust you again?"

"I'm sorry, Conny." Frankie reached out for her arm, but she jerked away. "I couldn't tell you. It's too complicated. I couldn't risk losing you again."

"I feel so stupid." She stomped her foot. "Our relationship is built on lies."

Frankie softened his voice. "Baby, I just came clean." He paused, looking directly into her flickering blue eyes. "Trust me. No more lies. I promise."

"I don't know if this is gonna work." She shook her head tightly. "I already accepted your checkered past." Her voice cracked. "But I actually thought you were being honest with me." Turning slightly, she covered her scrunching face with her hand.

"Come here." He reached for her arm.

"No." She dropped her hand, revealing her raw emotions.

The muscle on Frankie's cheek twitched. "Fine. I'll come to you." He took a step forward.

She turned her back to him. "Just leave me alone." She wiped the tears from each side of her face and then tried to choke down the rest of them.

"Kittenz," he whispered, slipping his arm around her waist and pulling her close. "I'm sorry. I love you. I'll never lie to you again."

Conny didn't say anything. She just kept sniffling with him behind her, literally breathing on her neck.

"What can I do to make you love me forever?"

She broke free and spun around to face him. "I do love you, *dummy*," she said and stomped her foot on the granite tile floor. "Can't you see how much I care?" She gestured to her overflowing eyes. "I can't live in a situation where I can't trust you. W-what else did you lie about? Did you lie about us being safe? What if the cartel is still coming for you? I-I got two kids to worry about, Frank." Pouring the rest of her wine down the drain, she dropped the glass just hard enough to shatter in the sink. "Don't you care about them?" Her head whipped around to face him.

"Yes, Conny. I promise." He opened his arms and she fell into them. "No one's coming for us." He squeezed her tighter. "I'm serious. We're safe. There's nothing to worry about."

She sniffled. "I love you."

"I love you, too, Kittenz." He lifted her chin and kissed her gently. Though she seemed reluctant to respond immediately, when his teeth nibbled at her lips, a soft sigh escaped her mouth as she relented to his embrace. With his hands cuffing her buttocks, she backed away.

"That's gross. I've been helping sick patients all day in these scrubs. Wash your hands and meet me upstairs."

*****

From underneath the covers, Conny's moans drowned out the volume of the TV in the background. When the noise came to a stop, only the news-man on the TV was heard.

With his lips next to her ear, Frankie whispered softly. "I love you."

"I love you, too."

Reaching for the nightstand, Frankie grabbed the remote control, aiming at the television. Before he pressed the OFF button, he squinted to read the headline at the bottom of the screen: *TWO RUSSIAN INTELLIGENCE AGENTS CAPTURED ON MEXICAN BORDER LAST WEEK. FOUR ISLAMIC MIGRANTS ARE ALSO IN CUSTODY. ONE IS COOPERATING.*

Frankie hit the power button and the room went dark. He held Conny tighter, and then he closed his eyes. *Terrorists and Russians on the same team,* he thought, rolling on-to his other side. With a slightly elevated heart rate, he tossed and turned, his restless mind swirling around the breaking news, the image of Ivan's dead body, and Conny. *Don't think. Don't think. Don't think…*

2

The Buccetti Compound
March 13, 2017

At the blissful feeling of Conny's hand patting his head the next morning, he groaned, burrowing into the pillows. Peeking out from under the thick down blanket, Frankie's voice was a thin plea. "Don't go." The room was dark.

"Don't worry, little Frankie," Conny said, sitting on the side of the bed. "I'll be back after work. I promise."

"But little Frankie doesn't want you to leave. He just wants to cuddle."

"Aww." She climbed further on the bed. "Poor little Frankie. Nurse Conny will take care of him later."

"Can't you just stay…a little bit longer?"

"I'm late. I gotta go." She leaned forward, gave him a quick peck on the lips, and then she was gone.

"I love you, Kittenz," he mumbled with closed eyes. *My life is so perfect.*

*****

Frankie's eyes cracked open to a dark room and the sound of his phone ringing. Groggy and annoyed by such an abrupt start to the day, he twisted and reached for the night stand.

Grabbing his vibrating device, he looked at the screen and muttered under his breath. "Why would Carlos call at 7:15 in the morning?" The phone rang again and he swiped the screen with his thumb. *Must be important.*

Pressing the phone to his ear, Frankie let out a dull, callous greeting. "Hello…"

"Turn on your TV!" Carlos Zapato said in a shaking voice. "W-we just got nuked!" His words were fast. His tone was loud, but not screaming.

Frankie ripped off the covers. "What?" he asked, rolling out of bed in just his boxer briefs. "You got to be kidding me?" Frankie, Carlos, and Mariani had been the closest of friends since they were kids. And Frankie couldn't remember a time when Carlos lied or pulled a prank. That fact elevated his heart rate.

"No! It's a terrorist attack!" Carlos said in low baritone.

Fumbling the remote, he pressed the power button, washing the room in a bluish glow. "Oh, my God." His free hand covered his mouth, his eyes exploding with shock and awe. "I love you, bro, but I'm gonna have to call you back."

The digital picture on the screen displayed a city that was black and smoldering, a tall mushroom cloud rising from the center. A dark purplish sky blocking out the sun.

He dropped his phone on the floor with a clunk. "Washington D.C." he whispered, his hands raising to the top of his head. His breaths were heavy. His heart was stirring. *The White House is gone!*

New words flashed on the screen, and the trembling question in his heart was answered as he read silently: *New York City, Chicago, Los Angeles, and Minneapolis all hit with tactical nuclear weapons.*

Minneapolis?

"Dad!" Frankie cried, scooping up the phone in his quaking hands. *No way.*

Dialing his dad's number, he snapped the phone to his ear. "Straight to voicemail." He took a deep breath. "Fuck!" He dialed the number again. Same result.

Letting out a huge sigh, Frankie dropped his butt down on the edge of his bed. With his jaw sunk in his chest, his left hand shot to his brow. His head was shaking in disbelief. "This isn't happening."

Frankie jumped to his feet with a clenched jaw, his hands balled into fists. Looking around the room for something to break, his eyes landed on the man in the mirror. He didn't recognize the dark beast he saw.

What are you gonna do, Frank? Thoughts were rushing though his mind. *Calm down.* He unclenched his hands and let out a long deep breath. *Channel your anger. Find out the facts.* He swallowed the knot in his throat. *Dad might have made it.*

A mild but sharp pain in his chest gave him pause. Looking down, he saw his hand pressing on his bare chest muscle, his fingers pressing in between his ribs on the left side. *I can feel it,* he thought as his pounding heart riveted against his middle finger. *Thank God I'm still ticking,* he thought. *A lot of people are dead right now.*

Spinning back toward the TV, he silently read the streaming text on the bottom of the screen: *PRESIDENT CLACHER IS IN A SECURE LOCATION. P.O.T.U.S.: A RETALIATORY RESPONSE IS IMMINENT.*

Frankie picked up his phone. *This is history.* He pressed an icon on the screen, and then started video recording the TV, narrating the footage with a single tear running down his cheek. "March 13th, 2017," he choked down the tears with a sniffle. "The enemy detonated multiple tactical nuclear weapons—" he said, struggling to hold the phone still, " —simultaneously in order to show sophistication. But who is this enemy? Al-Qaeda? Russia? China? ... All of the above?"

The known unknown caused a paralyzing cold chill to shutter down Frankie's spine, and then it took a hold of his entire body. His freedom-loving heart was pounding rapidly in his chest cavity, and his mouth was half-open. *This might spark World War Three!*

His eyes were wide, gazing at the flat screen TV that was so close he could have grabbed it, and smashed it on the ground.

His phone was still recording. Five sections now. Each showing live footage of black and gray mushroom clouds pluming into the sky.

"AMERICA UNDER ATTACK," Frankie read the screen out loud. Underneath that threatening phrase was a continuous stream of fine black print that flowed from right to left on the bottom of the screen. "The enemy is unknown.... Continuity of Government is secure.... President Clacher has a message for all American citizens and her guests: 'On this treacherous winter morning in America, freedom was tested but not defeated.... America will prevail, freedom will be restored, and peace will be made for all time.... A retaliatory response is imminent.... Absolute victory is on the horizon.... Soon, providence will shine a light down on us from above.... Please stay calm, please remain kind, please help your neighbors, hold your children, and most importantly...please pray for the United States of America to endure the unendurable."

Pressing the screen on his phone, Frankie switched from video to camera, and then snapped off a few still pictures. *I'll never forget this moment,* he thought. *I wish there was something I could do to help.*

The TV chirped and the screen went black. "What the hell?" Frankie tried to turn the TV back on, but there was no power. Crossing the room, he hit the light switch on the wall. Nothing.

Frankie dropped to his knees. "Father," he said out loud, besieged in near darkness, only a thin ray of sunshine angling through the cracks of the blinds. "Please forgive me for my sins…. Thank you for my many blessings…." He paused to think about the words he was about to say. "I have sinned against you my entire adult life. Please wash the sins from my wicked soul.

"Today…millions of innocent people were murdered. There's a good chance my dad was one of them. Please let my dad and my family down there be okay. If not, please accept them into heaven." His voice broke, a few tears falling from his closed eyes. "Please bless the injured, please give hope to those who are suffering, grieving, or displaced. Father…please bring forth peace on Earth, please bless America, please help restore freedom. And lastly, Father… please look after my friends, my family, and Conny and her kids. Please help us to survive this hell on Earth…. In Jesus name we pray." He paused to let the air out of his lungs. "Amen."

Frankie hung his head in quiet solitude. Taking a deep breath, he opened his eyes, rose to his feet, and then pressed the flashlight icon on his phone. A beam of light shone into his closet. *Clothes,* he thought, jumping into a pair of jeans and socks. The T-shirt and black fleece jacket from the day before was on the carpet. *That will do,* he thought, and then swooped them up, slipping into both. *Mariani needs to know what's happening.*

Aiming the phone light at the door, he swung it open, and then marched toward Mariani's room. As he rushed across the hallway, his mind was racing. *Mariani isn't gonna believe any of this.* He approached the door, lifting a closed hand. *How do you tell a guy the world is on fire?*

"Mariani!" Frankie pounded on the door five times. "I'm coming in." He twisted the knob, barging into the bedroom. His dear friend was curled up under the covers. Mumbling.

Striding up to his friend, Frankie's voice was a loud, low bark "Wake up!"

Giovanni didn't even flinch.

"G!" Shoving his friend on the shoulder, Frankie's voice only rose in retaliation. "Get up! Right now, man!"

"Leave me alone," Mariani muttered with contempt. When he tried to roll over, Frankie grabbed his arm, stopping his motion.

"Dude, America is under attack."

Mariani rolled over, tugging the blanket closer to his face. "C'mon, man. Please…let me sleep."

"No," said Frankie. "You don't understand…we just got nuked. You have to get up, we got things to do."

Mariani didn't respond.

Frankie reached for the dresser and grabbed a short glass of scotch that was half full. "Wake the fuck up!" He smashed the glass against the wall.

"Jesus!" Springing up at the violent sound, Mariani squinted at Frankie. "What the…!" His words coming to a close as his eyes adjusted to the dim light, his gaze remaining locked on Frankie's stubbled face. "What did you say?"

"Bro, nukes are going off in American cities."

Mariani's body was still under the covers, but his tattooed chest and arms were exposed. "When was this?" he grumbled as he got out of bed, reaching for his black wind pants.

"Like ten minutes ago."

"Who did it?"

Frankie shook his head. "I have no idea."

"Who got hit?"

"Washington D.C., New York, Chicago, L.A., and Minneapolis."

Mariani's face scrunched up. "Minneapolis?" he echoed with panic in his voice. "That's where my sister lives."

"I know," Frankie said, studying the vein bulging from the right side of Mariani's bald head. "I-I think it was a tactical nuclear weapon. Early reports said it only leveled the downtown area. Not the entire city." He turned the flashlight off on his phone and then handed it to Mariani.

At the sight of the picture on Frankie's phone, Mariani let out a heavy sigh. "She works at the university downtown." His free hand was clenched into a fist.

"Oh, man." Frankie reached out to touch his friend on the shoulder, squeezing sympathetically. "I'm so sorry. … I hope she wasn't there today."

Mariani shook his head. "Thanks, bro," he said, swallowing grief. "I'm gonna call her right now."

"The power's out, bro. No service on the phone either."

Mariani looked at the screen. "Fuck! You're right, no service." He gave Frankie's phone back, and then threw on a shirt. "She'll probably be okay." He paused, turning to face Frankie. "How 'bout your dad? He still live down there?"

"Yeah, he works downtown, too," Frankie said. "I called him before the power went out…and it went right to voicemail. I'm kinda freaking out. I don't know what to do."

"Fuck, I'm sorry, brother. This shit sucks."

"I hope we find them someday," Frankie sunk his head briefly.

Mariani smacked Frankie's shoulder. "Pick your head up, soldier. You know what happens next."

"World War Three," Frankie said, biting down on his lower lip.

"I bet the Stealth Bombers are in the sky already."

"There's a flip side to that coin." Frankie cracked his knuckles. "China might be coming."

"China's too smart. They'd hit us with a bioweapon."

"What if this is a false flag attack?"

"No way," Mariani shook his head. "Take your tinfoil conspiracy theory hat off. This is an act of war by a foreign enemy, and they'll be dealt with. Swiftly."

"I hope we survive."

"We're gonna survive," Mariani said from his gut. "And we're gonna keep our families safe, no matter what happens next."

"We got an underground bunker," Frankie said and tilted his head. "That's a good start."

"I think we might need more supplies. This could be a long war. We should go to town and get some shit."

"We got supplies here."

"I'd rather have more than we need than not enough."

3

Duluth, Minnesota
March 13, 2017

Diana Buccetti heard a car door shut outside of her house, and she reached for the shotgun on the coffee table. Rising to her feet, she waddled her short and stout body to the window. Peeking out the blinds, her curly white hair dangled in her face as three bulky college-age kids got out of an SUV. They were congregating on the snowy sidewalk, and another loud group was across the street. *What are they doing?* Diana kicked the bottom of the door. "Come on, mother fuckers!" she yelled, but the baggy- clothed young adults didn't hear her.

Setting the gun on the hardwood floor, she zipped up her red and black jacket, and then paced back and forth. "Where the fuck's my son?" Diana asked under her breath. "Where the fuck's Russel? No phone, no lights, no heat. And no one cares."

Plopping down on the couch, her round shoulders rose and fell with each wheezing breath. Her sixty-seven-year-old heart was thumping at a high rate. *There is no peace, only strife,* she thought to herself. *The end of the world is here, and I'm all alone. No one to protect me.*

Tensing suddenly, Diana's eyes swiveled toward a sound coming from outside. The crunch of footsteps on the icy porch.

"Oh God," Diana whispered, her hand going to her throat when heavy footfalls landed on each frozen step. Her fingers trembled as she positioned the shotgun at the giant silhouette on the other side of the glass door.

The man outside pounded on the door. "Diana!" He raised his voice. "Hurry up! Let me in!"

"Russel." Diana let out a breath of relief and unlocked the door.

Russel pushed the door open. "Did you hear about the bombing?" He swiped snowflakes from his full head of gray hair.

"Lock the door!" she barked.

Spinning, her common-law husband did as he was told. Turning back, he stuck his arm out. "Give me that gun." Russel's words were deep and slow.

"They hit Minneapolis, too." She gave him the shotgun. "I bet we're next. What took you so long?" Diana snipped with seething frustration. "What, were you gonna wait till I got bludgeoned to death? These punks around here are probably going to start robbing people soon. With no phones, no one can call 911."

"I was at work," Russel said, resting the weapon on the coffee table. "I'm sorry. I was up on the tenth floor. Vacuuming. No one told me what was going on."

"I can't believe this is happening," she said. "What are we gonna do?"

"You should pack some bags," he turned and looked out the window at the growing commotion outside. "We'd be safer out at Frankie's place."

Diana shook her head. "I ain't going nowhere."

4

Hermantown, Minnesota
March 13, 2017

Frankie tapped the brakes of his black SUV and then turned down the secluded gravel road that Conny lived on. "We'll make this quick," he said, eyes scanning the address numbers at the edge of the evergreen forest that was blanketed with snow.

"I still don't think it's your job to look over her kids," Mariani said from the passenger seat. "We need to get to the store before the rush."

"If Conny's still at work, her teenage kids are home alone," Frankie said over the loud hum of the tires at thirty-miles-an-hour. "They're probably scared to death with no phone or power. I just want to tell them it's gonna be okay."

Turning his head to the left, Frankie first saw Conny's house through a gap in the trees. Slowing down to turn in the driveway, he saw a big red truck parked in his spot. The driver-side door was swung open. Frankie's grip on the wheel tightened. A tall man in jeans and a black jacket was facing the house. Blue arms were wrapped around him. Brown hair was flowing in the air around his shoulders. "What the fuck?" A sharp pain entered his heart after the witness of betrayal.

"That's fucked up." Mariani said.

Frankie stomped his boot on the gas and the truck roared. "What a stupid fucking gash."

"She was in his arms, bro. You can't forgive that."

Frankie's seething breaths were loud. His hands were strangling the steering wheel. "I'll never talk to that bitch again." He pounded the palm of his hand on the wheel. A soft growl rumbled in his throat.

5

Location Unknown
March 13, 2017

Planted in a thick leather chair in the situation room — a thousand feet underground — President Tom Clacher interrupted the Speaker of the House. "Excuse me, Speaker Roth. … I decide."

"Mr. President," Speaker Roth said, her short silver hair dancing by her jaw-line as she spoke. "You need my consent before retaliating."

Eight remaining members of the continuity of government snapped their heads in President Clacher's direction. The commander in chief's face was gaunt with exhaustion, his forehead grooved with lines of worry. All the same, his red tie was snug, while everyone else's hung loosely around their necks; he was also sitting upright while everyone else sat slouched.

"You gave me your advice." The thin, white-haired president leaned forward, one hand absently grabbing the black key that was hanging around his neck. "I disagree. My decision has been made." The tension around the long oak table was thick. The grumbles were few.

"Sir," a black-haired woman spoke out of turn. "The enemy has underestimated the resolve of the United States military. Sir." Her tan hands were folded perfectly on the table. Her hair was tied in a bun. And her blazer was black like the rest of the civilians in the room.

"Miss Freeman, you're exactly right," President Clacher said in a lowered tone. "The enemy has made an irreversible mistake."

The door opened, and the Secret Service man closed it behind him. "Excuse my interruption, sir." His body was stiff. "Deputy Secretary of State Eugene Parker has an urgent message."

"Let him in," Clacher said.

The door opened again, and a tall heavy-set man rushed in with a briefcase. "Please excuse me," Eugene Parker said, sitting his rotund frame in the chair next to Speaker Roth. "Sorry, I'm late." His hand brushed over his deeply receding sandy blond hairline. "I-I just received new intel from one of the terror suspects captured on the Mexican border."

"I'm listening," President Clacher said.

Deputy Secretary Parker slid a leather folder across the table. "The ISIL soldier has spilled the beans. And our partners in Saudi Arabia have corroborated. T-they say ISIL has now taken responsibility for the attack." His face was blushing and his blue eyes were blinking rapidly.

The president opened the folder. "And you believe terrorists have that capability?" He snorted. "Because my intelligence report says the opposite."

Parker nodded. "I-I do, and historically…ISIL speaks the truth after manmade disasters." He pointed back at the president. "Don't you dare use nuclear weapons until you're certain who is responsible." His finger was shaking.

From the center of the table, the president twisted to face the yes man to his right. "Did he just say our enemy speaks the truth?" Clacher lifted his bony finger to chest level. "Don't answer that...." He paused, straightening to point at Eugene Parker. "I don't like your tone, Parker. You're fired!" Clacher swiped his hand. "Get him out of here."

Two burly Secret Service agents in black suits grabbed Parker and forcefully lifted him out of his seat. "Don't let him use nuclear weapons!" Parker shouted, kicking and screaming all the way to the door. "He's gonna get us all ki—" And the door closed.

An awkward moment of silence hung in the air. Clacher dropped a closed fist on the table. "That's exactly why the American people elected me in a landslide. Because we're led by weaklings like that." He paused to scan the men and women at the table. "We're about to go to war, people. Anyone who doesn't want to be a part of this...should leave now." He gestured to the door.

President Clacher looked around the room for defectors. One man in uniform stood up, saluted the president, and quietly made his exit.

"Anybody else?" Clacher asked, and then paused before turning to the Secret Service agent closest to him. "Detain them both. Until the end of hostilities."

One of the Secret Service agents gave a slight nod before exiting the war room.

"Mr. President," said the Acting Secretary of Defense Richard Secord. "We're all with you, sir... How would you like to proceed?" With the civilian-military leader missing after the morning attack of Washington D.C., Richard Secord filled the seat with experience and muscle. Now across the table from the president, he sat still in a black suit and tie. His brown hair was parted to one side, black rectangular glasses resting on his nose.

"In my briefing," President Clacher said, "I was told that it is the policy of the United States to respond to nuclear attacks by retaliating against all enemies at the same time. I was given three options." He paused for dramatic effect. "Do you concur?"

"I concur, Mr. President," Acting Secretary Secord said coldly. "There *are* no good options in this situation, sir. We are certain…Russia and China are involved." He tilted his right hand. "What Mr. Parker didn't tell you, is that two Russian intelligence agents were also being interrogated on the Mexican border. They kept their mouths shut, but our military intelligence has concluded that Russia is guilty. This means, because of their military alliance with China, Iran, and North Korea, all four nations must be dealt with."

"What option do you recommend?" President Clacher asked, looking at the straight-faced man who seemed to never blink.

"Option 'B' with the door open for option 'A'," Secord said as if he had rehearsed those words a hundred times.

From two seats to the left of the president, Speaker Roth smacked the table. "Slow down, Mr. President." She raised her voice. "Do you understand that Russia and China have at least six thousand nuclear warheads between them? They'll turn us into a parking lot."

The president's eyebrows lowered. "You're fired!" He pointed. "Get her out of here." The room erupted in gasps, but one sharp voice screeched loudly. Secret Service closed in.

"You can't fire *me*!" Speaker Roth stood up. "You've gone mad! I represent one-third of this government. I'm enacting the 25th Amendment, right now. This man is mentally unstable and unfit to lead. Raise your hand and save your country." She glared at Secord.

Richard Secord looked at every person in the room. No one budged. He shook his head slightly.

"Get her out of here!" Clacher demanded, and the Secret Service team carried her out of the room.

When the door closed, Acting Defense Secretary Secord straightened his husky frame. "Mr. President," Secord said. "Millions of Americans will die, but the goal here is to preserve the union. The time for peace is over. If we don't act, our enemies will be emboldened."

"Don't we have a secret program for this?" President Clacher asked. "You know…missile defense?"

At that moment, the female CIA analyst at the end of the table rose out of her chair. "Excuse me Mr. President," she said, standing in a black pantsuit. "Permission to give a brief presentation, sir?"

"By all means, Miss Freeman," Clacher said, tilting one hand open.

"Thank you," she said, stepping toward the huge screen across from the president and behind Secord. Reaching in her jacket pocket, she pulled out a black laser pointer. With her right hand, she pointed the red beam at the digital map, landing the red dot on Russia.

"Russia is *indeed* our greatest geopolitical foe," Steff Freeman said. "They have more than 5,000 nuclear weapons, but the consensus is…they *will* surrender after Moscow is destroyed." She paused, turning her athletic body to face President Clacher. "The Russian regime is intelligent. Our spies on the inside tell us that the political hierarchy understands that the capabilities of the United States are unique. The problem is…they have at least fifty nuclear submarines spread out in every ocean in the world. The hardliners in the Russian military might not obey orders from land. My fear is…they launch a counter strike from beneath the sea.

"However, we do have three thousand interceptor missiles. They *are* operational, but I'm afraid ten percent of projectiles *will* get through." She paused to let out an audible sigh. "What I'm about to tell you is beyond classified. Most of you will be learning about this for the first time. We *do* have a missile defense system. It's called: Stardust." She paused, watching the reaction from the president. "Yes, in fact, we have lasers on satellites orbiting the globe at all times. They've never been tested because we couldn't risk the enemy gaining this knowledge. *This* is what gives us the upper hand."

"So, basically, you're saying that plan 'B' should work?" President Clacher shrugged. "But some of their bombs will find a way to the homeland?"

"Affirmative, sir," the CIA analyst said. "Plan 'A' will not be necessary. We only need a limited nuclear attack."

Vice President Andrews cleared his throat. "Do you have data from a computer simulation on this precise scenario?" He shared a glance with the president, rubbed his bald head, and then returned his wide eyes to Steff Freeman.

Miss Freeman nodded. "Yes, sir."

"What's the projected death count on both sides?" VP Andrews asked.

Without looking at any notes or taking time to think, Steff Freeman opened her mouth. "Sir, twenty to fifty million Americans will parish at the hands of Russia and China. Ten million will die in Europe from Russia. Japan and South Korea will be vaporized by China and North Korea. And Israel will be destroyed by Iran." Pausing to swallow hard, Freeman exchanged glances with a black-skinned admiral at the end of table. "Russia will lose thirty million, China will lose a hundred million, North Korea will be vaporized, and ten million will parish in Iran. Once this happens, all of America's enemies will be no more.... And hopefully...there will be peace for all time."

President Clacher cleared his throat, and waited for Freeman to return to her seat. "Thank you, Miss Freeman. Thank all of you." He let out an exasperated sigh, his head swiveling from left to right. "I appreciate your service to our beloved country. I appreciate your input, opinions, and honor. I am *honored* to work with all of you to preserve freedom. I can only pray...the history books will treat us fairly." He paused dramatically before quoting the father of the atomic bomb. *"Now I am become death...the destroyer of worlds."* He tucked his chin in his chest. "May God forgive us for what we're about to do."

6

West Duluth, Minnesota
March 13, 2017

Frankie pulled his SUV into a parking spot at the grocery store and threw the shifter in park.

Mariani cursed under his breath. "Look at all those people," he said, pointing to the gathering crowd at the entrance. "What are they waiting for?"

"Looks like the doors are locked," Frankie said. "I'm surprised someone hasn't drove through yet."

Mariani smirked. "We should do it. Put the Tahoe to the test."

"Ughhh," Frankie grumbled. "That's a lot of effort."

"We need supplies, right?" Mariani pressed. "Come on, I'll drive."

"That's how we end up in jail."

"I ain't going to jail." Mariani cocked his black handgun.

Frankie tugged his black winter cap further over his ears. "Let's try *not* to get in a shootout. Our families are gonna need us."

"You're right, bro." Mariani shoved his gun in the holster underneath his black leather jacket. "I'm just saying. I will not hesitate."

Jets above the clouds shook the ground below. Frankie's body jerked at the sound of thunder, and then he tilted his head to the dark cloudy sky. "Ken Spatz might be up there."

Mariani gazed into the sky. "Nah, I bet Spatz is overseas. Probably about to drop some bombs on some terrorists."

Frankie nodded. "Yeah, last time I talked to him, he said he got promoted."

"He deserves it. Dude dedicated his entire adult life to the military."

"Ken's a true patriot in my book." Frankie picked at his fingernails. "A Marine, a CIA agent, and now a fighter pilot. Wherever he is, I hope he's safe."

"He's a survivor. I don't think nothing could stop him."

"Maybe he'll tell us some war stories sometime."

"Look!" Mariani pointed at a revving truck in the middle of the parking lot. "Them assholes are gonna ram the door."

"Those guys are nuts!" Frankie chuckled. "We'll let them do the dirty work. Then we'll walk in."

"You better be ready." Mariani gestured to the crowd. "These people are desperate."

Frankie nodded. "I was born ready," he said, letting out a breath before opening the door. His heart was pounding as he stepped down to the icy blacktop. Cutting through the parking lot, his heart slowed down because Mariani was at his side.

The sound of an out-of-date pick-up truck revving its engine made Mariani's mind crank.

All of a sudden, the truck screamed toward the glass front door of the grocery store. A trail of black exhaust smoke followed as it smashed through the entrance and barrelled into the store. Dozens of people blitzed the entrance, screaming and shouting like it was midnight on New Year's Eve.

Frankie's boots crunched on broken glass as he stepped into the dark building. Grabbing a cart, he pushed it to the right side of the store, and Mariani went to the left. LED emergency lights led their way.

Pushing his cart down the first aisle, Mariani grabbed a package of toilet paper and dropped it in his cart. As he reached for a second package, a woman's shrieks gave him pause. Snapping his head over his shoulder, his body followed. A gun was now in his hands. With long strides, he followed the voice of distress to the frozen foods section in the far corner of the store.

A tall and large man with a black jacket was smacking a blond college-age girl whose arms shot up to block the blows.

Mariani pointed the gun toward the ceiling and squeezed the trigger. The fiery explosion made the petite girl drop to the floor. "Back the fuck up and turn around."

The man turned to face him. He had pork-chop style sideburns and a snarl on his mouth. Taking a step toward Mariani, he spread his arms wide. "Why don't you mind your own business?" He flicked open a stainless-steel knife.

Scurrying away from her oppressor, the young woman hid behind Mariani. Her mouth was bleeding, and her diamond-studded nose was red. Her face uncommonly pale. Mascara running down her cheeks.

"Don't fucking move," Mariani said, his gun trained on the man's massive chest.

The man took a step forward. "You ain't got the balls to sh—"

Giovanni Mariani bucked his gun, the single report echoing across the supermarket.

"No!" the girl cried, jumping to her knees, reaching out to touch the bleeding man's scruffy face. "You didn't have to shoot him." Her fingers then covered the steaming hole in his chest. "Steve!"

The big man was on his back. Not moving.

"Consider that a favor." He scooped up the man's knife and then stuffed it in his pocket.

"He's an asshole, but I'm not just gonna let him die."

"Good luck." Mariani walked away and didn't look back.

*****

A stampede of looters had just fled the vicinity at the sound of Mariani's second gunshot. Frankie was creeping with his pistol in his hands. Adrenaline was pumping through his chest as he pushed and shoved his way up and down the aisles, frantically searching for his friend.

"Stugots!" Frankie hollered, dodging people and shopping carts until he saw a thin figure in black walking toward him with a gun at his side. The bald head and very gait identified Mariani from twenty feet in the dark.

"You missed it, bro," Mariani said, looking off to the side briefly. "I just caught a rapist in the act. Had to put him down like a sick dog. He was uncurable."

The two old friends met eyes.

"Damn, man," Frankie said, his eyebrows arching. "He's dead?"

"Yeah, I had no choice. He had a knife."

*****

Just before noon, Frankie navigated his SUV up a steep road in the middle of the city. "My mom ain't gonna want to go."

"Just tell her it ain't gonna be safe here," Mariani said calmly, his lips puffing on a cigarette. The smoke getting sucked out the cracked open window.

Parking in front of his mom's house, Frankie turned to face Mariani. "You wanna come in?"

"Nah, I'll wait here," Mariani said. "Hurry up. It's only a matter of time before this neighborhood gets wild. And I still need you to drop me off at my mom's house."

Frankie nodded. Pushing open the truck door, he stepped down to the snow-crusted sidewalk. Picking up his head, he saw cars coming and going at faster speeds than usual. He heard people screaming and yelling in the distance as if there was a keg party up the block. Reaching inside his parka, he touched the cold steel of his gun. *I hope I never have to use it.*

Walking slowly in the shadow of two giant evergreen trees, he noticed his mother watching him from behind the wood-framed glass door. By the time he reached the top step, the door opened. His mom's face raised, her eyes glinting. She held open her arms. He embraced her tightly.

"Mom," he whispered, bending low over her head. His hands were flat against her back.

"'Bout time," she muttered.

"I know, I wanted—Jesus!" Whipping his head toward the street, Frankie flinched at the intrusion of a loud siren.

The siren continued for a long moment, and then it was replaced with a slow-speaking computerized female voice that addressed the public at large.

"*...ATTENTION!*" the voice said loud and clear. "*THIS IS NOT A TEST.... REPEAT...THIS IS NOT A TEST.... THE UNITED STATES OF AMERICA IS IN A STATE OF WAR.... UNTIL HOSTILITIES EXPIRE, A STATE OF MARTIAL LAW WILL BE EXECUTED BY THE NATIONAL GUARD.... THERE*

WILL BE A CURFEW STARTING AT 1500 HOURS…. ANY PERSON SEEN IN THE STREETS WILL BE DETAINED…. I REPEAT…THIS IS NOT A TEST…. REMAIN IN YOUR HOMES UNTIL FURTHER NOTICE…. THE STATE WILL DELIVER INFORMATION AS NEEDED ON YOUR RADIO DIAL…99.9…. REPEAT…TURN YOUR RADIO DIAL TO CHANNEL 99.9…."

Diana stared at her only son. "We're all gonna die. I know it. The nukes are coming."

"We're gonna be okay, Mom," Frankie said. "But we got to get the hell of here, right now. Criminals won't obey curfew. They'll be looking for trouble."

"I'm not leaving," Diana snipped. "This is my home."

"Mom." Frankie shook his hands in front of his head. "You have five minutes to pack a few bags, then me and Russel are gonna carry you out."

"Leave?" Her head snapped backward. "If we're all going to die, I'd rather die here, thank you very much."

"Mom, we're not gonna die." He paused, reaching for her shoulder, speaking slowly to break through her early stages of senility. "I love you. But you *have* to understand…the roads are jam-packed, and it's only getting worse. We'll be safe at my house in the country."

"Diana!" Russel raised his voice. "Listen to Frankie."

Diana cursed all the way upstairs. Frankie started filling a bag with canned goods. *I ain't gonna give the looters a free lunch,* he thought. While rummaging through the over-cluttered kitchen, he noticed three small pieces of art hanging on the wall above the sink. It was three wooden squares: each with a life-size painting of the different forms of an apple. The first was pristine and red, the second had a big bite taken out of it, and the third was merely a core, with a little black stem sticking out of the top. Frankie smiled, grabbing the childhood memories and shoving them in the bag.

*****

Pacing back and forth, Frankie looked outside at the waiting truck in front. *This is taking too long.* Turning back toward the stairs, he shouted. "Mom! Let's go."

Stomping up the stairs, Frankie slowed down as he entered his mom's bedroom. "Are you okay?"

Diana was lying in her bed — weeping. "I-I don't want to go, Frankie." Diana cried with a shaky voice. "I-I can't leave. Everything I own is here. All my antiques, my pictures. My clothes."

"Mom," Frankie said with a light touch. "These earthly things can be replaced. Your life can't."

Diana took her arm off her face. "But the house will be ruined," his mother said, still weeping.

"We'll rebuild it, Mom." Frankie reached for her hand, thinking about the possibility of losing both of his parents. "I-I love you. I can't live without you. All I wanna do is survive…together with you."

7

Location Unknown
March 13, 2017
1:10 p.m.

The Acting Secretary of Defense Richard Secord placed two bulky briefcases on the oak table in front of President Clacher. As the cases were opened, he spared the others in the room a quick glance. Silence prevailed as the members in attendance watched the proceedings.

The president's eyes locked on the military-grade laptop computer. *Wow,* he thought, studying the black screen with the white flashing cursor. The black keyboard with the keyhole on the right. The red button beneath the keyhole.

Reaching inside his suit coat, Secord pulled a small code card from his breast pocket. It was protected by a thin plastic case. Snapping the plastic with his fingers, he pinched the paper card and slipped the case into his pocket. "R-U-4-86," he said and spelled it out. "R as in Romeo. U as in Uniform. The number four. And the number eighty-six."

"R-U-4-86," President Clacher repeated as he typed the first Cerberus Code. Locking eyes with Secord, he blinked repetitively, beads of sweat rolling down his sides.

"Mr. President," Acting Defense Secretary Secord lowered his voice. "At the count of three…press enter."

President Clacher leaned forward, hovering a finger just above the enter button on the keyboard. Turning his head, he saw Secretary Secord's finger actually touching the button.

"One," Secord said, glancing at the president's slightly twitching hand. "Two." His pause was brief but noticeable. "Three." Simultaneously, Secord and Clacher pressed down on the enter button.

President Clacher pulled out the second code card from his breast pocket. Taking it out of the protective jacket, it was his turn to read the codeword to Secord.

"Yorktown," POTUS said proudly. "Y as in Yankee. O as in Oscar. R as in Romeo. K as in Kennedy. T as in Tango. O, as in Olympics. W as in Washington, and N as in November."

Once they both typed in the password, they counted to three out loud.

The president pressed the enter key at the same time as the acting secretary of defense. Both leaders then removed the black lanyard from around their necks. Clacher gripped it tight, nervously looking down at the small black key in his fingers. *The death key.*

Following Secord's lead, President Clacher gently inserted the small key into the keyhole on the right side of the keyboard.

Clacher locked eyes with Secretary Secord. Compressing his lips, Clacher swallowed doubt.

"At the count of three," Secord said, "we both turn the key to the right. Hold for three seconds, and then let go."

"I'm ready."

Secord bit his lip. "I'm ready, sir."

Eyeing one another, both men spoke in unison. "One…two…three."

"Mr. President," Secord said gravely. "The weapon is loaded; the safety is off. All you have to do is press the red button to proceed."

8

Minneapolis, Minnesota
March 13, 2017

In the suburbs of the Mini Apple, Frankie's step-mom was frantically stuffing a suitcase in her bedroom. Her fourteen-year-old daughter was impatiently standing in the doorway, biting on her fingernails.

"Tina, why don't you go pick out a few of your favorite books," Elise said and zipped up her suitcase. "Get that one Frankie got you for Christmas." Elise was bundled up in a parka and woolen cap. Her curly brown hair was in a pony tail and resting on her back.

"Okay, mom," Tina said, and then ran out the door, her boots rapping on the wood floor in the hallway.

Elise Williams picked up a pen and began scribbling in a notebook on her husband's computer desk:

Tony,
I really hope you were late for work today. Then you missed the bombing downtown. It's getting too dangerous here for Tina. I heard gunshots just down the block. We're going to my aunt's house in Mankato. Please meet us there. Be safe. We love you!

Eternally yours,

Dropping the pen, she turned to Tina who was standing with a suitcase and two plump backpacks. "Did you get everything you might need?"

"Yeah, mom," Tina said softly. "I got some clothes, my toothbrush, books, and a pillow." Her skin was a shade darker than her tan winter jacket. Her smile was nonexistent.

"All right," Elise said, letting out a heavy sigh. "Let's go to auntie's house. She has a surprise for you."

*****

Elise shut the front door. Turning around, she grabbed Tina's hand and walked down the front steps. Pausing briefly, she gazed in awe at the setting sun behind the thick smoke from the smoldering nuclear explosion twenty miles east. The horizon was a dark shade of purple she had not seen before. The smell of soot was lingering in the air. The sound of car horns honking and people screaming and yelling kept Elise's head on a swivel.

Distant gunshots rang out, and Elise ran to the car, yanking her daughter's arm firmly. She opened the door. "Get in," Elise said. "Let's go! Hurry up."

Tina got in the front seat and Elise shoved their bags in the back. Shuffling around the car, she got in and let out a breath. Turning the key, she looked in her rear-view mirror and saw a parked car with broken-out windows and a littered street.

Taking her foot off the brake, she backed out of her driveway. Turning on the street in reverse, she shifted into drive and began rolling forward. A rugged group of young men was walking down the middle of the street. They were wearing dark puffy jackets and caring objects in their hands.

"Why are those people in the street, Mom?"

"I don't know." Elise cursed under her breath as she coasted toward them slowly.

The group kept walking forward. Elise slowed to a stop.

"They got bats, Mom."

From about thirty feet, Elise counted more than ten hoodlums. "They're not gonna let us through."

"Turn around, Mom. I'm scared."

The gang rushed toward them.

"I can't. No time for a three-point turn." She honked the horn and held it. The screaming men continued charging forward. Mouths opened. Arms flailing.

"Take your seatbelt off and hide on the floor."

"Why?"

"Just do it!" Elise yelled.

As soon as Tina was low. Elise slammed on the gas, accelerated, and then plowed through the people blocking the road. "Stay down!" Elise yelled at Tina.

Behind them, a loud gunshot erupted, and the rear window shattered. Ducking her head, she steered blindly until the loud popping stopped.

Picking up her head, Elise sped down the road. "Get in your seat." Her voice was shaky. "Put your seatbelt back on."

Tina jumped into her seat. "What's happening, Mom?" the kid cried, pulling her seatbelt across her chest. "Why do them people hate us?"

They traveled in the direction of the interstate highway heading west. After a right and a left, she slowed down and veered onto a roundabout leading them to 495 West.

Braking around the end of the loop, Elise smiled because they were safe. "Holy crap." She pumped the brakes, slowly coming to a complete stop behind ten thousand honking cars and trucks. "This is worst traffic jam I've ever seen."

"Mom, w-what are we gonna do. We're stuck."

"Everything's going to be okay, sweety. Don't worry. We'll make it to auntie's house. It might just take a little bit longer."

The freeway was backed up as far as the eye could see. Craning her neck, Elise looked in every direction. Nothing but parked cars and smoke plumes rising into the dark sky.

9

Fish Lake, Minnesota
March 13, 2017

Frankie parked his SUV in front of his garage. His mother and Russel pulled up next to him in their car. Letting out a deep breath, Frankie gazed at the house he built with stolen cartel money. Cherry wood siding and staggered stones are what he saw, but he envisioned the bunker underneath the house. *I wonder if we'd survive a nuclear attack on Duluth?*

Diana knocked on his window.

Frankie jerked back around, cracking the door open. "Welcome home, Mom," he said. "We should be safe here." He got out, placed an arm around her shoulders, and then guided her to the front of the house.

Diana cracked a thin smile, the chilled wind blowing her hair. "I really like it out here." She turned slowly, looking at the enchanted green forest that encircled the house, garage, and two-acre plot of flat snowy land. "Do you get deer out here?"

"All the time. Mariani feeds them." Frankie didn't dare tell her why he fed them.

"Nice place, Frank," Russel said slowly. "You did good."

"Let's go inside," Frankie said. "I'll get your stuff later."

Keys dangling in his hands, Frankie led everyone to the front door. The house was dark and cold as they entered, but Frankie was smiling. *Finally, home!*

Diana found her way to the lambskin sofa in the living room. She reclined her feet, placed her hands on her slightly plump belly, and then closed her eyes briefly. Snapping her eyes open, she barked out an order. "Turn on the radio!"

Frankie found a hand-sized radio and turned the dial to 99.9. Upon turning the volume up, a male baritone voice overpowered the static.

"*...was the worst afternoon in the history of the world,*" President Clacher said gravely. "*This day will live on until the end of time. As you all know, America has been attacked. You need to know...that more attacks are coming. As commander in chief of this nation, for the sake of national security, preservation of the union, and freedom for the world, I have ordered a retaliatory strike on the axis of evil. We will not surrender our freedom to such threats on our nation. On this, you have my word of honor.... I am not afraid to name this axis of evil. The enemy who faces the full might of the United States military is Russia, China, North Korea, and Iran. As we speak, operations are underway to achieve absolute victory. Unfortunately, we face a sophisticated, determined, and capable enemy with rogue elements in their hierarchy. This battle will not be easy, this road will not be smooth, the days forward will test our will as a nation to survive...and endure the unendurable. But, because you have not doubted my resolve, I will never doubt yours. We will rebuild this nation, we will rebuild the world, we will restore freedom to the oppressed, and we will give hope to those who are hopeless.*" The president softened his voice. "*We will do this together. I want to borrow a few words from my predecessor — President Lings — who was a victim in this morning's surprise attack on Washington D.C.: 'We are one people. One team. One vessel...in a sea of evil. We must endure for good.'*

"And with that, I wish you well. I look forward to speaking with you again...very soon. I'll explain my short-term plan to get every American the relief they will need for the tough months ahead. May God bless each and every one of you. May God continue to bless the United States of America."

And as a familiar song began to play on the radio, Frankie, Russel, Diana, and tens of millions of Americans listened with a tingle on their cheeks, and moisture building up in their eyes.

"O beautiful, for heroes proved.... In liberating strife.... Who more than self, their country loved, and mercy more than life... O beautiful for spacious skies, for amber waves of grain, for purple mountain majesties, above the fruited plain.... America...America..."

10

Location Unknown
March 13, 2017

President Clacher pointed at the flat-screen digital televisions on the wall. Leaning forward in his seat, his eyes squinted at the live satellite footage of three gray missiles. The first was a beast with lamb-like horns, coming up out of the earth. The second was seen rising from the ocean. And a third beast was rocketing above the firmament.

"What the hell was that?" President Clacher's eyes widened. On the center screen, a missile in outer space burst into smoke, breaking apart into several pieces.

"Mr. President," Vice President Andrews said. "Those Intercontinental Ballistic Missiles just deployed five nuclear weapons each. And now, they're re-entering Earth. They're descending on enemy coordinates at civilian and military installations in Russia. The missiles fired from our submarines are going to do the exact same thing but were given coordinates in Red China. As we speak, Stealth Bombers are in the clouds above Iran and North—"

Acting Defense Secretary Secord rose from his seat. "Ten seconds to first touchdown," he shouted. "Center screen."

The president stood tall, waiting, gazing at the screen and the thermal nuclear explosion he had ordered. The giant flash of light jerked his head back an inch. And then his eyes snapped to the next screen, soaking in the airborne fireball and black mushroom cloud. Sucking in air, he covered his mouth, exhaling hot breath on his hand.

The big screen behind the president displayed a flat digital picture of the globe with blue lines that represented each weapon's trajectory from deployment to destination. The smaller screens showed live satellite footage of each target city or military base.

Clacher looked from the live footage back to the trajectory screen. He squinted. "I believe…"

The sudden blare of the emergency alarm cut him off. All eyes swiveled toward the sound.

Admiral Grannis plopped his meaty hand on the desk, turning toward his commander in chief. "A dozen ICBMs from Russia and China are en route, sir." His black uniform was full of decorations.

VP Andrews raised his voice. "North Korea just unloaded their conventional arsenal on South Korea," he said, sinking his head. "And the State of Israel is no more."

No one spoke, but a few people shifted uneasily in their chairs. Someone sighed. Another person cleared their throat. No one looked at each other. All eyes were on the screens.

Black and orange mushroom clouds occupied each screen on the wall. Each representing millions of lives lost. The president, turned to read the global map behind him. Dozens of bold black **X**'s marked enemy targets destroyed.

A small speaker in front of Admiral Grannis chirped, and everyone turned to face it.

"The target is destroyed," an *SR-71 Blackhawk* pilot said from the *MiG* swarmed skies above Moscow.

Loud cheers erupted. Men and women in the room were rapidly clapping their hands. Smiles and nods were interrupted by another chirp from the speaker.

"Communism just died," Lieutenant Ken Spatz said in an *F22-Raptor* above the China Sea. "Beijing is gone."

Clapping her hands on the far edge of the table, Steff Freeman's eyes widened at the sound of Spatz' voice.

"The potbelly dictator in North Korea is on fire!" a pilot said with excitement.

Acting Defense Secretary Secord was pumping his fists. Admiral Grannis' arms were flexed in the air. President Clacher was exchanging glances at Steff Freeman.

"Sir," the vice president gently touched Clacher's arm. "Enemy projectiles are re-entering the atmosphere. There're more missiles than we thought!"

Gasps were heard. Cuss words echoed.

The president's head whipped to the center screen. "God bless our satellites."

"The Stardust Program is working, sir." Acting Secretary Secord pointed at the screen.

Vice President Andrews' eyes were locked on the map of the United States. "Mr. President, what was left of New York City is gone." Andrews was massaging his temples.

"Seventy-five percent of bogeys are down, sir," Miss Freeman said, studying her satellite computer.

"Mr. President," Andrews said. "Area 51 and the NORAD base are both gone. Do you know what that means, sir?"

President Clacher turned to his number two. "We're gonna take some hits, Andrews." He rested a heavy hand on his shoulder. "Let it ride."

"Ninety percent of enemy bogeys have been terminated." Miss Freeman said, her head buried in the computer screen.

"Chicago." Andrews covered his face.

Freeman cleared her throat. "Sir, out of fifty Intercontinental Ballistic Missiles, only five snuck through."

"American technology has no match." President Clacher cracked his knuckles.

"Mr. President," Secretary Secord said. "The president of Russia is on the line."

President Clacher glanced at Secord before straightening his tie. "What's your recommendation?"

"Mr. President, accept nothing less than absolute surrender," Richard Secord said.

The president nodded, reaching out for the big black satellite phone. "This is the president."

"President Clacher," the president of Russia said in his best broken English. "Unfortunate we speak under such dire circumstance."

"Indeed," Clacher said with contempt. "It didn't have to be this way."

"It did not," President Petrov said. "Collectively, it was out of our…hands."

"A lot of people died," Clacher said. "And a lot more could still die."

"Which is reason I call," Russia's president said. "War is game of chess. Your domination of outer space…is checkmate. I wish only…to stop bloodshed…save Russian brethren. And preserve fertile land for my grandchildren."

"President Petrov, absolute surrender is your only option," President Clacher said. "Absolute surrender or no deal."

"Mr. President," Petrov said. "I am prepared to surrender, under one condition. I trade coordinates of my submarines in return for immunity for my government…and myself. I will not be hung in tribunal."

"Coordinates?" Clacher said. "Did I hear you correctly? … You don't have control over your military?"

"My military on land understand stakes," Petrov said. "Men thousand leagues under sea, not so much…. They are…more…old school, KGB. They will never surrender."

"That sounds like a problem," President Clacher shifted his head to read a note given to him by Steff Freeman. "How many subs do you have?"

"Thirty-nine with ICBM," the president of Russia said in a smug tone. "I have coordinates to all Chinese subs, too."

"When will they launch?"

"They are reloading as we speak,"

"Immunity," President Clacher said without asking for advice. "You have a deal. Give the coordinates to my team."

"Thank you, Mr. President," President Petrov said. "You are strong adversary. Spine of steel."

11

The Buccetti Compound
March 13, 2017

Diana Buccetti pushed her empty plate forward. "That was a good burger, Frankie. Thanks."

"We're lucky," Frankie said. "Who else gets to barbeque, and then eat dinner with the lights on? And heat, too."

"We're not lucky," Diana said, her fingers crossed on her round belly, glancing at Russel who was still eating. "We're blessed. But why? … Why do we get to live like this?" Her jacket was zipped up tight. Frankie had set the temperature low to save gas for the generator.

"Mom," Frankie said, all bundled up in a jacket and watch cap. "We don't need to worry about that. Sometimes, you just got to stay positive. And this is one of those times. The world is on fire, for cryin' out loud."

"Stay positive?" Diana squinted an eye. "What about everyone else? Who knows how many are dead? How many are suf—"

"Mom, stop." He showed her the palm of his hand. "Please…just relax."

"I can't relax," she said, jerking one hand. "How do you not worry about your friends? What about Conny, and her kids?"

Frankie dropped his fork on his plate, standing up abruptly. "Thanks for ruining my dinner."

"What? What'd I say?"

"Conny left me, Mom." He started walking out of the kitchen, turning back to face her. "She ran off with another guy. You happy?" He sunk his head, blowing out a breath. "And there's more." His head leveled off. "I think my dad got killed in the attack on Minneapolis. And most of my friends are probably freezing right now." His voice lowered. "That's what you want to talk about?" He shook his head. "No. I was just starting to make peace in my mind. I'm just happy to be alive. Here…with you and Russel. Is that okay with you?"

Russel had been silent as usual. Rising more than six feet tall, he extended a hand toward Frankie. "Thanks for having us, Frank." Russel dropped a heavy hand on his shoulder. "I'm sorry about your dad. I'm gonna go get another load from the car."

"Thanks," Frankie said. "I'll come help you in a few minutes." Russel walked out of the room.

Diana was biting her lower lip. "Who does Conny think she is? What a little bitch."

"Mom, bad-mouthing her ain't gonna help nothing. It was probably for the best. She was always bitching and moaning anyways. I loved her, but…she made her choice."

"Next time you have a girlfriend, you better pay more attention to her."

"There won't be a next time, Mom. I'm a loner. I need to be alone."

"Come on, Frank." Diana gave him a big hug. "You'll never be alone. I love you." She rubbed his back then let go.

Frankie sniffled, and then wiped his nose. "Thanks, Mom. I love you, too."

"You got lifelong friends who love you. Where's Carlos and Jewelz?"

He let out a breath. "I don't know. He woke me up this morning. Told me about the terrorist attack. I haven't talked to him since."

"How 'bout that black boy? And his girl?"

"Who, Marcel and Mae?" His head shifted. "They probably went to their cabin. They'll be okay."

"Do you think Mariani will come back?"

Frankie nodded. "Yeah. He'll be back. He's at his parent's house."

"I like that one," Diana said. "He has a good heart. A good soul."

"He's one of a kind," Frankie said. "He's like a big brother to me."

She took a sip of water and coughed. "I bumped into that Native boy a couple of weeks ago, too." Her voice was strained.

Frankie squinted a little bit. "Who? Gordon Grayfeather?"

"Yeah, that's him." She nodded. "I saw him at the drug store downtown. He was polite, but he looked rugged. Long hair down to here." She gestured to her elbows.

"He just got out of prison a few months back. I've only seen him once. He was talking about some hard labor job he got. Cutting logs."

Russel walked back into the room. "That's one big guy," he said. "I'd hate to see him mad."

"He was with two other boys," Diana said. "They said you guys are friends."

"Probably Brice and Dennis. I don't know how many times they saved my ass in jail. I wonder what they're up to now?"

12

Duluth, Minnesota
March 13, 2017

Brice Rockwell removed the gun from his waistband and placed it under the driver seat of his rusty Toyota Camry. Turning the key with his tattooed fingers, he revved the engine just to keep the cold car running. "This is a bad idea." He turned the headlights on. The dark street lit up. People were walking in the distance, and large snowflakes were slanting in between.

"What, should we hide in the house and starve?" Brice's cousin, Dennis asked mockingly, his shoulder jerking into a shrug. Bundled up in a black winter jacket with the hood resting on his back, he sat with no seatbelt across his chest. His bearded head cocked in Brice's direction.

"We should just wait for the free shit," Brice said, shifting into gear. "The National Guard will be here tomorrow or the next day." All the same, Brice pulled onto the street, his boot pressing down on the gas pedal as they drove downtown in his shitbox car. Glancing in the passenger seat, he saw the closest thing he had to a family. And a grizzly beard a shade lighter than his.

Dennis tugged his black woolen hat over his ears. "Fuck the government. We need food…tonight. I'm out of smokes, too."

"Just remember, this was your idea." Brice slowed down, swerving around a group of men walking down the middle of the street. "Look at all these people." He honked once, cocking his head as he slowly drove past them. "It's like a gang of twenty. And they're holding fucking bats."

"We got guns."

A loud thud exploded the back window and both men ducked.

Brice slammed on the gas, cursing with his head low.

"Stop the car!" Dennis barked, his lowered brow facing Brice, one hand planted on the dash.

Brice stomped on the brakes, and the car came to a skidding stop on the icy tarmac. "What are you gonna do?"

"I'm gonna lay down the law." Dennis reached inside his jacket, pulled out a gun, and then kicked open the door.

"Dude, we ain't got time for that shit." Craning his neck, Brice saw a mob through the busted-out rear window. "Let's get the fuck out of here."

All the men in the mob were cursing at them.

Dennis extended his arms. "Throw a brick through my window, mother fuckers," he said under his breath, gun trained on the charging group of bat-wielding men. "See what happens." He squeezed the trigger three times. The ear-splitting eruptions sent men dashing in every direction. Except one.

"Let's go!" Brice yelled, his body leaning halfway across the passenger seat. His face almost red with muted anger.

Dennis hopped in the car and it squealed off before the door was even closed.

"What the fuck are you doing, man?"

"That brick could have hit one of us in the head." Dennis slammed his fist against the door panel. "Plus, this is World War — motherfucking — Three. Every man for himself. Survival of the fittest."

"Bro, I just got out of a coma." Brice made a sharp turn on the next block. "And I'm trying to stay out of prison."

Dennis nodded. "All right." He tugged on his light brown beard, his lips making a thin line. "I won't shoot no one else. Unless…"

"You actually hit someone?" Brice's head snapped to the passenger seat. "How do you know?

"Of course, I hit one." Dennis shoved his gun back in his jacket. "I'm a good shot. Left one dude on the street. His boys scattered like roaches."

"Just save your bullets, please." Brice's head was shaking. "We might need 'em sometime."

Brice put his right blinker on before he turned on First Street, a few blocks away from the neighborhood drug store. The one-way street was dark and relatively quiet compared to a few blocks up the hill. One car was driving in front of them. No people on the street.

"Watch out!" Dennis shouted.

Brice slammed on the brakes and a speeding car coming up the avenue smashed into the car in front of them. The T-bone crash didn't stop the car. Its engine revved, and it screamed up the hill.

"Don't stop," Dennis said, and Brice took a left down the avenue. "We got an angry mob looking for us."

Turning right down a dark alley, Brice slowed the car to a crawl. "I hope that dude in the wreck is okay."

"Look at that." Dennis pointed to the right. A motionless human body was face down, head resting on cement steps that were leading to the back door of a dilapidated house.

Brice tapped the brake. Coming to a complete stop, he turned his head, locking his eyes on the dead man. "That dude got curb-stomped. Only gang members do shit like that."

"There ain't no law out here. No cops. No order. A fucking free for all."

Brice let his foot off the brake, rolling past the frozen stiff dead man like you would road kill. "Let's not end up like that dude."

"I got your back no matter what, bro," Dennis said as the vehicle parked in a dark alley across the street from the drugstore.

"I got your back, too. But damn, brother. You just offed some dude like it's the old wild west." Brice killed the engine.

Both car doors opened. Brice got out, stuffing the pistol in his waistline. Tying a black bandana around the back of his head, he tugged it down so only his dark eyes were showing. Slipping thin gloves on his hands, he grabbed a flashlight and duffel bag from the back seat.

Dennis shoved a couple of large black contractor bags in his pockets. Reaching to the floor, he curled his fingers around an AK-47. "Just in case."

Brice blew out a heavy breath, and then ran up to the store, his cousin following in his footprints.

The red brick building had a black gate blocking the door. Dennis pointed at a narrow window with a hole in it, glass littering the pavement. "Look! Someone already broke the window."

Brice lifted his flashlight and broke out the rest of the glass. "Be careful, bro," he said, and then watched Dennis squeeze inside the store.

Brice stepped through the window, popping up on the other side. His flashlight beam landed on Dennis who was scanning the area with his rifle. "You get the smokes and water. I'll get food and toilet paper and."

"I'm on it." Dennis walked into the darkness.

Brice hurried for the refrigerated section against the far wall. Reaching low, he started grabbing sandwiches, dropping them in the bag one by one.

Behind the till, Dennis was stuffing cash in his pockets. Spinning on his heel, he saw cigarettes on the wall. After tossing several cartons in the bag, he darted for the cold drink section. He then loaded his bag until it was heavy. *Pharmacy,* he thought, dragging the bag with his left hand.

Walking toward Dennis, Brice lifted up his bag. "I think I got—"

The explosive sound of sudden rapid gunfire cut him off. Four echoing reports, and then a loud voice started running his mouth from the front window.

"What's up now, bitch?" a disembodied voice rang out. In the empty store, the sound reverberated off the walls surrounding Brice and Dennis. "You shot my nigga in da chest!" He fired off another shot. "Guess what happens next?"

From behind the wall of the pharmacy, Dennis had the front entrance way covered with the sight of his AK. He aimed and let off a steady stream of bullets, giving cover fire for Brice to come to him.

Crouching low, Brice's quick and scattered movements brought him to the front desk of the pharmacy. Tossing the duffel bag on the other side, he climbed over the top, and then took cover behind the wall. "What the fuck?" His brow was low. His ears were ringing.

Before Dennis could answer, that same voice continued barking threats from outside, protected by the brick wall.

"Got you surrounded!" the man shouted. "We gonna carve you up, trick!"

Dennis fired a few more shots toward the threat. "We need to create a diversion," he said to Brice, "I'm gonna lay down some cover fire. Go find the barbecue aisle. Spray lighter fluid everywhere. Light that shit…and get back."

"Then what?" Brice asked, huffing and puffing, his adrenaline creating a line of sweat on his brow.

"Then we go hunting," Dennis said, briefly locking eyes with Brice. Lifting his rifle, he squeezed the trigger repetitively. The bullets were smashing into the front wall. Some flying through the window they had entered just minutes before.

With all the haste he could muster, Brice shuffled low, finding the barbecue aisle. He tossed propane tanks and bags of charcoal on the floor. A mound formed, and then he doused it with lighter fluid. Pulling a lighter out of his pocket, he lit the corner of a bag of charcoal, and then crouched back to his cousin who was still firing his rifle.

Dennis stopped shooting. Twisting his head to look at Brice, he swore under his breath. "There has to be a second exit," he said, his eyes bouncing from the growing fire to the front of the store. His rifle popped five more times.

"There is a back door," Brice said, and then let out a deep sigh. "But I'll bet them punks are out there, waiting for us."

"Follow me," Dennis said and fired the last few shots in the forty-round banana clip. "I think there's a breakroom in the back.

Dennis crept to the back of the pharmacy where he found a door. Upon opening it, Brice walked through the doorway, and then Dennis locked the door behind them. The thud sound of bullets going through sheetrock walls made them both drop to the floor.

Dennis pulled a new magazine from his coat, and then fed his AK new life. Taking a deep breath of doubt, his heart pounded. *We're either gonna die from bullets or fire,* he thought. *One or the other.*

Brice hit Dennis in the arm. "Let's move these vending machines in front of the wall," Brice whispered. "Might stop a bullet. We need to come up with a plan."

They pushed the two machines against the wall.

"They got to be running out of bullets," Dennis said, his breaths short. "Maybe we could shoot our way out."

"Hold up," Brice said, scanning the room with the flashlight. The beam landed in the back corner. "Look at that. A ladder."

Dennis sprung to his feet. "You might have just saved our lives, bro," he said, nodding. "Let's get the fuck out of here."

Dennis climbed the ladder. Reaching the top, he pushed open the hatch and set his bag down on the snowy flat roof. Brice followed behind him.

"Shhh," Dennis said. "Listen...and they'll tell us where they are. I bet they got the building surrounded."

Brice nodded with his lips pressed together. They sat with their backs against the three-foot brick wall that wrapped around the square building.

Dennis shifted his head, swatting Brice in the arm. "You hear that?" he whispered.

Listening to the men down below, Brice took a deep breath. "I think there's only a few of them," he said, nudging Dennis. "We should take 'em, right now."

"We got the high ground," Brice said softly, letting out a breath that looked like a puff of smoke.

Dennis winked. "It's gonna be a turkey shoot."

"I'll post up over there," Brice whispered, pointing to the wall that faced the parking lot. "When I start blasting, they'll flee into your line of fire."

"I'll light 'em up."

Brice nodded once, and then army-crawled to his post. Behind him, he left a wide black streak from the snow he brushed away as he crossed the flat rubber roof.

When Brice got to the other side, he peeked over the ledge. Seven armed men stood underneath him.

He slowly rose and extended his arms downward. He fired his gun as fast as he could pull the trigger. Before they even heard the retort, several bodies crumpled to the snow. The injured groaned, and the rest of the mob fled.

As soon as they rounded the corner, Dennis fired and didn't stop firing until no one was standing or moving. The echoes repeated.

14

The Buccetti Compound
March 14, 2017

Frankie drew back his pool stick and tapped the white ball softly.

"Nice touch," Mariani said as the eight-ball slowly rolled into the corner pocket.

"Good game, bro," Frankie said and set the stick on the pool table. "I'm hard to beat."

Mariani lit up a cigarette. "I'll get ya next time."

"If there is a next time."

Mariani blew out a stream of smoke. "What do ya mean?"

"The president said a retaliatory strike is imminent." Frankie's expression tautened as he shook his head. "If we hit Russia and China, they'll hit us back. Duluth's been one of the top ten targets from Russia since the Cold War. We have the biggest shipping port in the world, and we probably have a strategic military base here."

"So, you think we're gonna get hit?"

"I hope not," Frankie said and let out a sigh.

Mariani tilted one hand. "I don't like the idea of not knowing what's going on. Waiting on the next radio alert."

"The only information…is what they give us."

"But they haven't said nothing since the president promised victory. Who knows what happened? Maybe we lost. Maybe we surrendered. Why else would the radio be silent?"

"I'm starting to think there's more going on behind the scenes. There are no coincidences. All major events are planned."

"C'mon, man," Mariani said, blowing out a stream of smoke.

"No, I think this war has been in the works for a long time," Frankie said. "The inner core of the onion, the elite of the elite. The *Illuminati*." He paused for a moment. "They've wanted a one world government for centuries. The blueprint calls for a three-war plan toward global domination."

"Blueprint?" Mariani's forehead was crinkling, his arms crossing in his chest. "What do you mean by that?"

"The Great Reset," Frankie said, lifting one finger. "Let me get the book." Crossing the room to his office, he came back holding a black hard-cover book with gold letters. When he sat back down on the green leather sofa, he opened to a page that was marked with a large paper clip.

"Order from Chaos," Frankie read the name of the chapter, handing it to his friend.

Mariani received the dusty old book. He took it in his hands, reading silently until he was interrupted by Frankie.

"Read it out loud for the class," Frankie said. "I haven't read it for years. Kinda stopped believing in that stuff."

"All right," Mariani said and cleared his throat. "*Tomasino Dimerco, a 33rd-degree mason, wrote a letter to Leonardo Roth that was dated March 13th, 1877. In this letter, he outlined his blueprint for three world wars which would ultimately bring forth a one world government.*"

Mariani paused, scrunching up his face as he started to put the book down.

"Keep reading," Frankie said, flicking a finger toward the book as he smiled cryptically. "It gets deep."

"How long is it?" Mariani said. "Sounds like some conspiracy-theory bullshit."

"It is, but it's two pages you'll never forget." He put his feet on the table. "March 13th. Can't be a coincidence."

"Whatever." Mariani picked up the book, lowering his eyes to the page. *"The First World War must be orchestrated perfectly, in order to warrant the Russian people to topple the Czars and fundamentally transform that country into a bulwark of atheistic Communism. The agents of the Illuminati must instigate turmoil and hostilities between the British and German Empires. At the conclusion of the war, Communism will be elevated and used in order to swallow all Eastern European governments."* He paused, squinting one eye. "This was written in 1877?"

"The debunkers would say it's a hoax like Bigfoot," Frankie said. "Keep reading, bro."

Mariani brought the book closer to his eyes. *"The Second World War must be orchestrated by capitalizing on the differences between the Fascist and the Jews. This war must be escalated so that Germany is destroyed and so political Zionism is showered with enough support from the west to give birth to a sovereign state of Israel. More importantly, Communism must expand its tentacles, in order to threaten Christendom, which will then stalemate until the time comes for a final solution to the human problem."* He closed the book, set it on the table, and then looked at Frankie. "So, you're telling me that this asshole predicted the future to a tee?"

"No." Frankie shook his head. "It wasn't a prediction. It was a blueprint, an order from the elite of the elite."

"And you believe that shit?"

"Read the next passage," Frankie said, tilting his left hand. "You'll see."

"You read that shit," Mariani said. "I don't buy it."

Frankie offered a smirk, then gently grabbed the book. *"The Third World War,"* he said, *"must be orchestrated by capitalizing on the differences between Christendom and the leaders of Atheistic Marxism. This War must conclude with the physical and economic destruction of all warring nations. We shall unleash the nihilists and atheists, and provoke a social cataclysm so great that the inhabitants of the earth will have no choice but to submit. Then the multitudes will be forced to receive a mark on their right hands or foreheads. Those who refuse to comply will be deemed to be an enemy of the state and exterminated. Christianity without direction and leadership will be ripe to receive the true light through the universal manifestation of the Light Bearer. After the destruction of Christianity and Atheism, after every nation is controlled by one entity, after every global citizen is marked, only then may the pyramid be capped."* Frankie then closed the book and set it on the table.

Mariani lit up another cigarette. "That's the deepest shit I ever heard," he said with a caveat to follow, "but…it sounds a little rich…. The whole manifestation of the Light Bearer thing."

"Satan got a toe hold of the world after World War One," Frankie opined. "Then he got a foot hold after the Second World War. And now, he has a stronghold over the entire globe and everything in it. In time, there will be an assault on Christianity…so that eventually every human *has* to worship Satan or die."

"That's ridiculous," Mariani said, "but World War III is pretty fucking real."

"Indeed," Frankie said gravely. "I just hope we win…and they lose."

Mariani met eyes with his friend. "How bad do you think it is on American soil?"

"The fact that Duluth hasn't got hit yet gives me hope."

"We don't know that," Mariani said. "We're thirty miles out. For all we know, Duluth is on fire."

"Don't you think a nuclear bomb would be loud?"

Mariani shrugged. "Maybe we should drive to town and find out?"

"We should save the gas for an emergency."

"I suppose. I'm just curious."

"It's hard to even imagine a nuclear strike from Russia." Frankie blew out a deep sigh. "Those bombs are like fifty times the size of the bombs used yesterday morning. Russia's bombs will take out an entire city and then some. We're talking about tens of millions of people dead across the nation."

"Without food or heat, things are gonna get bad for people up north," Mariani said.

"I'm sure the government will come to the rescue," Frankie said. "But let's just hope…chaos doesn't transform into tyranny."

"Tomorrow is another day, brother," Mariani said and got up. "Wake me up in the morning. Don't let me sleep all day. We got some prepping to do."

Frankie got up and grabbed his bottle of water. "You better check for reds under the bed," he said sarcastically. "The commies are on the move."

"What time is it?" Mariani asked before he walked up the stairs.

"I have no idea," Frankie said. "My phone's dead. It's late though, probably two or three."

"It's the little things," Mariani replied, "like knowing what time it is. Things we used to take for granted."

Frankie walked upstairs and slid under the covers in his bed. Lying awake in his room, he stared at darkness. His eyes were wide open. His body was cold. Every time he closed his eyes, all he could see were mushroom clouds and visions of human bodies burning to a crisp, and then bursting like ashes when the blast wave hits. *Don't think. Don't think. Don't think…*

15

Washington D.C.
January 20, 2017

Deputy Secretary of Defense Richard Secord closed the door to his office. Sweat pooled along his forehead as he reached inside his jacket and pulled out the plump yellow envelope.

It had been sitting on his front doorstep when he'd left the house that morning.

Waiting for him.

With trembling fingers, he opened it. "What the hell is this?" he said softly to himself as he emptied the envelope on his oak desk.

With a clunk, a small tape recorder landed in front of him. Picking it up, he pressed the play button and sat down in his thick leather chair.

"*Good morning, Mr. Secord,*" a shrill female voice said mockingly. "*Code word: Coffin. It is imperative that you destroy this tape after listening.*" The voice paused to breathe. "*I've been ordered to deliver you a message. On the thirteenth of March, at 6:45 a.m., you will arrive on foot to a location that will be delivered to you that week. Do not ask questions, just do as you are told. The favor you owe will be collected very soon. For this favor, you will be rewarded heavily. Further instructions will be delivered to you at a time of our choosing. Out of precaution, we will be watching you. Oh,*" *one more thing, a tiny recording device is taped to the cassette you're about to destroy. It's the size of a pill, and it's undetectable. You will hide it inside your ass…every time you speak with the new president."* She laughed shortly. *"Do not disappoint us. Remember, we have embarrassing pictures of you. And…. Well, you know what we're capable of."* The tape clicked.

"Fuck." Secord removed the tiny black recording device from the tape and shoved it in the breast pocket of his suit jacket. "Record Clacher?" His eyebrows lowered. "What the hell is going on here?"

Pulling a hammer from his desk, he smashed the cassette tape and ripped out the film. "I should have never got involved with these people."

16

The Buccetti Compound
March 16, 2017

Huddled around the radio, Frankie and his guests were sitting on the edge of an L-shaped sofa. "Shh," he said to his mom, leaning forward to turn up the volume. A screeching noise from the speaker repeated four times. A computerized female voice followed. The living room became silent.

"*This is not a test*," the dry voice said then quickly repeated. "*This is not a test…. This is the Emergency Broadcast System…. Stay tuned for a message from the President of the United States. Following that message, this channel will be transferred to your local authorities who will give you lifesaving information about locations that will provide food, shelter, and medical attention.*"

The screeching noise returned in four sharp beats. The small radio was resting upright on the center of the oak coffee table. Diana, Russel, Frankie, and Mariani were staring at it as if it were a TV. But Frankie was looking past the radio, his gaze locked on the pile of logs burning in the ledger stone fireplace.

"*Good afternoon, America,*" President Clacher said with the soberest tones. "*Three long days ago, I gave you my word that we would survive…. I promised that America would prevail. And today…I can guarantee that in every state in this union, a red, white, and blue flag is still flying in the wind. The flag is still there.... Victory has been achieved!*

"The existential threat to this nation is over, but regional enemy insurgencies will remain a challenge in the months to come. Russia and China have both surrendered unconditionally. ... I hope that will give you a little comfort....

"That said, we have challenges at home. Thirteen American cities have been destroyed by enemy missiles. The death count is staggering. The number of injured and displaced is unimaginable. The power grid is down. Americans are cold...hungry...and uncertain of the future.

"This is the responsibility of government to do everything possible to stabilize the union and provide emergency relief to those who need it. It is my personal goal that every city in America will have relief within one week. As the days, weeks, and months go by, we will stabilize. Our nation has prepared for nuclear war for decades, but reconstruction is not going to be easy. With your help and calmness, we can do this...together. We all have a role to play in the reconstruction of America. Once the power grid is repaired, the economy will snap back to life.

"Our goal is for America to have a sense of normalcy by Independence Day, this year. Out of chaos, comes order, and as of now, the only order is the United States Military, which I trust to perform this daunting task with honor. I understand it will be unsettling to see a military force on the streets of America, but this is the only way....

"Once we feel that the United States is stable, I give my word of honor that I will remove Martial Law, reenact Posse Comitatus, restore the Bill of Rights, and follow the Constitution. This might take one year, or it could take five, but freedom will be restored to become the beacon of light for the world.

"The United States of America can claim victory, but we have ashes in our mouths. In time, our mouths will be clean, our hearts will be strong, and our skin will be thick.

"*Thank you...for this great honor of my life...to serve as your commander in chief...during our darkest hours. I look forward to leading us to a warmer, brighter sun. May God bless each and every one of you. May God bless the dead. And may God continue to bless this land we call...America.*"

17

Duluth, Minnesota
March 23, 2017

Dennis peeked out the blinds of his second-floor apartment and peered down to the street. A sliver of daylight gave him a clear view of soldiers in woodland camouflage, marching down the slushy road. Stunned at the sight of troops on the street, he didn't even feel the cold glass pressed against his nose.

Spinning on the hardwood floor, Dennis pointed his thumb behind his shoulder. "Bro, they're going door to door," he said to Brice who was sitting on the couch. "We're fucked."

Brice hopped up and crossed the room, lifting a finger to the blinds. "You're right, bro," he said, and then turned back, his hands spread wide. "We can't let them in here."

"I know," Dennis said. With a glance, he took in the AK-47 resting on the table next to him. He grimaced. "We're not supposed to have guns."

"Holy shit," Brice said, tugging at his beard. "They're gonna take us to the prison camp."

"Hell, no," Dennis said, cocking the rifle with his right hand. "I ain't goin' back to prison."

Brice lifted up the cushions on the couch. "Wait. They ain't got time to search everyone," he said with a low defeated tone. "We hide this shit and play nice. They're just here to help."

"Are you listening to what you're saying? These mother fuckers don't give a fuck about us. They want our guns. And when they find out we're on parole…they'll either bring us to the FEMA Camp or shoot us on the spot."

"You have no faith in government."

"No," Dennis shook his head slowly. "I don't. Not at all."

At that very moment, a series of loud knocks at the front door traveled up the flight of stairs. A man's voice followed. "National Guard! Open Up!"

Brice's eyes were wide open, swiveling around the room. *Guns everywhere,* he thought. *On the table, on the floor, on the dresser.* "Let's hide this shit," he said, the instant rush to his voice matched his jittery hand movements. "We'll give false names."

"I ain't getting locked up, bro. Don't answer it."

Bro, we can't win a shootout with soldiers," Brice said, shoving a pistol under the couch cushion.

With a curt nod, he gestured for Dennis to do the same with the AK.

Shaking his head, Dennis begrudgingly placed his gun beside Brice's. "Never say can't."

After fixing up the couch, Brice quickly exited the room. His footsteps followed the pounding.

"I'm coming!" Brice hollered and the knocking stopped. Descending the steps, he turned the knob, and then pulled open the scratched and dented metal door. Trying to look innocent, he widened his nervous eyes, but they kept blinking. "I-I appreciate your service."

Two tall soldiers looked down on Brice. One black and one white. The pale soldier was holding a dark-green plastic box, and the other had a rifle pressed across his chest.

"Good morning, sir," said the soldier with the gun. His tropical accent was thick. "How many occupy residence?" The beard on his massive jaw was clean. Trimmed.

"Two." Brice's head shifted with his eyes. "Me and my cousin."

"Do you feel safe in residence?" The armed soldier's eyes were slightly protruding out of his skull.

"Yes, sir."

"You have ID?"

Brice shook his head. "No, sir."

"What's your name?"

"Mike Rotch."

"Mr. Rotch, what's your cousin's name?"

"Ben Rotch."

"Can we do a quick search of the residence?"

Brice looked at both soldiers. "I don't think that's necessary." He flashed a quick smile, slowly pushing the door shut.

The soldier blocked the door with his boot. "It's for your safety, sir. Please step aside."

18

Location Unknown
April 1, 2017

Sitting behind an oak desk in his subterranean office, President Clacher tilted a hand to Steff Freeman, who had just closed the door behind her. "Please, take a seat."

"Thank you, Mr. President." Steff Freeman from the CIA said, and then stiffly sat down on a thick leather chair. She was holding a black leather folder on her lap.

Clacher crossed his arms. "Vice President Andrews insisted I meet with you," he said, briefly studying her erect posture and CIA analyst attire. A black pantsuit with a white button-up shirt, and a top-level clearance badge hanging around her neck. "He said you have new intel about insurgents in China?"

"Yes, sir." She set the folder on his desk. "Our drones are finding underground tunnel complexes we were unaware of, sir." Unbuttoning two buttons on her blouse, she kept talking as she pulled a folded piece of paper from the inside of her bra. "The enemy lives like ants, sir." She pushed the folder across the desk. The note resting on top.

President Clacher cocked his head, reaching for the paper that resembled a love letter in junior high school. "What is this?"

"Intel. Sir."

"This room was just swept, Miss Freeman." He unfolded the note. "No need for precautions here."

Steff's eyes shifted. "Mr. President, have you ever heard the Roman saying: But who will watch the watchers?"

"Of course, Miss Freeman," Clacher said. "But I trust the Secret Service with my life. And they've done a pretty damn good job so far. They could have just let me die with everyone else in Washington, but instead, they brought me here."

Steff Freeman nodded. "I understand. Sir."

President Clacher's eyes lowered to the note which he read silently: *Mr. President, I am highly trained to detect deception, collaboration, weakness, and fear.* He paused, meeting her eyes, and then returning to the letter. *I am also trained to target valuable assets for compromise. Over the last two weeks in this bunker, I've attended dozens of high-level meetings. I've had countless off-the-record conversations with mid-level staffers. And it's my opinion that there is a shadow government whose plans do not align with yours, sir. I don't want to be a part of it. Many others secretly share my view. But there is something lurking that is so powerful, so invisible, watchful, that no one will even speak of it, let alone oppose it. High-ranking men in the military and intelligence agencies are scared shitless, sir. I could give you one or two names of suspects, but it's deeper than any one man, or group of men. That said, I have no proof of danger to your life, but you should not trust anyone in this bunker. Unleash me, sir. Let me capitalize on weakness when I see it. I might be able to get someone to flip and find out if you're in danger. All I need from you is a nod of approval, and a pardon with my name on it. I will do anything necessary to preserve freedom. Nothing else matters. Sir.*

The president sucked in a deep breath and blew it out. His eyes locked on hers, nodding. *She seems genuine,* he thought with his lips pressed together. *She's definitely on to something. I noticed the Deep State working against me, too.*

Leaning forward, Clacher rested his elbows on the desk and interlocked his fingers. His nod was slow but definite. His eyebrows low, the muscles on his jaw flexing. "I appreciate the new intel, Miss Freeman," he said with a lowered tone. Breaking apart his hands, he leaned back against the chair, the muscles on his face now relaxed. "I'll read it right away." He blinked. Twice.

"The Chinese have been digging tunnels for a thousand years, Mr. President." She cleared her throat. "It will take time to clear them. Is there anything else I can advise you on, sir?"

"That will be all, Miss Freeman. I look forward to your next report."

Steff rose, extending a hand.

President Clacher shook it. "Thank you, Miss Freeman." He winked. "Keep up the good work."

19

The Buccetti Compound
April 6, 2017

High in a deer stand attached to a pine tree, Frankie handed Mariani the binoculars. "I haven't seen nothing all morning." His voice was hushed as he grabbed the camouflage compound bow.

"Be patient," Mariani said, and then scanned the perimeter. Thick foliage and morning fog were all he saw. "We ain't leaving till we get one."

"How long does it usually take?" Frankie asked.

"It's different every time." He set the binoculars down on the wood floor. "We just hurry up and wait."

Frankie let out a breath, and the vapor cloud rose in the crisp spring air. "I got nothing else to do."

"I can tell you're stressed, bro," Mariani said. "Please tell me you ain't still thinking about Conny?"

"No. I got other stuff on my mind, too." Frankie tilted a hand. "We got about a month's supply of water. The world is on fire. My dad's probably dead. My mom doesn't stop talking shit. You want me to keep going?"

"But Conny shouldn't cause you any stress. She's gone. Forever."

"Look, bro. She double-crossed me." He shook his head. "I don't ever want to see her again." Frankie's shoulders lifted briefly. "But that doesn't mean she isn't on my mind. I want to know why she ran off with that dude. I need to know how long she was with him."

"Bro, we saw her in his arms. Do you think that was the first time? Second?"

Frankie's jaw muscle twitched. "No." He let out an audible sigh. "I-I guess I'm just a sucker for love. I deserved it. I was weak. Stupid."

"Nah, man. She dishonored herself." Mariani gave Frankie a firm two pats on the shoulder. "You won, bro. You got off the hook easy. No kids, no alimony. Shit, she did you a favor."

Frankie sunk his head. "It just hurts, man. I can't explain it. It's like, I kinda wanted to make a fam—"

Mariani's finger shot up to his lips. "Shh…" He then pointed forty yards in the thick murky woods.

Frankie lifted his head, shifting his body in that direction. "It's a doe," he whispered.

"There ain't no law out here."

Frankie pulled an arrow from his quiver. His hands were trembling.

"Breathe, brother. Take your anger out on the doe." Mariani rested a hand on his shoulder, squeezing tightly. "Channel all your hate and pain…built up through the years. And just let it go with the arrow."

Drawing back the wire, it locked in the ready position. As Frankie aimed at the doe, his elbow and forearm began to shake. "The wire is too tight."

"Take another breath. The wire is perfect."

Frankie took a breath and blew it out.

"Again."

Frankie took another. The crosshairs landed on the deer. Upon releasing the trigger, the wire snapped and the arrow flew forty yards in one blink of Frankie's eye. The doe darted.

Mariani picked up the binocs. Turning to the area, he zeroed in on the floor of the forest. Wet leaves. Tree roots. Mud. "Holy shit, bro. You got her! Nice shot!"

"How can you tell? She's gone."

"She left a trail of blood. We'll find her."

Frankie cracked a smile. "Dude, that was awesome. My adrenaline is still pumping."

"Told ya. All better now?"

"I'm a new man."

"No. You'll be a new man once you take a bite of the heart."

Frankie squinted his eye. "Wait, what?"

20

Astana, Kazakhstan
December 25, 1999

An elderly man in a fine black suit exhaled cigarette smoke. "Which of your recruits is best suited for the prelude to the Great Reset?"

A second old man in a black suit flipped the page of a picture album resting on a fine oak desk. "I have two remarkably proficient young men who could prove themselves useful to our operation." He pulled out a polaroid photo, setting it in the center of the desk. "Their loyalty is secure."

"Perfect." He held the picture in his pale wrinkled fingers. "I remember that day." The man's thoughts brought him back to 1989, back to that pivotal moment. He'd been in the cellar of an ancient cathedral—a dark room lit only by the light from thirteen candles. In front of him was an open coffin; two naked young men lay spooning inside.

Staring down at the men, he'd felt his lips pull into a snarl. "Silence," he said, raising an arm and capturing their attention. "Do this one act. Submit to your master, and forever reap the reward. You will reach the pinnacle of power and wealth. You will be immune from the law. You will be respected and feared. Men will envy you…and women will bow to you."

"Yes, Master," the thin, pale Eugene Parker said from inside the coffin.

"How about you, Secord?" the old man croaked.

Richard Secord squirmed in the coffin. "Y-yes, Your Grace."

"Good. Then let the ritual begin." He snapped his fingers twice.

The two men in the coffin started having sex. One was groaning. The other was panting.

Pulling out his camera, the man snapped several pictures of the men. Pictures sure to guarantee their loyalty. Silence.

" —Seth."

Hearing his name, Seth Roth snapped out of his reverie. "I do not doubt their sustained loyalty."

"Indeed, my brother under the skin." The corner of David Roth's mouth ticked upward. "Indeed."

21

Duluth, Minnesota
April 20, 2017

With one hand on the steering wheel, Brice crept up to a four-way stop sign in the business district of the city. "If they let us in the arena…" he said, pausing to wave at a camouflage Humvee rolling down the avenue. "…w-we should stay for a month. Till it gets warmer."

"I ain't staying at no FEMA camp, bro," Dennis said. "The plan was to get some food and clothes and get the fuck out of there. We can't leave the guns and ammo too long."

Brice let off the brake. "I was just thinking about how cold it was last night." His boot switched to the gas pedal. "Why not stay for a while?"

"It's almost May," Dennis said. "We can tough it out a few weeks. It hasn't been that cold."

"I'm sleeping in my jacket every night." Brice's head turned to the passenger seat. "It would be nice to sleep in a warm bed. Take a hot shower." He paused, both hands now strangling the wheel. "Don't you wanna eat a hot meal?"

Dennis punched the palm of his hand. "I'd rather starve than live in a cage again."

"It ain't gonna be nothing like prison. It will be like a country club. Women everywhere."

"Maybe a country club for now. But probably re-education camps later." He hit his hand again. "Then comes extermination."

Brice glanced in the rear-view. "You said the National Guard was gonna take our guns and shoot us on the spot. But they barely even searched the house. And they even smoked a cigarette with us. Those soldier boys were cool as shit."

"I'd rather take my chances out here." Dennis craned his neck as they drove through another intersection. "Holy shit, did you see that sidewalk? It was covered with blood. Someone must have got blasted by the National Guard."

"Or they had a run-in with some crazy ass gang members like we did."

Dennis stared out the passenger side window. "It's a dog-eat-dog world we live in."

"The National Guard must have a cleanup crew to pick up all the bodies." Brice rolled down the ravaged city block. Each building had its windows busted out. Graffiti tagged the brick walls. Some of the storefronts were black with soot. And a gas station was burnt to the ground.

Dennis smirked. "Looks like we weren't the only ones to set a fire."

"They probably did it for no reason. At least we had a purpose. Survival."

As they cruised down the road, they passed a set of blacked-out traffic lights and an empty intersection. To the right was the drugstore they had burnt to the ground last month. Brice brought the car to a crawl. The one-story brick building was a blackened heap.

"Feels like yesterday," Dennis said.

"I hope it doesn't come back to bite us."

"There's no way. The fire burnt all the evidence."

"What about security cameras?"

"No power. Remember?"

"Yeah, but some businesses have a backup generator for shit like that."

A wolfish grin grew on Dennis' face. "You did good that night, bro," he said. "I was impressed. Them pieces of shit wanted to kill us. And you stepped up to the plate."

"Survival comes natural to me." Brice took his eyes off the road. "When your life's on the line, you just have to act on instinct. Experience."

"And who taught you how to defend yourself?"

"You did."

"We done fucked some shit up, bro," Dennis said. "And we'll do it again if we have to."

Rolling past a bus stop, Brice's head shifted to a large figure standing inside the glass shell. It was a tall Native American man with long stringy black hair. The front of his white T-shirt was stained red.

"That's Gordon-fucking-Grayfeather!" Dennis insisted. "No fucking way!"

"Is it him?" Brice squinted to look closer.

"Yeah, it's him!" Dennis clapped his hands together. "We could use some more muscle around the house."

Brice stopped the car in the middle of the road. "That's another mouth to feed, bro."

"We'll send him out to get more."

"He's wild. Uncontrollable."

"I'll calm him." Dennis opened his hands.

"Fine." Brice got out of the car. He lifted his hands up. "What up, Gordon?"

The staggering man in question took two steps in the road and stopped. His arms were now flexed. His brow low. His face darkening. A defensive growl emanated from his mouth, and then he suddenly barrelled forward.

Brice planted his right foot back. "Gordon!" he barked, but the surging man didn't slow down.

Grayfeather suddenly stopped on the balls of his feet. His breathing was even and regular, his fists hanging down at his sides.

Dennis was on the other side of the car with a pistol in his right hand. He slowly crept around the front. "We on the same team, dog!" Dennis shouted.

With a demented sly grin, Grayfeather burst out laughing.

Brice and Dennis stared at each other for a moment. Dennis returned his gun to his waistband.

22

The Buccetti Compound
May 5, 2017

Frankie Buccetti opened the front door before his carpenter had a chance to knock. "Hey, Larry," he said to the husky man in an old red and black flannel jacket. "Come on in."

"I would have come sooner, but I—"

Frankie cut him off. "I'm sorry to take you away from your family." He closed the door. "I know during times like this…the world comes to a stop. I figured since the curfew got lifted, I'd see if you wanted to get back to work."

Larry Sobek shook his hand. "No. I'm actually happy to get out of the house." He adjusted his paint-stained ball cap. "The damn kids are driving me nuts. The wife, too. Plus, you said you could pay cash…*and* deer meat."

"Yeah, we got more deer than we can eat."

"That would be great. We've been living off government rations for the last month. Fucking disgusting."

"Well, thanks for coming," Frankie said. "It's good to see another human. I spend a lot of time alone." He lifted an arm, gesturing to the stairs. "Let me show you what I need to get done." He walked upstairs to his bedroom.

"How do you like the new house, so far?" Larry asked, one hand on the railing. "I bet the bunker was nice to have when the bombs started dropping."

At the top step, Frankie turned to face him. "I'm sure glad no bombs dropped in Duluth though."

"I know, right?" Larry paused, briefly tilting his head. "Minneapolis hit close to my heart. Had some family down there. They were out of the blast zone, but they had to leave everything and relocate up here. I guess the big city got dangerous once the power went down. They've been staying with my mom in Hermantown. I don't think I could handle any more kids in my house. They never shut up."

Frankie nodded slowly. "I'm glad they made it at least." He let out an audible sigh, his hand rising to press on his forehead. "M-my dad worked in downtown Minneapolis. I don't think he made it." He swallowed down a lump of grief. "Probably lost my sister and stepmom, too."

"Sucks, man." Larry shrugged. "But if they died, I bet it was fast."

Frankie's left eye scrunched up. "I-I'm gonna try not to think about it." He pointed at the gray wall across from his bed. "I need a secret room for my safe," he said. "But I want it to be like a panic room. You know…in case I wake up in the middle of the night to intruders. A place I can hide quick."

"How big ya want it?" Larry asked, a cigarette dangling from his lips. A flame in his hands.

"What do ya think?" Frankie shrugged. "Five by three?"

Larry glanced at the wall. "I think six by four would be better. You might want to fit a small mattress in there. Maybe some guns."

"What do you think it's gonna cost me?"

Larry exhaled a stream of smoke. "Do you still have left over wood, sheetrock, and paint in the garage?"

"Yeah. There's definitely enough supplies."

Larry's head shifted to the side and back. "Three grand." He exhaled a small cloud. "Good thing you have materials. I don't see the stores opening any time soon."

"I was listening to the president the other day, and he said the power grid should be up by July."

"You believe that idiot?"

Frankie's back straightened. "I believe I heard him say it. We'll see if it actually happens."

"I don't believe a word he says. He straight up started a nuclear war."

"But we got hit first."

Larry shook his head. "That was a false flag attack. Just an excuse to take over the world."

"Maybe you're right? I guess we're gonna find out."

"That we are, my friend. We have no idea what the world looks like. We might not ever know. Maybe they'll never turn the grid back on. No news, just propaganda from the radio."

"All the reason to build a panic room. Shit, I already got the bunker. Why not?"

"If you got the money, I'll build it."

"How 'bout twenty-five hundred cash. And seventy-five pounds of deer meat. My friend Mariani smoked it. It's bomb."

Larry nodded, his lower lip sticking out. "That sounds good to me."

"Great. When can you start?"

"Right away. Everyone else is sitting around on their ass waiting for government rations. I can't live like that. I'd snap. Probably end up beating my wife."

"Don't worry, I got plenty of work to get you through."

Larry nodded again. "Crazy times, eh? You never know what's gonna happen next. Nuclear war…or someone breaking in your house."

"I'm sorry you have to raise children in a crazy world like this."

"You want mine?" He pinched his cigarette butt with his fingers, shoving it in his jacket pocket. "Just kidding." He chuckled. "How's the Mrs. doing, anyways?"

Frankie's eyes narrowed. "It didn't work out." He shook his head, eyes studying the carpet.

"I'm sorry to hear that." Larry puffed out his lower lip. "She seemed nice. Nice looking anyways."

Frankie's jaw muscle condensed. *She didn't like you,* he thought. He said, "She had her moments."

"Women. You can't live with 'em. You can't kill 'em." Larry laughed shortly.

Frankie opened his safe and took out two stacks of twenties. "Here, take this." He dropped it in Larry's hands, and then reached back in the safe, pulling out five hundreds. "Now let's go load your truck with deer meat."

Larry smiled smugly, his eyes shifting to the overwhelming heap of cash inside the safe.

23

Duluth, Minnesota
May 14, 2017

Brice Rockwell crouched in the darkness behind a two-story house. A shotgun was in his hands. Dennis and Gordon Grayfeather were standing behind him. A wall of trees and bushes separated them from the next house.

"I'll take the back door," Grayfeather said, his hatchet dangling at his side. He was wearing a black T-shirt and black jeans.

"Wait for us to get to the front," Brice said, pumping his shotgun. "Remember. Find the money and get out."

Dennis cocked his pistol. "Two different sources told me they have kids chained to radiators. Have no mercy. Anyone in there is guilty."

Brice pressed the butt of the shotgun on his hip. Stepping around the corner of the house, he heard his jacket scratch against the rough wood siding. Muffled voices from inside traveled through the wall. Dennis was right behind him. Their black clothes blended in with the shadows of the house and trees.

Standing on the back deck, Grayfeather knocked on the glass screen door three times. His long black hair danced in the mild spring breeze as he stepped to the left. Just out of sight. He could hear commotion from the kitchen.

A few moments later, a scrawny pale man wearing a ball cap stumbled up to the door. "Who is it?" The man pushed open the screen door and took a step on the deck.

Swinging his hatchet, Grayfeather buried the weapon in the side of the man's head. The young man didn't say a word, he just fell with a thump. The hatchet was stuck in his skull. Grabbing the man by the ankles, he dragged him to the end of the porch. With his right hand, he yanked the hatchet out of his brain. Looking at the wet blood on the blade, he cleaned it off with his fingers and painted his face.

Returning to the door, Gordon knocked again; a streak of red blood stained the glass. Instead of hiding, this time he stood in front of the back door with his hatchet drawn back.

A tall, slender man with an untamed beard stumbled up to the door. His eyes squinted in question of the blood.

Grayfeather smashed the glass with his small axe. The man on the receiving end collapsed. Screams echoed. Chaos ensued for the people inside the home.

Gordon trampled over his second victim and reached for his hatchet. Scanning the kitchen, he saw two more scrawny men with big eyes and dirty clothes. They were quaking in their shoes. Hands in front of their faces.

"P-please stop!" a transient cried, his rotten teeth clattering.

Grayfeather growled. And then he descended on them.

*****

Dennis kicked open the front door and waived in his black handgun. Flickering candles and dead men were the first things he saw. Gordon Grayfeather was the second. Brice stepped into the foyer with low eyebrows.

"The first floor is clear," Grayfeather said. "I'll sweep the basement next."

The shrieks of a woman came from the second floor. Their heads swiveled up the stairs. Brice climbed the steps. Dennis was behind him with his pistol drawn. At the top of the staircase, one of the two doors was wide open. Brice peeked his head in the bedroom. Moonlight from the window revealed three young girls chained to the radiator. One lay still on the carpet with her bound arm twisted.

"Help us!" a skinny teenage girl cried. Her hair was dark. Skin fair. Eyes swelled shut.

Three gunshots rang out from above. Brice leaped back behind the wall.

"I bet the money is in the attic," Dennis whispered.

Brice nodded. Sneaking a look around the corner, he scanned the room.

The small girl started pointing to the closet. Brice crouched across the room. In a fraction of a second, he twisted his neck and saw Dennis had his back. Reaching for the knob, he quietly opened the door. A metal ladder was leading to a dark hole in the attic. The barrel of his shotgun was tilted upward. At the sound of voices, he decided to bend his ear.

"Who would be stupid enough to fuck with us?" the disembodied voice said with a low tone.

"It's gotta be one of our customers," said another voice.

"But who?"

"Go down there and find out."

"But—"

"Don't be a little bitch. I'll be right behind you."

As soon as the man placed both feet on the ladder, Brice exploded a round from the shotgun. The man fell to the wood floor of the closet. The girls screamed.

Brice pumped his shotgun and bucked it one more time.

From the attic, a man screamed. "You're fucking dead, bitch!" He fired two shots through the floor.

"Fuck you." Dennis returned a volley of bursts from his gun. "I'm gonna set this bitch on fire…. What you gonna do then?"

"Don't do it!" a loud voice shouted from above.

"We got ten of us down here," Dennis barked. "You got no way out."

"What do you want?"

"We want the fucking money," Dennis ordered. "A little bird told me everything. You sell meth. You sell stolen shit. And you kidnap little girls. Sell 'em off to the highest bidder. Fucking sick!"

"We ain't got no money."

Dennis pulled out a lighter. "Okay, I guess I'm gonna have to light this bitch up."

"No. Wait!"

"You have thirty seconds to drop it down."

"Okay! Okay!" the man from upstairs said.

At the sound of a soft thud, Brice looked down at the black duffel bag. It was laying on the dead man crumpled up on the floor. With the barrel of his shotgun, he dragged it out from the closet. When he looked in the bag, he saw a small mound of cash and jewelry. He then slid it to Dennis for his approval.

Dennis hollered up the stairs. "That's it, dog? That's all you got?"

"That's everything," the voice said from above. "Take the girls!"

Brice glanced at Dennis.

Dennis made a hacking gesture to his neck. "Fuck these punks," he whispered. "Let's burn this shit down."

Brice hollered through the ceiling. "All right. We're leaving. Just stay the fuck out of this neighborhood."

Dennis stripped the bed of its soiled linens and then dropped them on the dead man in the closet. Flicking his lighter to a flame, he lit the bedding on fire. Taking a few steps back, he smiled as the cotton fabric sizzled.

One of the girls was crying. "Hurry up, man," she pleaded. "Let us go."

Dennis wiggled the radiator back and forth. When it loosened, he rocked it harder until it fell to the carpet. "You're free. Go."

The fire had grown fast. The flames now climbing through the hole in the closet ceiling.

Cursing from the men upstairs erupted. Gunshots started ringing out from above. Bullets and shards of wood rained down through the ceiling. One girl got hit. The other ran out the door.

Brice and Dennis picked the girl up by her arms and dragged her down the steps. Loud bangs continued as they ran out the back door. The girl was gasping for air.

On the back porch they stopped, resting the bleeding girl on the wood deck. "Where the fuck is Grayfeather?" Brice asked.

"Let's go find him." Dennis opened the back screen door. "Bro!" he yelled, eyes scanning the dead bodies and blood in the kitchen.

"I'll check the basement." Brice took one step on the staircase and saw Grayfeather climbing the steps.

"What's up, bro?" Grayfeather asked, his lips lifting up on one side.

"The house is on fire. Let's get the fuck out of here."

They ran through the kitchen and out the back door. Dennis lifted the wounded girl and carried her across the grass on his shoulder.

In the middle of the back yard, Brice stopped. Turning back, he saw flames and smoke rising. *Damn.*

At the crash of a man falling from the sky, their heads whipped to the side of the house. The men from the attic were jumping from an open window. When they landed, their legs buckled and snapped like twigs. Four men were screaming. Rolling. Crawling.

Gordon Grayfeather pulled out his hatchet and started walking toward them.

24

Alone in his subterranean office, President Tom Clacher opened a leather binder and set it on his desk. Cursing under his breath, he picked up a fancy pen and leaned forward. *My brother needs to hear from me,* he thought. *And I don't care what anyone says. I'm the president, damn it.*

Clacher put pen to paper:

Ryan,

I hope all is well, Clacher wrote in cursive. *March 2017 was hard on the soul. So much death, destruction, and uncertainty. So much suffering. The death I can handle, but the suffering is what keeps me up at night. The war with our enemies is all but over, but here on the homeland, it feels like a warzone. Society without law and order is barbarism. A nation without an economy is unsustainable. A country with no freedom is no country at all. I long for the day I can relinquish my war powers, but the people aren't ready yet. Are they?*

It feels like everyone is just waiting to die. The power grid is still down. The National Guard has done its best to deliver rations to as many neighborhoods as possible, but naturally, many people have perished due to starvation. And last winter many simply froze to death. With no water to shower, I'm told that diseases have started to spread, and thousands have died of dysentery. The conditions are so bleak, but things could have been far worse. At least we won the war. I'd hate to be the president who lost to the Chi-Coms.

The American Military Force is robust in the big cities, but as we saw in Iraq and Vietnam, an insurgency ultimately becomes a quagmire in a short period of time. And that's how the military has confronted these high population centers: they approach them with counter-insurgency tactics which include regular deadly force to deter citizens from not complying. He paused to take a breath and let it out slowly. His right hand returned to the paper. *I've been told atrocities have happened. Rogue death squads. Gangs. Turf wars. The resistance and death count are growing by the day. I don't blame them for not trusting us. I can't trust anyone in this government. I'm thousands of feet below ground, in a den of vipers. My wife and kids are dead. You're the only person I trust. It feels like everyone is working against me. And lying to my face.*

There I go again, complaining about my life. Tell me your survival story. Tell me your vantage point. From my end, it's bad, Ryan. I've seen satellite and drone footage. The radioactive voids that were once thriving cities like New York or Chicago, still have smoke rising from the smoldering coals. The cities have been burning for two months now. Ninety-nine percent of those cities have been evacuated, condemned, and a physical perimeter has been made around each vaporized radioactive wasteland. These toxic areas have been marked and labeled. We call them: No Man's Land. Entrance to these cities is prohibited, but foolish looters enter at their own risk. Those who dismiss the warning, do so in order to steal material items. They might gain in the short term, but they are sure to suffer an agonizing death from radiation poisoning a week later.

Ryan, I have to figure out a way to rebuild this nation faster. Americans are counting on me to do better. The military brass informs me what they say I must do to preserve the union, but there has to be a better way than lock down and ration. You're a historian. What would Lincoln do?

Give my best to Liz and the kids.
Love always,
TC

25

Location Unknown
June 3, 2017

Standing in a stainless-steel elevator, Steff Freeman watched the newly sworn-in Secretary of Defense Richard Secord swipe his badge on the waist-high panel. After a beeping noise, he then pressed the *S15* button. Immediately, she felt weightless as the small box dropped deep underground.

"I've never been to that level, sir," Steff said, her black computer bag hanging on her shoulder.

Secord tucked his chin as they free fell faster than any elevator in the world. "Few have, Miss Freeman. Few have."

"I feel privileged, sir," she said, watching Secord in the reflection on the door. Black suit, white shirt, thin black tie. Hands interlocked in front of him. Perfect posture. No expression on his freshly shaved face.

The elevator jerked to a stop. A chime sounded. The door opened.

Secord extended an open hand. "Ladies first."

"Thank you, sir." Steff stepped into a well-lit white hallway.

"Follow the yellow line, Miss Freeman."

The two colleagues walked side by side down the white hallway at a fast pace. A bold yellow line stretched in between a red and blue line. Halfway down the hallway, the red and blue lines broke off in different directions.

"You're not going to tell me where we're going?" Steff asked. With her black blazer unbuttoned, her breasts bounced in her white blouse with each step.

Secord glanced at her. "Patience, Miss Freeman."

She nodded, her eyes locking on the big black door twenty yards in front of them.

"The new director of the CIA speaks highly of your I.Q., Miss Freeman. In this new and evolving world order, our agencies will have a greater level of cooperation than before."

"I look forward to working closer to you, Mr. Secretary." Her breath was elevated.

"Forgive me for being short with you in the past. Us army brats never trust politicians or spies."

"I don't blame you, sir. But you can trust *me*." She smiled, and then they stopped in front of a door that looked like a closed elevator.

"I don't trust anyone, Miss Freeman," he said coldly as he swiped his badge on the panel.

As the door slid open, two dozen men and woman in dark blue camouflage uniforms stopped what they were doing and saluted the civilian commander of the military. He saluted back. The moment he dropped his hand, they went back to work in the medium sized station with black walls and dim lights. Some were typing on computers. Others were pointing at screens. A few were barking orders into satphones.

Secord stopped in front of one screen.

Steff dropped her jaw. "Is that Mars?"

"Affirmative, Miss Freeman," Secord said. "We have hundreds of drones in the skies above Mars." He shrugged. "And a base under a mountain." He started walking again, and

Steff followed him past a row of gray desks and computer screens, all the way to a door in the back corner of the room. Covering the wall was a layer of black high-tech foam. The surface looked like a thousand tiny pyramids.

"After you, Miss Freeman."

"Thank you, sir." With a nod, she entered a room that resembled the president's office. The oak desk was glossy, and the leather chairs were thick. A picture of the late secretary of defense and the deceased former President Lings hung on the wall directly behind the desk. (Both were victims of WWIII).

"Take a seat, Miss Freeman."

Steff dropped down in the chair, noticing there were no picture of the current president. She placed her satchel by her feet, up against the chair.

"Now, that we're secure, I can tell you what you're doing here." Watching her closely, he paused to meet her squinting eyes. "We…are entering a new world order. No longer do we face an existential threat from abroad. We are the victors of the war to end all wars. We control all nuclear, biological, and chemical weapons on the planet. We're in charge of every major military on the face of the globe. We also control outer space and every satellite.

"Miss Freeman, our only threat will come from within the United States, or foreign nationals who penetrate our borders. The CIA will have a new role. It will monitor civilians unlike ever before. And that starts today. The power grid will be on tomorrow, and the internet will be full of dissent. It will be our job to determine threats from thought. Our computer systems will use keywords to dragnet millions of conversations on social media, email, phone conversations, text messages, and open conversations. Anti-government extremists will be the target."

"Isn't that domestic spying, sir?"

"Miss Freeman, after the war, the president wisely chose to suspend the Constitution by ordering Martial Law, rendering the Bill of Rights null and void. Until these war powers are lifted, the military and intelligent agencies will collect data in an attempt to stop future attacks on democracy."

She blinked twice. "And what will be my role?"

"Miss Freeman, as you know, the Pentagon and CIA headquarters were destroyed. We lost eighty percent of our bureaucrats. Both agencies will relocate to Philadelphia, Pennsylvania. This will be the new Capital of the United States. While the agencies recruit employees, staff, and management, you will be the CIA liaison to the Defense Department. You will have direct access to me and my staff. We will collaborate on current and future threats to our borders and interior. Your agency will monitor satellite, internet, and phone activity. And *you* will relay information to *me*…or my staff."

"Will I get a pay raise?" She smiled, winking slightly.

"Miss Freeman, your new position will be quite demanding." He adjusted the knot in his tie, and then said, "I'm sure the new director will compensate you appropriately."

"I'm super excited to get started, sir." She repositioned herself in the chair.

"Congratulations, Miss Freeman." He glanced at the sliver of cleavage her blouse provided. "Here's your new clearance badge." He handed her a small black card on a black lanyard.

Leaning forward slowly, Steff smiled, grabbing the key to enlightenment. "Thank you, sir." She sat upright. "This is an honor." She slipped the lanyard around her neck. "Truly."

"I am confident you will succeed."

"Unfortunately, sir, I think I already failed. We all failed, sir. We should have seen the nuclear attack coming."

"We didn't fail, Ms. Freeman. World War Three was inevitable. Frankly, we're lucky it happened now. In five years, we would have lost. As you know, China's economy, technology, and military were on the verge of surpassing us."

Steff flashed a quick smile, cocking her head. "I guess I never thought of it like that, sir."

"That's the difference between the CIA and military." He stared at her plump lips. "You try to prevent wars. We prepare to win them."

26

Buccetti Compound
June 14, 2017

While sitting at the picnic table on his back deck, Frankie's eyes were locked on his laptop computer. The morning sun and its gentle rays of heat beamed on his neck. Dressed in a dark brown golf shirt and gray sweatpants, Frankie declined to hit the cigar Giovanni Mariani tried to pass him. "No, thanks. I'm good."

"Why not?" Mariani brought the cigar to his lips.

"Pot is a demotivator," Frankie said, his eyes locked on his computer screen. "Now that the power grid is back on, I need motivation. Big opportunities are coming."

"What do you mean?"

Frankie smiled. "You didn't watch the president's speech on TV last night?"

"Nah." Mariani shook his head. "I was at my parent's place. What'd he say?"

"Let me read part of the speech," he said and grabbed his computer, eyes falling on the screen. "He just declared war against the big banks: '*The United States of America is going to abolish the Federal Reserve and create a new Central Bank.*'" Frankie changed his voice to sound more like President Clacher. "'*No longer will our monetary system be controlled by international* bankers. *The new bank will be a fiat system like the last, but it will be owned publicly instead of privately. It will be based on the full faith and credit of the United States of America. This form of monetary system has been tried in the past…during the Revolutionary and Civil Wars. This system was a success. There was no interest on the debt, and no tax on income…because it was not necessary to create revenue. Revenue will be collected in the form of a Value Added Tax on goods purchased, and by tariffs on international trade.'"* Frankie paused, glancing at his friend who had low eyebrows and one eye squinted more than the other. *"'Today…as the sole economic and military superpower – and victor of World War III – America will make this system work in the name of national security. With unlimited funds from our new Central Bank, we will rebuild the world and put every able-bodied man and woman to work. By the end of my first term, the American economy will be stabilized. Economic growth will be unlike anything we've ever seen. But I need your help.*

"'In order to start this bank, the United Stated will begin selling tax-free sovereign bonds to those who have cash on hand to invest in America's future. The first investors to capitalize on this opportunity will collect massive interest rates for patriotic gratuity as they will have helped to spark this flame…that we call America.'"

"What the fuck is that supposed to mean?" Mariani asked.

"Well," Frankie said with a victorious smirk. "That means, the president just fundamentally transformed America for the good. It *means* that he fired the robber barons who have had a stronghold on America for the last hundred years. It means…no New World Order! The book was wrong! They're not going to exterminate us!"

Mariani cracked a smile. "No one was ever going to get exterminated." He shook his head. "But what the hell is a robber baron?"

"You know," Frankie said. "The international banking families. They've financed all sides of all wars for the last three hundred years. The inbred royal bloodlines that can be traced back to the Dimercos or the Roths."

"The elite of the elite," Mariani said, blowing out a cloud of smoke.

"Exactly," Frankie said. "He just kicked out the vampires and werewolves, and publicly told them they are no longer welcome to suck the blood from the American people."

"If they're so bad," Mariani inquired, "why hasn't any president said this before."

"JFK hinted to an audit of the Federal Reserve," Frankie said. "And Lincoln actually created his own debt-free form of currency."

"Greenbacks." Mariani smiled and nodded as if he just had an epiphany. "And both of them got a bullet to the head."

"Apparently, our president has some balls," Frankie said with a short laugh. "We better hope he doesn't get assassinated, cuz you don't wanna know what happens next."

Mariani shook his head. "I don't give a fuck what happens either way. Fuck 'em. If we can survive World War Three, we can survive anything."

"Well, I got an idea you might give a fuck about."

"Yeah," Mariani said with a chuckle. "What's that?"

"We should buy some sovereign bonds," Frankie suggested. "We'd get beaucoup rich in a year."

"No way," Mariani shook his head. "My money is three feet underground, and that's where it's staying." His mind's eye flashed back to the winter a year in the past. Back when he and Frankie robbed the Flebotomia Cartel and stashed the money deep in Ivan's woods. Back when trained killers were hunting them. Back when he saved Frankie's life. Twice.

"Okay, but don't say I didn't ask."

Mariani tilted a hand. "You're not really gonna invest in that bullshit, are ya?"

"Hell yeah, I'm gonna invest. I think I could make a ton of money."

"You're on your own this time, brother."

*****

Two days later, Frankie walked into the car dealership and found Carlos Zapato's office. Turning his head over his shoulder, his eyes raked over a brand-new black truck with four doors. *That truck looks mean,* he thought as he knocked lightly on the office door.

"Come in," Carlos said, and when Frankie walked inside, he smiled. "Hey, Frank."

"Los," Frankie said, extending a hand. "Long time no see, brother."

The two men shook hands, and Carlos wrapped him up in his bear-like torso. After two hard pats on the back, Carlos pulled out a chair.

"How's business?" Frankie asked.

Sitting down in his thick leather chair, Carlos adjusted his sky-blue tie. "You're the first customer to walk in the door." His tie contrasted with his dark blue suit jacket and black, graying hair. "How 'bout you? How was the bunker?"

"It's peaceful out there," Frankie said. "Why don't you and Jewlz come up for dinner one of these nights? She might get a kick out of that bunker."

"That's a good idea," Carlos said. "She needs to get out of the house. It was a long winter."

"I know. It seemed like forever. But at least we survived to tell the story to our grandchildren someday. Millions didn't make it."

Carlos smiled thinly, a play of sadness in the quick upturn of his lips. "What brings you in today, my friend?"

"Three things: I wanted to say hi. I got a once-in-a-lifetime opportunity for us. And third...I got my eye on that truck out there."

"What's the opportunity?" Carlos asked, his beefy hand rubbing his freshly shaved chin.

Frankie leaned forward. "Did you read about the president's plan?"

"I did. I like the zero-income tax part, but without Congress, this law would be unconstitutional."

"Under Martial Law, the Constitution is null and void," Frankie said. "Until the union is stable, the president can use unlimited power. National Security is on the line."

"So, what?" Carlos said, "What's your idea?"

"Sovereign bonds," Frankie said. "We should buy some."

"Bonds accumulate small amounts of interest over a long period of time," Carlos insisted with a short laugh to follow.

"Historically, you're probably right," Frankie said. "But the government is gonna start its new central bank with a majority of bonds. If the interest isn't high enough, we could just invest in the stock market."

"*Now* you're talking," Carlos said. "That's where we need to be."

"Let's do both," Frankie clapped his hands together. "But first...I need that truck out there."

"What, the black Silverado?" Carlos chuckled.

"Yeah," Frankie said. "That's the one."

"Sold!" Carlos got up and escorted Frankie to the truck of his dreams.

*****

For the first time since the Great War, Frankie's friend, Marcel Taylor turned on the open sign to his mattress store. "Finally, back in business," he said to his wife who was smiling with her long sandy hair resting on her back.

Mae Taylor glanced out the window and saw cars cruising down the street. "I bet a lot of people will need a new mattress," she said, turning back to face Marcel. "Three and a half months with no shower. Them beds are nasty."

"Order another shipment," Marcel said, adjusting the black glasses on his nose. "Get some couches, too." He was of average height, but thin. His hair was short, but wool like. And his skin looked just like dark chocolate.

"After I place the order, should I pick up some lunch?" Wearing her typical tan capris and a blue company polo, Mae looked polished and professional. That had always been her style.

"Not today, babe," Marcel said. "I got a meeting with Frankie."

"Okay, tell him I said hi." She kissed Marcel on the lips, fixed the collar on his rippled white shirt, and then walked into the office.

"I'll be back in an hour or so."

Mae turned back. "Hey, I almost forgot." Reaching inside her purse, she pulled out the gold cross his mom gave him for Christmas. "I got your neckless back from the shop."

"Thanks, babe." He closed his eyes briefly, and then fixed it around his neck. "I felt naked without it." His mom had perished in the Chicago nuclear attack on 3/13.

Mae hugged him tight. "I'm sorry, babe." She rubbed his upper arm. "I miss her, too."

When his wife walked away, Marcel touched the cross, and then walked outside.

Frankie was parking his shiny new truck.

"Damn," Marcel said to himself, crossing the parking lot under a blazing sun. When he opened the door, he climbed in and shook Frankie's hand. "Whuuuud up, play boy!" Marcel said in a loud, high-pitched tone. "Nice truck, bro!"

Frankie smiled in turn. "Good to see ya, brother," he said. "It's been a minute." He threw the truck in gear. "How's business?"

"We just opened the doors."

"The people will be coming," Frankie said. "I'm glad to see you made it through the winter. How are the wife and kids doing?"

"Everyone's good," Marcel said. "Mae says hi. We been up at the cabin. It was peaceful. It had an old school fireplace."

"Nice," Frankie said. "What did you eat all winter?"

"My kids got plenty of hunting practice," Marcel said with a large smile. "Mostly deer, but they got a moose and a bear, too."

Frankie took his eyes off the road to glance at Marcel. "That's pretty cool. How'd the bear taste?"

"A little tough. I didn't really like it." "Bro, I got something you're gonna like," Frankie said. "Me and Carlos are about to blow up the stock market. You want in?"

"That's the best idea I ever heard!" Marcel boasted with a robust smile. "Buy when the stock market is at an all-time low, and sell when it's at an all-time high."

"We're gonna be rich!" Frankie said from the driver's seat. "It's gonna be overwhelming."

"When can we start?" Marcel said.

"Yesterday," Frankie said. "With each passing day, we're losing money. I think we should get a stock broker and invest every penny."

"How much you gonna invest?"

"I've still got a half-million buried," Frankie said in a slow and lowered voice, as if someone might be listening.

27

Astana, Kazakhstan
September 11, 2016

Heather Roth stood in her father's office with her uncle and dad standing on each side of her. A thick chrome briefcase sat on the oak desk in front of them.

Seth Roth blew out a stream of smoke. "Open it."

Speaker Roth leaned forward. Clicking two buckles open, she slowly lifted the top. Straightening herself, she gazed down at a tactical nuclear weapon. "It's beautiful," she said quietly, her thin eyebrows arching.

Heather's dad, David Roth wrapped his arm around her waist. "Five of them will be detonated simultaneously, in order to prove sophistication. It must look like Russia and China are responsible."

"The feeble-minded president will be given options from Mr. Secord," Seth Roth said. "And from there…global chaos will ensue."

Speaker Roth closed the case. "What if Russia and China turn us into a parking lot?"

"The American military has no match," Seth said. "Did you forget about our satellite capabilities?"

"No, Master. I am fully aware. It was just a question. But we shouldn't underestimate the ability for humans to fail."

"Enough questions," Seth Roth snapped his fingers. "The blueprint calls for a global cataclysm. And then, a seven-year transformation. We must minimize the threat from the armed American citizen. We need to make them beg for government to save them. Stalin and Hitler proved hard tyranny never works. The people need a soft dictatorship of the proletariat. We take them...not with brute force, but with the soft touch of incrementalism. Doses and doses of government, and soon...they will fall like a plump red apple...into our hands."

28

The Buccetti Compound
July 4, 2017

The flat-screen television showed President Tom Clacher waving and smiling behind bulletproof glass and a navy-blue podium that held the Great Seal of the United States of America. And Frankie Buccetti was sitting at the edge of his seat, listening.

"GOOD AFTERNOON, AMERICA!" the president hollered into the microphone, stepping back to wave at the hundreds of thousands of enthusiastic people who lined the streets in front of the new Capitol Building in Philadelphia, Pennsylvania. Clacher looked dapper in a black suit, white shirt, and a pale blue tie that matched the sky above. He kept waving and turning from side to side. "Thank you! … Thank You!" He continued waving and blowing kisses and pointing at people in the crowd that rolled like waves in the vast Atlantic Ocean.

"U.S.A! U.S.A.! U.S.A.!" Clacher shouted with a robust smile on his face, listening to the sound of his words being echoed by the people as it traveled through the streets and beneath the skyscrapers. The powerful chant continued for another solid minute until the leader of the free world began to speak again. "Before I get started…I want to take a moment of silence for the twenty-five million Americans who died as a result of World War Three." He tucked his chin in his chest and the crowd did the same. The silence continued until the president's voice sounded. "Rest in peace, my friends," he paused dramatically and then continued. "To those of you who lost a mom...or a dad. A child or a friend. To those who survived, but lost everything. To those who suffered in the aftermath of the Greatest War. I'm sorry." His right hand was pressing on the left side of his chest.

The president leaned on the podium for a long moment before nodding slowly. "I feel your pain," he said. "I lost my wife...Carla. Two adult kids, Blain and Robert. ... I lost my home. The White House. We all lost something. But *we* are the fortunate ones. *We* are lucky. *We* are blessed. Because *we* are alive."

Clacher's heavy sigh sounded like wind in the microphone. "Please, let's not let them die in vain. Let's rebuild this nation...and the world. ... And let's do it in the name of peace and love...and freedom.

"Together, we can do this. The wind is at our sails. The threat is over. The world is united. Freedom will ring...not only here in America, but in Russia and China, and every other nation on the face of the Earth. Ruthless dictators will be no more. And most importantly, international bankers will no longer have a stronghold over this nation's monetary system.

"I'm not the first president to kill the bank, but I will be the last. Let me read for you, the words of President Abraham Lincoln: *The money power preys upon a nation in times of peace, and conspires against it in times of adversity. It is more despotic than monarchy, more insolent than autocracy, and more selfish than bureaucracy.* I am confident that Honest Abe was telling the truth … I'm going to take his advice!" He briefly rose his fist in the air.

"Today…I'm here to declare victory in this Third World War! I'm here…to give assurance for the future of this great nation. Together, we survived the Greatest War in the history of the world. The hard part is behind us. But reconstruction will be a challenge."

Clacher paused, gazing at his supporters. "It's going to cost a lot of money to build new cities for displaced people to live. And since 1913, our money has been in the hands of a few rich men whose interests do not align with the American people. Their ultimate goal is to inherit the earth and everything in it. And I'm not going to let that happen." He shook his finger in the air. "No. I'm going to abolish the Federal Reserve! I'm going to create our own National Bank!" And the crowd cheered and clapped for a solid minute until they kindly allowed him to conclude.

"Together, we will climb this mountain. We will stride forward, shaping a more perfect union. All men and women will be created equal, receiving Life, Liberty, and the Pursuit of Happiness. That beacon of liberty. That illuminating star in the night sky that shines just a little bit brighter than the rest.

"On this birthday for our great nation, I want all of you to be grateful for what we have, hopeful for the future, but never forget…the past. Thank you! God bless all of you! And may God continue to bless the United States of America!"

Frankie's TV screen flashed back to the SNN studio. Two men and one silver-haired woman were sitting around a table. Former Deputy Secretary of State Eugene Parker, SNN journalist Alex Tarnowski, and Speaker of the House Heather Roth all wore frowns on their faces.

Frankie Buccetti watched intently.

"President Clacher needs to be removed from power. Today," Alex Tarnowski said. Shaking his full head of white hair at the camera, his lips briefly compressed into a thin line. "He has caused the death of millions. Rather tens of millions of people. No: hundreds of millions of people. *King* Clacher has made America a police state. And without Congress, he is making new laws as he goes along. Like a South American despot."

"I'd take it a step further than that," said Eugene Parker. "This president has accomplished something that has been tried over and over again throughout history. He has taken over the world and plans to make his fat cat friends rich while the rest of us starve. With every new law he passes without Congress, he proves that he is a usurper and a dictator. This man's illegal use of Martial Law has killed countless Americans and jailed even more without trail. Clacher is pathological…. He is Hitler times a hundred."

Speaker Roth's thin eyebrows formed a V. "We all know Mr. Clacher is destroying democracy," she said, and then dropped a closed fist on the table in front of her. "But the question is—what are we gonna do about it?"

"The responsibility of saving America will fall on us," said Eugene Parker. "It's up to *us* to let the people know that this is a post-constitutional president who is tyrannical in nature."

Frankie changed the channel to find the same style of coverage. Then he changed it again and again, until he turned the TV off and laid down on the couch. *Don't think. Don't think. Don't think.*

29

Washington D.C.
March 13, 2017

From the bowels of the White House, Secret Service Agent Pete Richardson jerked forward in his seat. Narrowing his eyes, he zeroed in on one of the many screens in the security room. A plain white van with black windows was parked on the road closest to the front gate. "Get someone to check on that van," the man ordered into his radio. "It's blocking traffic."

"Copy," Agent Johnson said on the other end of the radio.

Agent Richardson zoomed in with the drone camera to get a closer look. Just then, a second white van pulled up parallel to the van in question. The doors of the first van opened. Two bearded men with brown skin hopped out, rushed across the blacktop, and climbed into the side door of the second van.

"Code red!" Richardson yelled into the radio and hit the red button. An alarm sounded throughout the grounds of the White House. "Somebody get to that van. Two Arabs just jumped in a second van and sped off."

"Calm down," Agent Johnson said. "You just called for the evacuation of the White House. Call it off. Shut off that alarm!"

"Sir, you don't understand what I just saw. Terrorists just abandoned one van and took off in another."

Agent Johnson raised his voice. "My men are on it. Call off the code red. Now!"

Richardson spoke into his radio. "Wait, your guys just got there." His heart was hammering uncomfortably in his chest. His eyes were locked on the screen. Secret Service men in black were approaching the van with long guns drawn. One agent swung open the back door. He paused for a long moment and then climbed in the back.

Agent Richardson heard nothing but radio static. "What's going on? Tell me something."

Static.

"Speak to me!" Richardson said.

Agent Johnson barked into the radio. "Code red! Retreat to the bunker!"

"What is it?" Agent Richardson asked.

"A fucking bomb! Set to detonate in four minutes."

*****

Three minutes after the bomb was found, President Clacher was being rushed through the bunker of the White House toward a secret high-speed train. A dozen Secret Service agents were surrounding him. One African American admiral in a black military uniform had a thick suitcase handcuffed to his wrist.

The rear door to the train was open. Clacher followed an agent up the steps and inside the well-lit first compartment. Maroon leather seats were on both sides of the aisle.

"To the front, Mr. President." Agent Johnson pressed his hand against Clacher's back as they hurried in a single file line. No windows were on this train. Just white walls with mahogany panels on the lower half.

The president's head twisted back and saw more than a dozen agents with sub-machine guns in their hands. "What the hell is going on out there?"

"Sir, it's a bomb," Agent Johnson said. "Keep moving, sir. It's on a timer."

President Clacher quickly marched through two sets of doors to the front of the train.

Agent Johnson stopped the president just before the control room door. Swiping his security badge across the black panel on the side of the door, it beeped and slid open. "Right here, sir."

Clacher stepped inside the small suite, and his eyes bounced from the oak walls to a desk, to the long leather sofa against the wall. Dropping into the seat behind the desk, he let out a heavy sigh. The man with the briefcase sat across from him. As the train propelled forward, Clacher braced himself, one hand on his chair, the other against the desk. Four Secret Service agents sat down, guns still pressed against their chests.

"Where are you taking me?"

The magnetic levitation train was now speeding through the subterranean tunnel at two hundred and ninety miles-per-hour.

Agent Johnson held out a hand. "You'll get all the details soon, Mr. President. Right now, I need —"

All of a sudden, the train roughly jostled, and a thunderous grumble of an eruption was heard. Felt. The train shook violently but it didn't slow it down. The lights were flickering.

"Oh, my God." Clacher's left hand covered his mouth, and his wide eyes locked on Agent Johnson. "My wife and kids were at an event on Capitol Hill. How big is that bomb?"

"Mr. President," Agent Johnson said. "Only a nuke could shake the ground like that, sir. We're in a state of war. Sir."

President Clacher buried his head in his hands.

The man in the black military uniform rose and set the briefcase on the desk, opening it in front of the grieving president. "I'm sorry about your family, Mr. President," Admiral Grannis said in a deep baritone voice. "But your nation needs you. You must elevate the nation's readiness to DEFCON 1."

President Clacher leveled his head. His chest was rising and falling. Low eyebrows. Short breaths.

"Mr. President."

Leaning forward, President Clacher reached out a trembling hand, typed his password on the keyboard, and then poked the enter button. Then he pressed the number one. Before he punched the enter button again, he met eyes with the admiral.

"The United States Military is mobilizing, sir," Admiral Grannis said, closing the case and setting it on the floor next to his black boots.

"Where are you taking me?"

"Sir, we're traveling to a bunker in Montana. Sir." Grannis was the stiffest man in the room.

"We have tunnels all the way to Montana?"

"Sir, that is affirmative. Sir."

*****

An hour after the nuclear attack on Washington D.C., a second train was rocketing down the tunnel just behind President Clacher. Inside a posh suite, Speaker of the House Heather Roth was patiently waiting for Deputy Secretary of State

Eugene Parker and Deputy Secretary of Defense Richard Secord to finish reading the classified intel report she'd given them. Secord was the first to level his head.

"Madam Roth, this State Department report is vague with anonymous sources from Saudi Arabia," Deputy Secord shrugged. "This information is not credible. What's the purpose of this?" Secord had been given orders in advance to be with Speaker Roth on this day. He knew the Roth family was up to something. He knew he had no choice but to go along to get along. He knew the safety of his family depended on it. But he didn't know the extent of what she was planning.

Speaker Roth held up a threatening hand. "Let me fill you in, Mr. Secord," she said, adjusting the collar of her light gray pantsuit. "We both know this feeble-minded president is going to wage a nuclear war that will kill a billion people. When the dust settles in a few years, we'll leak this doctored intel and turn Congress against him. We'll say his actions were beneath the dignity of the presidency, and because of those actions, millions of Americans were killed for no reason."

Deputy Parker grinned, closing a black leather folder. "Madam Roth, *you* are a genius. If ISIS set the bombs — and Clacher retaliates against Russia and China — *he* is a war criminal. A pariah."

"Excuse me, Madam Roth," Secord said, shaking the piece of paper. "You really think *this* flimsy document would get him impeached and removed? And even if he *is* removed, Vice President Andrews will be waiting in the wings. He's less malleable than Clacher."

Roth twitched her pale finger and clicked her tong. "Trust me, Mr. Secord." Her head cocked. "My father has many tricks up his proverbial sleeve."

She's gonna take over the government, Secord thought, swallowing hard. "Pardon me, Your Grace," Secord said with a tremble crawling up his spine. "I-I meant no disrespect. You've summoned me here, but I'm in the dark. I don't know what you want from me."

"Mr. Secord, you and Mr. Parker are here…because my father trusts you." She cleared her throat. "Excuse me. I meant; he trusts the oath you made to the ancient fraternity. He is confident you will follow orders and fulfill your commitment." Roth leaned forward in her chair. "That said, you *have* been told very little up to this point. I understand your confusion. This mission is on a need-to-know basis. You're right. The time has come to give you new orders."

"Thank you, Your Grace." Secord blinked. "Please tell me what I need to know." He folded his hands on his lap.

Roth offered a coy smile. "Mr. Secord, you will be my eyes and ears in the Clacher Administration. You will use the device we gave you to record every meeting with him. Going forward, you will advise the president to implement polices we give you. In the meantime, Mr. Parker and I will build an army of bureaucrats, members of the media, and politicians to keep in my pocket. When the lights come back on, we will incrementally leak damaging information about Mr. Clacher…until the time comes to open up the dam. And eventually, he will be forced to resign or become the first president in American history to be impeached and removed from office."

Secord gave her a slight nod that didn't affect his stiff posture. "And then what?"

Roth winked. "That's all you need to know for now, Mr. Secord. If you play your cards right, you will have a significant role in the next administration. If not, your family will suffer. And you will watch."

The Deputy Secretary of the Defense Department bit his tongue and nodded his head.

"Mr. Secord, do I sense...animosity?"

Secord shook his head. "No, Madam Speaker," he said. "I'm with you. You'll make a fine leader." A vision of a future Heather Roth flashed in his mind: The same silver hair and Mao suit, sitting on a throne, placing a jewel-encrusted crown on her own head.

"Of course, I'll be a fine leader, Mr. Secord." Roth looked at both of her puppets.

"I serve at your pleasure, Madam Roth," Parker bowed his head.

Richard Secord let out a breath, staring into her dark eyes. "Madam Speaker, I am fully committed to the cause." *I should snap your frail neck.*

"I hope you two are ready to make history," Roth said. "Or should I say...*shape* the future?"

30

Duluth, Minnesota
October 24, 2017

Standing in his mom's vandalized house, Frankie Buccetti handed Larry Sobek a thick envelope. "Here's five thousand for the down payment," he said. "Thanks for fitting us in your busy schedule."

Larry shoved it in his jacket pocket. "No prob. Looks like the looters fucked it up pretty good."

"Yeah, this neighborhood got it pretty bad," Frankie said, shaking his head tightly. "She's anxious to move back home. And honestly, I don't think I could live with her too much longer."

"I know the feeling," Larry said, looking around at the broken windows, graffiti, and trash. "I couldn't live with my ma' for a week."

"How long do you think it will take to fix?"

"Probably a few days to clean it out, and about a month to remodel."

"Perfect. Thank you."

"It looks like there's some water damage. It might end up costing more than ten."

"Money won't be a problem," Frankie said. "Business has been super good. I'm gonna invest in some real-estate when I get back from traveling my bucket list. I'd like your team to do all my work."

Larry nodded. "It's always nice doing business with ya, Frank. Anything you need. Just call."

"Thanks. You do great work." Frankie shook his hand.

"Who's gonna be living at your house after your mom moves back home?"

"Just me."

"A big house for one guy."

"Silence is a virtue."

31

Duluth, Minnesota
December 14, 2017

Lying in a tilted hospital bed, Conny Bream held her newborn daughter in her arms. Tears were streaming down her blushing cheeks. The baby was all wrapped up in a lightweight cotton blanket, but her little tan face and big brown eyes kept her smiling. Conny's ex-husband and teenage kids were standing around the bed, smiling at the newest addition to their family.

"What's her name, mom?" Conny's younger son asked.

"Sethra," Conny said, and then her ex-husband cuffed his hands behind the baby's head and bottom, lifting her in his arms. As the baby started crying louder, he lightly rocked her back and forth with a soft bouncing motion. But to no avail.

The nurse came into the room with a clipboard in her hands. "Can I get you to fill this out, please?"

"Yeah, no problem," Conny said, receiving the certificate of live birth. Printing her name as the mother, her eyes fell upon the next line. *Father.* Her hand immediately began to tremble, but she managed to finish writing her last name.

Conny's ex-husband passed Sethra to their younger son.

Avoiding an awkward pause, Conny handed the clipboard to her reconciled ex-husband. And the tears continued to roll down her cheeks.

"You okay, mom?" the older son asked, reaching for her arm.

"I'm fine." She rubbed her eyes. "Just a little tired."

32

Fort Peck Lake, Montana
January 28, 2018

Steff Freeman squeezed the brake on her black snowmobile, and Ken Spatz flew right by. Twenty yards in front of her, Ken's yellow and black sled came to a skidding stop on the frozen lake. Taking her helmet off, she dismounted her seat and strutted toward him in her tight black snowmobile suit.

Ken hopped off his sled and set his helmet on the seat. Turning, he spread apart his arms. "You okay?"

As Steff walked up to her old friend, his tall, strapping features brought back many memories of their late-night romps at basic training, then Afghanistan, and then again when they both joined the CIA. Back then, his black hair was buzzed and his face was always freshly shaved. Now he looked rugged with a beard and long brown hair that was being taken by the icy wind. *Mmm,* she thought, biting her lip as she got closer. "Let's take a walk," she said and Ken followed her across the cracking ice.

"What's up?" Ken asked, trying to keep up with her pace.

Steff glanced but kept cutting through the snowfall until there was some space between them and the snowmobiles. Stopping and spinning on her boot heel, she lifted a finger to her lips. "Shhh."

Ken's eyes squinted.

Grabbing his black jacket, she took a step closer.

Ken wrapped his arms around her waist. "You missed me, didn't you?"

"Of course," she said, tilting her head. "But I brought you out here because I have something to tell you."

"Good," he said, and then swiped her legs from underneath her and pinned her on the snowy ice. Before she could say another word, her wet tongue was dancing with his, distracting him from the wind and snow; distracting him from anything that wasn't Steff.

When Steff felt his hand rubbing on her crotch, she whispered, "Stop."

"No," Ken said, gently placing his hand under her ear. "You started it."

From underneath him, she grabbed his jacket. "I mean, stop. I need to tell you something."

"Okay. What is it?"

"Put your ear close to my lips."

Ken twisted his head and lowered it slowly.

"Don't tell a soul." Her words were soft but sharp. "There's a plot against the president. My source says it's bigger than any one man. He says almost everyone is in on it. There's nothing we can do. America will be a full-fledged dictatorship within five years at the most."

"Why would you tell me this?"

"Because you're the only person I trust. And we need to start building a resistance."

"Sounds like a suicide mission."

"It is. But someone has to stop them. Why not us?"

"Just me and you?"

Steff shook her head. "No. I know a few patriots in the intelligence community, the Secret Service, *and* the military. But I need time to make sure. I need them to trust me, too."

"How are you gonna do that?"

"I have my ways." She rubbed on his groin.

33

The Buccetti Compound
April 4, 2018

Frankie opened his mail box and found junk mail, bills, and a red envelope that was bigger than the others. The return address came from Mankato, Minnesota, and it was hand written with neat penmanship.

"Elise!" Frankie said, dropping the other letters on the leafy ground. It was his stepmom!

Ripping open the paper, he found a card with a depiction of Jesus walking with His flock of sheep. A bright sun in the corner. A staff in His right hand.

A new horizon lies ahead, Frankie silently read the card and opened it. *As long as you have faith,* it said on the inside. Beneath the text was a folded sheet of paper. Upon unfolding it, he read the handwritten note silently:

Frank,

I'm so sorry it took so long to reach you. We lost everything, except for what we brought with us. Your sister had the Christmas card you gave her stuffed in the book about JFK. She loved that book! It helped get her through the long winter of 2017. Gosh, it was bad down here in the Twin Cities. Absolute chaos. We had to relocate to my aunt's house here in Mankato. Much safer! We're doing well, and living a peaceful life. I'm an economics professor at the college. And

Tina is in high school. Tenth grade! Can you believe it? She's doing well, but she's still struggling with depression after the loss of your dad. It must have been a tough time to be a teenager the last year. I sure bet you could cheer her up!

Frank. I'm so sorry for your loss. I truly wish we found that card faster. Your information is blocked and you're not on social media. I hope this letter reaches you in good faith. We love you. And look forward to talking to you on the phone or in person.

Your father died in the initial attack in Minneapolis on Marth 13, 2017. I loved him with all my heart. He was such a good husband and father. He spoke so highly of you. Frank, it would be so good to see you. I'm sorry a million times over.

Love,

Elise and Tina Williams

Frankie walked up the long winding driveway with tears in his eyes. *I love you, Dad,* he thought, sniffling down the pain of loss. *I only wish I knew you more. Now you'll get a chance to know me from above. I hope I make you proud someday. Maybe I should go spend some time with Tina this summer?*

34

Duluth, Minnesota
May 24, 2018

Sitting on a stool in a hole-in-the-wall bar, Giovanni Mariani tilted his half-full glass of whisky to his mouth, and then set the empty glass on the bar. "Is that Gordon Grayfeather?" he said under his breath, peering at a large man in a black T-shirt at the other end of the bar. Squinting, his head cocking a little to the side, Mariani tallied up the images: long black hair, dark skin, gigantic frame. "That's him for sure." Lifting himself off his stool, he treaded slowly toward the man in question.

Mariani had almost reached him when Grayfeather turned, almost as if he'd sensed an approach. The man's fists clenched down at his sides in anticipation.

"Gordon. It is you, brother?"

"What?" Grayfeather raised his shoulders. Ten years in prison, a year of surviving in a near lawless world, and a ten-drink buzz clouded his vision.

"Whoa, bro." Mariani stuck out the palm of his hand, warding off the big man who was staggering. "It's Giovanni." He shrugged one shoulder. "You don't remember me? Frankie's boy?"

Grayfeather took a step forward and let out a chuckle. "Mariani!" He wrapped him up in his long muscular arms, and then squeezed him so tight, he actually lifted his feet off the ground.

When Mariani's feet were both firm on the floor again, he smacked his old friend on the shoulder. "How ya been, man?"

"Let's go smoke. I'll tell ya all about it." Turning, Grayfeather marched to the back of the bar and out the back door. With a group of young men and women smoking in a circle, he kept walking in the dark alley until they were out of earshot. Puddles filled the potholes. Shadows from the tall brick buildings encompassed the two men. And wind was swirling around them.

Mariani lit up a cig. "So, what the hell ya been up to, bro?"

Grayfeather blew out a stream of smoke. "We been putting in work. We got the whole town on lock down. You should join us, brother. I could use another enforcer."

"Sounds like a risky job."

"It's simple, bro. Everyone's afraid of us. We basically rob chomos, then sell their shit on the black web. Cops got more important things to worry about."

"Paranoid chomos got guns."

"Zero risk, bro. In fact, we have so much fucking money, we loan it out like a bank. Big interest. It's like an endless cycle."

"What if they don't pay?"

"They all pay, plus interest. Trust me, bro. Me, Brice, and Dennis made a reputation around town. But, yeah, *some* people have problems paying. So, we send them to steal shit. And then we charge a fee for theft payoffs. See, it's just mo' money every day."

"What if they go to the cops?"

"Cops?" He laughed. "They don't give a shit what happens in the ghetto. After the war, the cops got lax. It's almost like a no-go zone in Europe."

"Why is that?"

"Crime is rampant, bro. It's everywhere. Look around in the bar. Everyone's spun out on drugs. Gun shots can be heard every night. Hookers in the alleys. We just capitalize. There's no competition."

Mariani nodded his head and blew out a stream of smoke. "Well, I'm happy for your success, bro."

"You want in?"

"No, thanks." Mariani shook his head. "All I do is hunt, fish, and drink whiskey. I like the simple life."

"The money is good, brother. You sure?"

"I got a little money buried. But I live off the land. Money isn't useful to me."

Grayfeather laughed. "How 'bout action? I could give you an address of a child molester once a month. Take out some aggression. I remember how much you like adrenaline."

"Thanks, bro, I've had enough action to last a lifetime."

"Yeah, I heard you and Frankie had a run-in with the Flebotomia Cartel."

Mariani nodded, tilting his head to the left briefly. "You could say that. Felt like a war though. We got lucky."

"Nah, man." Grayfeather shook his head slowly. "Them vatos are no joke. You got skills, bro. Brice said you took some dudes out with a bow?"

Mariani nodded. "You should try it sometime."

"That's a good idea. My hatchet is too messy."

"You use a hatchet?"

"My weapon of choice. Never fails me."

"Why don't you put the hatchet down for a weekend and come turkey hunting with me? I got an extra bow."

"How 'bout this, I'll go hunting with you, if you go hunting with me?" Grayfeather dropped a heavy hand on his shoulder and squeezed. "I'll make sure it's a repeat offender we take down. Dennis pays snitches to tell us where the sex traffickers live. We saved three little girls last summer. We're heroes, dog!"

Mariani flicked his cigarette against the brick wall of a building. "All right, bro. Let me think about it."

"Awesome!" Grayfeather smiled. "If you like it, I'll let you ride with me on a special operation. Some punk named Adoette gets out of prison soon. Dude raped my boy's son up in there. Turf war shit. I gots to handle that."

Mariani noticed Grayfeather studying his facial expression. "Bro, I love you," he said with a low brow. "But I really enjoy laying low." When he met Grayfeather's dark eyes, he saw a coldness he'd only seen in a rabid dog.

"It's all good, bro." Grayfeather shrugged. "Probably something I should do by myself anyway. Might get ugly." Grayfeather paused, smacking Mariani in the shoulder. "Hey, what the hell has Frankie been up to?"

Mariani shook his head. "I haven't talked to him much lately. He hit it big in the stock market after the war. Since then, he's been all business."

"Damn, the stock market. Frankie? I can't picture it. I thought he'd be digging ditches the rest of his life."

"Not anymore. Dude doesn't even wear jeans. He thinks he's gonna make a billion and save the world."

"Damn, bro. Sounds like I'm gonna half to bring him back down to Earth."

"Nah, I'm happy for him. He worked his ass off his entire life for nothing. The guy deserves a lucky streak. I just think, sometimes he forgets where he comes from."

"Tell that black bastard I said what's up."

"I think he's on some business trip. I'll tell him when he gets back."

35

Mankato, Minnesota
June 25, 2018

Frankie dribbled a small basketball in the driveway of his stepmom's new house. Meeting eyes with his teenage sister, he smiled. "What am I at? H-O-R?"

"No," Tina smiled. "You're H-O-R-S, Frankie. Quit trying to cheat."

"What are you at?" Frankie said, holding the ball in front of his sky-blue polo shirt.

"I'm at H." Tina's curly dark brown hair was resting on her shoulders. The kid was almost as tall as Frankie. She was wearing a white T-shirt and black gym shirts. And she had an athletic build.

"Damn, I'm getting smoked by a kid," Frankie said, aiming at the basket twenty feet out from the hoop. "I got this." He shot the ball and it bounced off the back of the rim.

"Horse!" Tina pointed. "You're a horse." She giggled and then ran after the ball. Scooping it up, she then dribbled between her legs and around her back, passing the it to Frankie.

"I'll get you next time."

Tina squinted one eye. "I thought you were leaving today?"

"I was, but…I'm starting to like it here. Let's go ask your mom if I can stay a little longer."

"You bought the house. I don't think she can say no."

Frankie smiled. "I've been here for a few weeks. You guys probably want me out of your hair. I just want a few more chances to beat you. I can't go home and tell my friends I couldn't beat a girl."

"But what if I keep beating you?"

"Then I'll never leave." Frankie smiled. "Something's wrong with me. I get obsessed with winning. Even against all odds, I can't give up. It might take me a while, but I'll find a way to beat you, sis."

Tina smiled, and then they walked into the house where her mom was serving dinner.

"Just in time," Elise said, placing a plate in the spot where Tina would be sitting.

"She beat me again," Frankie said, pulling out a chair to sit down.

"I haven't beat her since she was nine." Elise sat down at the table. "Do you like ribs, Frank?"

"My favorite," Frankie said.

Tina sat next to her brother. "Me, too," she said, cutting into the saucy meat with her knife.

Frankie took a bite of his riblet. "Wow!" His eyebrows lifted. "How'd you get that taste?"

"It's my aunt's recipe. Been in the family for generations."

"You could make some money with sauce that good," Frankie mumbled with a mouthful. "It's amazing."

"The sauce is good, but any business with food is difficult. Way too much of a risk for me."

Frankie looked at his stepmom. "I got a risk-free idea for ya."

"What's that?" Elise asked.

"You're an economics professor, right?"

"Yeah, why?"

"Well, I was thinking...I bet you could invest my money better than me. I mean, you must be like ten times smarter. Why don't I pay you twenty percent to invest my money?"

Elise laughed shortly. "Frankie, you've already done so much. You bought me a house and a car. Twenty percent would be grossly excessive. I could just give you advice for free."

"But I don't like all the technical stuff with the stock market and taxes. It's above my head. I thought it would be a good way for you to make a lot of money doing what you love."

"But my passion isn't money. It's teaching."

"Why can't you do both?"

"Frankie, I'm way so busy with Tina and basketball, and all of her other activities. I'm sorry. I will definitely teach you, though."

Frankie shrugged. "Why don't you teach Tina how to invest my money? Give her twenty percent?"

Tina's head shifted from Frankie to her mom.

"She's fifteen. And I won't raise her to be money hungry. Money is the root of all evil."

"It is, but there are very few people in this world with the opportunity we have. We could all get wealthy and make a difference in this wicked world."

Elise let out a sigh. "Fine, I'll do it for ten percent, but I'll teach Tina to do most of the work. And we'll put five percent in a trust fund for her college education."

Frankie smiled. "Thank you!" He brought his hand to his chest.

"No." Elise shook her head. "Thank you. Your dad would be proud."

"That's one of my goals," Frankie said. "I wish I could have made him proud when he was alive. I mean, I barely even visited him."

"Frankie. Your dad was so proud of you. He bragged about you all the time. You guys are exactly the same. He didn't travel much either."

Frankie let out a breath. "We can't change the past." He turned to face his sister. "But we can mold the future."

36

Northern Illinois
January 3, 2019

Frankie peered out the window of his first-class plane seat. The clear sky provided a panoramic view of the west side of Chicago—or what used to be Chicago. Now it was a city in ruins. A parking lot. Black rubble as far as the eye could see. The plane was flying alongside the Windy City heading south. Airplanes were prohibited from flying over it.

"Fuckin' Russians, eh?" said the old guy sitting next to Frankie. He was wearing a blue sport coat and jeans. Circular glasses were resting on his nose.

Frankie straightened himself. "I don't think we'll ever know exactly what happened."

"Trust me, son. My entire family is in the military. That was definitely Russia and China."

"You're probably right," Frankie admitted. "I just think there's more going on behind the scenes than they're telling us."

"Sounds like you're listening to that crazy guy on the radio." The man's head was bald on top, with gray hair on the sides. "Luke Easton."

"What's wrong with that?" Frankie asked.

"Nothing. I just think he's a conspiracy theorist. I like to deal with facts."

"Honestly, I think it's all fake news. But I like Easton better than Alex Tarnowski. That guy says he's a journalist, but totally sides with Heather Roth."

"I don't like none of them. I get my info from my nephew."

"I respect that," Frankie said, sticking out his hand. "Frank Buccetti."

The old man shook Frankie's hand. "Gary Spatz. Nice to meet you."

Frankie's head snapped back. "Spatz?" he questioned. "By chance, are you related to Ken Spatz?"

"I'm his uncle." Gary pointed at himself. "Do you know him?"

"Yeah, we go way back." Frankie met Gary's blue eyes, noticing the resemblance. "We were both into sports in high school. Baseball, basketball, football, and hockey. We got to know each other pretty good. And then he left for the military."

"You know what? I think I remember you in hockey. I never missed a game. You were the only colored kid on the ice. I remember you were fast as lightning."

Frankie smiled. "Yup, that was me. Do you remember Ken's senior year? The championship game? I got a slashing penalty."

"That was a long time ago, but if I remember correctly, it almost cost us the game. But you redeemed yourself with two goals."

"Those were the days," Frankie said, glancing out the window at the green plains of southern Illinois.

"Better view now, eh?"

Frankie nodded. "Thanks for taking my eyes off the ash heap. I was getting depressed."

"What kind of plans do you got in Florida?"

"Just a business trip. Maybe stick my toe in the ocean for the first time. And then off to the next stop."

"What kind of business are you into?"

"Commercial real-estate. Stocks. Sovereign bonds."

Gary flashed a smile. "You picked the right time for that. I hear property in Florida is at an all-time low."

"That's what my advisor says. So, I figure I'll give it a shot. Might be a better return than the stock market."

"I wish you luck, young man. Not my line of work."

"What do you do?"

"I'm a retired military lawyer. Snow bird. I live in Florida half the year."

"That sounds like a peaceful living."

"It is." Gary winced, sticking his hand underneath his sport coat.

"You, okay?" Frankie asked, his eyebrows lowering.

"Yeah, just gas. I need a drink." He pulled out a fancy silver flask and took a swig. "But anyways, I'm happy to see a young man like yourself find the path to success. Don't slow yourself down worrying about conspiracy theories. Go make your money while you're still young." Gary had a brief coughing fit. "The world will always sort everything out."

Frankie nodded in agreement, secretly questioning his own beliefs and wild theories. *Maybe the Great Reset book was wrong after all?*

37

The Buccetti Compound
August 18, 2020

Frankie Buccetti's eyes were locked on the TV and the highlights from the presidential debate that took place the night before. Standing behind a podium in a black suit and thick red tie, President Clacher cocked his head toward Speaker of the House Heather Roth. She was wearing a bulky gray pantsuit. And her mouth was flapping rapidly.

"Excuse me, Speaker Roth," President Clacher said, twisting from behind his podium to speak directly to her. "But my leadership saved this nation." Straightening himself, he gazed into the cameras and lowered his voice. "I managed the reconstruction of America *and* the world. Despite our obstacles, this economy is bullish. The stock market is at an all-time high. People are working again. And big industry is building—"

Speaker Roth smacked the notebook on her podium. "Stop!" She stuck her palm in his direction. "Mr. President, everyone knows that you're responsible for the death of hundreds of millions of people all over the world. And let's face it, *you* are a racist, sexist, bigot, homophobe." Her pale, bony finger was pointing in his direction. Shaking.

"That's ridiculous," Clacher said, his face reddening by the moment. "I defeated very capable enemies. My team rebuilt

America from the ashes. I love all Americans. How dare you lie to the voters like that. Shame on you."

"No. Shame on *you*, and anyone who supports you."

President Clasher clenched his jaw. "Madam Roth, you just insulted half the country. The voters will never forget that. And the American people will never forget how much money your crooked family made in—"

President Clacher's counter-attack was cut off as the screen switched to the SNN studio. A chime sounded, and the words: BREAKING NEWS, flashed on the screen. SNN anchor Alex Tarnowski was sitting behind a gray desk with a stack of papers in front of him.

"We have urgent breaking news," Tarnowski said with a straight face. "Multiple unnamed sources are saying that President Clacher acted improperly in the genesis of World War Three. The president dismissed intelligence from Deputy Secretary of State Eugene Parker that would have prevented nuclear war. Clacher then detained Parker for two weeks and had Secret Service agents threaten him for silence." Tarnowski paused dramatically. "Our sources tell us that the documents Secretary Parker gave the president that morning...proved ISIS had claimed responsibility for the initial attacks on the morning of March 13, 2017."

Frankie swore under his breath. "Unnamed sources?" As he stared at the screen, his head was shaking. "That's fake news for sure."

38

The new White House
Philadelphia, Pennsylvania
September 17, 2020

President Clacher reached for a gold-trimmed picture of George Washington and pressed a small button on the wall behind the frame. A narrow section of the Oval Office wall slid inward. With his right hand, Clacher gestured for Steff Freeman to enter.

Steff nodded and then stepped inside. The president followed.

As soon as Clacher's feet were planted in the firesafe room, the door closed. "This room is bug-free," President Clacher said, looking down at Steff Freeman's wide eyes. "Any electronic devise would trigger an alarm." The state-of-the-art box also had the ability to drop to the bunker in the event of an emergency.

"Mr. President," Steff said, "the source won't give any names, but he admits most of the government and corporate powers are working against you. He keeps saying the threat against you is political...not violent." Steff pursed her lips, slightly shaking her head. "But I can tell he's petrified of these people. His lip quivers when speaking about them. What they do to people who cross them. He says they don't need to kill you; they'll just destroy you in the media. And if you happen to win the election, they'll do everything and anything to impeach and remove you from office. But that's when he clams up. His eyes start shifting."

"We should take him down," Clacher said. "He knows where all the bones are hidden."

"Sir, I need more time to break him. He's trained in my tactics. The only reason he tells me anything is because he loves his country. And, because he's lonely."

"Treason isn't love, Miss Freeman," Clacher said. "I have to at least fire this guy. He can't be trusted."

"Sir, there's such thing as a triple agent. I think it's worth it to keep trying." Her hand opened and then dropped to her side. "If you fire him, we lose our only lead. We need him."

"That sounds good, Ms. Freeman, but how do—"

"If you take him down, you only have a pawn. We need to connect the dots and rid this government of the lingering shadow. This is our only chance."

The president punched his hand. "Every time I look at him, I want to punch his lights out. To think this asshole is a traitor."

"Don't look at him. Make yourself unavailable. He can meet with VP Andrews. Fire him after the election. I'll get names soon."

Clacher rubbed his temple. "Okay. What about the election? What kind of dirty tricks do they have up their sleeves."

"Mr. President, the polls are close. The intel leak gave her a bump, but your base is strong. Sir, you have something Speaker Roth doesn't have. You have a following. You have a base of World War Three survivors. A movement of patriots who are voting for *you* not the party. She's depending on the media. You need to go shake some hands and give some speeches. I'll get an October surprise for ya." She winked.

39

Duluth, Minnesota
November 3, 2020

On election night in America, Frankie was sitting with his mom at her newly remodeled house. Diana was reading President Clacher's closing argument on her smartphone. *"If you want a senile, drunk swamp creature to fundamentally transform America while lining her deep pockets, then go ahead and vote for Nasty Roth. A woman who flies to Pedophile Island twice a year. I got the plane manifest. I can't prove what she did there, but know it was disgusting."*

Diana Buccetti laughed shortly. "Too bad, it looks like she's gonna win. That little bitch makes me sick." She took a sip of tea and set it down on the marble coffee table Frankie bought for her.

"It ain't over till Ohio and Florida are decided," Frankie said. "Nothing else matters."

"But she's up in the popular vote," Diana said. "She's gonna win. I know it."

"Relax," Frankie said with a smirk. "The popular vote means nothing."

"We'll see what happens," Diana said with a great deal of pessimism in her voice.

Frankie pointed at the TV. "Boom!" He shot up. "Look." He pointed at the screen. "He won Ohio! And Florida. It's over! Clacher won!"

40

Duluth, Minnesota
February 12, 2021

After closing on a commercial real-estate deal, Frankie, Marcel, and Carlos popped into the Great Lake Saloon to celebrate. Drinks in hands, the men sat down at a table in the back of the bar.

"We got a really good deal on that hotel," Frankie said, looking dapper in a dark blue suit with no tie, just a white Oxford shirt with a sharp collar. Whereas Carlos and Marcel wore black suits with ties.

"You can thank *me* for that," Carlos said, his finger pointing inward. "I played football with the Hackett's grandson. They would have charged anyone else five million easy."

Marcel set his drink down. "You got the hookup, but I got the business credit. The three of us put our minds together, and made something big happen." He held his drink up. "Cheers!"

The Three friends tapped their glasses.

"Happy to be partners with you guys," Frankie said, sipping on a glass of water. "I been on my own for the last year or so. I had to travel and find out who I am. What I want. And I needed to build up my bank account."

"How much you got, bro?" Marcel asked.

Frankie smiled, leaning forward. "I got a million in property in Florida. A million invested in this hotel deal. About a million in the bank. I got a stock market portfolio worth at least two million. And a full safe at home."

"Damn, bro." Carlos slapped his hand on Frankie's shoulder. "You're rich as fuck! I only have a million in stocks, and the half mill I invested in the hotel. I've been living off the day job." He guzzled his beer and went for another.

"But this is just the beginning!" Marcel boasted, smacking hands with Frankie. "I got so many ideas. We're gonna make a hundred million fo sho."

"One step at a time, brother." Frankie nodded his head. "Inch by inch."

A one-hit wonder from the eighties was playing in the background as Carlos returned with two bottles of beer.

"We got to talk Carlos into transforming the hotel into a Vegas-style resort." Marcel smiled at Carlos who was sitting down at the table. "With a nightclub!"

"I like the sound of that," Frankie said.

Carlos shrugged. "What about a five-star restaurant?"

"Maybe that smokehouse Marcel used to talk about," Frankie said. "Together, we can do great things. I just want to do something positive in our hometown."

"We gonna take it to the next level," Marcel said and took a sip from his short glass of scotch. "We fittin to have a monopoly in dis town."

"What did that old guy say?" Frankie shrugged, flickering his fingers as his brain sputtered. "Competition is like sin."

Carlos tilted his hand. "I don't mind competition. It makes you better. It makes you want it more."

"There ain't gonna be no competition," Marcel said, shaking his head. "We gonna be the only real night club in

Duluth. And if we get a Mixed Martial Arts fight once a month, it's gonna be money."

Carlos took a swig from his bottle of beer. "Vadik Domechev for the Grand Opening is going to be huge. He's going to rip someone's arms out of their sockets. And the crowd is gonna love it."

"He's a beast in the ring," Frankie said. "I bet he draws a crowd."

Carlos set his beer on the table and looked at his watch. "I haven't seen that killer since college."

"All he does is work out," Marcel said. "I bumped into him at the gym."

"Your beer is empty." Carlos smacked Marcel on the back. "This rounds on me. Then I got to hit the road. I told Jewlz I'd be home an hour ago."

"Get me lemonade," Frankie said.

Marcel tilted his head. "You should drink a beer with us. This is a celebration."

"Alcohol is poison. Almost five years sober. You two should try it." Frankie looked at Marcel and the Los.

Carlos tilted his beer. "Never."

*****

Frankie was leaning on the pool table talking to Carlos and Marcel. Hearing the voices of women giggling, his head craned toward the bar where his eyes found a sleek figure walking toward him. Her familiar dark curly hair and blue eyes forced a rush of anxiety through him as he fixed his slouch.

She placed four quarters on the pool table. "You wanna shoot a game?" Her quick smile revealed pearly white teeth and something more.

"Rack 'em up, Tara." Frankie could almost hear his heart thumping in his chest. *Tara Barini,* he thought, biting down on the inside of his lip, his mind flashing back to the last time he saw her a year before the nuclear war. He remembered talking to her in the same exact place at the same bar. The night he decided to save himself for Conny who had just dumped him. The same night he choked Dane Fowler for the first time. *Holy smokes. I'm a fool for turning her down. Probably no chance now.*

Tara set her drink on the table Carlos and Marcel were sitting at. "You two want to play doubles?"

Marcel smiled, shaking his head. "Frankie already beat me three times," he said. "Good luck. I was just about to smoke." He put his jacket on and walked toward the back deck and Carlos joined him.

"We playing for money?" Tara asked, crouching low to place the quarters in the slots.

"I don't gamble," Frankie said, glancing down at the flash of pink panties creeping up her back. "But for this occasion, I'll play ya for a dollar."

Tara rose to her full height, five foot, five inches. "I can tell you're scared to get beat by a girl. I get it."

"I take on all comers," he said. "I better give you my A game. I heard nurse practitioners have a soft touch."

Smiling to meet Frankie's eyes. "How do you know what I do for a living?"

"That's classified." Frankie smiled. "But I'm happy for you. I know how hard you worked to get there."

"Frankie." She placed her hands on her hips, tilting her head a notch. "If you been keeping tabs on me, why didn't you ever call?" She then started placing balls on the green felt.

"After a year and a half in jail, I fell back in the Conny trap." Frankie gave a nervous short laugh. "And then we kinda had a nuclear war."

She snapped the balls in the wooden triangle, locking them in place. "I'm talking about recently, buster. You should have called."

"There's a flip side to that coin, Tara."

"No, there's not. I don't have your number." After she racked the balls, she stood back and Frankie took his stance.

Leaning forward, Frankie aimed at the balls before he broke. "The past is history, Tara. The future is a nightmare."

Tara smiled. "I guess…it's all about right now." She locked eyes with him, distracting his break.

Crack! And the cue ball bounced off the table.

41

Philadelphia, Pennsylvania
May 1, 2021

From the highest suite in the tallest building in Philadelphia, Seth Roth gazed out the window at the lights of skyscrapers and cars that were twinkling beneath him. "The time to act is now," he said, lighting up a cigarette with the cherry of the last. Turning to face his brother, he blew a stream of smoke upward. "Your daughter has been too patient. Tell her to use cunning to take what she wants."

"She'll use her position to bring Clacher to his knees." David Roth's mouth widened. "And I'll unleash my dogs in the media to chew on his vitals."

"Our ancestors were right." Seth straightened the bow tie of his black tuxedo. "Order can only be gained from chaos."

David Roth extended his hands toward the multitude of car lights flooding the roads of the new capital city. "The American subjects are prepared to be programmed, controlled, and systematically herded to the slaughter. Mr. Clacher is all that stands in our way."

"Clacher has shown incredible resilience. Somehow his supporters still love him."

"Once the senators are aware of the information we possess, the president's allies will turn on him."

Seth laughed a short cackle. "The future is ours. The world is ripe for the taking."

"Is operation Andrews still the status quo?"

"Have I said anything to the contrary?"

42

Duluth, Minnesota
June 4, 2021

Frankie pulled his truck next to a gas pump and parked. Before hopping out, he sat and listened to his favorite radio host finish his thoughts.

"*...supposedly, the Special Prosecutor has found evidence that President Clacher made a deal with the Russian dictator to end World War Three.*" Luke Easton's voice sounded off through Frankie's speakers. "*Apparently, the Russian government got immunity. So, what? The deal ended a nuclear war. Probably saved tens of millions of lives. This is a witch hunt in search of a crime. A sophisticated coup d'état.*" The radio host let out a heavy sigh into the microphone. "*Folks, it's not time to panic. But it's getting close. I'll let you know when it's time to panic. Excuse me. I'm up against a commercial –*"

Frankie tuned the key back and pushed the door open. "Coup d'état," he said to himself as he stepped out of the truck. Grabbing the pump handle, he put the nozzle in his gas tank. Glancing at the digital screen on the machine, he watched the dial spin for a minute or two until it clunked to a stop on fifty bucks. After returning the nozzle to the gas pump, he walked toward the entrance of the store.

In front of him, a muscular man in a black golf shirt was holding the door open for a little old lady. His black ball cap read: *TOP GUN* in white letters. And his face was covered with a brown beard.

"Is that Ken Spatz?" Frankie asked loudly, hoping Ken would hear him. It had been many years, and he looked a little different, but Frankie recognized his old friend. They had played hockey with each other in high school, and then Ken went off to Afghanistan with Giovanni Mariani. Because of a picture taken of a dead terrorist, Mariani came home. Ken Spatz on the other hand, made it a career.

The man turned. "Holy shit!" Ken smiled, stepping away from the door. "I haven't seen you in forever." He smiled, sticking out his hand.

The two men firmly shook hands and embraced one another.

"How you been, man?" Ken asked.

"I've been good," Frankie said. "I heard you served in the Greatest War. I appreciate your service."

"Thanks, man," Ken said. "I appreciate the support. No one gives a shit about veterans these days."

Frankie let out a breath. "Trust me, people are grateful," he said, meeting his blue eyes. "Hey, did your uncle Gary tell you I met him on an airplane?"

Ken shook his head. "No, he died a couple of years ago. Heart attack."

"Awe, man. I'm sorry to hear that." Frankie scrunched up his face. "He seemed like a good guy."

"Thanks." Ken put one hand in his jeans pocket. "I was pretty close with him."

Changing the subject, Frankie shrugged. "What else you been up to?"

"I took a job with a security firm," Ken said. "Been traveling around the country. Pays the bills."

"You still in the military?"

Ken shrugged. "No, I retired after twenty years," he said. "It's hard to transition, but I'll live."

"Well, let's get together sometime soon. We got some catching up to do."

Ken smacked Frankie's shoulder. "How 'bout you cook that lasagna Mariani used to brag about?"

"Give me a ring sometime soon." Frankie handed him a business card.

"What's this?" Ken asked, glancing at the off-white card that read *BTZ Resort* at the top.

"I bought a hotel with Carlos and Marcel. The remodel is taking forever, but the grand opening event is booked for October. Vadik Domechev is fighting for the Midwest MMA championship belt."

"That's awesome!" Ken said. "Good for you, bro. Count me in for the fight. Vadik is a badass."

The two men clasped hands and gave each other a quick hug.

"Take care, bro," Frankie said.

"Thanks. You, too." Ken parted for his truck.

"Hey, one more thing." Frankie closed the distance. "I gotta ask—since you served in the war—what do you think about the origins of the war? The president...and the impeachment hearings?"

"I wish I could tell you what I know." Ken winked.

43

BTZ Resort
Duluth, Minnesota
October 15, 2021

Inside a caged octagon, a tall, bald-headed announcer in a black tuxedo held a microphone in his hands. "ALLLLEJANDROOOOO!... HERNANDEEEEZ!" he screamed a rolling voice at the top of his lungs.

The reigning champion of the Midwest Mixed Martial Arts League was holding his golden belt above his head. Hernandez had brown skin, white and red shorts, and a bald head. The crowd was screaming and shouting and cheering. As soon as Hernandez found his corner, the song coming from the speakers changed to a hard beat, and the room became mostly dark. Muted.

I CAME TO BRING THE PAIN, HARDCORE TO THE BRAIN... The rap song rocked the ball room section of the BTZ Resort.

Standing close to Tara Barini, Frankie craned his neck to see his friend, Vadik Domechev strutting down the wide center aisle like an alpha male pit bull at the end of his leash. He was wearing black shorts with a white stipe running up each side. His chest was bare, and his girthy muscles demanded respect.

Compared to his Hispanic opponent, his skin looked pale, and his short-cropped hair looked light brown.

"Hailing from Moscow, Russia," the announcer hollered into the microphone, "trained in Duluth Minnesota. Fighting out of Crado's gym. He has a brown belt in Jiu Jitsu. A nine and one record, with three knock outs…three tap outs…and three referee-decided victories. Weighing in at one hundred and ninety pounds. The one, the only…. VADIK THE PIT BULL…. DOMECHEEEEEV!"

Frankie saw Vadik turn to the roaring crowd and lift his fist. The VIP section where Frankie was sitting was especially raucous. And he could tell the overwhelming cheers from Vadik's friends and family made him stand even taller in the center of the ring.

"Liver shot!" Ken Spatz pumped his fist in the air.

Tara leaned into Frankie. "Why does he want him to go for the liver?"

"It's painful," Frankie said, wrapping his arm around her waist.

Tara's face scrunched up.

Mariani extended a closed fist. "Kill him!"

Now in his corner, Vadik was facing his trainer who was on the opposite side of the cage pumping him up. Raising his gloves to chest level, Vadik's thickly chiseled biceps flexed. Turning back to the center of the ring, he threw sharp jabs in the air and slowly stepped forward.

Both men crept toward the referee.

"LLLLLLLET's get ready to BAAATTLLLLLLLLE!" the announcer screamed in the microphone and the crowd roared. The two fighters tapped gloves with their right hands and circled each other, slowly posturing, ducking, and throwing slight blows into thin air.

Vadik had small black fingerless gloves on his weapons of mass destruction. His left foot was pointed forward as he led with his left fist, testing his range and getting closer with each quick jab.

Hernandez was shorter than Vadik, but about the same build. Taking advantage of Vadik's high guard, Hernandez shot out a kick to the knee.

Vadik stumbled backward. Once he recovered, he then ran Hernandez back seven or eight feet into the chain link fence. Punching his face twice, Vadik then tackled him, pinning him in the corner with his left knee on his chest.

Every spectator in the house was on their feet, screaming and shouting with an electric pulse that replicated hysteria. In the VIP room, Mariani was the loudest by far, violently rooting on his old friend.

"KILL HIM!" Mariani screamed, then repeated it in case he wasn't heard. "KILL HIIIIM!"

Hernandez dodged a blow. Using momentum, he switched positions, briefly pinning Vadik's face against the fence. Hernandez landed a series of blows: left, then a right, then another right.

Vadik used all of his might to kick the aggressor off. Struck hard but not damaged, he bounced up with new vigor. Charging at Hernandez, he tossed a hard left jab that was blocked, then in almost the same motion, he gave a crippling blow to the liver which staggered the champion back. It looked like he was going to fall, but he didn't.

Vadik threw a barrage of stiff punches that were all blocked. Ducking low as he stepped forward, he sprung up and landed one on the chin, dropping Hernandez to the mat. Instead of celebrating, Vadik pounced like a wild cat on a mouse. Grabbing the hurt fighter's arm, Vadik spun on his back, slamming his thick legs on Hernandez's chest. With the man's arm in between Vadik's legs and his wrist in his grip, Vadik stretched back with all his might.

The crowd shrieked.

Alejandro Hernandez was squinting his face in pain. The referee was hovering behind Hernandez's head. He was about to call the fight. And then it happened: Vadik snapped the forearm like a small branch.

44

Philadelphia, Pennsylvania
December 14, 2021

Sitting in a swanky five-star restaurant, Secretary of Defense Richard Secord was eating breakfast with his heavy-set wife. She had dark hair, dark eyes, and fierce breasts peeking through her white blouse. Mrs. Secord still had a leash on his heart, even though he had a thing for young busty spies.

As Secord chewed his eggs Benedict, he thought about Steff Freeman and her fit young body. The secrets he told her. The exotic things she did to him in return. The danger. The risk. The power to get what he wants.

Interrupting his day dream, a tall blond woman in a black low-cut dress stopped in front of his table.

"Good morning, Mr. Secretary," she said, bending over while sliding a black flash drive toward him. "A man paid me to give this to you. He said it's important."

Secord's eyes bounced from the small device to her eyes in two seconds. "What'd he look like?" His eyebrows were raised. His voice rushed.

The young woman's eyes shifted away and then came back. "Um, an old white guy." She glanced at Secord's wife and blinked. "White hair. He was smoking a cigarette outside on the patio."

"Thank you," he said, and the blond walked away. Shoving the device in his pocket, his eyes landed on his wife whose face was blushing with emotion.

"Who was that, *Dick*?" She asked with a low growl, her eyes squinting. When he didn't say anything, she leaned forward. "Who was it?"

Secord looked around the restaurant to make sure no one was watching them. Lifting his hand to chest level, he whispered to his wife. "Peg, please don't do this here. I-I don't know that girl."

"Just like last time?" she whispered. "Or the time before that?" She shoved her plate forward, lifting her larger-than-average frame out of the booth. "Please don't come home tonight." Peggy shuffled away from the table.

Secord bit his lip and shook his head tightly. "Fuck," he said just under his breath. Placing a hundred-dollar bill on the table, he grabbed his briefcase, and then slowly walked out of the restaurant.

His driver and black SUV were parked in front, but he flagged down a cab heading in the opposite direction. He wanted to be far away from work when he found out what was on the flash drive. He might want to curse or cry or break something, and not have subordinates wonder why.

Slamming the cab door shut, Secord handed another hundred to the foreign driver. "Drive!"

"Where I go, my friend?" the skinny cabby asked, tugging on his bushy black beard.

"Just fucking drive!" Secord popped open his briefcase and opened his laptop. Breathing heavily, he jammed the flash drive into the USB portal.

When the file opened, his eyes widened. "Holy shit." Hundreds, if not thousands of classified documents and recordings filled the drive. *This incriminates me, the president, and members of Congress.* At the bottom, there was a memo with his name on it. Upon clicking on the small icon, he let out a slight moan.

"I'm a fucking patsy," he said under his breath, and then continued reading:

"There is only one step from the sublime to the ridicules." — *Napoleon Bonaparte*

If you want immunity, you will testify before the impeachment hearings, and you will hand this flash drive over to Congress. No one but a select few will ever see it, but its contents will force just enough senators to flip. They will turn on the president to keep this information secret. If you comply, you will inherit five million dollars. Don't forget about the pictures we have of you in the coffin!

Eternally,

Your Master

"Stop the car!" Secord said, and the cab pulled over.

Exiting the cab, a string of curse words erupted from his mouth. "Fuck that family," he said, his free hand making a fist. "No more. I've had enough. If they think they're going to use me for a scapegoat, they got another thing coming."

45

Philadelphia, Pennsylvania
January 20, 2022

In a packed congressional rotunda, the Chairwoman of the House Impeachment Committee, Heather Roth slammed the gavel three times and the room became silent. "Former Deputy Secretary of State Parker—did ISIS take responsibility for the initial attacks on the morning of March 13, 2017? Yes, or no?"

"The unarguable answer to that question is…yes," Mr. Parker said with contempt. "Nineteen intelligence agencies told me as much."

Speaker Roth leaned her plump red lips closer to the mic. "Was there any evidence that Russia, China, North Korea, or Iran had any involvement in the first attack?"

"There was absolutely zero evidence that Russia *or* any other nation-states had any involvement in the manmade disaster."

"It is my understanding," Speaker Roth said angrily, "that when you reminded President Clacher of this fact, he reacted inappropriately by firing you, and then jailing you for a month."

"That is correct, Madam Speaker," Eugene Parker said with another lie to follow. "It is also important to note that several times during that month, men in black suits—who I did not know — came to threaten me. They said, 'if you love your kids, then keep your mouth shut.'"

"I'm disgusted. No further questions."

After the chairwoman yielded her remaining time, the ranking minority member, Congressman Traficant cleared his throat. After taking a sip of water, he then offered an opening statement.

"President Clacher is unconventional," Traficant said, sporting a light gray suit jacket and a sandy blond comb-over. "He is unorthodox. He is bold, brash, harsh, crude, and sometimes wrong. But he *is*…a good man, who I know loves his country. That said, March 2017 was the darkest hour in American history. America was under attack; nuclear bombs were used to kill millions of people. The President of the United States, then followed U.S. Policy, clearly stating — that in the event of a nuclear strike on American soil — the president *shall* give orders to retaliate against all enemies, simultaneously as a matter of national security. If the former deputy secretary of state is accurate with his information, the president still had a duty to perform." He cleared his throat again, glanced at his notes, and then continued. "Five years later, we do have evidence that the bombs used on 3/13 were consistent with radioactive material found in North Korea after the war. It is a fact that North Korea proliferated nuclear material to Iran, and it is probable that Iran passed that finished product to ISIS. These nations are in a military alliance with Russian and China, similar to NATO. An attack on one is an attack on all.

"It is a mistake to think President Clacher acted in any way other than honorable. His leadership, with the advice and consent of the United States military fought and won World War Three in a swift and decisive manor. After the war, he led the reconstruction of the nation and the world. The economy we live in today is the fruit of the labor *this* great leader produced."

After his opening statement, it was his turn to ask the witness some questions of his own.

"Mr. Parker," Congressman Traficant said. "If the president's response to five nuclear attacks on American soil was inappropriate, what would you have recommended for a more…appropriate response?"

"I'm not a military strategist," Mr. Parker said. "My job as a career diplomat was to prevent war, not start it."

"I understand you don't want to answer the question," Traficant said. "Because you know, in that situation, there were no options for peace. There was only victory or surrender. Let me ask again in a different way. What is your understanding of U.S. Policy for that contingency?"

The former deputy secretary of state squirmed in his seat and then leaned into the microphone. "The contingency plan for that situation was in fact, exactly what took place." Parker said, letting out an audible sigh. "But President Clacher should have exercised restraint the way President Kennedy did with the Cuban Missile Crisis."

"Thank you for answering my important question," Traficant said with a touch of mockery, his lips tugging upward just a bit. "I'm glad we agree on U.S. National Security protocol. I like your historical reference, but during the Cuban Missile Crisis, no bombs were ever dropped. If one bomb detonated on American soil, I believe President Kennedy would have retaliated in the same way President Clacher did."

*****

Steff Freeman was striding down the marble floor hallway of the U.S. Capitol Building with a briefcase in her hands. Disguised as a male airman in a dark-blue uniform and garrison cap, she adjusted her glasses and pushed open the door to the men's room. *Good, it's empty,* she thought, crossing the checker tile floor to the far stall.

Opening the door, Steff bent over and reached for the tank lid, gently setting it on the seat. A Ziplock bag was floating in the tank. It was stuffed with documents.

Secord came through, Steff thought, and then grabbed the package. Unzipping the baggy, she emptied the contents in her briefcase. The black flash drive resting on the heap got shoved in her underwear.

A creak from the bathroom entrance sent a bolt of chill down Steff's spine. Men were laughing in the main part of the bathroom while she trembled in the stall.

A disembodied voice said, "That Parker guy is desperate to take down the president."

"This is just a witch hunt," a second man said, pausing momentarily as he tinkled. "I'll decide after I hear Secord's testimony. He holds more credibility in my world."

And then Steff heard the toilet flush.

"It ain't going nowhere," the first voice said. "I haven't seen anything to convince me the president did anything wrong."

The second toilet flushed. Steff sucked in a breath of air, but she waited until they were gone to let it out.

*****

At the end of the long day, emotion was swelling in the packed rotunda. Everyone looked at least a little bit drained: the participating members of Congress, the media, and those in attendance. Some were leaning back in their seats, some were yawning, and some were outright sleeping.

Speaker Roth leaned into the mic with a raspy voice. "Defense Secretary Secord," she said, gazing in his direction. "Did this president order a full-scale nuclear attack on the wrong enemy, creating a chain reaction that killed at least one hundred million people?"

"Madam Speaker," Secretary Secord said with a wrinkled brow. "My counsel has advised me to exercise my Fifth Amendment right to not answer any questions that may or may not be used against me in a future investigation." He paused dramatically, reaching into the inside pocket of his suit jacket. When he pulled out his hand, there was a small black thumb drive in his fingers. Standing tall, he held it up for every person and camera to see. "This flash drive…contains secret voice recordings of members of Congress, corporate donors, and the president. Charge me with a crime and it will be leaked!"

The lights from dozens of cameras flashed and twinkled. The gasps of shocked people took the air out of the room. The pictures of that information drive immediately went viral on the internet.

"Mr. Secord." Speaker Roth raised her voice, and the room quieted. "Be careful. I'll charge you with contempt of Congress."

"Test me, Madam Speaker," Secord said, and then dropped back into his seat. "Charge me with a crime. See what happens. See, I'm a realist. I am *certain* President Clacher is going to be persecuted. The charges against him and his subordinates like myself will be tried in a military tribunal like after World War Two. In Nuremberg, Hitler's minions were tried, convicted, and hung for their treachery. I have no intention to be hung for doing my job. So, Madam Speaker…put my immunity in writing."

"Thank you, Mr. Secretary." Speaker Roth laughed shortly. "Unfortunately for you—in this court room—*all* persons are subject to search and seizure." She paused, her dark eyes shifting to the side door. "Bailiff!" she barked. "Take him away! Seize all electronic devises on his person."

The room erupted in a rumble of commotion as the bailiff and all the guards enclosed on the witness. Secord's head swiveled back and forth. Squirming in his seat, he rose. "If I'm going down, I'm taking everyone with me!" He reached back his arm, and then chucked the flash drive into the crowd.

A desperate frenzy ensued. Men and woman were trampling over each other for the thumb drive. People were screaming, panicking, fighting.

"Order in the court!" Speaker Heather Roth hollered in the microphone and hammered the gavel several times. "Order in the court! Guards…lock those doors. Nobody in or out until that device is recovered."

46

Fish Lake, Minnesota
February 18, 2022

From inside a small wooden ice house, Frankie's fishing pole bent sharply. Flexing his muscles, his eyes locked on the hole in the ice.

"Pull that sucker up!" Ken Spatz said loudly. "You got 'em!"

"He's fighting!" Frankie said, struggling to reel it in. Yanking upward, he pulled the fish out with a splash of water.

"That's a good-looking fish," Ken said as it flopped on the wet ice. "Probably the biggest one of the day." He was wearing a black snowmobile suit and a woodland camouflage watch cap.

Between the propane heat and the fight with the fish, Frankie felt warm, so he unzipped his thick gray parka. "Should we keep fishing?" Frankie asked with the fish still flopping and opening its mouth in desperation. "Or is it lunch time?"

"I could eat," Ken said. "Let's go to the island and start the grill." He softened his tone to a whisper. "No phone."

Frankie nodded.

Pressing his pointer finger to his lips, Ken pulled out his phone and set it on the upside-down bucket he'd been sitting on.

Without saying a word, Frankie followed his lead. Zipping up his jacket, he then slipped on his gloves with a concerned look on his face.

Ken snatched up the stringer with four fish. One was still flopping. With a hammer, he clubbed it once. That's all it took.

The ice house was warm and toasty, but as soon as they stepped outside, the February bitter chill stiffened Frankie's body. Squinting his eyes, he blocked out the bright sun with his hand. A small island was about fifty yards away. Crunching on the hardened snow, they crossed the flat terrain of the frozen lake. Wind gusts swept away their footprints.

Upon the approach of the heavily wooded island, Frankie noticed a small camouflage tent pitched underneath a cluster of evergreen trees.

Ken set the fish on the snow. "Me and Mariani brought the picnic table out here when we were about fourteen-years-old. Feels like yesterday."

"I came out here with you guys once," Frankie said, shifting his attention to the machete shoved into the ice-crusted ground. "I think I was like nineteen."

"A lot changed since then," Ken said.

"I know. We didn't even have cellphones back then. All we wanted to do is drink beer and catch fish."

Ken took a step closer to Frankie. Placing a hand on his shoulder, he leaned toward him. "Bro, speaking of cellphones," he said. "I had you leave yours in the icehouse for a reason. The NSA is listening to every single phone call. Not only that, but it's recording, too. All the time. Every email, text, *and* voice message. All stored in a universe of data."

"I didn't know that," Frankie replied. "I assumed texts might be recorded. But phone calls, *too?*"

"Yeah, man," Ken nodded. "Your phone is recording all the time. Even your internet clicks are recorded. In all reality, they don't give a shit about what you say, but in the future, if they think you're a threat to national security, they could search every moment of your life through your phone. They can use code words to narrow it down, and find out your every thought."

Frankie let out a heavy breath and a vapor cloud shot out from his mouth. "That's terrifying."

"That's just the tip of the iceberg," Ken claimed, and then chopped the heads off three fish with three thuds from the machete. "You wanna hear a crazy story?"

"I like stories," Frankie said, and then Ken passed him the machete so he could cut up his fish.

"Good," Ken said. "I think you'll like this one."

"Is it classified?" Frankie asked with a cock of his head.

"More than classified," Ken said, then started cleaning a fish. "It's basically treason to speak about it. If you tell a soul, it could get my family killed. Then I'd have to kill you."

"You have my word of honor," Frankie said and stuck out his hand.

Ken shook his hand firmly. "Other than Mariani, you might be the only civilian I can trust."

"I appreciate that," Frankie said. "I'll never tell a soul."

"Okay. But, if it comes back to me, I'll know it was you."

Frankie nodded his head.

"Believe it or not, I have an inside source who saw the defense secretary's famous thumb drive." Ken paused to meet Frankie's blinking eyes. "It contains dark secrets. Unmasked voice recordings of presidents going back twenty years. Also, closed-door meetings and phone conversations with members of Congress. Emails, texts, classified missions, information about JFK." Ken paused briefly, looking over his shoulder out of sheer paranoia. "Most importantly, it held top-secret information regarding the attacks of 3/13 and the nuclear war to follow. And I'm told there are compromising pictures of people at the top levels of government." He filled his lungs with cold air and let it out before he continued. "Government is like a hotdog factory, bro. If the public had any knowledge of these things, they'd lose faith in the system. I don't think the public will ever see it. It's held tightly in the hands of Congress. But if Clacher doesn't resign, the president's enemies in Congress will use a closed-door hearing to impeach and remove him from the presidency. See, the drive has dirt on them, too. Senators in Clacher's own party will turn on him if it means this info never sees the light of day.

"I don't know when, but it is going to happen soon. And they might even remove the vice president. It will be a high-tech coup d'état: a regime change without violence."

"Hold up," Frankie said from the opposite side of the picnic table, looking into Ken's eyes. "I bet that Secord guy gave someone a copy. They'll leak it and everyone gets dirty."

"Honestly," Ken said. "I don't think it matters. If they leak it, the president would have to resign. If they don't leak it, he still resigns to spare the country a painful trial and removal. They win either way. My source told me this is all designed to take down the president at all costs. She told me that the NSA, CIA, and the State Department are filled with deep state permanent employees. Unelected bureaucrats. And they have it in their best interest to oust this president. The people I'm close with are of the few patriots left in this government…and they told me to prepare for the worst."

Frankie scrunched up his face. "What's the worst?"

"You know what it is," Ken said. "It's the nightmare scenario you told me about when we were in high school. The fundamental transformation of America. The end of the two-party system. And the capping of the pyramid. Just like the Prophecy Group videos we watched when we were kids."

"The Great Reset," Frankie said, nodding. His grand suspicions coming to fruition. "If Clacher and Andrews are both in jail, Speaker Roth would take her seat on the throne. With a majority in the House and Senate, she would have free rein to move forward with no opposition."

"Exactly." Ken clapped his hands. "But it's worse than that. The War Powers Act is still in motion. Dictatorial powers are at her finger tips."

"What did our history teacher used to say?" Frankie asked, but answered his own question. "*Power corrupts, but absolute power corrupts absolutely.*"

"Ain't that the truth."

"What should we do to prepare?" Frankie tilted his left hand.

Ken lowered his voice. "My boss at TRS Security is dying of cancer. He wants me to buy his company."

"What's TRS Security?"

"This company has been revered for decades, offering security to diplomats, politicians, and important businessmen. We've also been hired for nightclubs and concerts."

"Is it profitable?" Frankie asked.

"Uh, yeah. But I'm not in this for the money."

"What do you mean?"

"See, Frankie…Mr. Thoreson knows that the entire bureaucracy of government is controlled by a small group of men who are so powerful, so watchful, so technologically invasive, that people best not have a phone around when they talk shit about them. This seventy-year-old man wants me to watch them from the inside. He wants me to walk with the elite…and stalk them over time. He wants them to trust us."

"How can I be a part of this?"

"As of right now," Ken said, "I need an investor I can trust." He paused, letting out a breath. "But Mr. Thoreson won't settle for anything less than two million dollars. Trust me, this business is worth a lot more than that. He owns more than a dozen vehicles. He's got state-of-the-art computer systems, night vision goggles, body armor, weapons, electronic jamming systems, and much more."

"And you need two million?" Frankie asked.

"I'm throwing in a hundred thousand." Ken opened his hands. "I want skin in the game. But yeah. One point nine." He paused looking directly at him. "I heard you're sitting on a golden egg."

Frankie swallowed. "What percentage of equity?"

"I plan on running the day-to-day operations of the business," Ken said. "I have a lifetime of experience in the military, and I'm happy to do a service for my country. You'd be a silent investor. I'd need your help recruiting trustworthy people willing to commit treason if it comes to that. And on big jobs, I'd seek your advice and consent. Other than that, you'd just have to sit back and get a check for the rest of your life. I'd say 65/35, in my favor. How does that sound?"

"It sounds pretty good," Frankie said, "But one point nine million is a lot money. I'd have to sell most of my stocks. How 'bout 55/45?"

"60/40." Ken said then stuck out his hand.

Frankie grabbed Ken's hand firmly. "Deal."

47

Philadelphia, Pennsylvania
Federal Penitentiary
February 28, 2022

Richard Secord was sitting in a small visiting room. A thick sheet of plexiglass was separating him from his pregnant wife and seven-year-old son. Secord was wearing a navy-blue prison uniform and holding a black phone against his ear. One of his eyes was black and blue.

"They can't hold you like this," Peggy Secord said, tears streaming down her face.

"I'm sorry, Peg," Secord said, adjusting his black framed-glasses. "They're holding me indefinitely. My contempt of Congress charges can't see trial until the impeachment hearings are done. It's a process charge. Two years at the most."

"Your son can't wait two years." Her belly was huge. "And I'm about to have this baby. Who's going to help me? I can't nurse a baby and watch this one." Her eyes shifted to the skinny little boy with short brown hair and wire-framed glasses.

"Get a nanny. We got the money."

"That's what I wanted to tell you. They froze our bank account."

"What?" Secord pounded his hand on the desk. "Fuck!"

"Richard! I don't want your son to hear words like that."

Secord blew out a long sigh. "I'm sorry, son. You know I love you, buddy."

"I miss you, Dad. Please come home soon."

"I will, son. I promise. And when I get out, we're gonna go to a hockey game. Okay?"

"That's what I want to be when I grow up. A hockey player. I'll play for the Penguins."

48

Duluth, Minnesota
March 5, 2022

In the heart of the inner city, Frankie Buccetti stepped inside Brice Rockwell's front porch. An ashtray and several beer cans were sitting on a small table. He knocked on the door three times. A small chunk of lead paint floated down past Frankie's satchel, and then landed on the grimy floor. Pausing briefly, he knocked two more times as if it were a secret code.

"Who is it?" a husky voice asked curtly from the other side of the door.

Frankie took a step back. "It's Frank Buccetti." His black satchel swayed at his side.

The door creaked open. A cloud of pot smoke came rolling out. Standing in the doorway was a tall and large Native American man with long black hair and a black T-shirt.

"My nigga," Gordon Grayfeather said with a touch of mockery.

"Long time no see," Frankie said and embraced his old friend. The man's hug lifted him off the ground for a long moment, and then he dropped him on his feet.

"Come on in, brother." Grayfeather playfully grabbed Frankie by the jacket and yanked him inside the doorway. And then he shut the door. Locked the bolt.

Brice was standing in the dining room with a cigar in his lips. "Look what the dog brought in," he said with a wide smile, smoke rolling out of his mouth. "Where you been, man?"

"I've been lost." Frankie dropped the satchel at Brice's feet. "But now I'm found."

"What's in the bag?" Brice passed the cigar to Grayfeather.

"A gift from me and Mariani. A gesture of our appreciation."

Brice unzipped it and raised his eyebrows. "Damn, man." He shook the bag, making the bricks of money inside shuffle. "I don't know what to say."

Frankie spread apart his arms. "You saved my life back in the day."

Brice embraced him. "No, you saved my life." He squeezed tight with his bulky arms. "They said it was a miracle to wake up from the coma." He stepped back, patting Frankie hard on the shoulder.

"I was happy to hear the great news," Frankie said, letting a breath out as he shook his head slowly. "And then the war happened."

"Yeah, life been hectic since then." Brice set the bag of money on the brown leather sofa against the side wall. "I don't think Ben Crado would be too proud of me."

Frankie let out a breath. "Ben lived by the old school code. Man, I miss that guy."

"He was a good man. A good friend."

"A man of men."

Grayfeather shoved Frankie. "How the fuck did you find us, anyway?"

"Mariani. He told me a while ago. I'm sorry. It's been a crazy year."

"Yeah, I heard you been traveling a lot." Grayfeather looked him up and down. "Mariani was right. You don't wear jeans anymore."

Frankie smirked. "I know. It seems like I got a business meeting every other day. I can't remember the last time I wore jeans."

"Don't sellout, brother," Brice said, receiving the cigar, placing it in his lips.

"I'll never be a sellout, bro." Frankie gave a half shrug. "But I did buy into a great business. And I'd like you guys to consider joining my team."

"What kind of team?" Brice blew a stream of smoke toward the ceiling. "You be robbing trucks or something?"

Frankie shook his head. "No. I'm legit." He paused to look at the lowered eyebrows on Gordon Grayfeather's face. "My business is security. And I need a few solid guys I can trust."

"I bet Dennis will want to hear this." Brice hollered upstairs. "He'll be down in a minute."

Grayfeather playfully shoved Frankie again. This time harder. "Shiiit, you black bastard. We be runnin' shit…. We live like kings. How we gonna give that up? We got the whole Hillside on lock down. Look at all this stolen shit."

"Sounds profitable," Frankie said, gazing around the house at the plethora of flat screen TVs, bikes, and stereo equipment. "But I'm offering a better path."

"But I'm a beast," Grayfeather said gravely. "A menace to society. A danger to the general public. Look at me, bro." He paused and met Frankie's eyes. "I don't fit in your khaki world."

Beneath Frankie's gray cotton hat, his eyebrows lowered. Blinking, Frankie swallowed hard, unable to come up with words to say.

Dennis descended the flight of steps. "What up, doggy?"

"How's it going, bro?" Frankie said with a smile. "Long time no see."

The two clasped hands and embraced each other.

Standing in the living room, Frankie saw three sets of eyes locked on his every move. "Look, guys. We've been through a lot. I love you guys, but you can do better. We're in our forties now, and I think it's time to stop taking penitentiary chances. It's time to make money. Time to make a difference."

"We're doing pretty good for ourselves," Dennis said confidently. "I just got done selling a bunch of these TVs online. It's awesome. We pay for a list of child molesters, and then we rob them one by one. Cops don't give a fuck about these sickos."

"You could say that," Frankie said. "But another person might say…you're one bad day away from a life in prison. Or death."

"That's part of the territory," Dennis said. "It's all part of the game."

"Well," Frankie said. "I got a better game to play…and I need your help. All of you. It will require you guys to remain sober. Not even pot. And you'll have to refrain from any criminal activity. Especially violence." He gazed around the room at his criminal-minded friends. "Guys…I bought a security firm that has many moving parts. I need my contractors to start at the bottom, train hard, gain experience, and become reliable professionals."

"Hold up," Dennis said. "What kind of company is this?"

"TRS Security," Frankie said. "We offer security for nightclubs, and we also provide security to politicians and aristocrats."

"Damn, dog," Dennis said and lit up a menthol cigarette. "How the fuck did you come across that?"

"I know a guy," Frankie said. "He needed a partner, so I hopped on it."

"Did I hear you say the word: *contractors*?" Grayfeather asked slowly with a serious look on his mug.

"Yeah," Frankie said. "Other than administrative staff, we don't have employees, we have independent contractors."

"How much would we make?" Brice asked.

Frankie cracked a smile. "I can write each of you a check for ten thousand as a signing bonus. In the first year, you'll each make fifty thousand plus tips. Then, depending on your skill set, you could make a lot. A hundred thousand a year if you get on the congressional detail."

"Sign me up for a hundred thousand. I'm in." Grayfeather shrugged. "My skills are on point."

"You're a very capable man," Frankie said. "All of you are. That's why I'm here, but if you want to make the big bucks...you'll have to be trained to protect the elite. If that's what you want, I'll pay for your training."

"That sounds fair," Dennis said. "When would we start?"

"I'd recommend thinking about it over the next week or so," Frankie suggested. "Cuz once you sign my contract—your lives will change. Like I said before, this is my business. A lot is on the line: millions of dollars *and* my reputation. And much more I can't talk about right now. This is an opportunity to change your lives for the good. Think about it and get back to me."

Grayfeather started nodding his head, tugging the hair on his chin. A thin smile cracking.

49

The Buccetti Compound
April 1, 2022

Laying underneath the covers of their bed, Tara Barini rolled on her side and rested her arm on Frankie's bare chest. The faint glow of the alarm clock gave her just enough light to look directly into his eyes.

"What do you want in life?" she asked.

"Short term or long?" Frankie turned toward her.

"Long."

"Um, I-I want to serve my country…one way or another."

"In the military?"

Frankie shook his head. "No," he said, letting out a deep breath. "I'm no soldier. I just think I have some unique opportunities coming. I think God has a purpose for me."

"You always think so big. I don't understand why you can't just be happy with what you got. Why can't you just be happy with me?"

"Babe, of course I am happy with you. You asked what I want long-term."

Tara pursed her lips. "I love you, Frankie," she said with a sniffle. "We've been together a year now. You've made me so happy. Nobody's ever been so sweet. It's just, you're so busy, it feels like your business is more important than me. And now you're about to take on another business. How much money do you need?"

"I'm sorry, beauty. I love you so much. Just say the word. I'll sell my share of the hotel and just run TRS Security."

Tara shook her head tightly. "No. I'm sorry I said that. I'm busy, too. But we have opposite schedules." She squirmed closer, her hand dropping to wrap around his belly. "I come home from a long day at the hospital…and I'm all alone out here in the boonies. Then you come home and I'm in bed."

"Okay, dreamboat. I'll try to be here more." He kissed her lips. "I promise."

"I love you."

"I love you more."

"I doubt it," she said before climbing on top of him.

50

Duluth, Minnesota
April 7, 2022

Under a blanket of darkness and cold rainfall, Gordon Grayfeather popped the trunk of his stolen four-door sedan. The rotund man inside was unconscious. His skin was dark, and his face was badly bruised. Blood was pooling around his nose and mouth. With a grunt, Grayfeather pulled the heavy-set man out of the trunk and dropped him on the wet pavement. Grabbing the man by the collar of his jacket, he dragged him to a nearby park. Surrounded by a thick forest of tall pine trees, it offered an added cover to the shadow of nightfall.

Twenty yards ahead was a small stone bridge connecting the park to the forest beyond it. Rushing water could be heard. Grayfeather picked up the pace, dragging the man through slick grass. All of the snow had recently melted and found its way to the riverbed below, creating a twenty-foot-wide stream, rapidly flowing beneath the bridge toward Lake Superior. Grayfeather took three steps in the stream and re-gripped his hand to the victim's long hair, intertwining his fingers in unbreakable knots. His body was now anchored against the torrent of cold waist-deep water.

With the man floating in place, Grayfeather pulled a small bottle of rum out of his back pocket. Bringing it to his lips, he unscrewed the cap with his teeth and let the dark alcohol flow down his throat. Four gulps and the empty bottle fell to the stream and disappeared in the darkness.

Fueled by hard liquor and rage, Grayfeather punched the man in the nose and he woke up in a panic.

The first thing the man saw was his worst nightmare in the dark, hovering over him with his fist clenched. "What'd I do?" the victim blurted out as his last defense.

"You don't remember me from the joint, Adoette?" Grayfeather growled.

"No, I remember you." The man's eyes were wide.

"Do you know why I brought you here?"

"N-no." Adoette shook his head tightly. "I ain't got no static with you, niij."

Floating him upstream to a boulder in the middle of the creek, Grayfeather released his grip. "Get up."

"W-what do you want?" Adoette cried, his voice now sounding more like a girl.

Gordon lifted the man to his feet and let go. "Hit me. Give me a challenge."

Adoette clenched his fist and swung at Grayfeather who ducked, tackling him in the water.

They both were fully submerged. Water was splashing above. Grunts and screams muted out by the sound of the rapids.

Rising above the water, Grayfeather pinned Adoette underneath. After a few moments, he pulled him up for air and then dunked him again. Laying his back on the boulder, Grayfeather stood tall.

"Stop!" Adoette screamed at the top of his lungs. Begging and pleading. Whimpering.

Grayfeather smiled a sinister smile. "You raped my boy's son in prison." Reaching in his pocket, he pulled out a small knife. "I will never let something like that slide."

51

Palm Beach, Florida
April 22, 2022

Ken Spatz rolled off his lover and laid down on the bed beside her voluptuous naked body. "It's like a day hasn't passed." The room was dark except for the blue glow from the television.

"Soak it up, big boy," Steff Freeman said, dropping her hand on his muscular chest. "This might be the last time we see each other for a while."

Ken twisted on his side, leaning on his elbow. "Why is that?"

"Because it's happening…sooner than we thought."

"What?" He sat bolt upright. "The coup?"

"We believe so." She ran her fingers through her blond wig. "Ever since our mole went silent, we've noticed abnormal chatter. There's definitely an operation going on in Philadelphia."

Ken's eyebrows raised. "What kind of operation?"

Steff rolled out of bed. Reaching for a pack of cigarettes on the dresser, she put one in her lips. "It could only be an assassination." She lit it and blew out a stream of smoke. "There's a possibility that impeachment is just a distraction."

"Holy shit," Ken jumped out of bed and stepped into his jeans. "What if your mole sold you out?

"He hasn't." With the cigarette in her lips, Steff put on her pants and snapped on her bra. "I've set some traps. And I have a team of spooks watching my back. I'd know if I was being followed. But forget about me. This is happening in days not weeks. My superior officer has warned me to start taking precautions. That's why I'm here. To tell you in person."

"Are you going off the grid?"

"No. It would jeopardize the mission. They need me on the inside."

"What if he rats you out? They'll torture you till you give up your sources."

"I've made arrangements for that." Steff paused, setting the cigarette in the ashtray. "That's why I don't think we should see each other until we accomplish the mission." She slipped into her blouse and started buttoning it up.

Ken sighed heavily. "What kind of arrangements?" He bit his lip, lifting his eyes to meet hers.

"I have a cyanide pill taped to the inside of my bra. And I gave two loyal patriots instructions on how to reach you. An admiral and a general." She returned the cigarette to her mouth.

"How can I trust them?"

"You can't trust anyone. But if you want to serve your country, you'll take the leap of faith."

"Let's hope that day never comes. Either way, I have a team in place. The guys have heart. They're fearless, but they'll need more training."

Steff snubbed out the cigarette. "How long do you need?"

"A year."

"America will be unrecognizable in a year. Once the new regime settles in, they'll tighten the noose. Communication will be difficult." She tucked her blouse into her pants and slipped into a black blazer. "Our team will gather intelligence. We'll find a weakness. But we can't act until the regime's actions prove tyrannical. We need the American people to be fed up. Desperate for change. Accepting of drastic measures."

"Okay, I'll speed up the pace."

"Good. Train your team. Teach them security protocol first, then harden them with the training you learned as a Marine. Tell them nothing about the mission until you hear from me."

"Then what?"

"I'll let you know when the time comes. Until then, just get them trained with some experience."

"How am I gonna get ahold of you?"

Steff shook her head. "You won't." She made a gesture toward the floor. "Under the bed, there's a suitcase with two untraceable military-grade satphones. I'll call with updates." She took a step closer. "One more thing. The infamous flash drive is in there, too, with a stack of classified documents. Never leak the intel. Show no one. Just read it. Stash it. It might motivate you to never accept failure."

52

BTZ Suites night club
May 11, 2022

From the second floor of his night club, Frankie Buccetti sat alone in his office. His left hand was signing the last of four paychecks for his security team. All was calm and quiet until the earpiece picked up loud arguing from the security radio. Snapping his head to the computer screen on his desk, he saw six camera angles from the crowded bar. Leaning forward, he watched his black-clad security guards encircle a group of patrons.

Two blond women were standing next to three men. The largest in the group had long brown sideburns that took up half his face. His pale hands were spread apart. Two other men in their mid-twenties were flapping their mouths loudly.

"Break it up or leave!" Brice barked at the men who were face to face talking shit to each other. His freshly shaved baby face was mistaken for weakness.

"We ain't doin' nothing wrong," the sideburn guy said with a shrug. "We're just talking here." Wearing jeans and a light-weight black jacket, the man staggered a little, his pale face darkening by the second.

"I'm giving you a chance to walk away." Brice took a step forward. "You understand? … No fighting here. No shit talk either."

"Ya know what?" The big man with sideburns flipped him the bird. "Fuck you, bitch."

"You're done!" Brice raised his voice and pointed to the door. "Get the fuck out while you can still walk."

Mr. Sideburns placed one foot forward and drew his fist back. From behind him, Dennis stuck a taser in his side. The crackle of the electricity was muted by blaring techno music, but the voltage dropped the giant to his knees, and then to the floor. Seeing their friend in peril, his two friends jumped on Dennis. Brice instantly moved in. Gordon Grayfeather ducked his freshly shaved bald head and dove in the mix.

From the entrance, Vadik Domechev waved his hands. "Get back!" he yelled at the rest of the crowd. "Clear the way!"

Fists were swinging. Men were rolling around on the dance floor. And Dennis was stomping his boots on the big guy with the furry pork chops on his face.

Frankie barked into the walkie-talkie while running to the elevator. "Vadik, get in there and break it up before someone gets killed. I'll be right down for crowd control."

"I'm on it," Vadik said, looking for the greatest threat. He then made a beeline in that direction with long powerful strides.

By the time Frankie got to the bar, only brawlers remained on the dance floor. Turning his head, he saw the rest of the patrons congregating against the left wall. Snapping back to the action, he saw people laid out on the floor. Bleeding.

Some were crawling to safety. But the fight raged on. The security staff had forgotten their training, and were resorting to street fighting instincts. The college kids out numbered the four security guards. That was probably why Frankie saw Mariani and a few loyal cronies in the melee.

Frankie, Carlos, and Marcel escorted all remaining customers out the side exit. Carlos then locked the doors, leaving only the staff and brawlers. The lights came on. The music stopped. Frankie blew his whistle three times, and surprisingly the fight came to a halt.

"It's over!" Frankie yelled. "Security! Come stand next to me." The four bouncers rose and made a line next to Frankie, blocking any escape. Frankie studied what was in front of him, and saw three men limp on the floor, two sitting down holding their faces, and three on their feet with lowered eyebrows and flexed arms.

"The door's locked!" Marcel barked. "What's it gonna be? … You wanna go home or not?"

"We don't call cops around here," Frankie said. "You can leave now or get put in the ICU."

"I wanna go home," one of them said, wiping blood from his nose.

"Then pick up your friends and leave," Carlos said, pointing to the handful of injured young men on the floor. "And don't come back."

"One more thing," Frankie said. "We're not gonna press charges. I suggest you don't either. Our cameras don't lie. And our lawyers don't lose."

The big man with the sideburns crossed his arms. "We won't say shit."

Leaning up against the bar, Giovanni Mariani lowered his eyebrows, glaring at the big man with the wild sideburns.

Frankie escorted them to the front exit. As soon as Marcel unlocked the door, the brawlers left, and then Frankie sent the staff home for the night. The owners and security stayed.

"All right, men," Frankie said. "We won, they lost. I appreciate how you guys put your bodies in harm's way for the club...but we *have* to learn how to stop things before they get to that point. What if someone died, or lost an eye? ... What if next time we get sued?"

"Everything happened so fast," Dennis said. "They just kept coming."

"Vadik," Frankie said to his head of security. "What do you think went wrong here?"

"Uh, I don't know what we could have done differently," Vadik said. "Like Dennis said, they just started swinging. We had to defend ourselves. But I think we sent a pretty good message."

Frankie looked at his men. "Starting Monday morning, Ken Spatz will be training you every single day...until he thinks you guys are ready for the big leagues."

*****

An hour later, Frankie maneuvered his keyboard mouse to the security footage from earlier in the night. "We better delete the camera file." Frankie said to Mariani. "You broke a bottle over some dude's head. You got to be a little more gentle, bro."

Mariani's eyebrow lowered. "Yeah, burn that shit." He took a sip of whiskey. "Dude was big. Had to take him down the hard way."

"You could have killed him."

"Bro, get off my back. I'm gonna do what it takes to survive." Mariani had lines on his forehead. His arms were crossed. And sweat was forming on his bald head. "Plus, I think that was the mutt from the grocery store."

"What?" Frankie's left eye squinted. "What are you talking about?"

"The guy with the side burns." Mariani shrugged. "I'm pretty fucking sure that's the asshole I shot in the chest."

"No way. You said he was dead."

Mariani shook his head. "I thought he was."

"What makes you think it's him?"

"No one has sideburns like that."

"Do you think he recognized you?"

"I don't think so. That's why I hit him so hard."

Frankie clicked the mouse, deleting the security file in question. "Oops," he said. "Accidently deleted the footage. Forget about it. You'll never see sideburn guy again."

"I should have shot him twice that day. I won't make that mistake again."

Frankie felt his phone vibrating in his pocket, so he pulled it out. Looking at the screen, he shook his head. "My mom called like ten times in the last twenty minutes." His brow was lowered.

"Damn, it seems a little late for her. You better check on her."

"She's calling again. Let me get this." Frankie swiped the screen. "Hello?"

"I can't sleep," Diana said. "I've been watching the news all night."

"That's why you called me ten times?" Frankie said. "Cuz you're watching fake news?"

"Yeah." She let out a short laugh. "They're saying the president is gonna resign tomorrow."

"What?" Frankie said with an agitated voice. "Clacher?"

"Yeah," she replied. "I'm watching, right now: Sources close to the president regret the fact that he will resign tomorrow."

"That's fake news, Mom," Frankie said. "Don't worry about that shit."

"Turn on the TV!" Diana snipped. "It's on every channel."

"Hold on," Frankie said to his mom, turning on the TV.

The black screen flashed on, and a clear digital picture of a white-haired news anchor appeared. He was wearing a black suit, no tie, and a shit grin on his pale face. The volume was muted, but the headline told the story in seven words: *PRESIDENT CLACHER HAS BEEN FORCED TO RESIGN.*

Frankie slammed the bottom of his fist on the bar. "What the fuck?"

53

BTZ Suites
May 12, 2022

It was twelve noon, Central Standard Time. Frankie and Mariani were sitting on the leather sofa in Frankie's presidential suite. Frankie's eyes were glued to the flat-screen TV that was mounted on the hundred-year-old brick wall.

Frankie held out his left hand, gesturing to the caption at the bottom of the screen that said a resignation speech was imminent. "I can't believe he's not putting up a fight," he said. "They must have threatened him."

"Look at him." Mariani pointed. "He's doing it."

Silence took hold as the leader of the free world began to speak. Frankie and Mariani both leaned forward at the edge of their seats.

"Good afternoon, America," President Clacher said from the Oval Office, his hands folded on the dark oak desk in front of him. "This will be the last time I speak to you as your president. It has been the greatest honor of my life…not only to serve at the highest level of government, but to do so during America's most consequential moments. My first test as president was an act of war…in defense of liberty.

"That day, America was attacked without notice by an enemy who had no flag. We were blindsided by five simultaneous nuclear weapons that obliterated five once beautiful cities. Millions of people were murdered. Our very way of life was threatened. Freedom was one wrong decision away from being erased from existence. Our civilization was on a path fraught with peril.

"As president…I had a great many problems in front of me." Clacher cleared his throat and then continued. "But the first act of business was to stop the threat that faced us. There was no time for an investigation or jury trial. The threat was imminent, and it had to be stopped at all costs.

"From the war room, I was given four options as commander in chief. It was *I* that was given the burden to make an executive decision without wavering. Failure to act could have cost us everything. Weakness invites aggression. We gain peace through strength. Victory after surrender. I had no choice but to act. So, I did, and I have no regrets. I broke no law. I did not start this war, but I did finish it.

"Russia, China, North Korea, and Iran formed a military alliance just before the war. Our greatest generals were confident that I was making the correct decision. That said, a true leader will take responsibility for his actions. Even though I was right, I was also wrong. More than three hundred million people in the world are dead, and I have to live with that burden for the rest of my life. But worse—when the dust settled—about fifty million Americans died as a result of the war and the blackout to follow. And that weighs heavy on my heart. No man will ever be able to understand how I feel inside: the pain of guilt. But had I not acted…it would have been far worse. We could have lost a hundred million. Or maybe more. We could have surrendered or waited for the enemy to make a move. We could have waged war on ISIS and Al-Qaeda, and let our true enemies evade justice. No! Justice was served. We brought justice to our enemies, and we brought our enemies to justice.

"After World War Three was won, my team did everything humanly possible to save lives, provide food, and give comfort to a nation on the brink. With a nation in crisis, thirteen cities destroyed, and no electricity: order had to be restored. You and I had a rendezvous with destiny, and together as a team, we rebuilt America. Once the lights came back on, we fixed the economy, built new cities, created hope for the children, and helped to rebuild the world. Communism is no more, tyranny is history, and now there is only freedom and peace.

"With full confidence in Vice President Andrews and a bullish economy, I feel comfortable ending my second term early. As of 9:00 o'clock tomorrow morning, I will officially resign from the Office of the President of the United States. Let not your heart be troubled, because *you* will be in good hands. Vice President Andrews will lead us to providence in a smoother way than I ever could."

The president sniffled and choked down his pent-up emotion. "With my last words as president, I want you all to know that I love each and every one of you. I-I wish you excellent health and prosperity, long life and freedom…peace and blessings from above. May God bless our new president, may God bless the American citizens…and may God continue to bless the United States of America."

And the screen switched back to the cable news channel. Frankie turned the TV off.

Mariani lit up a cigarette.

"Give me one of those things," Frankie said.

*****

The very next day, Tom Clacher became the second president in history to resign. Immediately afterword, Vice President Andrews took the oath of office with his right hand on his wife's Bible. Once he became president, he shook hands with the Chief Justice of the Supreme Court and former President Clacher. Turning to kiss his smiling wife, President Andrews then pushed the door open and started walking with Clacher toward the *Marine One* helicopter. His entourage of staff, Secret Service, and media followed behind him.

The cameras were rolling as Frankie, Mariani, and the rest of the world watched history being written. The picture on the screen showed bright green grass and a large helicopter that was pale green and white with the Great Seal of the United States on the side. The former president now walked alone toward the helicopter, his successor waving behind him. As he took his first step on the white presidential staircase, he turned around and gave an iconic salute just like President Nixon did fifty years in the past.

From the lawn of the beautiful new White House, the 46th President of the United States gave a salute in return, then a long minute later, *Marine One* ascended into the air, flying off into the distance of the blackening sky.

President Andrews gave one last wave to the cameras. Turning back toward the White House, Andrews let out a breath. *Time to unite this country,* he thought, lowering his head against the stiff wind. His vice president was waiting to take his oath of office.

President Andrews flinched at the sudden explosion of thunder clapping. The Secret Service man next to him tackled him to the ground. Thunder rang out twenty more times in ten seconds. Everyone was laying on the grass. Many were bleeding. When the gunshots stopped, the media scattered like roaches. The Secret Service agents were surrounding the commander in chief who was not moving.

"Lay down cover fire!" Agent Johnson yelled into his walkie-talkie while on top of Andrews.

*****

Frankie's hands were pressing on the top of his head, eyes locked on the TV screen. "No!"

54

After being released from prison, Richard Secord's lawyer drove him to his two-story brick home in the middle of suburbia.

"Thanks again, Robert," Secord said, shaking his hand. "You're a life saver."

"I'm sorry it took so long to get you free," Robert Black said. "You got caught up in a political witch-hunt. It's over now. Enjoy retirement."

"Is my bank account unfrozen?"

"Yes. The only thing you're out of is a job."

"Thanks. I can't wait another second to see my wife and kids."

"Good luck to you, Richard. I'll send you a bill."

Secord got out of the black SUV and started running to his house. The door was cracked open. When he got into the foyer, he was surprised no one was there to greet him. Only a few tipped-over chairs and a cool draft.

"Peg! I'm home!" He ran up the stairs. Nothing.

Sitting on his bed was a large yellow envelope. Opening it, he emptied the contents onto the blanket. There was a car key and a primitive black cellphone.

The phone started ringing. *What the…*

Secord picked it up. Looking at the screen, he let it ring a few more times. Finally, he pressed the green button and brought the phone to his ear.

"Good afternoon, Mr. Secord." A hoarse voice said on the other end of the line.

"Who is this?"

"You know who it is, Mr. Secord," the man said. "It's your master. I need you to listen very carefully. Your wife and kids are counting on you."

Secord sat down on the carpet, leaning his back against the bed. Letting out a heavy sigh, he lowered his tone. "What do you want from me?"

"Mr. Secord, there is a maroon four-door sedan parked down the block. I want you to take the key and start driving toward the freeway. Stay on the phone. I'll give you instructions from there."

"Don't hurt them. Please."

"Mr. Secord, that all depends on your cooperation."

*****

In the dimly lit basement of his skyscraper, Seth Roth was watching Richard Secord get punched in the face repetitively. Two men in black were holding Secord up. And a bald man was teeing off. "Enough," he said, and the henchmen stepped back from Secord, whose body crumbled to the cement floor.

Seth took a long drag from his cigarette and then blew out a stream of smoke. "Mr. Secord, that was foolish of you to put your family in danger." He took a few steps closer. "All you had to do was follow orders. You would have been rich and powerful. Now, look at you. More pathetic than your romp with Mr. Parker...in the coffin."

Secord pressed his hand against his right eye. "L-leave my kids alone." He rolled his body against a brick wall and drooled blood on his filthy white dress shirt.

"Mr. Secord, we know there's a small network of rebels conspiring against President Roth," Seth Roth said, wiping ash from the chest of his three-piece black suit. "We never imagined you would join them." Roth stepped forward, hovering above the former secretary of defense. "Give me the names of your co-conspirators."

"I don't have any names." Secord said in a quavering voice. "I-I'm not part of any rebel plot." He propped himself against the cold wall. "I-I thought you were sacrificing me to get Clacher. So, I threw the flash drive into the crowd. I-I didn't want to be the fall guy."

Mr. Roth twitched his bony finger while clicking his tongue. "Bring out the wife and kids."

A door creaked open. Mrs. Secord rolled out in a wheelchair that was being pushed by a tall bald man in a light-weight black jacket. Duct tape was covering her mouth. Black mascara tracks were streaking down her beet red cheeks. Her wrists and ankles were bound.

Seth Roth smiled at the sight of her wide eyes shifting back and forth. Her pinkish fingers and hands fluttering with abject fear. "Calm down, Mrs. Secord. Nothing to worry about."

Two other light-skinned men in black coats were also pushing wheelchairs out the door. The first one had a newborn baby wrapped up in a small blanket on the seat. Behind it, a man was pushing Secord's sobbing boy. They parked all three wheelchairs directly in front of Richard Secord, and then returned to the door they came from.

Sitting in the shadow of two burly men, Richard Secord put his hands in the air. "Okay, okay, I'll tell you everything." His hands were shaking drastically. "Just don't hurt them."

"It's too late, Mr. Secord. You had your chance." Roth snapped his fingers, and the tall man came strutting up with a small torch in his hands. He stopped behind Mrs. Secord.

Richard jumped to his feet but got held back by the guards. "No!" Secord screamed, reaching out his arm. "Pleeease!" His hand never got closer than five feet to touching his wife. But his eyes connected with hers for a long moment. "Do it to me!"

One of the guards punched Secord in the gut and he went down. "L-let her go," he said but it sounded like a low grumble.

"Do it." Roth puffed on his cigarette.

The tall subordinate ignited the torch. The roar of the blue flame overpowered the crying from the family. The screaming from Richard Secord. The soft chuckle of Seth Roth.

The tall man in black aimed the flame just above Peggy Secord's head. After a brief pause, he slowly tilted the flame at her hair which sizzled. She screamed a high-pitched octave. Her head was whipping from side to side, and the wheelchair was teetering from her bucking heavy frame. Her gurgling screams, the ungodly screams of torture, filled the walls.

"No!" Secord whimpered from the ground. Both hands were covering his face but there were gaps in between the fingers.

The young boy was puking. The baby was crying.

Repositioning for a full-frontal assault, the bald man melted her face like a doll. Her head thrashed. And then, a few seconds later, Mrs. Secord's head sunk. The fire expanded. Black smoke climbed higher.

The man with the torch turned in the direction of the hyperventilating seven-year-old boy.

"Enough!" Roth barked, and the man walked away with haste. "I hope I proved my point, Mr. Secord."

Secord fully covered his face, sobbing like his son. "Yes, Master." His breaths were fast and heavy. His arms were now drooped at his side, his muscles limp. "Steffanie Freeman. She's part of the resistance. That's all I know. Just leave my kids alone."

Seth Roth lit another cigarette. "Good." He lifted the corner of his mouth. "My instincts were correct about you, Mr. Secord." Bending toward the little boy, he wiped the kid's tears with his pale finger. He then licked his wet finger, eyes shifting to Secord who now was sitting erect against the wall. His eyes were narrow but receptive.

Secord swallowed hard. "What are you going to do with my kids?"

"Don't worry, Mr. Secord. Your younger child will be at the perfect age of sacrifice in two years. His soul will serve Moloch for all of eternity."

"No!" Secord wailed, his head shaking tightly. "Please don't. Why? Why are you doing this to me?"

Standing behind Secord's older son, Roth's face took on a devilish grin. "Oh, I am *certain* it is your infant child's destiny." He laughed shortly. "But this one…is too old for the owl god. He will become *my* personal slave." He poked his chest.

"Why are you doing this?" Secord pleaded. "I gave you what you wanted!"

"But you betrayed the order, Mr. Secord. You knew the consequences and repercussions. Be grateful. It is a great honor to melt at the feet of a god."

"Please don't hurt my kids. I'm begging you."

"I will never hurt your older son… As long as he learns to appreciate my authority."

Secord wept.

"Oh, one more thing, Mr. Secord." Roth laughed shortly. "We tricked you. That flash drive we gave you was just a test to smoke you out. My brother bet me that you'd pass the test." He laughed. "I won."

"Why would you risk information like that?"

"Do you think we care about embarrassing politicians?" He shook his head. "We win either way. We just needed Clacher to resign. Now, thanks to you, my niece will rule with an iron fist."

55

Philadelphia, Pennsylvania
June 13, 2022

In front of a cheering crowd, Heather Roth placed her left hand on a thick black book held by her father, David Roth. The Chief Justice of the Supreme Court said the oath of office, and then she repeated it. Turning to face her enthusiastic supporters, she stepped behind a black podium with the reverse side of the Great Seal stamped on the front. Within the circle of the seal, an unfinished pyramid stood with the cap hovering just above the base. An all-seeing eye filled the triangular cap piece.

Raising her hand above her head, Roth waved and smiled, because *she* was the 47th President of the United States. President Heather Roth was the first woman president in American history. Short, thin, and frail, the woman in her seventies kept waving in her charcoal-gray pantsuit. Her shoulder-length silver hair was flowing in the light summer breeze. As she waved to the crowd, she kissed her fingers, blowing her love in every direction. And then rain began to fall from the black sky.

"Thank you!" President Roth said, then waved again. A frowning Secret Service agent held a black umbrella over her head while she spoke. There were only a few hundred paid supporters in attendance, but on television it looked like a hundred thousand. "Thank you … May the gods be with you."

She smiled robustly. "Four agonizing weeks ago," Roth hollered into the microphone, "America lost thirteen innocent souls who didn't deserve to die. Among them was a man who became president just minutes before.

"Let us take a moment for our fallen king, and those brave men and women who met the same fate." She pressed her bright lips together and bowed her head. Silence invaded the area. "Thank you!" she gave the crowd another minute for applause as she pretended to dry her crocodile tears with a white handkerchief. "Our founding fathers planted a seed of freedom in this great land. Over time, that seed grew into a vast forest of liberty. But today…we have the opportunity to plant acorns of equity across the entire globe." And the crowd went wild for another moment as she casually waited to continue.

"The fundamental transformation of America starts today!" President Roth said with a raised voice. "We must rebuild this nation to be the model for the world to replicate. This task will not be easy. I will need all of your help. I can't do this alone. It will take a village. In order to move forward and mold a more perfect democracy, you must educate yourselves on the issues, persuade your friends and family, convince your coworkers that weapons of war have no place in a civilized society!

"If you do that for me, I will deliver for you! Change is on the way and it starts today! When I sit down at my desk in the Oval Office, there will be an Executive Order waiting for my signature. It will prohibit the sale of human-killing weapons like the AK-47 and the AR-15!

"Never again will so many lives be taken in just two minutes by the hands of a crazed gunman."

The great orator went on for another hour with a long laundry list of policies, and then she concluded.

"Let's take a walk together toward our shared destiny of a new and evolving world order that works for all people on this green earth. Let's thrust forward together so that our children and grandchildren can live in a world of peace and equality for all time. May the gods bless America, and may the gods bless all the nations of the world to someday become one."

*****

From the confines of his office, Frankie Buccetti hit the power button and the TV went black. After five years of sobriety, he poured a glass of whiskey with no rocks. "Liberty just died…and no one cares."

56

Fish Lake, Minnesota
June 17, 2022

Ken blew his whistle from the top of a steep ravine. "Again!" he barked at his independent contractors in training. The sun was hot. The air was humid. Lunch break got skipped.

Gordon Grayfeather, Brice, Dennis, and Vadik Domechev scurried down the wooded hill. When they reached the bottom, they turned and climbed their way back up the hill with haste.

"Again!" Ken pulled out his gun and fired into the sky four times. "Pretend someone is shooting at you. Head low."

The sweaty men descended the steep hill with bullets flying above their heads.

"Lower!" Ken fired into the trees as fast as he could pull the trigger. When he was out of bullets, he reloaded and carefully shot around them as they climbed.

When they reached the top, each man was huffing and puffing. Vadik had his hands on his head. Brice, his knees. Dennis, his hips. And Grayfeather was wiping sweat from his freshly shaved head.

"Again!" Ken screamed, but the sweaty men shook their heads in protest.

"Fuck that!" Dennis raised his voice. "It's a hundred fucking degrees."

Brice wiped his brow. "Come on, man. We ain't training for war. We're fucking bouncers."

"Shut the fuck up!" Ken shoved his pistol in his holster and took a step closer. "You *are* training for war; you just don't know it yet."

"What you talking about?" Grayfeather asked, shrugging with a scrunched-up face.

"Huddle up." Ken waved them in. "Look, guys, you're doing great. Almost there. Only a few more months of training. I need you guys ready for battle. We might get a big job this winter. You'll be providing security for a member of Congress." He remembered Steff Freeman telling him not to tell them about the mission, but he had to give them a reason to train harder. "Anything could happen."

"Oh, I see." Dennis lifted his chin. "You want us to be sitting ducks? Like the Secret Service men who died with President Andrews?"

"No." Ken placed his hands on his hips. "I'm training you to assassinate a president who has committed treason!" He paused to look each man in the eye. "Are you in or out?"

57

Philadelphia, Pennsylvania
June 22, 2022

Steff Freeman paid the corner vendor for a cup of coffee and a newspaper. "Keep the change," she said, turning in the direction of the new thirteen-story CIA building. *I should go off the grid,* she thought, gazing at the creepy black building filled with people who still believed in the cause. People who were still loyal to the president. People who might change their mind after seeing the information she possessed. *Or maybe they wouldn't?*

Dressed in a black pantsuit, her strides were long as she shoved the paper in her purse. Taking a sip of hot coffee, her eyes studied each person on the crowded sidewalk as if they were an enemy collaborator who wanted to hang her for treason.

Since the rise of President Heather Roth, Steff's heart ticked up a notch every time she entered the front door of CIA headquarters. "Good morning," she said to the guard before scanning her badge. He was normally friendly, but today he looked stiff, only offering her a slight nod. *He's a little short with me today,* she thought. *I wonder what that's all about?*

She slowly took her gun out of its holster, set it on the conveyor belt, and then stepped through the x-ray machine.

"Thank you," she said, trying not to show her anxiety. "Have a good day." Steff grabbed her gun and returned it to its spot under her blazer.

As she crossed the shiny checkered floor to the elevator, Steff noticed a dozen people in the lobby, when a week earlier there were dozens. No one was congregating. Everyone was on the move. No one was smiling. *They all look afraid,* she thought, stepping into the elevator with three stone-faced men in black suits. "Thirteen, please."

A tall, bald man in casual attire pressed the button. "The lucky floor," he said, his chiseled jaw turning to face her. "I have a meeting there later."

The elevator shot up. "Maybe we'll cross paths," Steff replied on instinct.

The elevator stopped on the eleventh floor and the doors opened. The tall man briefly met her eyes. As he started walking, he looked back at her and said, "I sure hope so."

When the elevator closed, Steff lowered her head. *Definitely a field agent.*

Stepping onto her floor moments later, Steff took a deep breath as she milled her way past the cubicles to her office. Closing the door, she set her purse on the desk, took a sip of coffee, and then put in on a coaster. Pulling out the newspaper, she then plopped down on a leather chair.

"Holy shit," she said softly as she read the headline on the paper with wide eyes. *Defense Secretary and wife found dead in an apparent murder-suicide. The two children are missing. Fire destroyed half of the house.*

Exhaling a deep sigh, Steff set the paper down with a trembling hand. Her heart was pounding now, so bad that she actually pressed her hand to her breast. *Murder-suicide?* she thought. *No way. They killed her, and then he gave me up.*

Closing her eyes briefly, her lip began to quiver. *Time to disappear.*

*****

In the parking ramp, Steff thumbed the button on her key fob, and her black four-door sedan unlocked. *Hurry up,* she thought, dropping into the driver's seat. Pulling her gun out, she cocked it, pressed the safety button off, and then stuffed the barrel in the cup holder.

Unbuttoning her white blouse, she fingered underneath her bra. *There it is.* She pulled out a tiny canister, opened the top, and then slid the capsule into her hand. Rolling the pill in her palm, she popped it in her mouth and shoved it inside her lower lip with her tongue.

As she turned the key, two black SUVs screeched to a stop in front of her car. "Fuck," she said, the sharp zip of adrenaline rising to her neck. *This is it,* she thought. *I'm not going to make it out of this alive.* She reached for her gun.

A bald man in black casual clothes got out of the truck with his gun drawn. "Hands up," he barked loudly, the barrel of his gun aimed at her head. Two other men surrounded her vehicle.

"I'm fucked," Steff said under her breath, releasing the gun and raising her hands slowly.

"Get out of the car!" the tall agent from the elevator screamed. His face was stony. No emotion.

She opened the door and got out with her hands above her head.

"Face down on the ground."

Secord sold me out, Steff thought as she dropped to her knees. Lowering herself to the prone position, she pressed her cheek against the pavement. The pill was now clamped between her grinding back teeth.

"Don't fucking move!" The agent stepped toward her. "Traitor. Who are you working with?"

Steff's face scrunched up from the bitter taste in her mouth. The burning sensation of imminent death. *Good luck, Ken Spatz.* A tear rolled down her cheek. *You're our only hope.*

58

Driving to dinner with Tara, Frankie listened to his mom yell through his speaker phone that was resting on the center console. He wasn't expecting her to deliver bad news. "You got to be kidding me?" He grabbed the phone, turned off the speaker, and pressed it to his ear. Out of the corner of his eye, he saw Tara's head shifting from the passenger seat.

"No, I'm not kidding," Diana said with a lowered tone. "Gordon Grayfeather is the prime suspect in a grizzly homicide."

"No way. Couldn't be him." His left hand was gripping the steering wheel. He could feel Tara's glare.

"Why not?" His mom asked.

"Because he's been working with me. I know how much he likes his job."

"Great, I bet the cops will be knocking on my door any minute."

Frankie took his eyes off the road to glance at Tara who was watching him. "This must be a big misunderstanding," he said to his mom, hoping the disinformation would cloud Tara's thoughts while she listened to the conversation.

Diana sharpened her voice. "The last time you said something like that, I was visiting you in jail."

"Mom, please stop."

"Frankie, they found DNA under the fingernails of the corpse. No head."

He let out a breath. "I'll get to the bottom of this and call you back." Frankie hung up without saying goodbye.

Tara's voice rose louder than Frankie thought possible. "What the fuck was that all about?"

59

Duluth, Minnesota
August 31, 2022

Giovanni Mariani strutted down the sidewalk through a downpour of rain. The repetitive thumping of music from the bar greeted his approach. Shouldering the door open, he walked up to the bar and put a twenty on the counter. "Give me a whiskey on the rocks," Mariani said with a flick of his hand. "And a Jag bomb."

"Coming right up." The male bartender turned, reaching for the whiskey bottle.

Fuck it. Mariani thought. *It's my birthday, I can get drunk if I want to.*

Shifting his head, Mariani studied the long and narrow bar. The dimly-lit room housed more men than women. A few bikers were in the corner with beers in their hands. *Bikers.* He shook his head.

The bartender broke Mariani's thoughts by setting his change in front of him.

"Thanks," Mariani said, scraping up the pile of ones. Leaving two on the bar top, he shoved the rest in his pocket.

A vibration from his phone induced his hand back to the pocket it had just been. Pulling out the device, it stopped buzzing, but the lit screen read three missed calls. *Who the fuck is that?* he thought, not recognizing the phone number.

Punching the number with his thumb, he brought the phone to his ear and walked outside. It rang twice. A rusty SUV parking in front of the bar caught his eye.

"Hello?" A sharp baritone voice said into Mariani's ear.

"I just missed a call from this number."

"My brotha' from anotha' motha'," the voice said.

"This Gordon?"

"No, it's your daddy."

Mariani chuckled. "I heard you're in a little bit of trouble."

"Uh, yah…you could say that. Look, brother, I was wondering if you could do me a solid?"

"Anything for you, bro. I'm here for ya." Mariani pressed the phone harder against his ear.

"I just need some money to get out of town."

Mariani's head shifted away from the slender black-haired girl walking toward the bar. "Not a problem. We'd have to take a drive."

"Where ya at? I can come pick ya up."

"I'm at Fletcher's Tavern, downtown."

"Meet me in the alley in an hour."

"Sounds good, brother. Talk soon." He hung up the phone and re-entered the loud bar.

*****

After paying for his third round of hard drinks, Mariani took a shot, chased it with his whiskey, and then staggered though the growing crowd toward the back of the bar. He was heading outside, his steps trailing a stranger with an unlit cigarette in his hand, who appeared to have the same motive in mind.

Underneath a large canopy were two picnic tables, and Mariani set his drink on the one that was vacant. Rainfall was tapping the plastic above his head.

Lighting up a cigarette, he noticed one of the girls at the other table look back. Sitting next to her was an obese woman with long blond hair and guy with a clean beard, black hat, and white shirt that exposed his muscles. The woman in question now had her back to him. She was a thin gal with black hair and a gray hooded sweatshirt. *She looks familiar,* he thought. *Something about her.*

"Fucking rain, eh?" Mariani said, the slender girl turning to face him.

"Tomorrow will be better," she said, cracking a thin smile.

"Are you sure about that?" Mariani asked.

The woman, who upon closer inspection seemed in her earlier thirties, exhaled a stream of smoke in response. "I'm not sure about much these days." Her voice was scratchy and a little bit slurred.

The guy at the table stood up, faced Mariani, and then tossed his cigarette in a bucket. "For all I know, tomorrow I could be dead."

"I need a drink," the heavy-set woman said, dropping her cigarette in the bucket. "I'll be inside."

"Get me a beer," the man with the beard said. "I'll be right in." He leaned in and said something softly to the black-haired girl.

She nodded with her cigarette dangling from her lips. "I'll be in after my cigarette."

"All right," the man said, glancing at Mariani before grabbing the door handle.

The woman's blue eyes shifted to meet Mariani's. "You from around here?" she asked, and then took a sip from her beer.

"Born and raised." He blew a stream of smoke upward. "How 'bout you?"

"Me, too," she said. "I live up north, but I'm moving down here as soon as a job opens up for me."

"What do you do?"

She gave a half shrug. "I'm a nurse for people who live in group homes."

Mariani smiled. "That would suck."

"I actually like it." She smiled in return. "I like helping people." She paused, staring into Mariani's eyes. "Wait." She set her beer on the table and closed the distance. "I know you from somewhere."

Mariani tilted his head. "I thought the same thing about you. Where did you go to high school?"

"It is you." She covered her mouth, and then approached him with open arms. Her hug was tight.

"Damn, girl." He took a step back. "I think you got the wrong guy."

She shook her head. "I'm Katrina." She smiled. "You don't remember me? I used to be blond."

Mariani took a drag from his cigarette. "I'm sorry. I got a bad memory."

Katrina lowered her voice. "I met you in a grocery store on 3-13. You stood up for me."

Thinking back to that dreadful day, Mariani remembered a girl on her knees, crying over a man who was sprawled out on the floor. Bleeding. She was screaming for help. Pounding on the man's massive chest. Blond hair, blue eyes. Nose ring. *It is her.*

"I'm sorry I was such a bitch," she said, meeting his eyes. "That was traumatic for me."

Mariani chuckled shortly. "I kinda hoped I'd never see you again."

"Did you know Steve lived?"

Mariani lied. "No." He pursed his lips.

"Now I understand why you did what you did." She let out a breath. "I should have been more grateful. I should have asked you to put another bullet in his head."

"Why do you say that?"

"Because he's still up to the same shit. Putting his hands on me when he gets drunk."

"You're still with him?" His eyes squinted. "Why would any woman put up with that?"

She shrugged. "I don't know. I've been with him since I was fifteen. I don't know anything else."

"And he's here tonight?"

"He's on the way." She made strong eye contact with him. "I better go."

"Does he know anything about me?"

She shook her head. "No."

"I hope not," Mariani said, his heart elevating a few notches. "I don't want to—"

Touching his arm, she interrupted him. "Hey, I think we should keep in touch. What do you think?" Katrina ran her fingers through her hair.

"Probably not a good idea," he said, discarding his cigarette next to the bucket. "I don't need no drama in my life."

"Sorry I asked. I just..." She looked away. "Never mind." Her gaze met his again. "Can I at least say hi next time I see you?"

"I can handle that."

She shook his hand. "See ya around," she said, and then spun on her heel toward the door.

"Wow," Mariani said to himself, lighting another cigarette. "I should beat that chump." *I got more important things to do though.*

*****

Katrina sat down next to her oversized boyfriend, and she patted his thigh.

Steve swiped her hand from his leg. "Where ya been?" He chugged his bottle of beer.

"I went to the bathroom," Katrina said, squinting her eyes.

"I heard you were outside talking to a guy?" Steve's voice was deep. His brown hair was parted, and his sideburns were huge. His friend with the black hat and white shirt was sitting by his side laughing. And his heavy-set girlfriend was rolling her eyes. Another man at the table was tilting his beer back. His face was narrow with a gray goatee.

"He's just an old friend," Katrina said.

"Did you fuck him?" he asked while tugging on the collar of his black button-up shirt.

"What do you think?" Katrina's voice was sharp.

The big man's head moved toward her. "I don't like competition."

The guy in the black hat said, "She was extra friendly to him. That's all I know."

"Stop it."

"Nah." Katrina's boyfriend stood up. "I'm gonna mark my territory. You belong to me."

Katrina's face reddened. "Steve, leave him alone!"

"Stay here," Steve said. "We'll be right back." He got up and two of his friends joined him.

Katrina buried her head in her hands. The big-boned woman wrapped her up in her arms. "Sorry, girl. Let's get a drink."

*****

At the edge of the canopy, Mariani took one last drag from his cigarette and flicked it in the wet alley. His right hand was in the side pocket of his coat, brushing up against the cold steel of the pocket knife he stole from Katrina's boyfriend five years in the past.

When the back door opened, Mariani's head shifted. The first person who stepped outside was the man with the white muscle shirt from earlier in the evening. The second was a tall and large man with pork chop sideburns. And the third was a tall, wiry man who looked at least fifty.

No fucking way, Mariani thought. *Sideburn guy again. That bitch probably sold me out.*

Steve stood in front of his two friends. His fingers were flickering at his sides.

"You got a problem, big boy?" Mariani barked, his hand still in his pocket.

"Ya know what?" Steve took a step closer. "I got a big problem. I heard you got your eye on my woman."

"Who the fuck's that?" Mariani asked.

"Katrina." Steve puffed out his chest. "Just stay away from her. And we'll be cool."

"Hey, asshole," Mariani said. "Quick question for ya. … You ever been shot in the chest?"

"What the fuck you just say?"

"You heard me, fat boy." Mariani smiled. "That was me." Mariani pointed at his chest.

Steve took a step forward, eyebrows forming a thick V. "You're fucking dead."

"Go fuck your inbred mother."

Steve's friend tried to step in front of him, but got blocked by a big arm.

"I got this." Steve turned his head to face Mariani. "I'll give you a chance to fight me one on one. My boys won't jump in."

"You can't faze me," Mariani spit on the ground between them.

"This guy thinks he's tough!" the man with the white shirt said. "Let's fuck him up."

Steve took a few slow steps forward and then started rushing toward Mariani. Lunging forward, Steve tackled him on the wet blacktop. The guy in the white t-shirt and the third guy started kicking and punching Mariani.

Someone started screaming.

Mariani kept sticking the knife in Steve's side as fast as he could. Steve stopped fighting completely, but the other two continued stomping on Mariani despite his swinging knife. And then their revenge was interrupted.

From a dark shadow between the buildings, Gordon Grayfeather threw a small hatchet and it stuck in the side of the skinny man's head. The guy with the beard watched his friend crumple to the wet blacktop. The sight must have paralyzed him with fear because he didn't run when he had the chance. He just trembled in the shadow of the large man who was growling in front of him.

Gordon Grayfeather's eyes were black. His muscular forearms shot down from his wet black T-shirt. Fists clenched.

"I ain't got no beef with you, Chief," the small man with the muscle shirt said with a squeaky voice.

Gordon let out a devilish laugh. "I'm gonna pound your fucking face in."

*****

Grayfeather hovered above his battered victim. "What's your name, punk?"

"Aiden," the guy said. "P-please stop. I-I have three kids."

"Your kids will be better off without you." Gordon glanced at the hatchet and smirked.

"I have money!" Aiden whimpered as the shadow eclipsed him. "Anything you want."

"When I see you in hell, we're gonna do this again," Gordon said, and with a grunt, he smashed the hatchet in between the man's eyes.

Grayfeather's head snapped at the sound of the back door creaking open. *Fuck! Who's that bitch?*

60

Duluth, Minnesota
September 14, 2022

From inside the locker room at the gym, Frankie Buccetti set his bag on the bench next to Vadik Domechev. "Did you call the jail?"

"Yeah," Vadik said, nodding. "I've tried everything. They're not in jail. Not in the hospital. Shit, even Brice can't find either of them." Vadik was wearing gray shorts and no shirt.

"Hmmm." Frankie sat down and rubbed his bald head. "Maybe Mariani helped Gordon go on the run."

"That makes sense," Vadik said. "Gordon had to get out of town. Mariani's got money. Time to kill."

Frankie stepped into a pair of navy-blue shorts. "Yeah, Mariani took him out of state for sure."

"I bet he comes back, but I don't think we'll ever see Gordon again." Vadik tied his shoes.

Frankie switched shirts. "You're probably right. It's too bad though. I think he was turning over a new leaf." His shirt was now dark gray.

"He was good at his job. I'll give him that." Vadik slid into a black tank top. "In training classes, he works harder than any of us. He wants to be the best. He craves it."

They left the locker room and found the bench press. Vadik put two hundred pounds on the bar, and laid down on the bench. "No pain, no gain," Vadik said. "Let me show you how it's done."

Vadik took the bar, bounced it off his chest, and then pushed it up as he blew out air. Dropping it on his chest again, he repeated ten times. He then got up, put on more weights, and did it again. Hopping up with vigor, Vadik beat his chest three times.

"Beast mode," Frankie said, smacking his sweaty shoulder.

"You ain't seen nothing yet," Vadik said. "Come on, let's go to the ring. We can spar."

"I'm straight, bro." Frankie smiled. "That doesn't sound too fun."

"I'll take it easy on you," Vadik said. "Plus, we got head gear."

Frankie let out a short laugh. "Not today, bro. I just came to get a work out."

"All right, man," Vadik said. "But, when Mariani comes back, I wanna see you and him spar." Vadik smiled. "I wanna see who's tougher."

"I don't know if I could spar a friend," Frankie said. "I can't fight unless I'm angry. I can't get angry until my life's on the line."

61

Virginia, Minnesota
September 16, 2022

Katrina pulled a bandage from Mariani's brow. "Fuck," Mariani said. "I told you, I'm fine."

"It doesn't look fine to me," Katrina snipped. "You gotta clean this every day."

"Please, just leave me alone." Mariani crossed his arms and leaned back on the couch.

"Giovanni, you need to start trusting me."

"No, I don't." He lit up a cigarette. "I can't trust a woman who would be with a guy like Steve."

"I'm a loyal ass bitch." She sat down on the couch next to him. "If I'd stay with Steve and his abuse, just imagine how loyal I'd be with the guy who killed him."

Mariani blew out a stream of smoke. "Part of me thinks you sold me out that night at the bar. And you're helping me because you feel —"

"We've discussed this," Katrina said, interrupting his words. "Steve's friend told him I was nice to you. And then he got all jealous. Damn it, Giovanni, you've been here two weeks. I helped you *and* your Native friend with the bloody hands for a reason. You broke my chains. I owe you my life."

"You don't owe me shit."

"Fine. Can you at least drop the attitude? I'm not your enemy."

Mariani cracked a smirk. "Okay, but what if the cops question you? It's easy to not talk until you get questioned hard. They'll take one look at you and be able to tell you're hiding something."

"You don't know anything about me. I know how to deal with cops."

"Yeah, what will you say when they press you?" Mariani raised his voice to sound like a cop. "Why did you flee the crime scene? What did you see? What are you hiding?"

"How do you know I haven't already talked to them?"

His head snapped to face her. "What?"

"Yeah, I already gave a statement."

"When?" He blew smoke in the air.

"Right after we got you safe." Katrina snatched up Mariani's pack of cigarettes and lit one up. "Your boy told me to do it. He said if I mention you or him, he'd give me an acid bath." She exhaled a cloud.

"That sounds like something he would say," Mariani thought, nodding his head. "What did you say to the cops."

Katrina shrugged. "I told them three tall black men killed Steve and his friends. And then they beat me. The next thing I remembered was waking up in the ditch. Hitchhiking to the hospital to get a rape kit."

"And they believed you?"

"Why wouldn't they? I'm a white woman with bruises all over my body. *And* my boyfriend got killed trying to defend me."

Mariani spread apart his arms. "Why are you just telling me this now?"

"You've been such a prick; I was scared."

"Look, I was just minding my own business that night, and your boyfriend and his friends jumped me. It's kinda hard to be nice to you."

"I'm sorry, Steve was a jealous fuck. Wasn't the first time he tried to mark his territory. But I'm glad it was his last."

"How could you live like that?" Mariani's eyebrows were low.

"I grew up in the sticks," Katrina said, looking down briefly. "Steve was my neighbor. A few years older. Only boyfriend I've ever had. I was like the dog who got kicked a few times a year. I just took it. And got used to it. It wasn't bad all the time."

Mariani massaged his temples. "Well, I guess you won't have to take it no more."

"I'm free," she said. "Thank you. That's what I'm saying. I feel a strong connection to you."

"I don't believe in connections."

"You don't feel nothing between us?"

Mariani looked at her. "Look, I appreciate you helping me." He snubbed out his cigarette in the ashtray. "You're cool and everything, but when my boy comes to get me, I don't think I'll be seeing you again."

Katrina turned and stormed out of the bedroom. "I wouldn't close the door on me if I were you." She slammed the door shut.

*****

From the passenger seat of a stolen car, Gordon Grayfeather strapped on his seatbelt. "We need to ditch this car and get another."

Mariani threw the shifter into drive. "I need to grab some cash. I got it buried."

"You still gonna float me some cash to get out of town?" Grayfeather asked.

"Not a problem," Mariani said. "Do you think ten thousand would keep ya going for a while?"

"That would be awesome, bro. I just need to get out of state. I got people down south."

"Anything to help." Mariani nodded his head. "You saved my life. And you made Katrina lie to the cops. That was genius, bro. I think I'm in the clear."

"She did us a solid. I saw it on the news."

Mariani was gripping the steering wheel with one hand. "Why did you trust that bitch?"

"I held the bloody hatchet to her head and made her drive. Then I took her ID before I left."

Mariani chuckled. "Damn, man. She said you threatened her with an acid bath."

"Oh, yeah…that, too." Grayfeather lit up a cigarette and cracked the window. "On the ride to her house, she told me how she owed you a favor. She told me how you shot her boyfriend." He laughed shortly. "I thought she might be useful."

"Her dude was a mutt. I should've shot him in the head. None of this would have happened."

"He's gone now, brother. Don't dwell on the past. We need to keep moving."

Mariani's mouth stretched. "Thanks, brother. You had my back when I was down. I'll never forget it."

62

The Buccetti Compound
December 21, 2022

In Frankie's living room, logs were burning in the ledger stone fireplace. Frankie was leaning back on the sofa, fiddling with his pen, gazing at the fire.

Ken's late, he thought, returning his pen to the paper on the coffee table. *More time to write down my treasonous thoughts.*

...and the world is on fire, but no one feels the heat. We're ruled by a nasty old bag who dresses like a wolf, but speaks as if she is a shepherd guiding her beloved flock of sheep. The Constitution is being shredded more and more every single day. The midterm elections in November expanded their power. Their majority is basically unstoppable. The regime will be able to do anything they want. They could cut us to pieces, or send us off to the gas chamber. They could starve us or manipulate the people to kill each other over political differences. There are no checks and balances. No opposition. No objective media. Zero dissent. And I believe, there is no hope for the children. I feel bad for these poor kids. I feel bad for the masses that have no clue of what is coming. But I have no sympathy for the puppet masters who are pulling the strings. I so badly wish I could...

A flash of headlights coming from the driveway took Frankie's attention. He quickly tore the sheet of paper out of the notebook and crinkled it into a ball. Stepping toward the fireplace, he dropped it in the flames. Standing there, he watched it catch fire, then smirked at the words that were being erased from existence. *It's like they were never written.*

Frankie walked to the front door and unlocked it so Ken could just walk inside. When the three knocks came, he raised his voice. "It's open!"

The door creaked. "What's up, bro?" Ken stomped the snow off his feet. A long black gun case was in his left hand.

"How's it going?" Frankie extended his hand.

Ken shook it firmly. "Not good." He took a few steps inside. "We need to talk."

"Is everything okay?"

"Could be worse," Ken said with a grime smile. "You could be dead or without limbs like some of the guys I know."

"I know," Frankie said, pursing his lips. "I can't complain. I'm grateful that the Lord has—"

Ken put his finger to his lips and set his cellphone on the fireplace mantel. Frankie did the same.

"Can you get me a bottle of water?" Ken asked with a curt nod, gesturing to the door leading to the bunker. "I'm parched."

Frankie led him to the fridge. Grabbing them both a bottle of water, he led him downstairs to the sub-basement, then to the main bunker. In the gunroom, Ken set the gun case down.

"Can I get you to hang on to this for me?" Ken asked. "It's the safest place I can think of."

"No prob," Frankie said and pushed open the false brick wall in the back of the gun room. And then they descended to the RV that was buried twenty feet below ground level. They took a seat at the kitchen table where a chess board was resting with the pieces in a pouch next to it.

"I haven't played chess since before the war," Ken said.

"Let's play a game." Frankie poured out the marble pieces.

"Let's play and talk," Ken said. "I'm in a hurry, and there's things you need to know. Things you need to secretly tell everyone you associate with."

Frankie's eyes widened. "I'm listening." He gave his opponent the white pieces and himself the black.

"First things first." Ken lifted a finger to chest level. "As you know, Grayfeather is wanted for murder and mayhem. I need you to cut all ties, and delete any record of him working here."

Frankie nodded. "I understand," he said. "You should know…Mariani's gone AWOL. I think they fled town together."

"Fuck." Ken sunk his head. "I hope it don't end in a shootout with the cops."

"How do we proceed?" Frankie asked. "W-what can we do?"

"Nothing," Ken said. "When in doubt, do nothing. We need to keep on mission. We're short a guy now. Can't just train someone either."

"Three won't work?"

"I have a contract in the works. A congressman is requesting two bodyguards for an upcoming event, but we'll need four going forward."

"What can I do to help more?" Frankie made the first move with his pawn on the left side of the board.

"Just keep your men on a tight leash," Ken said, and then lifted his rook, setting it down on the right. "We need to get them more training."

"They're on notice," Frankie said and moved another pawn forward. "I told them to clear their schedules. Day and night."

"How long has Mariani been gone?" Ken moved his middle pawn forward.

"A couple months."

"What? Why didn't you tell me?"

Frankie shrugged. "Mariani is a peculiar individual. Sometimes I can't get ahold of him for a month or so. He calls it…hibernation."

"He's a big boy." Ken shook his head. "Hope he makes it out of this one. Anyway, you got to tell your guys to watch what they say at all times."

Frankie drew first blood, killing Ken's white pawn with his own. "I'm on it."

Ken killed Frankie's pawn in retaliation. "This is important to not slip up. The government's eavesdropping dragnet has expanded past phones. The police state is now in full effect. As I told you before, they can record everything you say and do with your cellphone, your computer, and even your TV. If it's new enough.

"I'm telling you this because we can't afford to have any of our guys get red flagged. You need to make sure they understand. It could affect all of us."

"I get it." Frankie lifted his rook for an L-shaped kill. "Big Sister is always listening,"

"Which brings us to the second part," Ken said and swooped down with his bishop to kill Frankie's rook. "This is between me and you. It's classified. Top secret. Tell no one.

"After the new Congress is sworn in next month, they'll have a super majority in the House and Senate. From there on, America will be transformed into something we will not recognize. All new laws will be authoritarian in nature. First Amendment: gone. Second Amendment: gone. Fourth Amendment: gone." He paused to let out and exasperated sigh. "Bro, they killed my source." He paused, his hands balling into fists. Luckily, she made a back-up plan. The new source just made contact. He said the military has been ordered to make plans to confiscate guns and silence anti-government extremists. UN peacekeepers are being shipped in from Haiti as we speak. They plan to eliminate the opposition.

"This is happening fast, Frankie. No matter how bad things get, we need to endure with our mouths shut. The government pays us. We will *Render to Caesar*...because the ends will justify the means."

63

Mt. Caca Island
April 20, 2023

Seth Roth stepped outside his tiki hut and lit up a cigarette. He blew the smoke into the night sky and gazed into the twinkling cosmos. *First Earth, then Mars, then…* His thoughts trailed off as his eighty-nine-year-old brother stepped out from his hut and straightened his white Oxford shirt.

David Roth walked up to Seth with his left hand in his pocket. "That boy was an exceptional ride."

"Did little Secord try to play hard to get?"

"No, he took it. But he cried like a baby."

"How old do you think the kid is?"

David cracked a smile. "Nine or ten. How about your boy?"

"Thirteen is my favorite number. Also, I find the ritual to be less difficult with older boys. Their brown eye of Satan is ripe for the taking."

"How will we celebrate the rest of Chancellor Hitler's birthday?"

"I thought we'd take a long walk down the beach. I have a great deal of top-secret information for you."

*****

Walking barefoot on the white sand beach, Seth stopped and put a new cigarette in his lips. Lighting it up, he blew out a stream of smoke toward the choppy Caribbean Sea. "The round table has decided to cap the pyramid ahead of schedule."

"But doesn't the blueprint call for a ten-year transition?" David Roth questioned the change of plans.

"Yes, but the wise men are confident the American subjects are weak." Seth scanned the line of coconut trees on the edge of the beach, and then stood squarely in front of David. "The first false flag attack will come very soon. After the second, your lovely daughter will sign an executive order banning all guns. After the third, she'll sign executive order nine hundred ninety-nine."

David kicked sand. "That's an aggressive agenda."

"I don't write the mission; I just execute it."

"Indeed. I'll trust the wisdom of the men at the round table."

Seth's smiling lips blew out a puff of smoke. "One year from tonight, we'll sacrifice the youngest Secord under the gaze of the Great Molech."

"And then the pyramid will be capped?"

"That is correct." Seth flicked his cigarette into the sea. "From there, the world will be one, and the liquidation can commence."

"Is the goal still two billion?"

"I believe so. One billion surfs…and one billion imperial subjects."

"A perfect world."

"Just as the blueprint dictates."

"I feel fortunate to help facilitate the plan our ancestors crafted."

Seth lit up another cigarette. "All six masters are pleased with our family's unique capabilities. They look forward to telling you as such at the Capping of the Pyramid Ceremony."

64

The Buccetti Compound
May 28, 2023

Emerging from the dark forest, a man in black made a beeline through Frank Buccetti's backyard. A small duffel bag was swaying at his side. Softly, he ascended the steps that led to the large back deck. Climbing on top of the picnic table, he reached for the roof and tossed his bag on the asphalt shingles. The tall and thin man pulled himself onto the roof. Rising to his feet, he crouched on the slant. *He said the window would be unlocked,* he thought, then lifted the window with one hand. *Dope, I'm in.*

Stepping one foot inside, he grabbed the base of the window frame for balance. Both boots now on the bathroom floor, he set his rectangular bag on the sink and pulled out a small flashlight.

Breathing heavily, his hands shook while he read the map silently. *First door on the left.* He folded the wrinkled paper and put it in his pocket.

Walking slowly, he turned the corner and approached a bedroom door that was half open. He pushed it with his hand and the door creaked. The beam of the flashlight scanned the room, landing on the walk-in closet.

"That's it," he whispered and hit the light switch on the wall.

He stepped forward. On the back wall of the closet was a row of fleece jackets hanging at eye level. Setting the bag on the carpet, he swiped the clothes to the side, revealing a false wood panel wall. On the right side, he found the hidden switch that allowed the narrow door to slide open.

The flashlight lit up the small area. A large safe appeared in the middle of the far wall. It was black with a bronze handle and a digital entry screen. "Time to pop that door off," he mumbled. "See what's inside."

The man dropped to his knees, opened the bag, and looked down, shuffling through the contents until he found what he needed. A mini welding torch.

Quickly screwing the brass nozzle on the tank, he dialed up the gas and clicked the ignition switch. At the roaring sound of the blue flame, the saferoom became bright. He then slipped a small blast shield over his head and approached the safe. Upon lowering the flame to the hinge, orange sparks started shooting in every direction. After a few minutes, the hinge became orange.

His eyes widened as the molten metal started flowing down the safe. Lifting the flame to the top hinge, he increased the power of the flame. More sparks flew for a couple of minutes. Killing the flame, he gently set the torch on the floor. A hammer and chisel appeared in his hand.

*****

Giovanni Mariani parked his car in front of Frankie's garage. A bright flash of flickering light was coming from Frankie's bedroom. Cocking his head to the side, he scrunched up his face. "What the fuck is that?" he asked himself. *Frankie's truck ain't even here.*

After gazing around the premises, he noticed the bathroom curtains were being sucked out of the house and waving in the wind. A sharp rush of adrenaline flowed through him, and he quietly got out of his car. Pulling the black snub nose handgun out of his shoulder holster, he cocked it and trotted forward.

Sprinting across the wet grass, he made it to the side door. With an elevated pulse, Mariani looked in the kitchen window, and then slipped the key in the hole. Slowly leaning into the door, he listened closely. A slight creek and the door was open. His arms extended the gun, and he crept through the dark kitchen. Stepping into the living room, he paused at the sound of metal smashing against metal.

"What the…" He said under his breath. With his widening eyes adjusting to the darkness, he slowly climbed the steps with a pounding heart.

The hallway at the top of the staircase formed a capital T, and the banging noises were coming from the right. The bedroom door was open. The light was on. Creeping toward the racket, he stopped at the entrance of the closet. His eyes exploded at the sight of a tall, wiry stranger with his back to him. *You're dead,* Mariani thought.

"Don't fucking move!" Mariani barked. His gun was trained on the intruder. When the man turned, Mariani met his eyes.

The burglar dropped the hammer and put his hands in front of his face. "Don't shoot!"

"I should put you down right now," Mariani said with a buzz of adrenaline flowing through his body.

"Please." The man's voice was shaky. "It's not what it looks like."

Mariani took a step forward. "Get on your knees. We're doin' this shit execution style."

*****

Frankie's mom handed her son a plate with two pieces of pizza. "This Roth bitch needs to drop dead," Diana scowled. "She smiles as she takes our rights away."

"Mom," Frankie said with a low voice. "Shh." He put his pointer finger to his lips.

"Who the fuck do you think you are?" Diana blurted out. "This is my fucking house. You're eating my food. And I don't like the bitch."

"They're listening, Mom," Frankie said so softly that he thought maybe just maybe the listening devices in her phone and TV couldn't record him. "You have to watch what you say."

Diana laughed hysterically. "HEATHER ROTH IS A WHORE!" Diana screamed louder. "I WANT HER DEAD!"

Frankie quickly stood up and led her to the kitchen by her arm.

"Ouch!" she snipped, yanking her arm loose. "What the fuck is wrong with you? Are you smoking that shit again?"

"Just listen to me for a second." Frankie opened a drawer, grabbed a pen, and then scribbled a note on a piece of paper. "Here, just read it."

"I can't read this," Diana said. "Your handwriting is pathetic. And I don't have my glasses."

"Well, go get them." His hand smacked against his gray slacks.

"They're upstairs."

"Oh, my gosh. Go get 'em."

Diana slowly walked upstairs. When she came back down, she was wearing glasses and lines in her forehead. Inclining her head, she began to read. It took her a minute, then she looked at Frankie and gave a very short laugh. "Who told you this?"

"Just trust me." Frankie took the pen and scribbled out what he wrote, and then he went back to watch the TV.

Diana followed him to the living room. "I don't believe it," she whispered.

"It's just a precaution," Frankie said softly. "That's all."

"I still don't like that stupid bitch." Diana picked up a piece of pizza.

They both gazed at the image of the first female President of the United States on the cable news show. Her shoulder-length silver hair was contrasted by a black pantsuit that looked too big for her. She was laughing and smiling. Her diamond earrings were glinting.

She's the most powerful person in the history of mankind, Frankie thought. *She has under her thumb, the control of every nation on the face of the earth. The United States is her baby that she doesn't love.* He kept thinking of what he wanted to say. *She wants to change America instead of loving her. She wants to rule the people, not lead them. She wants to indoctrinate them, not teach them.*

His thoughts were cut off by a sudden announcement on the television. Pointing at the large digital screen, Frankie stood up and started reading the caption. "Breaking news! Shots fired at a campaign rally for Congressman Traficant from Minnesota." He dropped his jaw in disbelief.

Frankie turned up the volume on the TV: "*Just minutes ago, two gunmen shot their way past security,*" the female reporter said with a trembling voice. "*They stormed in the arena, then took aim at the minority leader and his family.*"

"Mom, I got to go pick up Tara and go home. I love you."
He hugged her tight. "Watch what you say. Please."

*****

Mariani closed the thick, iron blast door of the bunker. Turning
to face his prisoner, he lifted the flashlight into the man's eyes.
"Who sent you?" There was a dark hole in the brick wall
behind the man in question.

"No one sent me," the narrow-faced man said from the
cold cement floor, leaning up against the wall. "I rob a different
house every week." The man shook his duct-taped wrists in
protest. "I'm sorry."

"What type of person do you think I am?" Mariani said
softly. "Do you think I can't break you?"

"You already broke my nose," the burglar said. "What's
next? My arm?"

Mariani tilted his head briefly. "Okay. Your choice." He
jerked the man by the collar of his jacket. Dragging him fifteen
feet inside the tunnel, he let go and dropped to a squat. "No
Miranda Rights in here."

Raising his hand, Mariani hit him on the nose with the butt
of the flashlight. The man rolled on his belly.

"How'd that feel?" Mariani said, poised to hit him again.

"I-I told you; I work alone."

Mariani straddled the burglar's back and scraped his face
on the rough cement floor. And then he grabbed him by the
hair, squishing his head on the cement with both hands.

"Fuck you!"

Mariani punched him in the liver. "Start talking, or I'll
smash your fucking head in."

"Suck my dick."

Mariani pulled out his survival knife. Stradling the man's back, he poked the back of his neck.

"Stop!"

"I'll stop when you tell me who sent you." He broke the skin with the tip of the knife.

"I can't."

Mariani backed off the guy. "All right, I got a better idea." He crawled out of the tunnel. "Don't go nowhere, now. I'll be right back." A few moments later the tunnel went pitch black.

*****

Frankie and Tara walked into Frankie's house. "Do you smell that?" He sniffed.

"Something's burning," Tara said, flicking the light switch on the wall.

 Frankie ran up the stairs and felt a draft. *It's cold,* he thought. What the…

Tara followed him into the master bedroom and stopped. She found Frankie standing by the busted safe, crouched before it, confusion marring his features.

"Someone broke in my safe, but the money's still there."

"That doesn't make sense."

Frankie grabbed the pistol from the safe. "Lock yourself in the saferoom," he said. "I'm gonna search the house."

She wrapped her arms around him. "Be safe." She kissed him. "Do you want me to call the cops?"

"No cops. I'll be okay."

Frankie pivoted on his heel and ran down the stairs. *Who could it be?*

Crossing the living room, Frankie's heart jumped as the basement door handle turned. Stopping on a dime, he lifted the gun, a slight tremor in his hands as he aimed at the door. At the first creak of the door swinging open, Frankie popped off three shots and a figure in black dropped to the carpet, hands going over his head as he yelled out.

"Stop shooting!" Mariani screamed from the floor. "It's me!"

Frankie dropped the gun and ran to his side. "Are you hit?"

Mariani hopped to his feet. "No, but holy shit." He was breathing heavily. "What the fuck are you doing?" His gaze fell on the three holes in the door.

"Man, I'm so sorry." Frankie let out a breath, dropping a hand on Mariani's shoulder. "I-I thought I was shooting at the intruder."

"I'm lucky you got bad aim." Mariani rubbed his chest. "Guess what?"

"What?"

"I caught him in the act."

"Who?" Frankie asked, his head snapping to the opened door that led downstairs. His eyes widening by the second. "Is he dead?"

"Nah, he's in the bunker. Won't tell me who sent—"

Mariani's words were interrupted by a female voice. "Frankie, you okay?"

Frankie walked toward Tara. "I told you to hide in the saferoom."

"I cracked the door and heard voices."

"I almost shot Mariani."

"Who's in the bunker?" Tara asked.

"No one."

"I just heard you guys talking about a guy in the bunker." She pulled out her phone. "Should I call the cops?"

"No!" Frankie lowered his voice. "No cops."

"Why not? What are you gonna do with him?"

Mariani's brow lowered.

*****

From the living room of the bunker, Mariani set two plastic jugs on the table. One large and green. The other, small and black. Antifreeze and motor oil. "You sure she ain't gonna call the cops?"

"I talked to her," Frankie said. "She ain't happy, but she won't call the cops."

"How do you know that?"

"She loves me, and she's Italian. She knows the code."

"I hope you're right, bro," Mariani said. "I'm a little worried." He grabbed the jugs and headed for the gun room. The prisoner was waiting.

In the gun room, Mariani eyed the wall of rifles, stopping to gaze at a black M4-A1 assault rifle with a grenade launcher attached to the barrel. "How the hell did you get this?"

"Ken's stashing it here," Frankie said. "It's fully automatic. Military clearance."

"Nice, I'm gonna have to test this bad boy out sometime," Mariani said. "But right now, my prisoner needs my attention." Marching to the ledger stone wall in the back of the room, he reached for a gray rectangular stone on the right side of the wall. Clicking it down came with a clunk. He then pushed the wall inward, just enough to walk through.

Frankie followed him with the flashlight in his hands. Lighting up the side wall, he found the escape tunnel and aimed the beam in the hole. A man sitting upright started blurting out F-bombs.

Mariani set both jugs on the lip of the tunnel. "Shut the fuck up!" he shouted. Climbing inside, he crouched forward with a jug in each hand, scraping them on the cement.

The man's legs and hands were bound. "Fuck you!" he shouted. "Bitch."

Frankie shook his head and stepped into the tunnel with the flashlight. "Bro, what are you gonna do?"

"What do you think I'm gonna do?"

"I think you're about to make a big mistake." Frankie pictured the force-feeding of antifreeze. And the reality of a dead man in his house.

Mariani craned his neck to face Frankie. "A mistake? This asshole just broke in your house."

"You don't understand; I can't get in any trouble right now. I have a lot on the line."

"You're going soft, bro." Mariani raised his voice. "This dude would have killed you and your girl if it wasn't for me." He pointed, shaking his finger at Frankie. "I think that gives *me* the upper hand."

"I'm not gonna let this go down."

"How ya gonna stop me?"

Frankie let out an audible sigh. "Bro, you don't have to do this. He's a petty thief, not a prisoner of war. Let's just turn him in."

"Bro, this is happening." Mariani bounced the bottle of oil off the burglar's head. "He saw my face. I'm about to feed him some antifreeze. You should leave unless you wanna hold him down for me."

"Torture never works."

"Cuz they don't do it right."

"I'm not gonna be a part of this."

"His people know where you live. They could be coming here right now. We need to find out who sent him."

"They're thieves. Not the Flebotomia cartel. Look at this skinny punk."

"What happened to you, bro? You're acting like a little pussy."

Frankie dropped the flashlight. "You better clean up your mess," he said, turning, and then crouching out of the tunnel.

"Oh, I will!" Mariani shouted. "This ain't my first date!" His attention returned to the man beneath him. "Just me and you, tough guy."

"Let me go…and they won't kill your family." The man was breathing loudly. "They know who you are. You're Giovanni Mariani, Frankie's best friend."

Mariani swore under his breath. "My best friend would be pinning you down right now," he said, grabbing for one of the jugs beside him. Hoisting it up for the burglar to see, he twisted off the cap. "Thirsty?" The cap bounced on the concrete.

"Hold on, hold on."

Gripping the man's head forcibly, he dropped a fist on his already busted nose. "Last chance."

The man groaned in pain.

Kneeling on his chest, Mariani grabbed the man by his hair.

"No!" the man was bucking and thrashing himself as the green liquid splashed on his lips.

Letting go of his hair, Mariani pinched the man's bloody nose. "Stay still, asshole." With his left hand, he started tilting the jug. The green fluid was cascading on his sealed lips.

Mariani heard muzzled groans.

"That's ok." Mariani kept tilting. "You're gonna need some air in about ten seconds."

The safe cracker's eyes were shifting back and forth. The moment the man's lips cracked open, a surge of coolant found the crack. His head shook, but the antifreeze kept coming. After a gurgling noise, the man coughed up green fluid, a few drops landing on Mariani's chin.

Mariani set the jug down and let go of the burglar's nose. "You ready to talk?"

The burglar turned his head and puked green fluid. Coughing deeply, he dry heaved. Then spit. Then dry heaved again. And again. With a green string of drool dripping from his mouth, he kept gagging.

In the beam of the flashlight, steam was rising from the burglar's mouth.

Mariani cleaned the man's eyes and face with a dirty rag. "You're pretty tough, kid. But I'm gonna find out who you're working with." He paused, lighting up a cigarette. "In about two minutes, I'm switching to motor oil. That won't taste as sweet."

"I'm sorry," the man said, panting for air. "I can't tell you. Please, just kill me and get it over with."

"I don't think you understand," Mariani said with a low tone. "Until you cough up the info, there will always be a threat out there." He flicked the cigarette off his face. "Time's up." Grabbing the quart, he twisted the cap.

The man started crying and sniffling.

Mariani pinched the guy's nose. As he tilted the jug, the man began twisting and shaking his head. The oil was splashing off his lips.

"Okay, okay!" he begged, spitting and snapping his head back and forth.

Marinai set the jug down.

"W-whatever you want. Please just stop."

"What's your name?" Mariani growled.

"R-Ryan Lancaster."

"Who sent you?"

Ryan closed his eyes, scrunching up his oil-slicked face. "L-Larry Sobek," he said, breathing heavily. "Frankie's carpenter. I'm his cousin."

Mariani cleaned the oil off Ryan's face with a dirty rag. "You better be telling the truth, or I'll feed you to the rats." Mariani laughed shortly. "And trust me, there *are* rats down here."

"I'm sorry," Ryan said. "It wasn't personal. Larry got extorted by some bad people. He panicked."

"Larry fucked up," Mariani promised. "Give me the address."

"I don't know the address," Ryan said softly. "I'd have to bring ya there."

Marinai pulled out his knife and cut the tape around Ryan's ankles. "All right. Let's go. You try anything, and I'll put a bullet in your ass."

*****

Mariani parked in a dark alley behind Larry Sobek's garage. Pulling out his handgun, he screwed on a large homemade silencer and set it on his lap. He tugged a black ski-mask snug over his head, craning his neck to look at the man in the back seat with duct tape wrapped around his wrists.

"You're gonna hang tight," Mariani said. "If you told the truth, I'll set you free."

"What if his wife answers the door?" Ryan asked.

Mariani knocked him on the head with the butt of the gun. "You didn't say nothing about a wife."

Ryan shook his head. "Please don't kill her. Not the kids either."

"Kids? How old?"

"Five and ten."

Mariani lowered his voice to a growl. "Who else will be in there?"

"As far as I know, it's just him and his family."

Mariani pointed the pistol at Ryan. "Don't give me a reason to put a hole in your head."

"Trust me." Ryan shook his head. "I-I don't want to die."

"I don't trust people." Mariani pushed open the door and stepped out.

The grass was wet. The entire backyard was thick with trees and leafy bushes. Sprinting to the side of the house, Mariani scraped his jacket against the wood siding all the way to the front. He listened closely. Peeking around the corner, he saw a blue glow in the window and heard the TV. *The moment of truth.*

Mariani stepped on the front porch, raised his knuckle, and knocked three times.

A dog started barking. *He didn't say nothing about a dog either,* he thought. *Now I'm gonna have to dump him in the swamp. Or maybe I'll cremate him in Ivan's furnace.*

The door creaked open.

Mariani tucked his gun close to his chest. Taking a deep breath, he moved in a single, smooth motion. Shouldering into the door, he charged forward. Gun pointed straight ahead, he had time to watch the lone figure duck to the floor.

"Oh God. Don't shoot. Please, don't..."

Aiming his gun, Mariani's eyes narrowed, his finger pulsing on the trigger.

The sudden inclusion of a low growl interrupted him. Turning, Mariani found the source of the sound: a large rottweiler running at him.

Squeezing the trigger three times, the dog dropped and let out a high-pitched yelp. The silencer had muffled the shots. Shifting back to the man, he took step closer. "What's your name? Don't lie."

"Larry Sobek!"

"Where's your wife?"

"She left me."

"Good." Mariani held Larry at gunpoint. "You tried to rob the wrong mother fucker."

"I'm sorry," he said, his breath rushing to push out his words. "I had no choice. A corrupt UN peacekeeper pulled me over. He said I have one week to pay him ten thousand, or he'd kill my family. Frankie is the only one I know with cash like that."

"You definitely had a choice," Mariani said, and his weapon clacked three more times. "I'm the one who didn't have a choice."

65

The Buccetti Compound
June 11, 2023

Hiking side by side with Frankie on a narrow path, Tara Barini brushed her hand against a pine tree. "That's not it. I just think the world would be safer without guns."

"Babe, the Traficant Bill abolishes all guns," Frankie said. "And that's just the beginning. That's what I'm trying to tell you. These people are hell-bent on global domination."

"Don't be crazy." She playfully shoved him into a thornbush.

"Damn, girl." He plucked a clump of pricker balls from his shirt and held it in his hand. "You need to inform yourself before it's too late."

"I am informed," she said. "But unlike you, I don't get my information from a tinfoil hat conspiracy theorist like Luke Easton."

Frankie flashed a smile. "Where do you get your information from?"

"Mostly on the internet. I'm so busy at the hospital these days, I don't have time for much else."

The trail split in two. Frankie stopped at the fork in the road. "We've never really talked politics. I-I guess I keep my thoughts about government to myself. I'm not anti-government. But I think liberty needs checks and balance. And someone has to put them in check…before government gets too big."

"Who? You?"

"No. I'm just saying, this regime is out of control. I hope someone stops them."

She spread apart her arms. "Out of control? Maybe the abolition of guns might seem extreme to some people, but the economy is setting records. The unemployment rate is low. And Roth ended the problem of homelessness in America."

"Forget about it. I can tell you drank the punch."

Tara's head snapped back. "Punch? Who do you think you are, anyway?"

"Let's take a step back." Frankie held up one hand. "We disagree on politics. Big deal. The problem *is* that some people can't tolerate other people's views. And someday…it might become a crime to think differently."

"So, you think someone should assassinate the president?"

"Shhh." Frankie put his finger to his lips. "I said no such thing, and you know it."

Tara pointed her finger in Frankie's direction. "You might not be a terrorist, but you kind of think like one. But what's really bugging me is what your friend Giovanni did to that man in your basement. He killed him, didn't he?"

"No." Frankie's eyes darted to the side.

"I knew it. I should have called the cops."

"If you *ever* call the cops, Mariani *will* find you."

Tara gave Frankie the middle finger. "You just threatened me." Her finger extended closer to his face. "We're done." She turned in the dirt and started walking back toward the house.

"It's not a threat." Frankie raised his voice. "It's a fact. Do *not* call the cops."

She turned back. "You asshole." Charging at him, she hissed and started clawing at his face.

Frankie wrapped her up in his arms and squeezed tightly. "Calm the fuck down. Okay?"

Tara thrashed her legs and bit his hand. "Let me go!"

"Ouch!" Frankie dropped her at his feet. "What's wrong with you!" He tossed the clump of prickers in her hair.

Tara bounced up with tears in her eyes. "Don't ever threaten me again. You don't know what I've been through."

"I don't want to fight you, Tara."

"Bring me fucking home. You drove me here."

Frankie tossed her the keys to his truck. "It's yours. Severance package. Never say a word."

"Don't worry, Frank. I'll keep your skeletons in my closet. I think I'll throw a camper on my new truck." Her eyes were squinting. "The hospital owes me vacation time. I'm going camping. Something you would never do with me."

66

Duluth, Minnesota
July 14, 2023

Driving down the road, Ken Spatz heard his satellite phone vibrating in the center console of his truck. *Here we go,* he thought as he tapped the brakes. Grabbing the phone, he pulled over to the side of the road. This call demanded undivided attention and extra precautions.

"Hello," Ken flung open the door and started walking away from his truck.

"Are you confident in your surroundings?" the unknown male voice asked.

"I'm on foot." Ken turned his head over his shoulder, then back forward as he picked up the pace.

"Codeword: Valley Forge.

"Affirmative. Codeword: Mount Vernon, sir." Ken's breaths were audible.

"Affirmative." The admiral's voice lowered to a growl. "Listen very carefully. I don't have time to repeat myself. The new congressman from Minnesota is going to hire a security team. I need you to apply ASAP. My person on the inside will doctor their digital resume and make sure your team gets the job."

Ken pressed the phone to his ear. "Yes, sir."

The man cleared his throat. "The governor will appoint Eugene Parker next week."

"I understand, sir." Ken let out a heavy sigh.

"This could be the connection we've been waiting for. Parker is tight with the Queen of Spades. Everything is depending on you, soldier."

"I won't let you down, sir."

67

St. Paul, Minnesota
August 1, 2023

From inside a black limousine, Congressman Eugene Parker was pressing his phone against his ear. Brice and Dennis were sitting on the seat facing the congressman. Because of the long phone call, he had not said a word to either of them on the entire ride from the suburbs to the capitol building.

"You look pretty in that suit," Brice said softly to Dennis with a wink and a crooked smile.

Dennis snorted and shook his head.

Brice straightened his black tie. "Just kidding, cuz. You look dapper."

As the limo pulled up to the capitol building, Congressman Parker slipped his phone into his pocket. "I appreciate your service," the congressman said to Brice and Dennis. "It was short notice, but this is an important event."

Brice nodded in return. "It's my honor, sir."

Dennis opened the door. Stepping outside, he shielded his face from the sunlight as he scanned the crowd.

Brice got out behind him. Turning to face the congressman, he waved him out of the vehicle.

Congressman Parker waved to the cheering crowd. The limo drove off, and then the congressman walked between his guards to the podium where he shook hands with the governor of Minnesota, two senators, and four members of Congress.

Brice and Dennis joined the other security guards on the side of the granite steps. Another hundred police officers with yellow vests mixed with the throng of people. Circling the perimeter, dozens of UN peacekeepers in camouflage uniforms and pale blue helmets were standing with long guns at the ready. Snipers were on the rooftops. Drones were watching from above as Congressman Parker spoke from behind the podium.

"It is the *honor* of my life to fill the seat of Congressman Traficant," Parker shouted into the microphone. "Thank you for trusting me with this seat, Governor Peck. I will vote and advocate on behalf of the first female President of the United States. I will support her agenda one hundred percent!" He paused for the crowd to cheer.

Dennis yawned.

*****

Halfway through Congressman Parker's speech, Brice took his eyes off the crowd because the congressman's fast hand gestures looked Hitleresque.

"The threat to America is real!" Parker said, pausing to let the crowd roar. "As your congressman, I will do everything in my power to liquidate this cowardly enemy. The anti-government terrorists and those who give comfort to them will be hunted down like vermin." His right hand tapped his chest before shooting out to full extension.

Brice's head shifted to the left. Protesters were holding white signs with the word Roth in a red circle, and a red diagonal line was crossing out the word. *Oh, she does have an opposition,* Brice thought. The anti-Roth protesters were massing near the barrier that was guarded by a line of UN peacekeepers.

The peaceful protesters were now face-to-face with the soldiers. Those in front started pushing the guards. The men in blue helmets pushed back. The protesters were now shoving.

The congressman stopped speaking. *What the…*

Several protesters wearing black garb breached the security line. Brice and Dennis drew their guns. The protesters dropped their signs and ran toward the podium. Backpacks were strapped to their backs. Each man was holding something small in their hands.

Dennis started shooting rapidly.

Brice tackled the congressman. Reaching up, he tipped over the podium for cover.

Dennis fired two more shots, and then jumped behind the podium to reload. The wounded attacker detonated his device and exploded into a giant fireball. Shrapnel shot out in every direction. Two more attackers detonated their bombs simultaneously. The fireball expanded.

68

Buccetti Compound
August 2, 2023

Frankie's one hour of sleep on the sofa was interrupted at 7:00 a.m. His satphone was ringing on the coffee table. Rolling over on the couch, he grabbed the buzzing phone and pressed the green button. "Hello," Frankie said, sitting upright on the couch, staring into the TV. *200 dead at the Minnesota Capitol Building,* he read the caption on the screen. *Including the governor and two members of Congress.*

"Are you sitting down?" Ken asked.

"Yeah," Frankie said. "What's up? Are they okay?"

"No," Ken said with a low tone. "Um…it's not looking good at all. Brice and Dennis are in critical condition. The doctor doesn't think either of them will make it. They're on…life support."

"Oh, my God." Frankie dropped his head, his breaths speeding up. Clenching his free hand, Frankie's blood burned. Breathing didn't seem like enough. Fury raged as he turned blindly, reaching for something, anything to break. A coffee glass. "Fuck!" He smashed it against the fireplace.

"They saved Congressman Parker's life. They killed a handful of terrorists. Your men are heroes."

Frankie sat down on the couch. "I can't believe it."

"I'm sorry. I know you were close with them guys."

Frankie stood up. "I ain't giving up, yet." His voice was a low growl. "I've seen Brice wake from the dead before."

"We need to go over some paperwork. How soon can we meet?"

"Right now."

"Two hours. Same spot as last time."

*****

From deep in Frankie's bunker, Ken Spatz poured a glass of whiskey. "Their plan is in motion," he said gravely. "The decision has been made. The New World Order is about to take its mask off."

"Prison Planet?" Frankie asked, his eyebrows low.

"They're about to tighten the noose," Ken said. "Once the nation is disarmed, it will be too late." He took a swig from the glass. "And, even if we could get close, we have no men."

"We still got Vadik," Frankie said. "And we could find more."

"It's too late to train them. The congressman needs security right now. He'll go elsewhere."

"You got training. You and Vadik could do it."

Ken shook his head. "I've been a soldier my entire adult life. I bought this business to be the general, not the assassin."

"I was just coming up with ideas, man."

"Do you know what happens if I ended up like Brice and Dennis?"

"What?"

"The mission is over. That's what." Ken met Frankie's eyes.

Frankie shrugged. "Well, we don't have a lot of options. Do we?"

"No, we don't." Ken rubbed his forehead. "And one guy ain't enough. Fuck, I'm gonna have to do it." He slammed the bottom of his fist on the table. "Fuck!"

"What can I do to help?"

"Nothing. My source won't talk to anyone but me."

"Why can't you get the info, relay it to me, and then go on the job?"

"Sure, I can do that now. But when the big job comes, my commanders would need me to transmit info in real-time. With all due respect, they won't speak to you."

Frankie's left hand opened. "Let's worry about that when the time comes."

"How bout I give you something to worry about now?" Ken finished his drink and poured another. "During Martial Law, the Constitution and the Bill of Rights are null and void. The regime can do anything they want. It's only a matter of time before they start rounding up the opposition."

"Do you think American soldiers would round up their own people?"

"The puppet masters pulling the strings have foreseen this problem: sympathetic soldiers. They plan to deploy America's military to hot spots throughout the world. UN peacekeepers will enforce law and order on the homeland."

"What about underground militias?" Frankie asked. "The patriots?"

"Any force that has any strength will be labeled terrorists, and destroyed with drones or fighter jets."

"What, are they gonna round up Christians like Nazis did the Jews?"

Ken shook his head. "No. This enemy is too cunning for that, too subtle to round people up. No, no. They will order every American to have a computer chip put in their right hand," he said, pausing to point to the fatty spot between the thumb and pointer finger on his hand. "Anyone without the chip will be deemed a terrorist, and evacuated to prison camps where they'll be 'liquidated.' Just like Congressman Parker said. Christians who are true believers will refuse to get the chip.

"Those whose faith is weak, or those like us who have to survive will render to Caesar, and welcome the chip."

"Whoa, whoa, whoa," Frankie said and put his hands up to interrupt. "I can't do that."

"You have to, Frankie," Ken said, letting out a breath. "Or we already lost."

"That's a hard pill to swallow," Frankie said. "It's a one-way ticket to hell."

Ken spread apart his hands. "The chip will come out after the mission is accomplished."

Frankie shook his head. "I can't."

"It's essential none of us raise suspicion. We're in the heart of Congressman Parker. And we want to keep it that way. We don't need any distractions."

"Under the radar." Frankie let out a breath and dropped his head.

"You have to. We're almost there, brother."

"Fine."

69

Virginia, Minnesota
August 5, 2023

Katrina looked out the peephole in her front door. A bald head with blue eyes was staring at her. *Giovanni,* she thought, reaching for the doorknob, the lock, and then the doorknob again. Opening the door, she met his eyes. "I thought I'd never see you again."

"I shouldn't have left like that," Mariani said. "I'm sorry."

"I'm really happy to see you," Katrina said, waving him in. "But, why are you really here?"

Mariani walked in the door and shut it behind him. "Look, I might be in trouble with the law. I got two options. Drive until I find a new place to live, or…"

"Or what?"

"I had some time to think about what you said. About loyalty. You told me to imagine how loyal you'd be…to the man who killed your abuser." He took a step toward her. "So, I imagined it."

"What did you imagine?"

Mariani lit up a cigarette. "Sometimes it feels like I can't trust my own friends. I think they have higher loyalties. Bigger obligations. I need someone who stays loyal to me." He pointed at his chest.

"And you think I'm that gal?"

"That's what I'm here to find out."

Katrina smiled. "If you respect me, I'll give you the world. That's all I ask."

"You already earned my respect." Mariani stuck out his hand. "Now you have to earn my trust."

Katrina shook it. "How do we start?"

"I need to fake my death."

70

Philadelphia, Pennsylvania
August 13, 2023

Congressman Eugene Parker was sitting across from President Roth in the Oval Office. "Madam President," he said. "The protests are getting out of control. I'm afraid some of them are becoming riots. What if they start an uprising? Or a revolution?"

"That would be good," President Roth said, leaning forward. "That's exactly what I want. Through chaos, we gain order. Each protest that becomes violent in nature…helps our cause. We'll label them terrorists, and crush them into submission."

"I understand, but what if—"

Roth raised a menacing hand, cutting him off. "Let me show you, Congressman Parker." She spun her laptop computer to face him. The screen was showing aerial footage from a drone above the U.S. Capitol Building. Thousands of protesters were massing right up against a barrier guarded by blue helmet peacekeepers.

President Roth picked up her satphone, dialed a number, and then pressed the speakerphone button. It rang twice.

"At your service, Madam Roth," Lieutenant Burr said.

"Good afternoon, Lieutenant," Roth said to a member of a secret branch of military intelligence. "Execute Order 101."

"Yes, Your Grace."

"I need it done…immediately."

"You should start seeing results within the hour."

"Make it ten minutes. Or I'll have your head." She hung up the phone.

Parker let out a breath, glancing at the president. "Madam Roth, may I ask what Order 101 is?"

"Congressman Parker, as we speak, the Christian terrorists are protesting in front of the U.S. Capitol Building here in Philadelphia, *and* capitol buildings in almost every major city. We have operatives in the crowds, the Capitol Police, and the UN peacekeeping force. Explosives have been planted in the doorways. And someone on the inside will accidentally prop a door open. Our people embedded in the protest will gin up the crowd and instigate aggression. Some of the peacekeepers will step aside and wave protesters in."

In less than ten minutes, the computer screen showed a throng of protesters in front of the capitol building breach the perimeter and climb the steps.

With a remote, President Roth zoomed in. The river of people was bottlenecking in the front doors of the capitol building.

Congressman Parker was covering his mouth with his hand, watching the stampede of angry protesters march into the capitol of the nation. Suddenly, an explosion flashed from the entry way. Fire and black smoke followed. Bodies were scattered. Survivors were running. Peacekeepers were shooting.

Roth closed the laptop. "You just witnessed a violent insurrection. And it was organized in ten capitol buildings at the same time. That's an act of war. The Christian terrorists have now become an existential threat to national security.

They must be stopped. And the citizens must give up a little bit of freedom for the promise of security."

71

Duluth, Minnesota
August 15, 2023

Cruising up a steep hill in his new black truck, Frankie turned the radio up a few notches and listened closely to his favorite radio host, Luke Easton sound off.

"My friend just sent me a video from the capitol building riot the other day," Easton said through Frankie's speakers. *"I'm sharing this with you because the mainstream news channels left a very important part out. I'm going to try to post it on social media, but I guarantee they'll shut me down. So, I'll just tell my twenty million listeners right now. Never forget, you folks got it here first."* Luke let out an audible sigh, and then he continued. *"Okay, it shows an out-of-control protest that spills over into the capitol building. And then...out of nowhere...there's a huge explosion. Dozens of protesters...dead. Just like that. And then missiles started raining down from the sky. I can hear gunshots. And they want us to believe these people blew themselves up —"*

There was a moment of pause, and then Easton spoke. *"Folks, there is a m-man who just entered my studio. He has a gun with a silencer. I-I'm not kidding."* His heavy breaths were heard by millions. *"I-I always said I'd let you know when to panic. That time is now."* His words sped up. *"The regime is going to silence the op —"* Radio silence was followed by a radio advertisement.

Frankie swallowed hard. Pressing on the gas, he hopped in the fast lane, heading to his house on the outskirts of town.

Reaching for his phone, he dialed Vadik's number and pressed it to his ear.

"Hello," Vadik Domechev said.

"Hey, are you busy?" Frankie asked.

"Kinda. Just got back to town. Been working with the guy all weekend. Crazy shit."

"I know. Can I get you to stop up? I need your help with something."

"I'm on the way."

*****

Frankie sat down in the living room of the bunker, and Vadik plopped down on the sofa, making himself comfortable.

"What's up?" Vadik asked.

"Shit's about to hit the fan," Frankie insisted. "An assassin just killed America's most listened to radio host live on the air. They have no shame. Dictatorship is coming, and we're not prepared. Grayfeather's gone. Brice and Dennis are still in the hospital. That means...I need *you* on top of your game. I know you been doing good on all levels. I'm proud of you. But going forward, there will come a day that the weight of the free world will fall on your shoulders. And we're all going to be counting on you to do what it takes to succeed. I'm confident in you, brother. I just want to express your importance. You're like...the last best hope for mankind. Do you understand the stakes?"

Vadik's eyebrows raised. "Frank. I've never been better. I'm dead sober. I'm focused. I run five miles a day. Two hundred push-ups. I've been training hard with Ken. And I'm still practicing Jujitsu. Throw me in coach. I'm ready."

"You're already in. Congressman Parker is close with Roth. It's only a matter of time."

72

The White House
Philadelphia, Pennsylvania
August 23, 2023

President Heather Roth was standing behind a black podium in the East Room of the White House. Her silver hair was cropped short, just above the shoulders of her oversized black suit coat. Two armed soldiers in black stood erect at her sides. A long bright red carpet with gold trim was shooting out behind her. Looking directly into the camera, it zoomed in, and then her cherry-red lips began to part.

"Good evening, citizens of America," President Roth said eloquently under the gloom of a dim red light. "I requested your attention tonight about a matter that has plagued America as of late. Anti-government Christian extremists have declared war on America. They have used weapons of war to assassinate President Andrews and Congressman Traficant. They used suicide bombers to kill Governor Peck, three members of congress, and hundreds of innocent men and women at the capitol building in St. Paul, Minnesota. And less than two weeks ago, these cowardly terrorists invaded the U.S. Capitol Building here in Philadelphia, Pennsylvania, *and* twelve other capitol buildings across America. After this invasion, the belligerent aggressors detonated bombs in each capitol building simultaneously. These heinous attacks on democracy killed dozens of UN peacekeepers and six members of Congress. These enemy combatants have established hundreds of sleeper cells all across the nation. And they are plotting as we speak.

"All twenty intelligence agencies have warned me…that *this* terrorist network has recently acquired biological weapons. I've seen the evidence. They plan to release a deadly biological agent any day. Given this unfortunate information, I have no choice as commander in chief, but to eliminate this threat to democracy. This was the hardest decision I've ever made, but my generals and military advisors have told me that we must thrust forward immediately.

"Right now, you're probably wondering what does this mean for me? You're probably wondering what you can do for your country?

"The answer is: If you comply with the state, and give up a little freedom for a thousand years of peace and security, then your lives will change very little. On the other hand, if you choose to walk with the terrorists, then you will meet their fate.

"For two thousand years, religions have committed every atrocity known to man in the name of their fabled religion. Genocide, slavery, and wars of aggression, all have been perpetrated in the name of God. I have painfully come to the conclusion, that *God* is a myth. There is no God, there is only the universe.

"America, I want you to gaze out to the night sky. You'll see that the stars are in alignment, the moon is full, and the solar system is ready for a new and evolving world order — free of religion.

"If you were a Christian yesterday or today, you can be forgiven for your crimes against humanity. Right here, right now, I fully pardon every Christian who is willing to discard their Bible and volunteer to implant our new Universal Identification System. Information will be sent to every household in the coming weeks. This is your duty as a citizen. It's for the greater good.

"After a designated amount of time has been given to receive this ID, UN peacekeepers will go door to door to check each house for terrorists. This chip in your hand will be the only way to prove you are not an enemy of the state. It will prove you are not a Christian, Jew, or Muslim.

"Why is this chip important? Because no terrorist will ever allow this chip to be inserted inside their body. They think it would go against their Bible. And a terrorist would not want their movements tracked. Now, if you're not a terrorist, what do you have to hide? If you live an honest hard-working life, or if you choose to be a ward of the state, then *you* will live in peace for the rest of your life.

"This chip." She held a tiny RFID chip in her fingers. "This chip will end all crime, end paper currency, end the need for a wallet or a purse. It will end poverty. You will no longer need a driver's license, a credit card, or a government food card. Your children will never get abducted because we will track them, the very moment they are reported missing. Take this chip and you will receive a stimulus payment of two thousand credits on your account!

"Follow your Big Sister...and together...we will bring forth a new civilization that will triumph for a thousand years.

"Please be wise when it comes to your reaction to the necessary change. Be smart, stay calm, and utopia will await you all. Goodnight, my village. Sweet dreams." President Roth kissed the tips of her fingers, blew into the camera, and then turned for the dark wood door at the end of the long hallway.

73

Duluth, Minnesota
September 9, 2023

Sitting in his mom's dank basement, Frankie hit the table. "Mom, you gotta do it," he said. "No options."

"You really think I'd put the mark of the beast in my body?" Diana asked, then laughed a short laugh. "Never! Did you hear me? Never!"

"You don't understand," Frankie said. "They'll take you away and do God knows what."

"All you think about is your earthly needs," Diana said.

"Mom," he said, lowering his voice as if someone could possibly hear. "It's bigger than just us. There's a lot on the line. The forces of good need patriots like me. Someone has to fight this enemy through stealth and cunning."

"You're gonna fight them?" Diana laughed again. "You already lost. Look at us, hiding in the basement so no one can hear us talking shit about our evil government."

Frankie pointed his finger in her direction. "Never doubt me, Mom."

"I'm not putting a chip in my body!" Diana said and looked at Russel. "And neither is he."

"Huh?" Russel said. "What did you say?"

"I said: you ain't getting no fucking chip in your hand," Diana barked. "What, are you deaf?"

"Leave him be, Mom," Frankie said. "I'm trying to help you. Don't you get it? They'll kill you."

"You're not trying to help me," Diana snipped. "You're trying to tempt me. The demon has penetrated your heart with flaming darts of evil. He has a stronghold of your soul, and I'm not going to be tempted." She stormed upstairs.

74

Duluth, Minnesota
October 5, 2023

Rolling into the parking lot of the high school he graduated from, Frankie Buccetti parked his truck facing the school that now served as a chip implementation center. A dozen vehicles were parked next to them. Three of which were black patrol cars that had UN license plates.

"Haven't been here for a long time," Frankie said. "What are the odds of this being the place we get the chip?"

Vadik Domechev unbuckled his seatbelt. "I can't believe we're doing this, bro," he said, pressing his hands on his face.

"This is gonna suck," Frankie said, gazing at the red, white, and blue flag that was waving in the wind. A dark gray sky was funneling above.

"You've been warning me about the chip since we were kids," Vadik admitted.

"As a kid, conspiracy theories pulled me in." Frankie let out a breath. "After twenty years of no chip, I started having doubts. But in the back of my head, I always knew it would happen sooner or later."

Vadik was gazing at the front doors of the school. "And here we are. The moment of truth. The point of no return."

"I hate it. But if we're gonna infiltrate the system, we have to blend in. We can't make waves. We have to swim through shit, or sink to the bottom."

"I hope your plan works."

"Do you have any last questions about the chip?"

"We went over everything pretty good," Vadik said. "You sure wearing a glove will muffle the voice recorder?"

"That's what Ken's source in the military said. But now we're about to find out."

"We sure will."

"My advice would be: watch what you say. If it's not treasonous, you'll be fine. When we have our meetings, we'll take other measures, too: loud music, wrap our hands with towels, and maybe submerge our hands in water. Sometimes we'll have to write down our thoughts. Just remember — every step you take, every word you say, every dollar you spend *will* be recorded. They can't keep tabs on every person all the time, but the recording will be used against you in the new court of law."

"I love Big Sister," Vadik said, playfully smacking Frankie's black fleece jacket.

They met eyes and then exited the truck.

"Any word on Mariani?" Vadik hollered over the wind.

Frankie stopped walking. Turning to face him, he shook his head. "No. No one can find him. It's like he fell off the map. *Again.* I talked to his mom: she's starting to get worried."

"Man," Vadik said. "I hope he's okay. I love that dude."

"He'll be all right." Frankie started walking toward the school. "Probably didn't want to get the chip."

"It's like the crew is on its last leg. G and Grayfeather are missing. Brice and Dennis are still recovering."

Frankie sunk his head. "Man, I feel bad for them guys. Glad they made it, though."

"It could have been me. Makes me think, ya know what I'm saying?"

"I'm sorry, bro. I can't believe I put my friends up to this."

"Don't talk like that. You gave us a great opportunity to make money. Now we're on a path to—"

Frankie cut him off with a "Pssst." Looking ahead, he saw the entrance of their old high school. Two extremely dark-skinned UN peacekeepers stood guard. They were both wearing camouflage uniforms. One was tall and stout with a baby blue beret, and the other looked malnourished with a pale blue helmet strapped to his head. "I'm starting to think we got in over our heads."

The tall muscular guard opened the door. "Welcome," he said with a strong tropical accent. "Please, take a seat. I bring clipboard. Application." The beard on his face was neatly trimmed.

"Thank you," Frankie said and they found the back row of chairs up against the wall.

The large common area was lined with a few dozen chairs. Only a handful were occupied. Mostly women and young children. The room was surprisingly quiet.

"Them people look scared," Frankie whispered.

"I'm scared." Vadik pursed his lips. "This ain't right."

The same peacekeeper approached them with two clipboards in his hands. "Fill this out," he said, handing them each an application and pen. "When complete, give to woman at window." He leaned inward, opening his protuberant eyes wider, almost like he was trying to intimidate them. "Good day, mate." He then turned around and returned to his post at the entrance.

Frankie's eyes lowered to the paper form. Grabbing the pen, he began filling in his name, birthdate, and address. Below the contact information was a series of questions.

"Do you feel safe at home?" Frankie read the first question quietly.

"Do you have firearms in your home?" Vadik read the second question.

"Did you vote for President Roth in 2020?"

The white clock on the wall ticked a quarter of an hour before they completed the five-page application. Frankie rose to his feet and Vadik did the same. They walked in a line to the brick wall with a window. Frankie slid the clipboard under the thick bullet-proof glass.

Behind the window, a wrinkled gray-haired woman received the paperwork. Glancing at them, she pointed down a hallway on their right. "Head that way. A nurse will escort you to the operating room."

"Thank you," Frankie said and they slowly walked toward the well-lit hallway.

The white floor was shiny, just the way Frankie remembered it from the last time he walked down that hall. The red lockers still lined each side of the long hallway. The trophy glass was still there, but the championship trophy Frankie won now appeared only as a foggy memory as he walked by.

Their past was now behind them. A tall female nurse was walking in front. And they followed her to the future.

Frankie walked into room 101. Vadik 102.

Frankie's eyes flickered from the elevated bed to the small desk with a laptop computer resting on the surface. Sitting down in a chair next to the desk, Frankie's jaw dropped at the sight of a digital poster projecting a 3D President Roth. In her right hand she held a golden pyramid, and on top of the pyramid was a small triangle with an All-Seeing Eye that never stopped staring at him. (Except for when it blinked once every minute.)

THE EYE SEES EVERYTHING, the caption read at the top. *THE PYRAMID WILL SOON BE CAPPED!* It read at the bottom.

Frankie's jaw dropped. *Holy shit*, he thought. *They have no shame.*

There was a sudden knock at the door, and then it creaked open. Frankie's heart sank, and his head snapped to the middle-aged man in the doorway.

"Good afternoon," the doctor said, his blank face pale against his white lab coat. After he closed the door, he sat down in front of the computer. Adjusting his black-framed glasses, he turned to study Frankie who was massaging his hands nervously. "Mr. Buccetti," he said. "Thanks for finally submitting. What took you so long to comply?"

"Uh...I-I'm super busy with work," Frankie said, his breaths speeding up by the second.

The doctor leaned toward the computer screen. "Yes, I see you are a successful man." He typed something on the keyboard. "Two businesses, ten properties, stocks, sovereign bonds." The doctor nodded his head. "Most impressive. Do you have any questions before we proceed?"

"I-I just want to know what I'm getting myself in to. I've never done anything like this before."

"It's nothing," the doctor said, tilting his hand to show Frankie the red dot that glowed through his skin. "It takes a minute to insert, but it will be with you for the rest of your life. It will register you to buy or sell goods. It will serve as your driver's license, Universal ID, *and* bank card. A wallet will no longer be useful to you."

"Thanks." Frankie opened his hands. "But, does it listen to my conversations?"

"I'll send you home with a pamphlet," the doctor said, snapping on blue surgical gloves. "This won't hurt at all."

"Time for the chip, huh?" Frankie let out a breath.

The doctor showed Frankie a small devise that looked like a silver gun. "Give me your right hand."

Frankie did as he was told.

"For the first week, your hand will feel a little uncomfortable," the doctor said. "Like a sliver in your skin. But afterward, you won't even notice it."

The doctor started rubbing a wet cotton swab on the meaty part between Frankie's thumb and forefinger. "This will numb it, so the Novocain shot won't hurt as much." The doctor grabbed a big needle. "Can you feel it starting to get numb?"

"Oh yeah," Frankie said and turned his head.

"Good," the doctor said and poked his hand, slowly pressing the injector down. "Now just relax for a minute or two."

Frankie's eyebrows lowered. "Okay."

"Mr. Buccetti, you seem a little nervous. Don't you trust President Roth?"

Frankie cracked a smile. "Yes…sir. I love the Dear Leader. She is…the last best hope for mankind."

"Good," the doctor said and grabbed his hand. "Keep your hand steady. I'm going to insert the chip and scan it into the system. Then you're free to go."

75

The Buccetti Compound
October 30, 2023

After a long day and a hardy dinner, Frankie laid back on the couch in his living room. No fake news. No complaining girlfriend. No nagging mother. Just silence. Deep thought.

Just as Frankie shut his eyes, his shoulder jerked at the sound of people walking up the steps on the front porch. Swinging his feet to the carpet, four loud knocks at the door jolted his heart. "What the...."

Sprinting for the front door, he looked out the small narrow window. It was Mariani, Gordon Grayfeather, and a younger-looking woman with black hair who he did not recognize.

Frankie scrambled for the lock, frenzied to let them in.

Opening the door, Frankie pressed a finger to his lips. "Shhh," he said, pointing to his hand, turning to grab an insulated glove from a small table next to the door. He then waved them inside. The boys nodded in understanding.

"What's up, Strunz?" Mariani said. "Long time no see, brother."

Frankie wrapped a thick towel around his gloved hand. "I got the chip, but I'm told the glove muffles voices. I take extra precaution though." Frankie embraced his old friend. "Where ya been?"

"You don't wanna know," Mariani said, gesturing to the lady. "But the good news is…I got a new girlfriend." He rested a hand on his lady's back. "Katrina, this is my brother from another mother, Frank Buccetti."

"Nice to meet you." Frankie shook her hand.

"I've heard a lot about you," Katrina said, studying the luxurious home.

"I hope it was all good," Frankie said. "Happy to have you on the team." Frankie turned to brace himself from Grayfeather who was approaching him in a playful fighting stance.

Grayfeather relaxed his posture, showing his bare right hand. "We're chip-free, bro." He smiled, snatching Frankie up in a bear hug before dropping him on his feet. "And we're actually dead. Should be in the newspaper tomorrow."

Frankie put a finger to his lips. "Let me give ya a tour of the house." He led them down the first flight of stairs and gestured to the pool table. "This is my rec room. No appliances down here." He gave a half-shrug. "It always feels like Big Sister is listening to me upstairs."

"It's that bad?" Mariani asked with a tone of disbelief. "I could see phones. But TVs?"

"Ken said any modern appliances have RFID chips. Just like in my hand."

Katrina sat on a stool at the bar behind the pool table. "This is nice down here. Its peaceful."

"Thanks," Frankie said. "Make yourself at home. The scotch is for guests. Water in the fridge."

Grayfeather grabbed the bottle and poured himself a drink. "I like your house, man."

Frankie tilted a hand. "Thanks, you've only seen the tip of the pyramid," he said, letting out a sigh. "So, what happened to you guys? How did you die?"

Mariani squinted one eye. "The three of us got drunk. And then I drove my SUV off Skyline Parkway. Piece of shit caught on fire at the bottom. A fucking tragedy."

"When did this happen?"

"Tonight," Grayfeather said. "We lit the fire about an hour ago. It was kinda fun pushing it off the cliff."

"Tonight?" Frankie plopped his hand on his forehead. "Holy crap. Who was in the Jeep?"

Mariani put up a hand. "Don't worry, bro. We went grave digging up in Hibbing."

"Worry?" Frankie's eyebrows were arching, but his voice remained calm. "I mean, I owe you my life and everything, but damn, bro. I can't afford any heat, right now."

"I'm sorry, brother," Grayfeather said. "We had nowhere else to go. But trust me, if the UN peacekeepers come up in here, I ain't going down without a fight."

Frankie swallowed his contempt for the predicament. "Let's hope it never comes to that." Glancing at Grayfeather, he saw the big man's eyebrow twitch, and then his upper lip began to curl. "How will they identify the bodies in the Jeep?"

"The Jeep's in my name," Mariani said. "Katrina left her ID and cellphone. And Grayfeather pulled out a tooth. No one will question it."

"What about the dental records from the bodies?"

Grayfeather gripped Frankie's shoulder. "We're two steps ahead of you, bro," he said, applying pressure. "I ripped out the teeth with some pliers. We just needed a few bones."

Frankie's face scrunched up. "Sounds like you guys got it all figured out. But, what does this have to do with me?"

"We were hoping you'd let us lay low for a few weeks," Mariani said. "Without the chip, we can't buy anything. My money is worthless." Mariani opened his hands before he continued. "Will you help us or not?"

Frankie shook his head. "I don't know, man." His voice was soft and slow. "I'm really close to the government right now. It might not be a good idea."

"Come on, bro," Grayfeather said. "You won't even notice us."

Frankie blinked. Twice. "The thing is, my mom won't get the chip either. So, I got her and Russel both here. They're in the lower level of the bunker most of the time." He pointed downward.

"Your mom loves me, bro," Mariani said. "She won't mind."

"How 'bout this," Frankie said. "Why don't you guys post up at Ivan's house for a while? I'll drop off some food and water."

"That works," Mariani said, nodding. "I appreciate it."

"The place is a dump." Frankie let out a breath. "Feel free to fix it up. I'll pay for time and materials."

Mariani smiled. "I'm a pretty good carpenter. But not as good as Larry Sobek."

"What's that supposed to mean?"

"That's the dude who robbed you, brother. I put two bullets in his head."

Frankie's mouth opened but no words came out at first. "Well, thanks. But—"

"But what? You don't seem too happy."

"Bro, our security firm just took a job with Congressman Parker."

Mariani shrugged. "So what?"

Frankie lowered his tone to a whisper. "Any heat could mess that up. We got a lot on the line."

"I took precautions," Mariani said. "And I faked my death just to make sure it didn't come back to you."

"I appreciate your loyalty," Frankie said, throwing his hands in the air. "I can't believe Sobek turned on me."

"He tried to make some lame excuse. Whatever."

Frankie massaged his temples.

"You okay, bro?" Mariani asked

"Yeah," Frankie dropped his hand at his side. "It's a lot to take in. The nation has fallen into the hands of a tyrant, my carpenter had someone rob me, and then on top of that, something happened to Brice and Dennis."

"What happened?" Mariani asked.

Frankie looked at Mariani and then Grayfeather. "Look, guys." He paused with pursed lips. "You been out of the loop. And uh…Brice and Dennis. They um. They were working with the congressman, and uh…they got caught in the middle of a terrorist bombing. I-I think it was a false flag attack."

"What?" Mariani asked. "Are they okay?"

"They made a miraculous recovery." Frankie's fingers came close to his cringing face as he tried to describe the injuries. "Burns and shrapnel were bad. The boys are still at the Mayo Clinic."

"That's fucked up," Grayferather said. "Can you give them my best?"

Frankie nodded. "I will when I can." He softened his voice. "Communication is tough with the chip. But our boys earned the trust of the congressman. If they ever go back to work, they might get close enough to take out the top vegetable."

"That's a lost cause, bro. You should give that up before you get your friends killed."

"I can't do that."

Mariani shrugged. "Why not?"

"Because I've made a commitment to Ken and the nation. We're the last hope for freedom."

"Let me know if I can help," Grayfeather said. "I got people all over the nation. They got people ready to go to war."

"We don't need a war quite yet. But we did need you on the job. We were counting on you, bro."

"Sorry, brother." Grayfeather shrugged, almost as if he was genuinely remorseful that he let Frankie down. "Mariani was in trouble. I had to split some wigs."

Frankie let out a heavy breath. "You guys are safe. That's all that matters."

"I still wanna work." Grayfeather opened his massive hands. "Maybe I can do some covert shit?"

Frankie nodded slowly. "I'll keep you in mind. Thanks. Your muscle might come in handy someday."

"I'd like that." Grayfeather winked. "Mariani gave me some money to get out of town, but cash is worth shit. I need to earn some food and smokes."

"This government is out of control," Frankie said. "You can't do shit without the chip nowadays. I got mine cuz of my business. But I plan on taking it out as soon as we overthrow the tyrants."

"Good luck, bro," Mariani said. "But that's impossible. I've been in the military. I know what you're up against."

"Nothing is impossible. Ken has people embedded in the military *and* Secret Service. They're ready to make a move. They just need us to get close enough to cut off the head of the snake."

"And then what?" Grayfeather asked.

"I'm not sure, but I'm assuming a revolution. That is, *if* it's true the military still has a few patriots left."

76

Astana, Kazakhstan
December 21, 2023

Chancellor of the world Heather Roth sat down across from her father in his study. A glossy oak desk stood between them. Her uncle Seth was standing off to the side in a black tuxedo with a cigarette in his fingers. A perpetual cloud of smoke was hovering around his head.

"We're pleased with your progress," David Roth said, gently placing his hand on the petrified wood desk. "Seventy percent of people have implanted the RFID chips in their hands. UN peacekeepers have fully replaced America's police force. And most importantly, millions of recalcitrant Christians have been liquidated."

Chancellor Roth nodded slowly. "Thank you, Your Grace. I have followed the blueprint to a T."

"Indeed, you have," Seth Roth said, blowing out a stream of smoke toward the ceiling. "But now it's time for phase two." He ashed his cigarette in the human skull ashtray on the desk.

Heather Roth bowed her head. "Yes, Master. The systematic assault on Christianity will continue. The schools will train children to spy on their parents. Incentives have been given to subjects who turn in Christian terrorists. And of course, we reserve the right to eliminate the enemy with error."

"Good," Seth Roth said. "But my brothers under the skin have decided to speed up the process a few notches." He stooped closer to her, lowering his voice to a growl. "There *is* no opposition. *We* control the media. Dissent *is* outlawed." Seth rose tall again, returning his voice to the usual arrogant intellectual tone. "*Surely*, you could become more *aggressive* with depopulation. Who's going to stop you?"

David Roth raised a shaking finger. "Be creative." He croaked. "We want the multitudes to be terrified. We need them to submit or die."

"I fully understand, Father."

David Roth stood up and shuffled around the desk, placing a hand on Heather's lower back. "My first-born child, you've made me so proud." He coughed into his arm. "We're only a few steps away. The pyramid is all but capped. But the population of the world must be cut in half. Four billion people is all earth can sustain. Eventually, two billion is the goal. Use all means possible: biological and chemical weapons. Terrorist bombings. Tamper with the water and food supply. Give the UN peacekeepers a license to kill. We want to create order from chaos! The more they revolt, the more force we'll use."

"Yes, Father," Heather said, her voice soft like a child. "I won't disappoint you."

"I am confident in your resolve," David Roth said, passing her a glass test tube that was full of a thick red liquid. "Now drink, my child. Drink."

77

Duluth, Minnesota
December 25, 2023

Driving on the freeway, Marcel Taylor passed a large billboard with the word Christmas crossed out. A cigarette was burning in his lips, but he rolled the window down and flicked it toward the sign in disgust.

"Ridiculous," he said under his breath, turning the radio up a few notches.

One hand keeping time with the beat, Marcel was opening his mouth for the next verse when something flashed in his rear-view mirror. Blue and red cherries were flashing behind him.

"Fuck!" he barked while tapping the brakes of his SUV. Pulling over on the shoulder, he parked the vehicle.

Grabbing his phone from the center console, Marcel called his wife. The line rang three times before she answered.

"Hello," Mae said.

"Babe." Marcel killed the engine. "Don't panic, but I just got pulled over." He glanced in the rear-view mirror to see a black squad car with UN plates parked behind him. "I just want you to know how much I love you."

"Oh, Marcel, I love you so much," Mae said with a shaky voice. "You're gonna be okay."

"I'm scared. I got a bad feeling about this."

"Shhh," Mae said, but the tremble in her voice gave her away. "Just, no fast movements. Be polite and come home."

Marcel kept his narrowing eyes on the mirror. "Thanks, but I'm just kinda freakin' out. I heard some dude got shot last week by the peacekeepers."

"Be strong. It ain't gonna happen to you."

"Do you have a pen?"

"Yeah, why?"

"Write this plate number down," Marcel said as the door on the squad car swung open. "UN 33. It's a Black Dodge Challenger. The pig is big as fuck. He's black as fuck. And has a clean-cut beard. Oh, one more thing…he's wearing a baby blue beret."

"Got it."

"If I don't come home, give that shit to the hockey player."

"I will."

"Tell the kids I love them. And wish them a Merry Christmas."

"Stay calm," Mae said. "I love you."

Marcel set the phone down on the center console and pressed a button. "I'm putting you on speaker phone. Don't say shit. Here he comes. I love you. Bye."

The UN peacekeeper approached the driver-side window.

Marcel rolled his window down. He then placed both hands on the steering wheel. "What's up, brother?" he said to the large authority figure in camouflage who was hovering outside his window.

"I'm not your brother," the UN peacekeeper said with a noticeable foreign accent and bulbous white eyes. "Next time you see lights." The man pointed at Marcel. "Pull over…immediately."

With a pounding heart and wide eyes, Marcel nodded slowly. "Yes, sir." His hands were strangling the wheel.

"Get out of vehicle."

"What'd I do?" Marcel asked, his hands spreading apart in a tight shrug. Lowering his brow, he quickly returned his hands to the steering wheel.

The man leaned toward the window. "Cigarette almost hit squad car," the peacekeeper said with broken English. "Littering is global warming crime. Get out."

Marcel pulled the handle and pushed open the door. Stepping on the pavement, he slowly raised his hands above his head.

"Hold out right hand. I scan chip." The man's height and girth dwarfed Marcel.

"It was just a cigarette, bro." Marcel surrendered his right hand. "I'm sorry."

"No matter," the peacekeeper said, and then pulled out his black laser scanner. "You might be enemy of state." The man smiled thinly. "I find out quick."

With one swipe of the hand, the device beeped, and the information was downloaded on the small screen. "Marcel Taylor," the officer said. "Forty years old. No felonies." He took a step closer. "Wife, Mae Taylor." He lowered his voice. "Four children. Owner of multiple businesses." He paused to place a heavy hand on his shoulder. "One million, six hundred thousand credits in bank account."

Marcel glanced down at the hand on his shoulder. "Damn, man. You can see my bank account?"

"I know every detail of your life." The peacekeeper snapped the device back on his belt. "My discretion. I could say you are Christian terrorist…who resist arrest. I could shoot you in da face."

Marcel's nostrils flared. His jaw clenched. "What do you want from me?"

"Lucky for you, *brother*," the peacekeeper said, giving special enunciation to the last word. "I'm not bad guy. I just want few thousand credits. For me." He shifted his head. "And my comrade."

Marcel noticed a shadow out of the corner of his eye. Craning his neck, he saw a second soldier— gun drawn— creeping behind the rear of the truck.

"Is that legal?" Marcel's eyes were squinting. Face scrunched up. Head slightly tilted.

"Don't ask questions." The peacekeeper pulled out his black handgun. "Only terrorists ask questions."

"Terrorist?" Marcel said. "How am I a terrorist?"

The foreign peacekeeper grabbed Marcel's jacket. "Last chance. Pay…or my partner kill family. Make you watch."

"How am I gonna pay you?" Marcel said, his heart riveting against his chest cavity.

"I have app for that." The officer pulled out his phone and scanned Marcel's chip again. "How much? Hmm. I think ten thousand. For now."

After two beep noises from the man's phone, Marcel dropped his arm to his side. Raising his chin, he said, "Don't spend it all in one place."

"Don't be proud," the peacekeeper said with a slightly raised voice. "Be grateful. You go home. Love family. Cost very little."

Marcel's body stiffened at the threatening tone. "I understand, sir."

"Good," he said. "But I keep address saved in phone. I come collect every month."

"Please," Marcel said, his throat thick with emotion. Glancing down at his feet, he added. "Please, stay away from my family."

When he looked back up, Marcel caught a funny expression playing out on the officer's face. "You pray to God?"

At the chilling words, Marcel shook his head forcibly. "N-no. Of course not."

"Yes, you do." Reaching forward, his movement so fast Marcel hadn't realized his intent until it was too late, the officer's finger snatched Marcel's necklace from his neck.

Marcel's eyes widened. He'd forgotten to take it off before leaving the house.

"You have Christian blood." The peacekeeper raised the chain and cross high enough for his partner to see.

Marcel shook his head tightly. "No, sir."

"You lie," the officer barked. "Christian!"

Marcel's eyelids widened. He could hear the second peacekeeper stepping behind him. Turning his head, he saw lightning. Heard crackling. Felt a jolt of electricity, and then the cold icy blacktop cutting into his face.

78

Ivan's old house
December 26, 2023

Standing next to Frankie and Mariani, Gordon Grayfeather punched the palm of his hand. "What? They got Marcel?" The muscles on his face condensed.

"Yeah." Frankie let out a breath. "His wife just dropped me off a note. She was freaking out. Poor gal was on the phone with him when he got pulled over. She said the cop was screaming at him."

"We need to break him the fuck out," Grayfeather barked. The lines on his forehead were pushing his eyebrows low. As his lip curled upward, he showed some of his teeth. And the black gap where one was missing.

Frankie put his gloved finger to his lips. "Shhh." He quickly buried his hand under his arm pit. "We *can't* do that," he whispered with an arching brow.

"What about that congressman you work for?" Mariani asked. "I'd say call that piece of shit."

Frankie shook his head. "Negative. I'm a silent partner. I don't talk to congressmen."

Katrina's head was shifting from Frankie to Mariani with cigarette smoke spilling from her mouth.

"Call Spatz then." Mariani's hands shot out in frustration. "They could be killing Marcel, right fucking now."

"Ken is fully aware of the situation. He said he'll try to pull some stings. But most likely Marcel's just in lock up. They aren't killing everyone who gets arrested."

"I'm calling Ken." Mariani pulled out his burner phone.

"Please, don't. Phones aren't safe."

"Fuck!" Mariani stomped his boot on the late Ivan Mortensen's hardwood floor. "I'm gonna put an arrow through a peacekeeper's neck. Fucking foreigners come here and snatch up our boy for no good reason."

"This sucks, man," Frankie said, lifting both hands in the air, shaking them slightly. "Trust me, I got my lawyer on it." He dropped his hands to his side. "I'm trying to get some info...or bail. Anything. Look, guys...if Marcel doesn't come home soon, I'll give you the peacekeeper's license plate number."

"What?" Mariani took a step forward. "You got this asshole's info? Give me that shit."

"I can't."

Grayfeather lowered his head to Frankie's level. "Why the fuck not?"

Frankie swallowed hard. "Bro, Marcel gave her the license plate number over the phone. If that dude ends up dead, they'll be able to listen to the conversation. She'll be next. And then me. And then you. Please, be patient, guys. Let's be smart here."

Katrina rose from the couch. "Why don't you give me the info?" she said. "I could find him, watch his moves. You guys take him out a few months down the road. By then, he surely would have arrested other people. They'll never know it was us."

79

BTZ Suites
Duluth, Minnesota
January 3, 2024

From the kitchen of his hotel suite, Brice Rockwell slipped a thick glove on his chipped hand before speaking to Dennis. "Frankie's coming with a present for us," he said softly, staring at Dennis and his pinkish marred face that was just a level worse than his. Both men were still recovering from the suicide bombing that scorched them with fire and punctured their bodies with shrapnel.

"Probably just some credits," Dennis mumbled then lit up a cigarette. He, too wore a glove on his right hand, just in order to speak freely. "This is the second time he's visited us since we got back from the hospital. Both times he comes with money. It's like he thinks money will take these fucking scars away."

"What else could he do?" Brice blew out a stream of smoke.

"Nothing," Dennis barely said. "I don't think he gives a shit."

"Of course, he does," Brice said with a low voice. "We took this job knowing what we were getting ourselves into. Frankie saw the tunnel and drove through it."

"Correction," Dennis said. "Frankie saw a tunnel, and *we* drove through it. After he gave us the order, the tunnel blew up in a big fucking ball of fire. We're just his pawns in a game of chess. I want no part of it. We can't win. Look at it out there." Dennis pulled the curtain from the window of the top-floor condominium. It was a no-pay lease from Frankie. A gesture of good faith until they fully recovered.

Brice got up and limped his way to the window overlooking the Aerial Lift Bridge. It was broad daylight in the middle of the winter, and snow was falling from a gray sky. When Brice looked down, he saw a stream of protesters marching down the street with picket signs. To Brice, they looked like ants, about to get swept up by UN peacekeepers. But at the time, he only counted four squad cars blocking access to the bridge. The vocal group of freedom fighters chanted: *Bill of Rights!* Over and over again.

Closing the curtain, Brice looked at Dennis. "Look, cuz," he said softly. "I love Frankie. The man took us off the streets and gave us a purpose. He saw our talent, and unleashed us."

"Yeah, I just hope…"

Three soft knocks at the door interrupted Dennis' thoughts. Brice opened the door. Frankie was standing with a pizza box in his hands. His dark gray wool coat was hanging to his knees.

"What's up, brother?" Brice took the pizza and set it on the granite kitchen counter.

"Not much," Frankie said, shifting to acknowledge Dennis. "What are you guys up to?"

"Chillin' like villains." Dennis shook his gloved hand.

"How do you like the view?" Frankie asked.

"I hate it," Dennis said softly. "Look out the window. Protesters and pigs. Everywhere."

Frankie walked up to the pane of glass. Looking down to the street, he saw blue and white lights now in multiple areas. Hundreds of picketers marching for unalienable rights. "I know," Frankie said with a lower tone. "That's good. The people are fed up. The problem is…not many are brave enough to stand up to tyranny. Everyone else is petrified." Frankie handed a yellow envelope to Brice.

"What's this?" Brice asked.

"Two checks for both of you," Frankie said. "It's on top of the insurance money. Just a bonus from the company. And a tip from me."

"A hundred thousand dollars from TRS Security," Brice said, holding the checks, "and a hundred thousand from you?"

"I wanted to make sure you wouldn't have to work for a long time," Frankie said, slowing his voice down to express importance. "You have no idea what you did for this company. And your nation. I honestly can't even tell you."

"Thanks, brother," Dennis said softly with his eyebrows raised. "This money is definitely gonna help make life easier, but it's not gonna bring my face back." He sighed heavily. "It ain't gonna take away the pain. I don't want money, I want revenge." His lip curled. "I want blood. I should go take it out on a blue helmet right now."

Frankie stood taller. Noticing a pen on the kitchen table next to a small yellow note pad, he grabbed it, and then wrote down a note for his friends to read:

Ken says the congressman has been asking about you two, the note read. *He asked if you guys are coming back to work. You should think about it. Then give me the word when you're ready. Parker trusts you. We're hoping someday, he hires you for an event with the puppet masters who staged that false flag attack. Only then, you will get your revenge. They did this to you! They did it to Marcel. And they won't stop until everyone is dead, a slave, or a government employee. Down with Roth, and her blood-drinking friends! Flush this note down the toilet! Thank you. I love you. You will both go down in history as the brave patriots who sparked the flame that saved the free world.*

80

Philadelphia, Pennsylvania
January 10, 2024

Ken Spatz closed the door of the limousine from the inside. Sitting down, he nodded to Vadik Domechev and then met eyes with the former congressman from Minnesota. "Congratulations, sir," Ken said with a nod. The limo took off.

Now that Heather Roth had a stronghold over the nation and the world, she handpicked her cabinet with yes-men like Eugene Parker. She appointed him truth czar and put him in charge of global propaganda and compliance.

Czar Parker returned the nod. "Thanks," he said, spreading apart his hands in a rare moment of humility. "I wouldn't be here…without the bravery and expertise of your men."

"It's our honor to protect you, sir," Ken said, hands folded on the lap of his black wool coat. For the job, he trimmed up his hair and shaved his beard. He looked like a Secret Service agent, and so did Vadik.

The czar pressed his hand against his heart. "Your team is my lucky charm," Parker said. "Brice and Dennis saved my life. I didn't get a scratch. And I'm confident you'd do the same."

"Mr. Spatz trained us well," Vadik said. "We take all the scratches."

"Brice and Dennis got more than a scratch," Czar Parker said. "How's the recovery going?"

Vadik jerked his left shoulder. "They can walk and talk and laugh," he said. "They're grateful to be alive. But the scars are unsettling. Their families barely recognize them, and they scare people when they go in public."

"I feel horrible," Parker said. "I gave them the best medical treatment in the world. It just makes my blood boil. Those filthy Christians terrorists. Don't you just want to kill them all?"

Vadik sucked in some air. He felt a gaze upon him as he met the czar's blue eyes. Vadik swallowed his pride. "Permission to speak freely, sir?"

"Go ahead, young man," Parker said. "Speak your mind. If you have hatred in your heart, let it out."

"I used to be a Christian," Vadik said, "but when that happened to Brice and Dennis, something changed inside of me. It was Christians who did that to them. They would have done that to me. I want them all to pay a heavy price."

"Don't worry, my friend," Parker said. "I can't tell you much…but your dream might just come true. The liquidation of terrorists has commenced. This administration will no longer tolerate violent threats against its citizens."

"It's the only way." Vadik pursed his lips.

The truth czar pointed at Ken Spatz. "I owe TRS Security my life. And…as long as I have influence, I'll give you my word…that your team will have job security *and* immunity."

Ken's chin cocked slightly. "Immunity?"

"In the months to come," the czar lowered his tone. "President Roth will be putting her boot on the neck of the enemy. Unfortunately, some good citizens will get caught up in the mix. I'll upload an asperous to all your profiles when I get to my office. That will keep the UN peacekeepers off your back. When you get pulled over, tell them you have diplomatic immunity, and get your chip scanned. They'll have no choice but to release you...because *you* work for the Department of Truth." He pointed at his chest. "The Dear Leader trusts my judgment."

"That will definitely make life easier for my men," Ken said. "How can I repay you?"

Parker rubbed his chin. "I want your men to work exclusively for me. And I want Brice and Dennis back to work. I don't care what they look like, they're exceptional body guards."

Ken nodded. "I'll make that happen." He held up a single finger. "One question, if you don't mind, sir."

"Of course."

"What if I said..." Ken shrugged. "...one of my friends got picked up a couple weeks back?"

"Why didn't you say something?" The czar sat upright, his eyes exploding. "I could have done something.... Oh, my providence. I hope it's not too late."

"We didn't want to bring a burden like that to you, sir," Ken said. "It didn't seem appropriate."

"Mr. Spatz," Parker said. "Write down his name and the city he was arrested in." He nodded. "And I will *personally* see to it that he is released immediately."

*****

In the back of a re-education camp bus, Marcel Taylor had his face in his hands, elbows on his knees. Eyes on the floor. The sobbing wail of a woman forced him to look up. He glanced at her. Hysterical. She had her hands high, shaking her chains. Shrieking.

"Shut up, bitch!" A guard in camouflage shouted from behind a gate. A shotgun was in his hands.

The screaming came to a halt. Only a low uneven hum of emotion remained. Men and women alike were both crying. Rumors had been buzzing around the camp: firing squads, guillotines, wild animals.

Sitting in the back of the bus, Marcel turned his gaze out the rear window like he did when he was twelve-years-old, blocking out the noise of the other kids.

Eventually, his mind wandered back to the interrogation on Christmas Day.

"Do you have a God?" Marcel remembered the female interrogator asking him.

"No," Marcel said, shaking his head. He looked past the dark-skinned woman in a tight camouflage uniform and pale blue beret. What he remembered seeing was a mirror and a black dome video camera.

The sleeves of Marcel's red jump suit were cut off around the shoulders. His wiry arms shot down like two black pipes. And his hands were cuffed together, shackled to his feet.

"One lie is a thousand lies," the female interrogator said, standing up from the other side of the table. "And I've seen a thousand lying terrorists *just* like you." She pointed a finger at him.

Attached to Marcel's temples, neck, chest, and wrists, were wires that connected to a lie detector and a computer that was resting on the table between them.

"What do you want from me?" Marcel's chin was slightly raised.

"Mr. Taylor. I represent your last chance at freedom. I want to re-educate you."

"For what?"

She walked around the table and leaned toward him. "The new world needs people with business management experience." She rose, dropping a hand on his back. "Someone has to give orders to the proletariats for the state. The blind can't lead the blind." She returned to her desk. "But first, to be an upper-class citizen of the world, you must assimilate. You must admit your crimes of religion."

"Okay, I was a criminal. But not anymore. I have no God."

"Mr. Taylor, you lied again." She spun the screen so he could see the zig-zag line of deceit.

"Okay." Marcel lifted his hands, palms facing up. "God is in my heart. Help me get him out."

"Good," she said. "Now you're ready for the trials." She walked toward the door but not without giving him a last parting glance before leaving.

For a moment, Marcel's eyes studied the room, and then they landed on the video camera.

Through the intercom, the same female voice sounded. "Start praying to your God for warmth. I'm gonna drop the temperature."

Chilled air shot down from ceiling vents. Marcel's eyebrows lowered at the sight of the mist and the noise it made as it exited the vents. It sounded like air being let out of a tire. But louder.

The intercom started playing country music.

"Of course, they know I hate country," Marcel muttered, crossing his arms.

After a minute, Marcel could feel his body begin to shiver. He could see the goosebumps on his arms rising. Instinctively, his body curled in on himself. Cuffing his hands, he brought them close to his mouth and breathed heavily with hopes of providing warmth.

One loud country song ended and another began. The volume increased. Marcel's teeth were clattering. His chains were jingling as his body quaked. The blaring speakers kept playing song after agonizing song.

With no warning, the music stopped. "Do you still believe in Jesus Christ?" The interrogator's question rang out through the intercom. "Yes or no?"

"No!"

"You lied! Don't you understand? I can read your lies."

"I can't win with you."

"No, you can't. But if you tell the truth, express remorse, and truthfully vow atheism, you will live."

"Fine." Marcel touched his heart. "I still love Jesus. But I vow to erase religion from my heart."

All of a sudden, the volume of the music got louder. More mist flowed through the vents, and then the door creaked opened. A gray ball of some sort came rolling in before the door slammed shut again. Marcel's eyes followed the ball until it stopped.

"What the fuck is that?" Marcel blurted out. Jumping to his feet, his eyes locked on the nest with black and white wasps crawling all over it. Marcel shuffled to the corner and curled up in a ball.

"I'm allergic to bees!" Marcel yelled. "Let me out!"

The music came to a sudden stop. The wasps were crawling on the floor. They didn't fly because of the freezing temperature.

"All we want is truth and compliance," she said. "I will give you one more opportunity to convince the computer that you renounce God and vow to remain a law-obeying citizen of the world."

"Yes!" Marcel said. "I renounce God. I will live by the law of the land."

"There will be no further questions," the interrogator said through the intercom. "We will evaluate your score, and determine if you are curable. Then, if you're eligible, you will be evacuated to a re-education camp."

The loud country music returned. The temperature rose.

After a few minutes the room became warm. The wasps started buzzing and swarming. A sharp flash of fear took a hold of Marcel. He couldn't even swat the insects because of the chains that bound him.

When the bus came to a stop, Marcel snapped back to reality. They had reached their final destination. Sitting upright, he didn't see a re-education camp like the guards had told them. Instead, Marcel saw the bottom of an iron ore mine and massive yellow dump trucks. The earth in the mine pit was a shade of orange he had not seen before.

The driver exited the bus, and the guard followed him. Voices of bickering prisoners competed with each other. Some people were screaming. Others were cursing. Outside on the dirt, a dozen UN peacekeepers in camouflage uniforms, black respirator masks, and pale blue helmets were standing in a line. They looked thin, stiff, and emotionless with assault rifles pressed against their chest. The first soldier in the line wore a sky-blue beret and held a loud speaker instead of a gun.

"Attention!" the officer barked. "We will be working in the mine today. You will shovel ore until dark. If you act accordingly, you will be given a ration box and two beers. But, if you make one step out of line, we will shoot the lot of you. When I stop talking, I want you to slowly exit the bus."

After a few panicked screams, gasps, and grumbles, the first person stepped off Marcel's bus. The man was guided into a long and narrow pit set in the ground. Systematically, they all slowly exited the bus. Marcel was the last in line. At the first sight of the six-foot pit lined with white powdery lye, his eyes popped wide open. At that moment, Marcel felt his heart jackhammering harder and faster than at any point in his entire life. Feeling light headed, he opened his mouth for air and suddenly felt a dry, mild burning sensation on his tongue.

Rolling his head, Marcel tried to make direct eye contact with as many soldiers as possible. "Fucking cowards," he said under his breath as he descended further into the tomb.

Returning his eyes to the long line in front of him, Marcel's thoughts were whirling. Each dragging step flashed a different picture of his wife and kids and friends. And then once the line slowed down to a stop, Marcel thought about the family farm, and how they herded pigs and cattle to the slaughter.

Marcel was now crammed elbow to elbow in the white pit. The blond gal next to him turned her head and looked at Marcel with tears streaming down her face.

"We're dead," she said softly, her jaw quivering. "T-they're gonna s-shoot us all."

A loud speaker sounded from above. "Attention," the peacekeeper shouted from the edge of the pit. "When I release the nerve gas, it will kill you instantly. You will feel no pain. It will just make you fall asleep. Your faith in your God brought you this fate. Where is he now? Go ahead and pray if you wish."

Loud whimpers and wails cried out from the bottom of the pit. Shaky voices of the damned were praying out loud with quaking mouths. Marcel had tears in his eyes now. Looking at a woman with her red face scrunched up, he smiled. His calm presence eased the lines on her forehead. She came closer and hugged him tightly. Sobbing.

When the VX nerve gas canister opened, the toxin rolled out in the form of a black cloud.

Marcel dropped to his knees. He said a prayer for the Lord to look after his friends and family.

After the short prayer, his eyes snapped open. His throat burned. Like everyone else, his hands shot around his neck. Gasping for air, he let out a weak cough. Foam started seeping from his lips. Collapsing to the white dirt, he began thrashing like a fish out of water.

81

Duluth, Minnesota
February 3, 2024

"I pledge allegiance to the flag," the class of first graders said in unison, *"of the United Nations of the world. And to the empire for which it stands, one world over God, indivisible with peace and equity for all."*

Sethra Bream was holding her right hand over her heart. Brown eyes locked on the pale blue digital flag that flew on a high-definition TV in the front of the room. She had recited the words because it was mandatory, but now her mind wondered what it meant. The song and the flag.

Gazing at the left corner of the flag, Sethra saw a golden pyramid with a small triangle capped at the top. What had caught her attention was the All-Seeing Eye that kept blinking once every minute.

Whose eye is that? Sethra thought, sitting down in her desk with the rest of her classmates. They were all wearing the same uniform. A black sport coat, black slacks, and black shoes. A white button-up shirt under the jacket. Most of the kids had brown, black, or blond hair, but Sethra's curly golden locks and light tan skin made her unique.

"I'm going to take roll call," the female teacher said with a gentle touch. "Please put your right hand in the aisle. I'll walk by and check you in." The teacher then slowly walked down each row, her black scanner beeping after each child was registered into the system for daily attendance.

"Now that attendance has been taken," the teacher said from behind her desk, "we can continue our studies from last week." The woman smiled, her head shifting to make sure all the kids were paying attention. "Big Sister trusts that each and every one of you is a great citizen of the world. She loves all of you more than she loves herself. She adores you, and she knows that none of you would ever betray her. Unfortunately, she understands that some of your care takers still cling to the religion of hate. She knows that you love your family members, but she wants you to know that it is your duty to watch them very carefully.

"Some of them might be hiding illegal guns or bibles. They might secretly pray to a debunked God, or they may hide secrets from the state. They might speak in condemnation against our Dear Leader, or they may conspire against her with secret groups of violent extremists.

"This is not acceptable, and Big Sister wants you to know that if you come forward with fruitful information, you will be rewarded. Just imagine a life with no parents nagging at you. Imagine a home with as much candy and video games as you wish. This could all be yours if you only catch your family in crimes against the state." She paused to study the children's eyes and lips.

"Does anybody have any questions?" The teacher smiled robustly. "Does anyone have any secrets to reveal?"

At first, no hands rose. "It's okay, don't be shy."

All of a sudden, three kids raised their hands.

"My d-daddy has a gun," a little boy said. "H-he keeps it under his bed."

"Good job, Timmy." The teacher brought him three bags of gummy bears and a soda pop. "See how easy that was? Anyone else?"

"My mommy doesn't like her job," a cute little girl said with a squeaky voice. "And she doesn't like Big Sister very much."

"Big Sister will convince her," the teacher said sharply. "Yes, that's how we achieve peace and equity. We must teach people how to get with the program." She then gave the girl a handheld video game. The girl smiled.

Sethra raised her hand. "What would happen to our parents? If we tell?"

"In most cases," the teacher said, "they would be re-educated in one of our many facilities for the soul criminal. Why? Are there any problems at home?"

"No, ma'am," Sethra said. "I was just wondering."

*****

Sethra opened the back door to her mom's car and hopped inside.

"Hi, sweety!" Conny said, craning her neck to look into her daughters' eyes. "How was school?" Conny smiled gloriously, with hope Sethra wouldn't protest her dentist appointment.

"We didn't really learn anything." Sethra buckled her seatbelt. "I just want to learn. I guess I'll just have to read books at home."

"What did you do all day?" Conny asked. Turning back to face the road, her short blond hair danced as she threw the car in drive.

"They've been teaching us how to be good citizens of the world," Sethra said. "They want us to spy on our families, and then tell on them when they go against Big Sister."

Conny lifted her hand and placed a single finger on her lips. "Shhh," she recited the code of conduct as if it were scripted. "We have to live by the law of the land. Big Sister wants us to remain obedient, in return for peace and equity."

"That's what my teacher told us," Sethra said. "I-I guess I just don't understand."

"You will, my sweet. You will."

They drove for about ten minutes on the dark and blustery day. The dentist's office was located on top of the hill. As they pulled into the parking lot, Sethra started stirring.

"I don't want to go to the dentist," Sethra said. "My teeth are fine."

"I know," Conny said. "When I was your age, I didn't like the dentist either. It's just something you got to do. They're just going to clean your teeth and check for cavities. That's all."

"Only cuz I love you, Mommy."

"Awe. I love you, too. You're so sweet." Conny was smiling. "What do you want for dinner?"

"Can we cook lasagna? And garlic bread?"

"Anything you want, my sweet," Conny said, and they both exited the car.

Holding hands, Conny and Sethra cut through the icy wind with haste. Mom opened the door, and daughter walked inside. Placing a hand on Sethra's back, Conny guided her to the reception desk.

"We have a 4:00 appointment for Sethra."

"Very good," the female receptionist said. "Fill this out. We'll call her name when the doctor is ready."

"Thank you," Conny said. Turning, they walked toward the waiting room. Only one man was sitting in the room, and his finger was scrolling on his smartphone. He had dark tan skin, a black fleece jacket, and a gray winter cap.

When Conny and Sethra got near, the man respectfully pulled back his legs and inclined his head to face them.

When their eyes met for the first time in seven years, Conny's heart sank. She stopped in her tracks. *Oh, my God,* she thought. *He's going to hate me.*

Frankie shot out of his seat. "Conny."

Conny's eyes started blinking rapidly. Opening her mouth, no words came out at first. "Hi, Frankie," she said, offering a half smile. "Wow. Uh." She gave a nervous short laugh. "I wasn't expecting to see you today." She brushed her jaw-length blond hair behind her ear.

Sethra was standing next to her mom with her little head tilted upward in question.

"Who's your friend, Mom?" Sethra asked. "He kinda looks like a Christian terrorist."

Conny pulled her close. "Sethra! Don't talk like that to people."

Frankie was not aware Conny had another child, so he dropped down to one knee in order to introduce himself. A ray of sun light was angling from the window and shining on her doll-like face.

"Sethra, this is Frank Buccetti," Conny said, pursing her lips. "An old friend of Mommy's."

Frankie's head tilted up to see tears flowing down Conny's blushing cheeks. Lowering his gaze to the blank face of the young child, he smiled. "Sethra." He stuck out his hand. "What a beautiful name. It's an honor to meet you."

Sethra hesitated but extended her little hand. "Thanks," she said, wrapping her other arm around her mom's leg.

Conny wiped the tears from her eyes. Her secret was at the tip of her lips, but she couldn't speak it.

"It's okay," Frankie said to Sethra. "I might look like a soul criminal." He smiled. "But if everyone is soul criminal, then no one is a soul criminal." He paused, tilting the palm of his hand upward. "Let me see your hand."

Sethra gave him her hand. Frankie took it and turned it over so that both of their palms were facing up.

"Look at those three lines on the palm of your hand. Then look at mine."

Sethra studied both hands. "They're the same! But isn't everyone's the same?"

"No." Frankie shook his head. "Soul criminals only have two lines."

"How do you know that?" Sethera asked.

From the other side of the room, a door creaked open. "Sethra?" said a woman in maroon scrubs.

Conny raised her hand. "She'll be right with you."

Sethra was smiling at Frankie. "I hope you're not a terrorist." She chuckled. "Just kidding. It was nice to meet you, Mr. Buccetti. Have a nice day."

"You too, Sethra," Frankie said and offered his knuckle. She bumped it and then turned toward the dental assistant.

Frankie rose, standing face to face with Conny.

Conny sniffled, locking eyes with Frankie. And then her eyes darted before her hands covered her face.

"What?" Frankie asked, one eye scrunching shut. "What's wrong?"

Grabbing Frankie by the hand, she pulled him out the doors and into the snowfall and whistling wind. "I can't hold this inside anymore. I have to come clean."

"Hold what inside?" Frankie tugged his woolen cap snug over his ears.

"You promise not to get mad?"

"How can I—"

"Sethra's yours, Frankie," Conny interrupted him with a trembling voice. "I'm so sorry. I-I never wanted to hurt you."

Frankie's hand pressed against his chest. "What?" he asked with a contorted face. "She's my…my daughter?"

"Oh my—" Conny bit her tongue. "How will you ever forgive me?"

Frankie brought his hand to his forehead, turning away completely. Letting out a heavy breath, he spun to face her. "I-I forgive you, Conny." His arms spread wide. "But I'll never be able to forget."

"That's fair. But you have to understand. When the war happened, my ex-husband came to my house. He said America was being invaded, and we had to go to the base. I was so scared. I just took the kids and went with him. I'm sorry."

"It's been like seven years." The hand in his pocket squeezed into a fist. "Why didn't you find me?"

"Colten still thinks he's the dad. It would crush him."

"What about me, Conny? What about Sethra?"

Conny's face scrunched up and a cascade of tears gushed down her face. "I'm sorry." She stomped her foot. "I don't know what to do." Plopping her hand on her face, she sobbed. "How am I going to tell Sethra?"

"Calm down," Frankie said, placing a gentle hand on her shoulder. "Everything's gonna be okay. We'll figure it out."

With her mind spinning in a tornado of pent-up emotions, she fell into Frankie's arms like it was 2017. "What if I got a divorce?" She sniffled. "Would you take me back?"

"I'm sorry, Kittenz. You fooled me twice. The shame is already on me."

82

Philadelphia, Pennsylvania
February 13, 2024

Sitting behind her desk in the Oval Office, President Heather Roth smiled at her puppet running the Department of Truth. "I want you to fly in two hundred thousand more UN peacekeepers," she said. "As you predicted, the protests have transformed into riots." She flashed him a hint of a smile. "And as *I* predicted, with each riot, each uprising, we gain more power. We just need more boots on the ground. Foreigners with no sympathy for the people." Her black pantsuit had noticeably broader shoulders than usual. Her face more pale. Her lips more red. Her eye makeup darker.

Truth Czar Eugene Parker smiled briefly. "As a global collective, we can relocate troops to America, but that will leave a vacuum somewhere else."

"We've been over this before, Mr. Parker." Roth dropped a fist on the table. "America is the priority. Third-world nations can burn. And then we'll send the U.S. military to nation build."

"Forgive me, Madam President," Parker said, speaking fast. "I fully understand your orders. I believe I misworded my statement. I was simply reminding you the UN peacekeeping force has reached full deployment status." His suit was black as coal. His tie red.

"Make it happen."

"Yes, Your Grace." Lowering his eyes to the gold pyramid lapel on her bosom, he noticed the All-Seeing Eye blink.

Looking at Parker, Roth slid a leather folder across the table. "Here's the next task I have for you."

"My honor," Parker said, picking up the folder. Upon opening it, he read the executive order calling for a string of fires at food transpiration facilities. "A promising idea. I'll get a team on it right away."

"The great Joseph Stalin proved that starvation is the most sufficient means of depopulation."

"Between the extra troops and the food shortages, this might just work. That said, Madam Roth, Mr. Stalin had a softer resistance. And he had hardened Soviet troops loyal to Mother Russia. We have armed militias resisting. And we're fighting them with low IQ mercenaries."

"Shut up!" Roth barked. "Through chaos...we gain order." The dictator raised her voice. "Mr. Parker, if you ever doubt me again, I'll have your head on a platter. I could drop bombs on every single uprising, but that is not the plan. First, we confiscated most of the guns. Second, we chipped eighty percent of the people. Now, we are establishing the ability to respond to insurrections with overwhelming force. This is scaring half the people into compliance. Next, we will starve everyone into submission. The fifth stage will be a deadly virus to thin the herd, and a vaccine to keep them dependent on the state. From there, the remaining citizens will be so weak, so sick, so exhausted, that they'll be grateful for the life we give them in the final stage."

Parker shook his head. "I would never doubt you, Your Grace. It's my job to explain the good *and* the bad."

"I am fully aware of all possibilities. We have to move like lightning. You have two months to damage the food supply, then we release the virus in late April. Make sure your people in the media turn up the rhetoric. Blame everything on the Christian resistance."

"Of course, Madam Roth."

The president placed her bony hands on the desk. "We *cannot* sustain this current situation. Depopulation is too slow. Seven billion is too many. Too many parasites sucking all the earth's resources. If by the end of the year, the global population shrinks twenty-five percent, I will reward you with a bonus of one hundred million credits. And more importantly, I will put a good word in for you with my father. He'll need a loyal and capable leader to govern the New World Order when I retire."

"Your Grace," Parker said, softening his voice. "Is everything alright with your health?"

"I feel like I'm thirty. But my father is aging. He needs me to take over the family business once my mission is accomplished."

"It has been my life's honor to serve your family, Madam Roth." Mr. Parker bowed his head. "I am most impressed with your leadership skills. Thank you for blessing our world with your expertise."

"Compliments get your everywhere, my old friend," Roth said with a bat of her eye. "I have an important event coming around the corner. You will be at my side. Only a select few…distinguished gentlemen will be there. Men from banking and oil. Media."

"I would love to accompany you, Madam Roth. When is this?

"April 20th," Roth said, her lips tugging upward. "Adolf Hitler's birthday. I will be the first woman to ever attend this event, and I'd like you to be my personal guest. It will give you leverage above the other options…for chancellor of the world."

"Thank you, Your Grace." Parker shifted his head. "I am so fortunate. This is the greatest day of my life."

Roth rose, slowly walking around the desk, gently placing her pale hand on his shoulder. "Mr. Parker, you are my only subordinate who has earned the privilege to stand at my side." She slid her fingers to his throat, and then behind his ear, before pulling her hand away. "After the event, there's an orgy you might enjoy." Her voice became a low growl. "I'll make sure you get to *fuck* me first."

Parker swallowed a lump in his neck. "Yes, Your Grace. I look forward to the privilege."

"You, me, and eleven enlightened men will participate in this special day," Roth said. "The hosts will be providing security, but you will also be permitted to bring four of your own detail."

"It sounds like the safest place on earth."

"This will be the most consequential evening of your life." She locked eyes with him. "Here's the invitation packet. The contents include the rules, code of conduct, and a blueprint of the property. Brief your security team, so they're familiar with the surroundings."

"Thank you, Your Grace."

"I trust your judgment, Mr. Parker. Silence will be a virtue. Consider this event classified. Leaking details will become a death sentence to the entire family of the leaker."

"I understand, Madam Roth." Parker bowed his head.

83

Duluth, Minnesota
February 17, 2024

Gordon Grayfeather and Giovanni Mariani were trudging through knee-deep snow, up a steep wooded ravine in the middle of a massive city park. Grayfeather was carrying a rock the size of a baseball and Mariani had a compound bow strapped to his back. With their free hands, they gained leverage by pulling themselves from tree to tree.

Grayfeather got to the top first. Peeking his head out from the bushes, he scanned from left to right. "Here little piggy," he said, cracking a smile. The icy road in front of him was void of cars and houses. But a large reservoir was on the other side of the street, and it was flush with tall shrubs and small trees.

Mariani reached the top. "Game time," he said. "I better get across the street. Katrina said he comes a few minutes early sometimes."

Grayfeather looked down the street then faced Mariani. "Try to not kill them. I want them to feel some pain. Fear."

Mariani nodded and then sprinted across the street with his bow in his hands. Dressed in all black, he climbed the bushy reservoir hill and crouched behind the thickest shrubs near the top. Pulling an arrow out of his quiver, he sucked in a deep breath and blew it out. And then he did it again.

"I'm in position," Mariani said into his earpiece. "Waiting on your move."

"Affirmative," Grayfeather said. "Any minute now."

"Going silent." Mariani's heart ticked up a few notches.

After a few more deep breaths, his body jerked to the sound of Grayfeather's sharp voice.

"Tango, he's on the move. Three o'clock your way."

Mariani rose to full height as a black UN patrol car rolled down the hill to his right. Drawing back the wire, he held it taut, waiting, watching as Grayfeather's rock sailed through the air, striking the squad car. A loud thud sounded and the car screeched to a stop. The driver's side door swung open and a large man with extremely dark skin jumped out wearing a camouflage uniform. His beret was pale blue. The side view of the tall and big man walking showed his clean-cut beard.

Mariani's hand trembled slightly as he aimed lower. "Right there," he said, releasing the arrow. The man went down fast. The second peacekeeper hopped out of the passenger side of the squad car and turned to look in the bushes where Mariani was pulling out another arrow.

Drawing back the wire of his bow, Mariani aimed at center mass. "'Merica," he said proudly, just before releasing the arrow. In a fraction of a second, the man in the crosshairs let out a yelp, and then spun around, crumpling to the ice-crusted road.

From the bush, Mariani watched Grayfeather emerge from the ledge of the ravine. One peacekeeper was squirming on the snow, trying to get back to his car. The other man was still, a growing circle of slushy blood pooling around his torso.

Stooping low, Grayfeather grabbed the bigger man by the collar of his uniform, jerking his body forward. The wounded man's loud screams cut the early morning silence. A red streak in the snow led to the weeds on the ledge.

"Marcel Taylor was my friend," Grayfeather said, showing him the drop-off.

"No!" It was the last word that the peacekeeper would say.

"Holy shit," Mariani said to himself as he watched his friend hurl the man down the rocky ravine. Trotting down the slope of the reservoir, Mariani saw Grayfeather at the ledge looking downward. The second peacekeeper was lifeless. Mariani grabbed him by the ankle, and then dragged him to the edge. Dropping the man's leg in the snow, he looked up to Grayfeather.

"Toss him down, brother," Grayfeather said. "It's my new favorite thing to do."

Mariani nodded slowly.

84

BTZ Suites
February 27, 2024

Frankie was sitting on his couch eating breakfast, watching what he thought to be propaganda on the news. Another terrorist sleeper cell had been neutralized. The white-haired anchor looked like he was holding back a smile. He had just accused the Christian terrorists of burning down a dozen food transpiration centers across the Midwest.

An unsuspected rap on the door made his skin jump. Whipping his head to the entrance of his suite, he sprang up and crossed the kitchen floor. *Who could it be?*

Squinting in the peephole, Frankie saw brown locks of hair and bright blue eyes. *Tara.* His heart dropped because part of him still loved her. As his trembling hand turned the handle, a surge of memories flowed through his mind. Her laugh, her moan, her fits of anger.

"There she is," Frankie said with a gentle smile, leaning on the half-open door.

"I brought a peace offering," Tara said, handing him a steaming cup of coffee. "Here." She looked warm in a light-gray ski jacket and blue knit cap.

Frankie took it. "Thanks, come on in."

"Burrr. Freezing out there." She closed the door behind her. Setting her coffee on the granite kitchen counter, she blew out an audible sigh. "I was in the neighborhood, and...well. Um." She touched her nose, eyes skirting off to the side. "I uh...came to the conclusion...you were right."

"About what?"

"Everything." She sighed heavily with a shaking head. "M-my friend and her boyfriend were—"

Frankie put a finger to his lips. "Hold on a second." He set the coffee on the counter, and then pulled a pair of gloves out of the drawer. "Try this on." He gestured to his right hand.

"What's that for?" she asked with a puzzled look on her scrunching face.

"I'll tell you in a minute."

Tara pulled the glove on her right hand.

"Just a precaution we use around here. The chip. It records."

"I kinda wondered about that."

"The glove helps, but other things record, too. The TV. Your phone."

"That's good to know." Tara gave him her phone.

Frankie opened the fridge and set it inside.

"Look, Frankie, my friend and her boyfriend were killed last week." Her soft voice cracked, and then she sniffled. "I took a job at a hospital in California, but came home for the funeral. I've been back for two days, and already heard dozens of stories just like that. People are saying it's not just in Duluth, but all over the country. And there's not a peep on the news about it. The only way people know is from word of mouth."

"I know. They're killing us off. The food supply is next."

"You predicted it," Tara said, pursing her lips. "I'm sorry I ever doubted you."

Frankie took a sip of coffee. "I didn't predict anything." He shook his head. "I just read a lot about history. Tyranny and slaughter are the natural human condition. Look at Greece, Rome, and Great Britain. Those in power will always crave more, and once they have total power, they try to eliminate the opposition."

"I'm scared." She looked down. "What can we do?"

"Not much. We just have to hope for a miracle."

She sipped her coffee. "What about your security business?"

"What about it?"

"I remember you hinted at some sort of big plan. Remember?"

Frankie's eyes shifted to the left. "It didn't work out."

"You're lying." Her eyes narrowed.

"No, I'm not." He shook his head, and then looked at the floor.

"Bullshit, you don't think I remember that look?"

"Tara, it's classified. Let's just leave it at that. I should have never told you."

"You trusted me then. Why can't you trust me now?"

Frankie shook his head. "Trusting women hasn't worked out too well for me. Last I remember, you left me when I needed you most."

"I made a mistake." Her hands flung in the air. "I'm sorry. What, you never make mistakes?"

"I try not to make the same mistake twice. Plus, even if I forgave you, what do you expect me to tell you?"

"Frankie, I know you got a plan. And I want to help."

"It's above your head. Shit, in all reality, it's above my head."

"If this becomes a war. Your team is going to need a doctor, right? Medical supplies? Blood?"

"You're a nurse practitioner."

Tara reached for and grabbed the back of Frankie's elbow. "What's the difference?"

85

The Buccetti Compound
March 2, 2024

Surrounded by friends in his bunker, Frankie raised a short glass of whiskey. "To our brother, Marcel Taylor."

"To Marcel!" Mariani, Carlos, Brice, Dennis, Vadik, Grayfeather, and Ken said in unison. Tapping glasses, the group of stone-faced men took the alcohol down.

"M-marcel was a g-good man," Frankie said, dropping his chin in his chest, shooting his hands to his face to hide the tears from his friends.

Mariani rested his arm around Frankie's shoulders. "He's right," he said. "The man worked his ass off his entire life. He raised a family the right way. And no matter what, he stayed loyal to *us*." He patted Frankie's back a few times. "It's all right, brother. He's in a better place."

The tight circle spread apart. Cigarettes lit up. Even Frankie was smoking for the first time in many years.

Ken Spatz raised his voice. "What happened to Marcel won't happen again. All of you now have diplomatic immunity. With the exception of Mariani and Grayfeather, of course." His head shifted to the ghosts. "They're dead."

"A little late for Marcel," Dennis said, leaning his back against the wall with a cigarette dangling from his discolored lips.

Ken took a step toward Dennis. "I don't like your tone."

"Get fucked." Dennis flicked his cigarette at Ken.

Ken lunged at Dennis, tackling him to the carpet. Dennis started swinging. Brice jumped on Ken.

"Break it up!" Frankie barked.

Grayfeather peeled Brice off Ken. Vadik pulled Ken off Dennis.

Dennis bounced to his feet. "You're fucking dead!"

Carlos got in his way and held him back. "Calm down, bro."

Ken pointed at Dennis, but his forward progress was blocked by Vadik who held the line.

"That's enough!" Frankie shouted. "We're all on the same fucking team! I know emotions are high right now. Marcel's gone. Please, let's respect that. This is his day." He shook his head tightly. "We can't bring him back, but we *can* channel our anger toward the tyrants." Frankie unrolled a blueprint and placed it on the granite kitchen counter. "But we only get one shot." He watched the circle of men tighten, and then he continued. "Ken has instructed me to tell you this is not only classified, but it's treason. And you could be executed just for listening. Feel free to leave now if treason is not on your mind."

"Treason is my middle name," Dennis said softly.

The others simply nodded.

Ken glared at Dennis briefly. "We are a team. Together, we've accomplished a major objective. We earned the trust for the big job! Security Detail for the Truth Czar…Eugene Parker, at a party with the Queen of Spades. And people even more powerful than her." He paused, looking around the room. "That's right, boys. Heather Roth." He took a moment to swallow the heaviness of the name. "If we follow the plan me and Frankie made, we will give the military what it needs to invade America. They will successfully overthrow the rest of the government. We cut off the head of the snake...and the military will do the rest."

"What do you mean by that?" Brice asked. "If you cut off the head, another will grow in its place."

Frankie looked at Brice. "Long before President Clacher stepped down," he said, "Ken told me the deep state had plans to remove Clacher and take over the world. And that's exactly what happened. He told me he had contacts in the military and intelligence communities. He informed me about two deep states. One hell-bent on tyranny, and the other...determined to restore freedom.

"The deep state Ken is connected to has been deployed all over the world. Roth is smart. She and her puppet masters know American soldiers would never kill, torture, or police their own people. She knows as long as the military is far away, they will never stop her evil plans for depopulation."

Ken Spatz cleared his throat. "My source...has assured me that the patriots have a plan ready for a military invasion. Land, air, *and* sea. Everything has been in place for a long time. But they can't act without Heather Roth dead. *And* they need the backing of the American people." He paused dramatically. "I'm pretty sure the American people are just about fed up."

Frankie handed Vadik a copy of the invitation. "This is where you guys come into play."

"April twentieth?" Vadik said, reading the document. "That's Hitler's birthday."

"Yeah, these are sick people," Frankie said. "You have to kill them. And, after Ken gives me the good word, I'll relay the message to his contact in the military."

Brice raised his hand. "How do we kill people protected by Secret Service?"

"Ken has a plan," Frankie whispered. "Since Grayfeather is out, Ken has volunteered to step up. Let me make this clear, Ken is in charge of this mission. He has immense combat experience, *and* knows how to mount a surprise attack."

"For the next few weeks," Ken said, "we'll prepare night and day. Wars are won with cunning. We will create a diversion, and confuse the enemy. The chaos will create a small opening."

"Sounds like a suicide mission," Dennis said. "What's the exit strategy?"

Frankie chimed in. "Me and Ken are planning the extraction. We need a safe house and a doctor. We might have both."

Ken turned to face Dennis. "I'll be perfectly honest with you." He paused, looking around the room. "This mission might become a death trap. The place will be crawling with heavily armed security. But we have intel that says some in the Secret Service might sympathize with our cause. Even if only a few patriots join the fight, it would confuse the enemy and give us an edge."

"I don't really like the idea of being shipped off to die," Dennis said.

"I heard you want revenge?" Ken asked. "You want honor? If this mission is a success, you'll save your nation, avenge your enemies, and carve your name in the history books. Your great-grandchildren will read about you in school."

"This is our D-Day," Frankie said. "We need to know who's in…and who's out. Right now."

"I'm in," Vadik said without hesitation.

Carlos opened his hands. "I'll help in any way I can."

"I got an army of thugs that will do whatever I tell them." Grayfeather dropped a heavy hand on Mariani's shoulder. "And I got Mariani by my side. We could cause some ruckus downtown."

Mariani nodded, looking around the room. "I've been against this plan for a long time." He met eyes with Frankie. "But after seeing what happened to Marcel, I see the big picture. This is *our* moment. And I want to be a part of it." He raised a clenched fist in the air. "'Merica!"

Brice and Dennis exchanged glances.

"I'm in," Brice said.

"You can count me in." Dennis extended a hand toward Ken Spatz. "I'm sorry about earlier. It won't happen again."

Ken clapped his hands together, and then bro hugged Dennis with aggression. "We got a team!"

86

Orick, California
April 20, 2024

After shutting the driver-side door, Frankie turned toward Tara Barini in the passenger seat. "Are you ready?" His voice tight and carefully controlled. Tara gave a slight nod, her trembling lower lip giving her away as Frankie started the truck.

The low grumble of the Chevy Silverado revved slightly as Frankie rolled out of Tara's dark, secluded driveway in northern California. No radio was playing in the background because it had been removed.

"Take a right at the end of the road," Tara said with a soft shaky voice. "Head north to the Redwood State Park."

As the truck picked up speed, the small camper bolted to the bed creaked in response. Though it was old, the exterior sporting a couple dents and slightly rusted, the inside was a marvel of ingenuity. A small bunk bed on each side. Cupboards full of first-aid kits, drugs, and medical supplies. IV polls were bolted to each bed. And the make-shift ambulance even had a compartment with blood transfusion bags just in case.

Frankie placed the satphone on the center console. "I'm expecting an important text from Ken around 12:30," he said.

"But it could come sooner. If I'm driving when it beeps, I need you to read to me what it says."

Tara swallowed nervously, her eyes skipping to the phone before she answered. "Yes. Yeah, I can do that." She strapped her seatbelt over her black fleece jacket. "It's a little after eleven, right now. I'll keep my eye on it."

Frankie accelerated to speed on the narrow country road. "We'll pick up Carlos and Katrina a little after midnight. Then we wait in the campground."

"Katrina did pretty good the past few weeks in training. I think she'll make a capable nurse."

Frankie glanced at Tara. "I hope you know how important you guys are to the team. It gives our men confidence, knowing if they get shot, they might have a fighting chance."

"Let's hope they come back without a scratch." Tara picked at her fingernails.

"Hope ain't enough," he said. "We need a miracle. But if we don't hear from them, we'll have to go with plan B."

"What's that?"

Grabbing the satphone, Frankie held it up, shrugging. "Call in the calvary. Lie if we need to."

"Lie to who?"

"Sorry, girl." Frankie entered the highway, accelerating as he merged in front of a speeding semi-truck. "It's best you don't know. Plausible deniability."

"What, you don't trust me?"

"It's not that. Just a precaution. The less you know the better. They have ways to make people talk."

She let out a short laugh. "Is it too late to change my mind and go home? Just kidding."

"We burned that bridge when we cut the chips out of our hands."

Tara cracked the window.

Tapping the brakes, Frankie looked at her. "Are you okay?"

"Yeah, just a little hot." She swallowed reality. "I'm just a small-town nurse practitioner. I'm not used to suicide missions."

"You're not *just* a nurse practitioner. You're a soldier, Tara…on the greatest battlefield in the history of mankind."

Tara shifted to face Frankie. "I-I feel honored to be a part of this. I'm just a little scared is all."

"I'm scared, too," Frankie reached for her hand. "It's natural, but what defines your character, is how you channel that fear when things don't go as planned." He smiled when he felt her squeezing back. "Instinct kicks in. You'll adapt. And I'm confident you'll be ready when the time comes." He paused, taking his eyes off the road to meet hers. "I know exactly how you feel. Now, take some deep breaths. Stay positive. One way or another, everything will be okay. Ken is an elite soldier, and the rest of the team has a lot of heart. They might just make it."

"My heart is pounding so fast." She plopped her hand on her chest. "I've never even stolen a pack of gum. But I feel like we just robbed a bank. And we haven't even done anything real yet. Shit could go sideways so fast."

"I always hope for the best and prepare for the worst." Frankie cracked the window, and they listened to the sound of the wind and the hum of the tires.

*****

Ken Spatz hardly felt the sting of needles pressing against his tuxedo-clad knees as he crouched low at his station on the eastern banks of the redwood forest. Truth Czar Eugene Parker had ordered them to guard the perimeter fifty yards away from the ancient ritual. No security was allowed any closer.

Gazing out through a small pair of binoculars, Ken was aware only of the images magnified before him: tiki torches surrounding a line of robed men. And a small fire pit at the foot of a thirty-three-foot-tall owl god carved out of a gigantic redwood tree.

Behind him, Ken could hear Brice, Dennis, and Vadik whispering about the dozens of armed security guards and Secret Service agents lurking in the woods. "Shh," he said. Craning his neck, he saw his three men in black tuxedos freeze still. Now silent in the thick dark foliage. Submachine guns were hanging on straps around their necks. Ken turned back to the blaze.

"There she is," Ken said softly as he scoped Heather Roth and Eugene Parker. "The Queen of Spades is in the center." He watched the single-file line of pagans drop to their knees, submitting to the owl god.

Ken handed the goggles to Vadik Domechev who was second-in-command.

"I see her," Vadik said, slowly scanning the targets and the ritual platform they were kneeling on, ringed in on three sides by stairs. Zooming in, he studied the owl god and the two colossal redwood trees that stood guard on its left and right. Zooming out, he noticed stone gargoyles guarding the steps, a tall obelisk shooting out from the center of the platform, and an altar between the owl god and the obelisk.

Brice swatted Vadik's shoulder. "You gonna pass that shit?"

"Hold on." Vadik zeroed in on the marble altar overlooking the fire. On top of the altar was a wicker basket. Resting inside was a still baby. Naked.

Vadik lowered the binocs, shaking his head in repulse.

"To her left is the Jack of Hearts." Ken glanced at the digital watch on his wrist. *11:55*

Dennis squinted his eyes. "How can you tell?" He reached for the binoculars, but Vadik was already handing them to Brice.

"Height differential," Ken said. "Parker's tall. Roth is short. And Parker told me he would be on her left-hand side."

Vadik handed the goggles to Brice.

Brice turned away from the ceremony. Flipping the switch for thermal imaging, he scanned the countless heat signatures of Secret Service men further down the tree line. "The security is thicker than I thought," he said, turning back to scope the commencement of the pagan ritual. "My God, they got a damn baby on the altar."

"A baby?" Dennis asked, reaching for the goggles.

"Give me a minute, bro. You'll get your turn."

"What the hell?" Dennis stomped his foot on the dirt. "What the fuck are they gonna do with a baby?

Ken shook his head. "Nothing."

"They're doing something," Brice said, his lips twisting in disgust. "Looks like a sacrifice to me. A bunch of sick fucks kneeling in front of a fire and a big-ass owl."

"That's the *sickest* shit I've ever heard," Dennis said, his face scrunching up, one eye squinting more than the other.

"It's a mock sacrifice," Ken said. "It's a doll."

Brice gave the goggles to Dennis. "I think I just saw its leg kick."

Dennis took a long scope at the pale baby. Lowering the binocs, he set them in Ken's hands, leaning in close enough for him to hear his whisper. "I can't let this happen."

"You will *keep* the status quo." Ken squared up with Dennis, grabbing his arm firmly. "You understand?"

"Fuck that." Dennis spun away from Ken's grip, flinging his arms in abject frustration.

Brice dropped a gloved hand on Dennis' shoulder. "Bro, clam down. Look at the big picture. Freedom or tyranny? You go now, you're gonna fuck up our only chance."

"Not to mention, get us killed," Ken barked softly. "You saw all the security, right?" he lowered his tone. "Don't even think about it."

Dennis shook his head and lifted his chin. "Don't tell me what to do."

"I'm in charge here, soldier." Ken pointed at Dennis. "We will stick to the plan. You understand? This is bigger than one baby. It's a whole future of babies. We fuck this up, they'll never be free."

Dennis clenched his jaw, looking Ken in the eye. "Fine, let them kill the baby." He mumbled something as he put some distance between himself and the team.

Ken's eyes followed Dennis.

Vadik flicked Ken's tux with his hand. "Who's on the right side of Roth?"

"The King of Hearts. Her dad."

*****

Tara pointed at the green sign on the shoulder of the highway. "Take that exit," she said. "Turn right, and then in about ten miles, take another right on Owl's Peak Road.

Frankie veered on the off-ramp and drove the dark country road until his headlights flashed over the sign indicating the destination. "Carlos and Katrina should be parked on the side of the road somewhere around here."

Tara's breaths were heavy and fast. Her hands were gripping her knees.

Frankie's eyes were searching the road, his fingers tightening on the wheel. His long exhale added to the fog on the windshield. "There! Yes, there he is." He pointed through the descending nightfall at the rusty car on the side of the road. The hood was up.

Frankie pulled over behind the car. "Hang tight." He glanced at Tara.

Climbing out of the truck, Frankie strutted up to the front of the car. "You guys, okay?"

Carlos winked and nodded, flinging his hand toward the junker. "Yeah. The car ain't gonna make it though." He kicked the back bumper. "Piece of shit."

"Hop in with us." Frankie waved his hand, playing along with the act, just in case a drone was watching from above.

Carlos and Katrina followed Frankie, and they all got in the four-door truck.

"The diversion is set," Frankie said. Leaning over, he tossed the C4 detonator to Carlos in the back seat. "Car's all set up, right?"

Carlos nodded. "As instructed."

Frankie gestured toward the detonator. "On my word."

*****

Ken pulled three small rectangular C4 blocks out of his pants and then handed them to Dennis. "I want you to walk thirty yards straight behind us." Ken lifted his hand to chest level. "Slowly." He leaned closer. "Stick the explosives on three different trees. Make it quick. Don't draw attention." He paused, attempting to read Dennis' eyes. "Come back zipping up your pants like you just took a piss. Just in case anyone happens to look in that direction."

Dennis nodded. "Yes, sir." He swallowed a lump of pride, and then shoved the devices in his pockets. Turning around, he walked until disappeared into the darkness of the thick murky forest.

Ken turned to Brice. "You shouldn't have given him the goggles. He didn't need to see that baby."

"My bad." Brice returned the binoculars to Ken. "What are they doing now? I saw small cups in their hands."

"It's blood," Ken said under his breath.

"No," Brice said. "They ain't drinkin' no blood?"

"That's what they drink, man," Ken said in a low, raspy tone. "Probably baby blood. They think it will keep them living forever."

"Shhh." Vadik pointed. "Something's happening."

At the foot of the massive owl, the group of thirteen cloaked individuals rose and began chanting:

"CREME OF CARE!" the choir chanted in unison. "WoOOOE OH! CREME OF CARE! WoOOOOE OH!"

An actor's thunderous voice exploded from a speaker inside the owl god. "HALT!" the ominous voice demanded. "WHO ART THOU…WHO DISTURBS THY REPOSE!"

"We are not worthy." A female voice hollered into a microphone in front of the altar. "We come to serve you a blood offering. Please accept this sacrifice. We seek admittance into the glorious afterlife."

"BRING IT FORWARD!" the menacing voice inside the owl ordered. Loud chimes echoed throughout the forest.

*****

Dennis reappeared next to Brice. "We're all set." He was breathing heavily. Wide eyes. Open mouth.

"Catch your breath," Ken said. "Right after the fireworks ceremony, I'll hit the button. After the second explosion, we deploy smoke grenades and the M80 fireworks. That should be enough distraction to sprint toward the owl. Heads low. Hold your fire until we get close. I'll be at the back of the pack. Halfway there, I'll stop, turn back, and lay down cover fire."

"You don't think—" Dennis got cut off.

Ken pressed his finger to his lips. "Shhh!"

In accordance with the script, a loud thunderclap erupted from the owl god, representing a decision made by the deity. The echo shook the forest like a bomb. A thick cloud of smoke rolled out the bottom of the dark owl, engulfing the people kneeling in black robes. Chimes sounded. When the smoke cleared, a naked Heather Roth rose, holding the naked child in her arms. Her robe now lay discarded at her feet.

"I AM MOLECH!" the voice from inside the owl said loudly. "SON OF RA, GOD OF SUN … I ACCEPT YOUR OFFERING … I AM PLEASED."

Just then, the woman returned the child to the altar. Holding out a hand, she waited as a tall, robed man placed a curved dagger in her palm. She lifted it with both hands, hefting it high above her head. The men beside her chanted to their god for blessing.

"BEHOLD, DARK ONE!" the twelve members chanted loudly. "THIS MORTAL BEING MUST PERISH...SO WE CAN LIVE FOREVER!"

"LET THE BLOOD FLOW FROM THE GUT OF THE DOOMED SOUL," the owl god ordered.

*****

Hidden in the thick, bushy foliage surrounding their post, Dennis kneeled right next to Ken. Letting out a heavy sigh, he cursed under his breath. "How are you gonna sit here and watch them stab that innocent little baby in the gut?"

"Follow the mission plan," Ken said to his subordinate. "We need the fireworks for cover."

"Fuck that," Dennis said with a low tone, gesturing to the ritual. "That kid will be dead by then."

"Wait for the fireworks at the end," Ken barked with a low rumbling growl, and then he grabbed Dennis' bicep.

Dennis jerked his arm free. "Don't fucking touch me."

Ken pointed at Dennis. "Stand the fuck down."

"I can't let them hurt that kid." His lips were curling into a snarl.

Ken took a step forward. "We don't need this right now. They could be watching us."

Dennis stood nose-to-nose with Ken. Vadik and Brice separated them.

Spinning free, Dennis ducked his head and darted out from the wall of bushes before anyone could blink.

Ken's eyes and mouth widened. His arm reaching for Dennis but he was already gone. In pursuit of the innocent child.

Brice shifted his head to Ken. "Sorry, bro," he said and then charged after Dennis.

"Fuck!" Ken said, frantically pulling out the detonator for the C4.

Vadik tossed a smoke grenade in the path of Brice and Dennis, with hopes of providing cover. And then he tossed two more.

Ken pressed the button, and a redwood tree thirty yards behind them exploded. A huge fireball lit up the forest. The echo must have been heard ten miles away.

Ken froze when footsteps came running past their den of bushes. Looking at Vadik, he put a finger to his lips.

"Over there!" A loud unembodied voice barked orders at a group of security guards a few trees behind them.

Other than the man's voices, Ken didn't hear anything else over the blind numbing beat of his heart as he pressed the second button on the detonator. Another fiery explosion shook the ground. Men screamed.

Ken drew his gun. Cocked it. "I thought Dennis was under control!"

"He's uncontrollable."

Rapid popping from nearby gunfire kept their heads low.

"He fucked up the whole mission." Ken pulled out his satphone, shaking his head in frustration. "I don't think we're gonna make it, bro." He hastily typed Frankie a message: *Send the Codeword!!!* And then he hit the send button.

Vadik pulled out a grenade. "I'm with ya, brother. Till the end."

"It's now or never!" Ken exploded the third tree. Pulling out a long string of fireworks, he lit the fuse. And then he pulled out two smoke grenades. "Blitz!"

Vadik rose to his feet, tossing grenades in every direction, charging forward with his head low. Ken chucked a smoke grenade in the path of their assault and then sprinted behind Vadik as the bullets carved through the smoky air around them.

*****

At the sound of explosions and gunshots, half of the robed men before the giant owl collapsed to the ground. The other half scattered like reptiles in the dark. Eugene Parker grabbed Heather Roth and the baby, and then darted off the stage. "Go, go, go!" he shouted at the empress who had no clothes.

"Someone betrayed us!" Roth screamed. Gunshots were ringing out and echoing through the ancient forest.

"Keep moving," Parker said from behind her. Craning his neck, he turned back and saw muzzle flashes from the darkness surrounding them. Ducking his head, he heard the staggering buzz of submachine gun fire. Straightening himself, he noticed a pause in the gunfire as he slithered into blackness. Suddenly, the sound of agonizing screams filled the void. The pain in the voices made him cringe.

The ground shook from another explosion deep in the woods. The loud rapid popping continued from near and far. Blood-curdling screams were reverberating off the giant wall of trees surrounding the sacrifice platform.

President Roth stopped, reaching out to touch Parker's arm. "I got a spot. Follow me."

Parker was ducking and dodging bullets as they ripped through the branches above their heads. Pushing forward, he kept his fingers on Roth's bare sweaty skin as he followed close behind her. The president's pale legs led him down a narrow trail that took them behind the stage.

*****

While pulling into a campground occupied with dozens of campers just like theirs, Frankie's satphone beeped.

Tara picked up the phone and nervously read the message from Ken. "S-send the codeword," she said with a shaky voice. "Three exclamation points."

Carlos and Katrina were silent in the back seat.

Frankie parked the camper. "Give me the phone," he said, sticking his hand out. Snatching up Ken's satphone, he scrolled through the contacts. When he found Ken's source, he punched in the top secret codeword with his thumb: *Lilith is sleepeth.* He read out loud as he typed.

Pausing to glance at his friends, Frankie hit the send button. "That's that." He let out a long deep audible sigh.

"Does that mean Roth is dead?" Carlos asked.

Frankie shook his head. "I don't know," he said gravely. "Either that...or they're in big trouble. Ken isn't taking any chances. He told me in private that we'll lie to the admiral if we have to."

*****

Twenty yards out from the obelisk, Dennis dropped to one knee, firing a short burst of bullets at the men in robes scattering. Two went down. "Die, mother fuckers!" He rose to a crouch and continued squeezing the trigger as he inched forward. He knew Brice was behind him, slowing down the advance from guards creeping in from the fringe of the forest.

Whipping around, Brice saw a robed figure crawling away and fired his weapon into his back. Shifting to the left, he shot at three pagans fleeing the platform. When they fell, there were no more targets, so he ran to the steps leading to the fire pit. Several men in robes were curled up on the stone floor. The glow of the fire revealed puddles of blood flowing through the cracks of the timeworn bricks. Brice did not discriminate. He shot men who were crying, bleeding, or stiff.

Releasing his magazine, Brice reloaded in three seconds flat. A wrinkled old man with white hair and a wet hole in his robe was leaning his back up against the marble altar. A burning cigarette was in the man's lips. His right hand was resting on another old man with white hair who was lying right next to him. Dead.

"Where's Heather Roth?" Brice barked with a low growl, his gun barrel pointing at the old man's head.

Two streams of smoke shot down from Seth Roth's nose. "She's in the afterlife," he croaked out. "Don't shoot. I can make you rich beyond your wildest dreams. I can make you king of an island with *countless* virgins...if that is what you request."

Brice extended his sub-machine gun. "No, thanks," he said. Upon squeezing the trigger, a three-shot burst spit out, and the bullets tore through Seth Roth's chest. The old man tipped over. Brice then fired another burst in the back of the old man's head.

*****

Crossing the smoky stump-riddled area between the treeline and the owl god, Ken Spatz felt a bullet hit the back of his leg and rip through flesh. Grunting, he collapsed to the ground, rolling behind a thick tree stump. He briefly scrunched up his face, but the familiar sounds of battle quickly numbed the pain.

"Fuckin' A," he said, reaching for the back of his upper leg. At the ear-splitting sound and fury of automatic gunfire, he twisted his head, trying to locate where it was coming from. "Fuck," he whispered under his breath. A dozen men were creeping toward him. Only smoke, stumps, and darkness provided any cover.

From the prone position, Ken took down one man with two shots, and the rest hit the dirt. Laying down a steady stream of cover fire made it more possible for Vadik to reach the sacrifice area. Scanning the treeless bowl and woods behind it, he saw flashes of light crackling in every direction. His first reaction was to frown at the reality of certain death, but then he realized they weren't shooting at him.

"They're shooting at each other!" Ken realized, the first smile of the night gracing his lips. "Half the security forces switched sides!" He removed his belt, fastened it around his thigh, and then yanked it tight. *That should stop the bleeding,* he thought, and then packed the wound with dirt.

Ken blasted off another forty shots in the area of the man he killed. And then he tossed his last grenade. Turning on his belly toward the stage, he began crawling on his elbows, using the fire in front of the owl god as a beacon in the dark.

Kaboom!

*****

From Main Street in downtown Duluth Minnesota, Giovanni Mariani and Gordon Grayfeather marched with a large mob of angry protesters. The local United Nations headquarters was in sight. It was the small hours of the morning, and half of the people were carrying torches. Grayfeather and Mariani were hiding weapons under their long black jackets, and many others followed suit. Some had guns, but the majority had bats, rocks, or knives.

The group of almost a thousand people stopped in front of the government building. Loud unorganized rumblings, curse words, and threats unified under one chant led by Gordon Grayfeather: "FREEDOM! NOW! ... FREEDOM! NOW! ... FREEDOM! NOW!"

Mariani was on one knee in the middle of the energetic mob. His weapon was cradled in his hands. Rising with an M4A1 assault rifle pressed against his shoulder, he aimed the grenade launcher at the double door on the front of the building.

Grayfeather fired a shot in the air and the sea of people parted. Mariani fired a grenade at his target.

After a loud whistle, a giant fireball exploded inside the entrance. A hole in the brick wall appeared. The angry mob of a thousand men rushed the building. Gordon Grayfeather gave his handgun to a stranger on the street, and then he pulled out his trusty hatchet from the small of his back. He gripped it tight in his right hand. Bending his knees, he began to growl.

"Slow down, bro!" Mariani hollered. "There gonna start shoo—"

A buzz of fully automatic gunfire came from a top-floor window. Mariani threw himself to the ground as protesters scattered in every direction. As the deafening gunshots continued to ring out, he looked forward. Bodies were being mowed down, but Grayfeather kept running forward without pause. "Fuck," he muttered. On instinct, he took cover behind a car, training his rifle on the window.

Muzzle flashes from the fourth floor were sparkling in the dark.

Mariani popped off three shots, and then the gunman tumbled out of the window. The mob ripped him from limb to limb.

Mariani continued laying down cover fire, taking aim at one window after another. After forty shots, he reloaded and then laid down a rope of gunfire as the mob breached the limestone building. His eyes shifted to find his friend, but Grayfeather was now lost in the haze of battle. "Go get 'em, boy. You were born for this."

*****

Brice Rockwell heard gunshots behind him and collapsed to the ground. "Ahhh," he grunted. "I'm hit!" He reached for his side and felt wetness.

Dennis dragged Brice behind the stone obelisk. "How bad?" He reloaded his gun.

"Got through the vest somehow." Brice's breaths were short and fast. "It burns."

Screams and gunshots and ricochets were all around them.

Dennis dragged Brice down the steps and into the foliage surrounding the platform.

"They're fucking everywhere," Brice said. "You're gonna have to leave me. I can't walk."

"That's not an option," Dennis said. "I'm not leaving you behind."

"I love you, brother," Brice grumbled in pain. "But you have to find Roth. You're running out of time."

Dennis nodded. His gaze was set on the blood pouring through Brice's fingers that were pressed on his wound. Taking off his tux jacket, Dennis ripped it to pieces with his knife. "Here. Keep putting pressure on it. I'll come get you after I kill that bitch." He got up, gun in hand. "Save your energy. I'll be right back."

"I-I feel cold," Brice muttered as Dennis darted back to the action.

Dennis crept to the front of the owl god where he saw Vadik taking cover behind the obelisk.

"Where's Brice?" Vadik asked.

"He got hit. He's in the bushes." Dennis met eyes with Vadik. "Where's Ken?"

"I don't know." Vadik shook his head. "How 'bout Roth?"

Dennis looked at all the dead bodies. "She was naked. Shouldn't be hard to find."

Vadik squinted his eyes as he scanned the area. "They're probably gone," he said, his gaze landing on the enormous owl god that had been carved with great detail. "Wait." He leaned in toward Dennis. "I bet there's a mechanical room in the owl," he whispered. "Remember…that thing had a voice?"

Dennis nodded his head in agreement. "Let's find out."

Crouching around the side, Vadik and Dennis approached the back of the owl.

Dennis stopped at first sight of the door on the back side of the fat redwood tree. "Psst." He pointed at Vadik with widening eyes. He then swung his gun at the door.

Vadik crept up to the door. Reaching for the handle, he shoved the door open, and then jumped off to the side.

Dennis stiffened his arms, aiming the gun in the doorway. It was dark, but he saw the silhouette of a man. "Don't move!" He took a step closer to see President Roth and Truth Czar Parker shivering in each other's arms. The baby lay on the dirt floor. Still.

With his finger on the trigger, Dennis only hesitated because the baby was so close.

"Don't do it, Dennis!" Eugene Parker said. "I was good to you."

"And then you tried to sacrifice a child," Dennis said, staring down the short barrel of his submachine gun. He didn't hear Parker's last desperate pleas. As he squeezed the trigger, he released all the hate and pent-up emotion in his heart. Three explosive bursts of automatic fire left Roth and Parker twisted in a pool of blood.

The baby started crying, and then Dennis swooped him up.

*****

On the steps of the ritual platform, Vadik was lifting Ken to his feet. Glancing at the edge of the forest,

he took in one last look at the gunfight still raging on. The constant loud flashes in the dark gave him hope that the side fighting for freedom was winning.

With his flexed arm wrapped around the lead man's waist, Vadik retreated down the trail leading behind the owl god. Dennis was sitting on the ground, tying a knot in a makeshift baby sling he had made from Eugene Parker's black robe.

"Brice is hurt bad," Dennis said, rising with the child in the sling hanging around his neck. "But if you lift him up, I can help him walk."

Vadik set Ken down for a rest. Stooping low, he grabbed under Brice's armpit. "You're gonna be all right, bro," he said, heaving the pale man to his feet, setting him in the grasp of Dennis. Wiping Brice's blood and sweat on his tux, he returned to Ken.

Brice was leaning on Dennis heavily as they staggered further into the dark void of the dense forest.

After ten minutes of the trek, Dennis stopped. Gently laying Brice on the damp forest floor, he readjusted the baby swaddled in the robe. "I don't think I can carry Brice and the baby for a mile and a half. He's struggling. I might have to put him on my shoulder."

Vadik looked down at Brice who was pale and sweaty with blue lips. "I'll take the baby," he said. "But Brice doesn't look good at all. There's got to be something we can do. The man's gonna bleed out."

Ken studied Brice and his bleak condition. "Pack his wound with dirt," he mumbled, his mind flashing back to similar situations in ugly battles in the past. He remembered the miracles when soldiers made it, and the pain he felt when they didn't. "It will stop the bleeding." This was the first time he was experiencing a critical wound of his own. His breaths were short and heavy. His words hard and labored. "I-I need to send Frankie a m-message. He...he needs to know we're gonna be late."

*****

Twenty minutes after reading the text message from Ken, Frankie pulled out of the campground with a pounding heart and quivering jaw. Turning the wheel to the left, he drove the truck down a dark and vacant gravel road running parallel with the main drive that circled Owl's Peak. "Detonate the car bomb," he said to Carlos who was sitting in the passenger seat. "It will draw attention to the other side of the mountain. Give our boys a diversion."

Tara and Katrina were in the camper, setting up the infusion pump, wound-cleaning station, and preparing tools for emergency surgery.

Carlos rolled the window down and pressed the red button on the C4 detonator. "Done," he said and listened to the echo of an explosion in the distance.

"Good," Frankie said. "Now keep your eye on that compass. Dead west should be about a mile down the road."

"I'm on it," Carlos said, pulling the compass out of his pocket. The arrow was bouncing closer to the big W with each passing second.

Frankie was cruising just under the speed limit. "We got to get them in the camper quick. And hightail over to the cave."

"I hope they're okay," Carlos said staring out the passenger window.

"Me too, bro. Me too."

"I can't imagine what they just went through," Carlos said, returning his eyes to the compass.

"The bravest men I've ever met," Frankie said with a shaky voice, turning the wheel around the curve of the heavily wooded country road.

"We're there!" Carlos shouted. "Dead west, right now."

Pumping the brakes, Frankie pulled the wheel to the right, coming to a stop on the shoulder. Jerking the shifter into park, he killed the lights but left the engine running. "Let's go get our team." He pushed open the door, jumped out, and then ran to the back of the truck. Squinting his eyes, he searched the forest and saw nothing but darkness and a thick layer of fog hovering around the tree trunks. Carlos was standing at his side.

"You hear that?" Frankie asked, and then shifted to the sound of brushes being trudged through.

Before Carlos could speak, Vadik broke out of the mist with a lump on his chest and Ken Spatz propped up on his right side. A moment later, Dennis staggered down the path with Brice on his shoulder.

Frankie's heart sunk at the reality of a man being carried. His eyes averted to Ken and his wincing face. Frankie rushed up and took Ken off Vadik's arm. "You all right?" Frankie asked Ken who was hobbling and desperately hanging on his neck.

"I-I don't think so, man," Ken said softly, looking up at the camper. "I-I lost a lot of blood."

"Don't give up, brother," Frankie said, shuffling toward the truck with a friend in his grip who was getting heavier and heavier with each step. "Tara's gonna fix you up, real good."

"W-we got Heather Roth," Ken mumbled. "The witch is dead."

At the staircase leading to the back of the camper, Dennis bent forward, lowering Brice to his feet but still holding on to his near limp frame. "Almost there, buddy," he said, waiting for help lifting him up the narrow stairs and doorway.

"I got him," Carlos said and took an arm. Together, they heaved him up on the threshold.

Tara and Katrina were waiting in the doorway of the camper. The girls dragged him inside.

Climbing the steps, Dennis breached the camper and grabbed Brice under the armpits. Tara and Katrina both grabbed a leg, and the three of them lifted him on the bottom mattress on the driver-side bunk bed.

"What can I do to help?" Dennis spread apart his blood-soaked hands.

"Cut his shirt off!" Tara said, reaching for Brice's wrist. "Katrina, get that I.V. ready." She then made eye contact with Dennis. "No pulse. I'm going to give him CPR."

Dennis pulled out a buck knife and cut Brice's shirt. A tiny hole on his right side was smothered in dark blood and dirt.

At the doorway, Frankie helped Vadik lift Ken into the camper. Once Katrina pulled him inside, Frankie slammed the door and sprinted to the cab of the truck. Carlos and Vadik followed behind him.

As the truck took off, Tara thrust her interlocked hands downward on Brice's chest thirty times, and then she desperately blew all the air from her lungs into Brice's mouth. Nothing. So, she tried it again. And again. And again.

Letting out a trembling choppy breath, Tara looked at Dennis. "I'm so sorry." She shook her head, briefly shutting her eyes. "He's gone." She slowly folded Brice's arms, and then shut his eyelids. There was nothing more she could do, so she let out another sigh, quickly turning to see Katrina cutting Ken Spatz's pants with scissors. He was pale, bloody, and motionless. But his eyes were blinking!

"Stay with us, Ken," Tara said, rushing to his side. "Keep fighting. You're gonna be okay."

"T-thank you." Ken said softly, his breaths heavy. Short.

Dennis was hovering above Brice. Sobbing. The guilt from sabotaging the mission was weighing heavy on his heart. Reaching out a trembling hand, he touched his cousin one last time.

In the cab of the truck, Frankie pressed down on the gas pedal. His eyes were bouncing from the dark road in front of him, to the driver-side mirror, to the rear-view where Vadik was looking down on a sleeping baby. "Bro, what the hell happened out there? What's the status?"

Vadik's breaths were fast. "The Secret Service guys started shooting at each other," he said. "It was awesome. Gave us an opening to find Roth and her people. Roth is dead. I watched Dennis light her up. Parker, too."

"What about our guys? Do you think they're gonna be okay?" Frankie asked.

"You saw 'em." Vadik paused, letting out a slow heavy sigh. "They got caught in the crossfire. Brice is dead. Ken's probably not far off."

"No. No way." Frankie shook his head. "Tara will save them."

Los craned his neck from the front passenger seat. "I carried Brice. The poor guy was lifeless. Cold. I don't think he's gonna make it."

"What happened to Ken out there?" Frankie's voice was a low rumble of desperation. Glancing in the rear-view, his mouth tightened as he saw the truth in Vadik's eyes.

"He got shot in the back of his thigh," Vadik said, letting out a heavy breath. "It's bad, bro. He's lost too much blood."

"Tara and Katrina will fix him up." Frankie sucked in a breath that felt sharp in his lungs.

"I don't think so, bro." Vadik's voice cracked. "Ken's white as a ghost." Removing his left hand from the baby, he pounded the door panel. "Fuck! It should have been me."

Frankie turned down a gravel road. "Don't lose faith, brother. Tara stole some bags of blood from the hospital." He glanced in the rear-view mirror, meeting Vadik's eyes and wrinkled brow.

Vadik nodded in response.

"When we park in the cave," Frankie said, raising his voice over the hum of the tires, "we'll get an update on Ken and Brice."

"I don't know if I want an update." Carlos lit up a cigarette. "I'm afraid it won't be good."

Frankie took a sharp left down another dirt road that was only wide enough for one vehicle. "Almost there, boys. Then we wait for Ken's source to tell us the regime has been toppled."

"The problem is, we'll be sitting ducks till then," Vadik said. "What if a drone followed us?"

"Ken installed an electronic jammer on the truck." Frank slowed down as the truck rolled over a bump in the road.

"That don't stop thermal imaging," Vadik said.

"Relax, bro," Frankie said. "Hundreds of people are camping in this area. We blend right in. Plus, the Air Force is on the way."

"I know, but Ken said it could take hours."

Frankie cocked his head to glance at Vadik. Before he could open his mouth, the earth-shaking rumble of thunder made Frankie flinch. And then the high-pitched screech of supersonic jets ripping through the sky above their heads came and went. A few seconds later, a cluster of roaring explosions shook the ground like an earthquake for what seemed like a solid minute.

Frankie's eyes shifted to the driver-side mirror. A gigantic fireball brightened the dark sky above Owl's Peak. "They got 'em! It started!" Frankie smiled, his tightly closed fist pumping in the air.

Carlos clapped his hands together. "Yeah!" He joined Frankie with a raised fist. "What do you think's going to happen next?"

"I'll tell ya what's gonna happen," Frankie said from his gut. "The sleeping lion just woke up. Our patriots in the military are gonna bomb the shit out of them. Right now, a thousand military hackers are bombarding the regime's infrastructure with cyber-attacks, viruses, and malware. They're tapping into their communications with misinformation and disinformation to confuse all chains of command. Our submarines are obliterating vital satellites in orbit all around the Earth. And don't forget about the millions of people like Mariani and Grayfeather who are attacking the UN headquarters across the nation."

"But won't the regime fight back?" Vadik asked.

"Of course," Frankie said. "We can't underestimate the enemy. But I want to believe in the resilience of the American will to win. We've been dancing with the devil far too long. We did our part. And now…it's time for the military to deliver."

"If we do win," Carlos asked. "What type of government will we get?"

Frankie cracked a smile. "Ken told me the new American government will follow the Constitution and Bill of Rights," he said. "It will be a Republic, my friend. I hope this time…we can keep it."

"Me, too." Carlos nodded his head.

Frankie handed Vadik an old but trusty pocket knife. "Give Los the baby. I want you to cut that RFID chip out of your hand. Then toss it out the window. It will be liberating."

EPILOGUE

Duluth, Minnesota
July 4, 2024

Frank Buccetti parked the truck in front of his childhood hockey rink. Glancing at Tara in the front seat, he smiled and then turned to see his daughter in the back. "I got a gift for you."

"What is it?" Sethra asked.

With his fingers, Frankie gently removed the blue silk ribbon from around his neck, and the gold medallion with a red, white, and blue star swayed back and forth. "It's called the Medal of Freedom," he said, turning fully to face her as he set it in her hand. "President Clacher just gave me this honorable medal the other day. And I asked your mom if I could see you, so I could give you this special gift on Independence Day. I want you to never forget how important freedom is."

"Why did the president give it to you?" Sethra asked.

Frankie smiled. "Because I was part of a secret team who helped destroy the enemy."

Tara turned to show Sethra the medal around her neck. "I got one, too," she said with a wide smile. "The president gave one to me because I helped save the leader of your dad's team."

Sethra's eyes got big. Examining the medal closely, she felt its weight and looked at each side. She then put it around her neck. "Thanks, Daddy. I'll take good care of it. I promise."

Frankie opened the door. The girls exited the truck. The space between them and the outdoor hockey rink was covered with freshly mowed grass. Behind the dry rink was a wall of leafy trees.

"When I was your age," Frankie said, pointing to the rink, "I skated here every day during the winter. It was my passion."

"What's your passion now?" Sethra asked.

Kneeling down to her level, Frankie gently reached for her elbow. "You're my passion, kid." He hugged her tight. "What's your passion?"

"I like to run." The young girl smiled, bouncing in the grass.

"Well, let's race then," Frankie said. "If you're my daughter, you must be fast as lightning."

Sethra shook her head. "I'm pretty fast, but I don't want to race today. Let's go for a walk."

"You come from a long line of athletes. I want to see how fast you are." He clapped her shoulder. "Come on, let's race. I bet you could almost beat me."

"I'm only six and a half, dad," Sethra said. "I could never beat you."

Tara giggled. "Come on, Sethra. We'll beat him together. He ain't that fast."

"Don't be a little buster," Frankie said encouragingly. "Never say never. That's a defeatist attitude. You got to think positive. But if you ever find yourself at a disadvantage…you have to find a way to win. Find a weakness in your opponent. Exploit it."

"Okay," Sethra said, smiling at Tara. "I'll beat ya both."

"That's my girl," Frankie said. "First, we should stretch."

Frankie stretched his arms and legs, and Sethra copied him.

"Ahhh!" Sethra suddenly screeched, her eyes large as she glanced over at her dad.

"What happened?" Frankie asked, reaching out for her shoulder. "Are you okay?"

"I'm okay." Sethra pointed. "It's just a spider on your mirror. I hate spiders."

"Oh, don't worry about him," Frankie said. "That's just a baby spider."

"Daddy," Sethra said in a scathing tone. "That little itsy biddy baby spider is gonna grow up to be a big mean spider someday. And then he's gonna bite us."

"So, what should I do?" Frankie asked.

"You have to destroy him," Sethra said with a cold look on her face.

"Sethra…" Tara put her hands on her hip.

"Okay." Frankie let out a breath. Opening the back passenger door, he pulled out a spray bottle of cleaning product. Aiming at the passenger-side mirror, he sprayed the spider on the web until it shriveled up and fell to the grass.

"The enemy is terminated!" Sethra said, jumping up and down. She then moved in for a warm hug.

Frankie hugged her tight, and Tara joined in. "Come on, now. Let's race.… Do you see the sign on the box that says: Home Team?"

"Yeah, I see it."

"Run as fast as you can," Frankie said. "First one to sit in the home team box wins."

"I'm gonna smoke you, Dad."

"Good luck," Frankie replied.

"I don't believe in luck." Sethra laughed.

Tara spread her arms apart. "Why don't you two race? I'll be the judge." Tara raised her arms high. "On the count of three — go!"

"Okay," Sethra said. "I'm ready!"

"One, two," Tara paused, wondering what the kid was doing near Frankie's feet.

Frankie shot Tara a wink and a proud smile, and then he looked down at his daughter.

Sethra had abandoned her starting line stance to untie her dad's shoelaces. She then tied the two shoes together in a double knot.

"Three!" Sethra said, bolting toward the home team box as fast as she could.

Frankie dropped to his butt to untie the knot. Gazing at his sprinting daughter's hair flowing in the wind, he smiled at the resilience and speed of his child. "She did what she had to do. To win."

A stark warning for all citizens of America: *It's only a matter of time before government grows bigger than we bargained for.*

A stark warning for all tyrants on Earth: *Freedom will always push back.*

About the Author

Nick Campanella is the author of *Path of Affliction* and *Order From Chaos.* His early years were spent on the hockey rink, and his later years flew by as he scratched out a meager living. Hard labor, retail, mental health. Along the way, he found his passion: creating a story that stays with each reader for a long time. When Nick is not writing or working, he loves to spend time with his family. His favorite book is Darth Bane.

More information at www.nickcampanella.com

CPSIA information can be obtained
at www.ICGtesting.com
Printed in the USA
LVHW012149041222
734578LV00003B/68